To Dear
Ve

August 2010.

AIDEN TRAYNOR

Hell Bent

Order this book online at www.trafford.com/06-2906
or email orders@trafford.com

Most Trafford titles are also available at major online book retailers.

© Copyright 2007 Aiden Traynor

All rights reserved. No part of this publication may be reproduced, stored in a retrieval system, or transmitted, in any form or by any means, electronic, mechanical, photocopying, recording, or otherwise, without the written prior permission of the author.

Note for Librarians: A cataloguing record for this book is available from Library and Archives Canada at www.collectionscanada.ca/amicus/index-e.html

Printed in Victoria, BC, Canada.

ISBN: 978-1-4251-1147-2

We at Trafford believe that it is the responsibility of us all, as both individuals and corporations, to make choices that are environmentally and socially sound. You, in turn, are supporting this responsible conduct each time you purchase a Trafford book, or make use of our publishing services. To find out how you are helping, please visit www.trafford.com/responsiblepublishing.html

Our mission is to efficiently provide the world's finest, most comprehensive book publishing service, enabling every author to experience success. To find out how to publish your book, your way, and have it available worldwide, visit us online at www.trafford.com/10510

www.trafford.com

North America & international
toll-free: 1 888 232 4444 (USA & Canada)
phone: 250 383 6864 ♦ fax: 250 383 6804
email: info@trafford.com

The United Kingdom & Europe
phone: +44 (0)1865 722 113 ♦ local rate: 0845 230 9601
facsimile: +44 (0)1865 722 868 ♦ email: info.uk@trafford.com

10 9 8 7 6 5 4 3

For Alicia and Ruth

*Go, my songs, to the lonely and the unsatisfied,
Go also to the nerve-wracked, go to the enslaved-by-convention,
Bear to them my contempt for their oppressors.
Go as a great wave of cool water,
Bear my contempt of oppressors.*

Ezra Pound, Commission

PART ONE

The Conditioning

1

January 1947

Fr Galvin edged his thin white legs off the narrow bed and placed his small bony feet on the cold linoleum. It occurred to him that it was the first Monday in January. The thought, and the ice invading his feet, made him shiver slightly. It crossed his mind that he should regard this small discomfort as a source of grace, a small suffering he could offer to God for the sins of his fellow man, and woman.

The weather, during the previous few weeks in Dublin, had been the worst in living memory, with biting winds and icy rain. Icicles hung like long skeletal fingers from the gutters on every house. Fr Galvin moved gingerly the few steps towards the bedroom window and, squinting through the drawn curtain, saw that the ground on this first week of 1947 was covered in a foot-deep layer of snow. He ran his eye along the road that sloped down to the crossroads, no more than one hundred yards away, around which the village of Glenawlin huddled. Snow everywhere. He would have to phone the Parish Priest right away about whether or not to leave the National Schools closed because of the weather, so he could make the announcement at the eight o'clock Mass. His house lay between the church on one side and the schools on the other, and as curate in this small rural parish in the foothills of Dublin's Three Rock Mountains, it was his duty to attend to such matters.

In a small terraced house, on the Dublin side of the crossroads, at the same moment that Fr Galvin's feet were touching the floor, young Alan Logan raised his head from his pillow, reached for the little red torch on his bedside locker, clicked it on and, turning, shone it through the chilly darkness towards the watch that hung on a hook on the wall beside him. Seven fifteen …and eighteen… nineteen…twenty seconds. The second hand fascinated him more than the minute or hour hands. It was so precise, so accurate, so … definite. He loved the accuracy of the numbers; arithmetic was the only thing he liked about school, really. This watch was his proudest possession. It was the old pocket-watch his Dad had given him a few months earlier for his twelfth birthday. His father, Jim, was a train driver and very particular about time, bearing in mind that his working life revolved around timetables. Alan peered through the softening darkness at his baby brother's bed - he'd be two next week - in the far corner, and then at the curtain that divided the room in two, and behind which his two younger sisters, ten and six respectively, slept. It was too early to switch on the light and waken them all. He would stay quiet, and warm, until he heard his mother moving about around a quarter to eight.

As he turned to replace the torch on the locker a sudden feeling of panic seized him. Oh God! There it was again, that cold stickiness on his legs and the dampness in the bed. It wasn't the first time this had happened. Every two or three weeks for the past few months, the same thing. He had never been a bed-wetter, and now he was confused, and embarrassed. When Dr Tracey came to him before Christmas, when he'd had the 'flu', he'd hurriedly mentioned the problem to him as soon as his mother had left the room, but the doctor just carried on as if he hadn't heard him.

He lay there close to tears as the minutes ticked past. Eventually he heard his mother on her way downstairs. He slid out of bed, ignored the shock to his feet as they touched the cold oilcloth, straightened up the bedclothes, and quickly washed himself, glad to rid his body of the offending messiness.

Half an hour later, as he sat at the breakfast table with his two young sisters, working his way through a steaming bowl of porridge smothered in sugar, a knock came to the hall door. His mother looked in his direction with raised eyebrows, as if by this conspiratorial gesture they might figure out who was there before opening the door. It was Mrs Reilly from a few doors down the street on her way home from morning Mass, with the news that Fr Galvin had announced from the altar that the Parish Priest, who, like all parish priests, was the State appointed manager of the National Schools, had decided that the schools would remain closed today in view of the terrible weather, and would those who had come to Mass tell those who hadn't. Alan's heart leapt for joy at the reprieve from school, which he hated, especially on Mondays. His life seemed to be spent, during school terms, in a continuous state of countdown from Monday mornings until four o'clock on Friday afternoons, when the last class of the last school day of the endless school week finished, and life could be enjoyed for a couple of precious days before the whole miserable process began again.

Fewer people than usual had turned out for Fr Galvin's eight o'clock Mass that Monday morning. It was always the same for a few weeks after the Christmas period, he thought to himself as he picked his steps carefully along the slippery pathway from the church to his house next door. People had not settled back into their routine, and then of course there was the bad weather to put some of the regulars off. People were so easily put off, he thought; would they never realize that a day without Mass and Communion was a day wasted? No point in getting upset, he argued to himself, as he fished out his hall-door key and fumbled with numb fingers to unlock the door. The house was freezing.

He hung his coat on the hallstand and set about lighting the fire. Having removed yesterday's ashes, he piled a few sods of turf on top of some sticks and paper, set a match to the paper and headed for the kitchen and, still cupping the same match in his hands, switched on two rings of the gas stove, one for the kettle and one for the frying pan, and set them alight. Into the pan he dropped a sliver of dripping and two slices of bread. Fr Galvin did not have a housekeeper. He declined the offer when the Parish Priest had told him he was entitled to have one, as he and Fr Deering, the 'P.P.', lived in separate houses. Privately Father Galvin disapproved of priests having live-in housekeepers, being of the opinion that having a woman under the roof could be a source of scandal and cheap tongue-wagging.

Alan's 'no school' induced happiness continued throughout the week as the snow piled up and the schools remained closed. The weather, however, did not prevent his mother taking the ten-minute walk to the church on Monday night for the Miraculous Medal Devotions, accompanied by himself and Terry, the elder of his two sisters. Alan liked this particular ceremony. The church always seemed to be at its cheeriest for this service, warm with the crush of the packed congregation, and filled with the blaze of a myriad penny candles adorning every shrine. He liked the hymns to Our Lady too, and the happy atmosphere – the most gladdening of all church ceremonies – and the way everyone sang out wholeheartedly. He especially liked the fact that there were no sermons about losing your soul into hell forever, or the weakness of the body and the temptations of sex. This service was always conducted by the Parish Priest himself, an elderly man, who, by contrast with his curate, invariably had about him a characteristic air of quiet contentment. He seemed to believe that all we had to do was ask Our Lady, and she with her great motherly love for all God's children, would persuade Jesus to let us all into heaven somehow. The fire and brimstone was Fr Galvin's preserve, and reserved for Sunday Mass and the Men's Sodality, which Alan had started to attend with his Dad on the second Friday evening of each month, now that he was twelve. These were sombre, serious affairs, where the atmosphere was heavier and the singing doom-laden and subdued. Usually he came away feeling uneasy and fearful.

The severe weather lasted a full six weeks, and the snow piled up in the village to a depth of over three feet, which was unprecedented in living memory. The schools remained closed, and life generally slowed to a pace where people attended to the necessities of life and little else. During this period the subject of Alan's education became a recurring topic between his father and mother at mealtimes. It became clear that they felt uneasy about the teaching standards in the local National school, and that Alan's education was suffering as a result. Eventually it was decided that they would try to get him into the nearest Christian Brothers' school, even though this would mean daily bus journeys. The Brothers had a reputation for getting good academic results and, even though Alan would benefit from this for only a couple of years before finishing his primary education, it was felt that it would be the wise thing to do. Alan listened to this with mixed emotions; he regarded the local school as hopeless, and would like to improve, but from what he had heard from others about the Brothers' methods, he was apprehensive. Would he be exchanging the drudgery and boredom of school life at present for something a lot more disagreeable?

It was mid-February before the snow and ice cleared from Glenawlin. The village, with its scattering of houses huddled around a crossroads between Dublin city to the north, Bray to the south, Blackrock and Dun Laoghaire to the east, and the mountains to the west, gradually shook off its toper and returned to normal. The villagers moved about as before between the two grocery shops, the newsagents, the hardware store, the butcher's, the barber's, the shoemaker's, the library, the church and the schools, and the two pubs. And the filling station with its two pumps came back to life.

Alan regarded the fact that he had had a perfectly legitimate reason for not going to school as a heaven-sent piece of good fortune. During those weeks he started to read more and more, something he had not bothered much with previously, except for the adventure comics with their thrilling stories of fictional heroes of the football, motor racing and boxing worlds. His mother had been on to him for ages to join the local library, and he decided he might as well see if it was any good. He had never read a 'big book' and felt it was about time he proved to himself that, like other boys in his class, he was capable of doing so. His first selection from the Children's Section nearly put him off reading forever. It was called *Through Three Campaigns,* and was about a soldier who had fought in three wars in Asia in the eighteenth century. It was long and boring, but he persisted till the end. Fortunately, the librarian sensed his problem and took an interest. Soon he was into the world of *Tom Sawyer* and *Huckleberry Finn,* of *Black Beauty, The Pathfinders, Robinson Crusoe, Treasure Island* and *Gulliver's Travels.* He had entered the world of books, a world he grew to love and enjoy.

These weeks were not, however, entirely untroubled. Alan had been learning in his religion class about sin – how there was venial sin and mortal sin and how mortal sin killed the soul, and if you died in mortal sin you went to hell for all eternity. And hell was a place where you were always in flames worse than any flames you could imagine on earth. This started to prey on his mind. After all, sometimes he didn't say his prayers, or he didn't think about what he was saying, and it said in the Catechism, which the Archbishop had written himself, that 'If our distractions at prayer be wilful, our prayers, instead of pleasing God, offend Him, and are an abomination to Him.' Was he offending God? Was he 'an abomination' to Him? That sounded very serious, like it could be a mortal sin. But how would you know? He'd have to go to Confession and get absolution.

At Confession on Saturday morning he told Fr Deering he

missed saying his prayers sometimes. The priest asked him 'how often?', and told him to say three Hail Marys and say a good Act of Contrition. He came away thinking that this wasn't much of a 'penance'; maybe the priest hadn't understood; maybe he hadn't told him properly. Maybe he'd made a bad Confession and was deeper in sin than he'd been before. He could never be certain whether or not he would go straight to hell if he died then.

One Monday morning a couple of weeks after the school reopened Fr Deering came in to talk to the boys about he called 'the holy season of Lent'. Lent, he explained, would start in a couple of days time on Ash Wednesday and last for six weeks until Easter Sunday. It was a time to remember that Jesus was crucified and died for our sins and then rose from the dead so that we could all go to heaven when we died. Everyone, he told them, should go to the church on Ash Wednesday to have ashes put on their foreheads to remind them that they came from dust and would return to dust when they died. It was a very good thing, he said, to give up something you liked during Lent, to make a little sacrifice to show Jesus we loved Him.

Alan decided to give up eating sweets and chocolate, which was easy by comparison with having to eat fish every day or two because meat wasn't allowed during Lent except on Sundays. Alan's Dad used to call this 'starving the butcher'. Alan hated the taste, the smell and the look of fish, but there was no escaping it until Lent was over.

Midway during Lent the parish was more or less taken over for two weeks by two priests from a Religious Order, called missioners, who came to give the annual 'retreat'. This event occurred like clockwork about this time every year. Each evening they took it in turns to preach a sermon in the church. Everyone was expected to take this event very seriously as, according to the missioners, this was a time of great privilege for everyone in the parish, as God was visiting them in a special way. The first week was exclusively for women, and Alan's Mum, like virtually every other woman in the parish, was in her place in the church by eight o'clock each evening, and again for the finale to the women's week - the Benediction service at four o'clock on the Sunday afternoon.

Alan, who'd been playing football that afternoon, arrived home at the same time as his Mum. As they entered the house they were greeted by his Dad's teasing comment,

'The ladies were in great voice this afternoon.'

'What are you on about?' his Mum countered.

'Oh, just that on the walk home from watching Alan's match I thought you'd all raise the roof of the church with the *Tantum Ergo*.'

'Very funny. I hope the men will give as good an account of themselves.'

Jim laughed and then in a more serious tone asked her if it had been a good week.

'Well, yes, I suppose all in all it was.' After a few moments she added, 'Much the same as every other year, really. A mixture of God's love on the one hand and fire and brimstone on the other.'

'Are you going tonight Dad?' Alan asked.

'Oh I suppose I'd better, or I'll probably be booted out the door by your mother,' he replied with mock resignation.

'Can I come with you?'

'Well, son, I think it would be time enough for you in another year or two.' A more serious tone had entered his voice.

'Ah, Dad,' Alan protested.

'Leave it go for this year, son. Okay?' The note of quiet firmness in his voice meant that was that.

And indeed, as his wife had done the previous week, Alan's Dad was in the church to hear what the missioners had to say for the next seven days.

With the departure of the two men who had held centre stage, or at least centre pulpit, for the previous fortnight, the relative excitement they had created subsided and Glenawlin settled back to its normal everyday activities.

For Alan the focus shifted to Easter, now only a couple of

weeks away, and the cheerful prospect of two weeks holidays from school. Easter was good for another reason also; it heralded the shortest term of the year and the long summer break - six weeks of glorious holidays - 44 days if you counted the weekends - away from the drudgery of having to attend school.

Alan's escape from the classroom that summer was overshadowed, however, by his concerns about the new school he'd be attending come the new school year. Three weeks before the end of term he and his mother had travelled by bus to the Christian Brothers' school in Dun Laoghaire to be interviewed by the Principal, to see if he would be accepted as a pupil. The atmosphere in the building was cheerless, Spartan and functional, and there was something else about it that Alan would identify later as a sour mixture of tension and fear. As they sat waiting on a bench outside the Principal's room, Alan was suddenly petrified when the place was filled by the sound of what seemed like the roars of a man who had completely lost his temper, coming from a classroom nearby. This harangue had been going on at full blast for about five minutes when the tall, black-robed figure of the Principal, Brother Laffin, appeared at his door, and asked them to come in. He directed Alan's mother to the only other chair in the room, besides the one behind his desk, leaving Alan to stand.

'Well, Mrs Logan, you want to transfer this young gentleman in here from Glenawlin National School?' Mrs Logan found his attempt at light sarcasm more confusing than funny.

'Yes, Brother.' She didn't risk a smile.

He turned his attention to Alan, and then to the papers on his desk.

'Well, …..,' taking another glance at the papers, 'Alan, an bhuil aon Gaelige agut?

Alan had no idea what he was saying, except that he was being asked something in Irish.

'They don't teach Irish very well where he's been going, Brother. That's one of the reasons we'd like to change him from there. But he's very good at maths,' said his mother, trying to recover the lost ground.

'Do you know your the twelve times tables?'

Alan rattled them off in a flash, which genuinely seemed to surprise and impress the inquisitor.

The interview probably lasted less than two minutes, and ended with Mrs Logan being told to have her son report to Class 5A by nine o'clock on the first Monday in September.

Despite Alan's pleas that there was no way he wanted to go to that school, his parents insisted, and his fate was sealed.

2

October 1947

'Mother of God protect us!'
It was his mother's voice coming from out of the darkness. She was clearly in a state of alarm. It took Alan a few seconds to realize that it was still the middle of the night, and that the house seemed to be filled with noise. He jumped from his bed and ran to his parents' bedroom in the front of the house. The light was on and his mother was now leaning out of the bedroom window, still beseeching heaven for protection. Sirens blared and it seemed extraordinarily bright outside for the middle of the night.

'Millars' house is on fire', his father explained in a low voice, his apparent calmness, as he pulled on some clothes, acting as a balance against his mother's agitation.

'We're in no danger. The fire is too far away. The Brigade is here already and they'll get it under control', he added reassuringly.

He tied his bootlaces quickly, walked over to where his wife stood at the window, and, putting his arm around her shoulders said quietly,

'Don't worry, pet. We're not going to come to any harm. I'm

going down to see if I can be of any help.'

'Can I come with you Dad?' Alan asked, as his father headed for the stairs.

'Go and waken up the girls first, and tell them to get dressed. Then put on some warm clothes yourself, and come and stay beside me.'

'Annie,' he called over his shoulder to his wife, 'get the kids wrapped up in case we have to leave the house. Alan will be with me'.

Alan ran to his sisters' half of the divided bedroom. Terry, the ten-year-old, was already sitting up wide-eyed.

'What's happening?' she asked, her voice and eyes full of anxiety.

'There's a fire down the road, and we have to get dressed in case we have to leave the house.'

'Is it morning?' This time it was the voice of six-year-old Amy, barely audible from beneath the bedclothes where she had, as usual, virtually cocooned herself.

Alan put his hand where he judged her shoulder might be and gave her a little shake,

'Come on Mimi,' - this had been her first attempt at her own name, and it had stuck – 'you've got to get up quickly now and get dressed.'

'Why?' she sleepily protested.

'Dad says so.' Another little shake. 'Please, Mimi, you've got to hurry.'

Reluctantly the chubby figure of his younger sister emerged from beneath the bed covers, looked about, and climbed from the comfort of her nest, drowsily mystified by the strange workings of the adult world.

Satisfied that his sisters were doing as they were told, Alan returned through the shielding curtain to the boys' half of the room, where his mother was endeavouring to pull some clothes on to the loudly protesting Barry. Alan broke his own record for getting dressed quickly.

'Put your coat on, Alan,' his mother called after him as he ran downstairs. Once outside, he located his father among a group of about a dozen men and a few boys, most of whom he recognized as near neighbours. The women and girls huddled together separately, among them the distraught Mrs Millar along with some of her own children.

The Millars lived a few houses beyond Reilly's in the same row of terraced houses as Alan's family. Apart from the parents there were five children aged between eighteen months and fourteen years old in the family. By the time Alan ran into the street the Millars' home was engulfed in smoke and flames. Alan had never seen or imagined anything like it. The ashen-faced Mrs Millar's piercing screeches of anguish transcended all the other frenzied activity in the street: Mr Millar was being restrained by firemen from re-entering the house. A grimy grim-faced fireman struggled from the building carrying a girl of about seven.

'She's okay. She'll be alright,' he shouted in answer to the unasked question in everyone's eyes.

'It's little Deirdre,' someone called out. Her mother made an instinctive rush towards her daughter, but the fireman was already heading for the waiting ambulance. In response to Mrs Millar's cries he shouted over his shoulder

'We've got to get her to the hospital right away. Her leg needs attention.'

By now the roof had fallen in and the heat being generated was intense. Alan was rigid with fright and helpless fascination. Feeling the heat on his skin from the safe distance he stood from the blazing building, he tried to imagine what it must be like to be trapped in those terrifying flames and have no way of escaping? Being roasted even for a few seconds would be the worst torture imaginable.

Another piercing exclamation tore him from his dire imaginings.

'Declan! Little Declan! Jesus, Mary and Joseph where is he!?

It was the distraught Mrs Millar again. Declan was about three years old and the second youngest of the Millar children. He was nowhere to be found. *He must still be* inside. But the Fire Chief was adamant that no one was to enter the building until he declared it safe to do so.

While the efforts to control the flames continued apace, the atmosphere among the onlookers became more and more sombre. Jim, warning Alan not to move any closer, returned to his own home a couple of times to check on Anne and the rest of the family. Finally, about half an hour later, the fire crew was permitted to resume its search of the interior. Within a few minutes the crowd beheld the tragic sight of a solemn-faced fireman emerging from the smouldering ruins carrying all that remained of the toddler. His little body was wrapped in a grey blanket. It seemed that he had crawled under his bed as far as he could go in his piteous attempt to escape from the flames. One of the onlookers knelt down and started to recite the rosary and gradually others followed suit and joined in. Alan's attention was fixed on everything that was happening. Although his body was stock-still his mind was racing – shock, fear, distress, disbelief all swirling about like leaves in a storm.

By 7 a.m. the fire engines and ambulances had left the scene, and the neighbours had returned indoors. An unnatural silence hung over the street. By eleven o'clock the only indication of what had happened was the blackened shell of what had been the Millars' family home splitting the terrace of houses, and gaping at the world like a mouth full of jagged carious teeth.

A little over twenty-four hours later Fr Deering faltered through the funeral Mass for young Declan. He stood at the foot of the tiny white coffin and tried in his gentle homily to comfort the parents and family of the innocent victim of this tragedy, which seemed to touch everyone in the local community. He spoke of how Declan was already with the angels, smiling down from heaven even now on the broken-hearted parents whom he loved and who loved him, and on everyone gathered in the church, because he was a little baptized soul who never knew sin in any way. He spoke of how Declan would be there at the gates of paradise to greet his parents who, in their present heart-broken state would find it hard to be comforted by this thought on this sad morning, but would surely find comfort in this knowledge in time to come. He thanked God that more lives had not been lost, and prayed for the complete recovery of young Deirdre, who was still in hospital being treated for the burns she sustained to her legs when her nightdress caught fire. Fr Deering, in his compassionate way, seemed to be as afflicted as anyone in the church. Alan, who had hardly spoken a word since witnessing the soul-stirring spectacle two nights previously, was also distressed. He kept imagining how frightened the little boy must have been, and the pain from the fire burning him.

After the funeral service, people gathered in small groups outside the church while waiting to depart for the graveyard. As Alan stood with Mimi beside his mother and some neighbours – Terry had drifted off to join some of her classmates - they were joined by Mrs Reilly. She was a large hefty woman who would have made two of his own mother despite the fact that his mother was, if anything, the taller of the two. It was Mrs Reilly's hat that had caused Alan's mind to drift idly on to speculating about which of the two women was the taller. In fact it was not so much the hat as the long green feather attached to it that fascinated him, as it wagged about insistently while she spoke. It seemed impatient to escape and resume its prematurely curtailed freedom in the sky above.

The formidable Mrs Reilly was able to acquaint the group with the fact that Declan's grandfather, who had lived in England, had died only three months ago and 'maybe he was lonely in heaven and had asked God to send little Declan, who he was especially fond of, up to him'. That anyone in heaven might possibly think of making such a selfish request, and the idea the God might have listened to it, filled Alan with amazement.

As the tiny white coffin was carried from the church to the

awaiting hearse, Mimi buried her curly blond head in her mother's coat and started to whimper softly. Alan put his hand on her head and whispered in her ear,

'Don't cry Mimi.'

'I don't like it,' she said disconsolately, without raising her head from the relative solace of her mother's thigh.

'I know,' Alan tried to comfort her. 'We'll be going home in a minute.'

'I don't like them putting Declan in that box,' came in muffled sobs.

Noticing this little drama, Alan's Mum, glad of the excuse to avoid going to the graveyard, said goodbye to the little knot of chatting mourners.

'There, there, Mimi. We'll get some sweets in the shop on the way home. Alan, will you find Terry and follow us home?'

'Okay.' But he made no move to do as he'd been asked. Instead he said hesitantly,

'Mum?'

'What is it Alan?'

'Mum, I was just thinking during Mass – you know when we're saying our prayers we ask our Guardian Angel to protect us. I was just thinking - why didn't Declan's Guardian Angel protect him?'

His Mum looked at him with a concerned expression on her face. After a moment she said,

'I really don't know, Alan. It's very hard to understand why these things happen. All we can do is believe that God must have His own reasons for letting some things happen that don't seem right to us.'

His Mum's answer was honest, but it didn't help him feel any less confused.

* * * * * * * *

It would take several weeks for the pall of gloom that had settled over Glenawlin in the wake of the tragedy to start to dissipate. At the time it had happened Alan had already been attending the Christian Brothers' school for almost two months. It had not taken him long to realize that the regime he had now become subjected to represented a startlingly radical change from what he now recognized to have been, by comparison, a sleepy lackadaisical attitude in the local National School in Glenawlin. Here the teachers seemed to believe that constantly roaring and shouting at the pupils and brandishing sticks and leathers, which they had no hesitation in using for the smallest infringement of discipline or hesitancy in answering a question, was the way to educate those young boys in their charge. Their avowed conviction with regard to producing properly educated boys seemed to be that 'the only way to succeed is to beat it into them'.

Alan quickly grew to hate every minute of it. His life now consisted of two very distinct elements. There was the time he spent in school, which was a state of continuous fear and tension, during which he scarcely seemed to breath; and there was the rest of his life outside the school environment, during which he experienced an ever-diminishing sense of relief depending on how much free time was left before he had to enter the school gates again. The final countdown came each morning as he numbered to himself every one of the ninety-three steps he trudged between the bus stop and the school gate. Although he did not receive anything like the worst of the punishment meted out in class, the regular and customary beatings which were the intrinsic routine of the classroom affected him just as much as if he were the one at the receiving end of them. Every so often an incident occurred which resulted in this conventional level of ingrained violence being made to seem like a mild chiding.

It was late October and Billy Matthews, who sat beside Alan in class, had not been seen for three days and no reason or excuse had been communicated to the school. On the fourth morning, as Alan made his way to class, there was Billy sitting outside the Principal's room, shrunken in the carapace of his heavy oversized overcoat, looking scared to death. He had been caught playing truant, known locally as 'mitching'. The news spread throughout the classrooms like an electric current. As the tension mounted a frozen silence descended on the entire place as every boy was gripped with his own fear about the grim drama that was unfolding. The uneasy silence was broken by the sound of the bell for the first class of the day, Religious Instruction. Brother Corbin swished into class 5A in his long black soutane. Everyone stood and Morning Prayers began. The next thirty minutes were devoted to the Catechism, as they were during this first period each day. In an environment where there was generally an undercurrent of tension this initial period was usually among the least tense of the day. This morning it was different. Everyone knew something ugly was about to happen, and the foreboding and dire anticipation caused minds to stall and attention to wander. Every few minutes Brother Corbin was obliged to let out a roar in order to restore some level of concentration.

At 9.30 the bell for the end of class sounded and Corbin left the room with an admonishment that there was to be 'No talking.' Despite this warning the level of murmuring and whispering started to mount and one or two hollow, mirthless, giggles fractured the petrified atmosphere. Noise from the corridor beyond the classroom door heralded the reappearance of Corbin, followed by a timorous line of boys from the adjoining 5B class. They filtered in and stood nervously, shuffling and shifting beside the walls. Everyone knew that the Production – The Public Shaming and Chastisement of Billy Matthews - was about to begin. Everyone had to be a witness to what was to follow, so that the lesson about discipline would be clearly driven home.

Corbin called for silence and held the door open as the Principal, Brother Laffin, nicknamed 'Lasher', six foot two and face like flint, strode in with the frightened Matthews by the ear. From his free hand dangled a fifteen inch-long piece of leather-encased steel, two inches wide and thick as a man's finger. Laffin, who, like Corbin and all Christian Brothers, attended Mass and received Holy Communion (the ways to grace and perfection in holiness and Christianity) every day, let go his victim and placed the chair from behind Corbin's desk in the centre of the floor facing the assembled captive audience of rigid eleven-year-olds. Alan could scarcely breathe as tension gripped his entire system like a vice. Why did he, and all these other boys who had done nothing wrong, have to witness this repulsive scene?

Turning to the hapless Matthews, and delaying just long enough to maximize the panic being felt by young Billy, he lifted the leather slowly and tapped the boy on the shoulder.

'Remove the coat'

'I'm sorry Sir' Matthews blubbered.

'You're sorry Sir' mimicked Lasher. 'It's a bit late for that Sir. Now take off the coat Sir, and be quick about it Sir'

'I'll never do it again……..Sir,' pleaded Matthews

'I dare say you won't Sir'. The leather now flashed through the air and struck Matthews on the bare skin on the back of his legs below the short trousers which, like every boy in the class at that time, he wore. 'Now, take off the coat!' blazed Laffin.

Each horror-stricken boy in the room seemed to form part of a grotesque tableau, unable to move a muscle, each of them silently thanking God that he was not the one on the receiving end of Laffin's justice.

The grey-faced Billy was now shaking so badly that he was having difficulty undoing the overcoat buttons.

'Hurry up, boy!' shouted Laffin. 'We haven't got all day'.

Eventually the coat was off. Billy seemed to have wizened and shrivelled in the process of its removal.

The leather slashed the air once more and caught Matthews on the same tender spot at the back of his legs again. He leapt with pain, and a communal gasp escaped around the room.

'The jacket, boy! Remove the jacket too', roared Laffin.

Billy was wearing a dark brown corduroy jacket and short

trousers that had seen better days. The jacket, its threadbare sleeves streaked with mucus, was the zip-up type, but the zip had either been left open or was broken. It came off easily revealing Billy's emaciated frame and the thin ragged white shirt that was his last remaining covering. Laffin made a show of noisily repositioning the chair. When this prop was set to his satisfaction he placed his right foot firmly on it, and instructed the trembling Billy to bend over his knee. The boy, whose backside was now facing the class, was too short to position himself while keeping his feet on the ground. Laffin hauled him up into position. Holding his prey firmly by the back of the neck with his left hand he now took careful aim with the weapon, tapping Matthew's backside a couple of times before lifting the leather high and delivering the first blow. Billy jerked and yelped. Laffin let him settle down before the next assault. Another yelp from Billy. By the sixth or seventh battering Laffin had succeeded in reducing the boy to tears in front of the class. A few more measured swings from the powerful arm and Billy was sobbing uncontrollably, which was Laffin's avowed intention from the start.

This splendid scene of Christian love and compassion for all God's creatures, especially children, continued until Laffin, jaws clenched and sweat pouring from his excited red face, had relieved himself of a full twenty four lashes of the vile extension to his powerful arm. The victim of this sanguinary, sanctioned and unquestioned violence was by now virtually incapable of movement. Laffin slipped the leather into a pocket in his soutane and lifted Billy from his leg. The boy's knees gave way and he fell against Corbin's table, somehow managing to stay on his feet.

'Well, Matthews, do you think you've learned your lesson?'

Through his pain and tears Billy managed a faint 'Yes Sir'. Whether this was from fear, relief, or pure hatred, it was impossible to tell.

'Then back to your lessons; and the same for all the rest of you'. Lasher, having performed his duty and set the world to rights, left the room.

What made this all the more traumatic for Alan was the contrast between what he had just experienced and what he was used to at home, where neither his Mum or Dad ever laid a finger on the children.

Billy was twelve years old, the third of a family of eight children whose father was long-term unemployed. Billy had spent the previous three days caddying on the local golf course trying to earn some money. The overcoat was his elder brother's. Alan slid from his place, picked up Billy's coat and jacket, folded the coat into the form of a cushion, and placed it on the seat where Billy sat beside him in class. It would be many days before he could sit there without some form of padding.

Although Alan realized that his own terror was as nothing by comparison to what Billy Matthews had suffered he hated being forced, like every other fifth-class pupil present at school on that wretched day, to witness this gut-wrenching stomach-churning performance by the head Christian Brother.

That night Alan slept fitfully and dreamt of black-garbed creatures chasing him through a forest. He didn't know what they would do if they caught him, but he knew if they did he was dead. Fear itself was enough to keep him beyond their hideous reach.

The following morning as he sat at the breakfast table, feeling even more cheerless and ill at ease than usual about the prospects of the day ahead at school, Mrs Reilly again made an early morning call on Alan's Mum, in a great state of excitement. She had been on her way to Mass when she saw a crowd of people gathered outside the parish priest's house. The news was that Fr Deering had died late the previous evening. Mrs Reilly had gone up to the house looking for Peggy, Fr Deering's housekeeper, with whom she was very friendly.

'When Peggy brought him in his cup of cocoa around ten o'clock last night, there was Fr. Deering, may he rest in peace, slumped in his armchair with his book lying on the floor beside him. Poor Peggy! It took her ages to realise he was dead, and she nearly fainted with the dreadful shock she got.'

Mrs Reilly went on to tell how Peggy had phoned Fr Galvin when she'd pulled herself together, and he'd immediately taken charge of the situation. The doctor came first, followed soon after by an ambulance, and Fr Deering's remains had been removed to Loughlinstown hospital.

Mrs Reilly delivered this news with an air of excited confidentiality, as if, somehow, she was its sole privileged possessor. She relished being the first with any news and spread it so fast that Alan's Dad used to say that as long as Mrs Reilly was about they'd have no need for newspapers. As she hurried away to spread the news along the street she had one other singular detail to deliver,

'And do you know what he had been reading before Peggy found him? A book about Fatima! Hadn't he a great devotion to Our Lady altogether? I'm sure she's taken him straight to heaven.'

Alan's first thought, for which he immediately felt guilty, was whether this might mean getting the day off school. It didn't, but the children attending the local National Schools were sent home because, not only was Fr Deering the Parish Priest but, like all parish priests in Ireland, he was Manager of the National School. When Alan learned later of the other children's good fortune in being off school for the day, he felt, quite irrationally, hard done by. He was, however, allowed to miss a few hours school three days later in order to attend Fr Deering's funeral Mass.

On that morning his mother took her place in the church, accompanied by Alan and his baby brother, Barry, half an hour before the service was due to start, so as to make sure she got a good seat. Alan thought this was overdoing it but, as it turned out, the church filled up very quickly. All the children from the local schools had been assembled and were marched in, his sisters among them, and every other local organization was strongly represented. By the time Mass was about to start the church was jam-packed. At the appointed hour the attending priests (Alan counted twenty-three of them) filed on to the altar, and a hush fell on the congregation. Fr Deering's purple-draped coffin seemed almost lost in the sea of vestments surrounding it.

As if on cue there was a flurry of activity at the church entrance. Heads turned and necks were craned. The word 'Archbishop' floated like a slow-moving wave through the church. In the reverential hush that followed, the assembly was graced with the flowing presence of the auspiciously-initialled J. C. McQuaid, Archbishop of Dublin and Primate of Ireland, arrayed in his gorgeous canonicals. He processed regally, accompanied by his acolytes, along the aisle and took his place on the throne-type chair that had been erected to the left-hand side of the altar. And there he sat throughout the proceedings, mitred and resolutely holding his ornate crosier before him, every inch exuding steely authority, as befitted the most commanding personage in the land. Alan wondered to himself how this splendid vision fitted in with what he was being taught in school about Jesus, who was a poor man and told his listeners to be humble and not to be concerned with fine clothes. But then again, the Archbishop had written the catechism he was learning this from, and such an important man must be right no matter what he did.

Alan was not entirely unfamiliar with Archbishop McQuaid. On the day of his Confirmation a couple of years earlier it was the Archbishop who had stroked him on the cheek, to symbolize that he would be prepared to suffer and die for his faith if necessary, and who had asked him a question from the catechism. He remembered it vividly as a very alarming encounter.

Alan had also seen the Archbishop's curtained limousine pass along the main Dublin/Bray road quite often in the late afternoon on its way from the Archbishop's Palace on the city's north side, to his residence in Dublin's most prestigious residential area overlooking Killiney bay. On a couple of occasions Alan had even caught sight of him, when the limousine had stopped so that he could call into the local shoemaker's shop. The shoemaker had the privilege of hand-making the Archbishop's footwear.

The sound of the organ brought Alan back from his reverie, and momentarily stopped his baby brother, who was blissfully oblivious of the solemnity of the occasion, from squirming about on his mother's lap. The choir followed the organ's cue in solemn tones. The singing continued intermittently throughout the Mass, during which one of the visiting clerics delivered a long eulogy to the late Fr Deering, while the Archbishop presided austerely.

At one point, however, the solemnity of the proceedings was temporarily interrupted in Alan's area of the church. As the congregation stood to join in the singing, Alan's Mum put Barry sitting on the kneeler at her feet. Before she realized it, bored baby Barry had crawled away through the legs of those in the rows of pews in front of him, which was vastly more interesting than sitting at his mother's feet, until it dawned on him that he was totally lost, and set up an ear-splitting howl. Barry was retrieved from the floor and passed back over the seats to his red-faced, apologetic mother. Barry now clung to her like a leech, and was rewarded with the whispered, idle warning,

'Just wait till I get you home.'

The Mass ended with the customary prescribed prayer: 'St Michael, the Archangel, defend us in battle; be our defence against the wickedness and snares of the devil. May God rebuke him, we humbly pray; and do Thou, O Prince of the heavenly host, by the power of God, thrust into Hell Satan and the other evil spirits who prowl about the world for the ruin of souls. Amen.' The words of this prayer seemed a bit odd to Alan. He couldn't figure out how if Satan had been sent to Hell, from where there was supposed to be no escape, he could be free to 'prowl about the world'.

Alan's musings were interrupted at this point by the sight of the Archbishop rising from his throne and making his majestic way through the assembly to his waiting limousine. He had not spoken one word during the ceremony, but his demeanour had spoken volumes on the subject of authority.

The dramatic events of the previous few weeks – the death of young Declan Millar in the house-fire and the unexpected death of Fr Deering in quick succession – made a telling impression on Alan's mind. They were his first real encounters with death. It was no longer a grim ritual: is was a reality.

Alan had been fond of Fr Deering. He used to fancy that when he himself got old it would be nice to be like Fr Deering. When he remembered that Mrs Reilly had mentioned that Fr Deering had been reading about Fatima when he died, Alan decided he would like to read about that for himself. He knew a little bit about Fatima already. It was in Portugal, which he'd learned about in his geography class. Our Lady had appeared to three young children there in 1917 and told them some secrets, and said they would have to say lots of rosaries, and two of them died soon afterwards and had gone to heaven because Our Lady had promised them that they would when they died. The third one was a nun now and she still kept one of the secrets to herself, and everyone wondered what it was.

He found what he was looking for in the 'Religion' section in the local library. The book was very frightening. It told of how the three children had reported that when Our Lady had been speaking to them she held out her hands and the earth had vanished and they found themselves standing on the edge of a sea of fire. As they stared into the vast lake of molten liquid they saw a great number of devils and damned souls. The demons resembled black animals, each filling the air with shrieks and screams. The bodies of the damned souls leapt about despairingly in the flames. And Our Lady explained to the children,

'You have seen Hell, where the souls of sinners go.'

Later in the book Alan read what had been written in 1941 by the one who hadn't died, and who was now called Sister Lucia:

'The secret is made up of three distinct parts, two of which I am going to reveal. The first part is the vision of hell. Our Lady showed a great sea of fire which seemed to be under the earth. Plunged in this fire were demons and souls in human form, like transparent burning embers, all blackened or burnished bronze, floating about in the conflagration, now raised into the air by the flames that issued from within themselves together with great clouds of smoke, now falling back on every side like sparks in a huge fire, without weight or equilibrium, and amid shrieks and groans of pain and despair, which horrified us and made us tremble with fear. The demons could be distinguished by their terrifying likeness to frightful and unknown animals, all black and transparent.

We then looked up at Our Lady, who said to us so kindly and sadly: 'You have seen hell where the souls of poor sinners go.'

Because, on account of his upbringing, it never occurred to Alan to doubt for an instant that every word of what had been written by the nun was true, this account was acutely alarming. The visualizations of what had been so vividly portrayed ran through his mind like a repeating horror film. For weeks afterwards he was half afraid to go to sleep for fear of dying and finding himself in hell.

During those weeks Fr Galvin was the only priest functioning in the parish. This meant that on Sunday mornings Alan's Mum had no option but to attend his Mass, something she had long avoided. His sermons always seemed to her to be slanted towards blaming woman for all the bad things in the world, of which, of course, there was an almost infinite abundance. Relieved from the late Fr Deering's restraining influence, his censures had now become even more pointed and strident.

'That man has lost the run of himself entirely since Fr Deering died. If it's not Eve succumbing to the Devil to tempt Adam it's Salome's lustful dancing causing the beheading of John the Baptist. You'd wonder if he ever had a mother himself with the way he's always criticizing women.'

Each Sunday she seemed to bristle more and more, and such comments were delivered with increasing resentment.

'Did you hear him today chastising the women of the parish for wearing the New Look, and ranting about 'Fashion'. After all the drab clothes we've had to wear through the war years. Dressing immodestly my foot!' This was a very sensitive subject with Alan's Mum, who always tried to look well and keep up with the fashion trends as best she could, with the meagre resources available to her. The priest had touched a sore point when he launched into his criticism 'of those who would go out into the world dressed in the vanity and folly and ostentation of what is called 'fashion'. I wonder by what name it will be known at the last Judgment? Have the Holy Angels got an equivalent word, and will 'fashion' be written down in the book of God's remembrance? What will it be called? Vanity, wilful tempting of others, vainglory, luxury, self-exhibition, aye, and all of this often to the peril and danger of those who look on. This tendency towards, this distraction with the cult of the body is a vile blight on society.' And so on.

'I've a good mind to stop going to Mass altogether until we get a new priest!'

Alan was astonished to hear his Mum say this. He knew that to miss Mass, unless you were sick, was a mortal sin and if you died then you'd go straight to hell. Also, he had never heard anyone question the word of a priest before.

'Will I start looking for a house in another parish, Annie?' his Dad would ask, jokingly.

The appointment of a new parish priest, Fr Burke, shortly afterwards saved the day. His Mum's disposition was restored to normal. The idea that she might stop going to Mass, and the consequences for her of doing such a dreadful thing, had worried Alan.

The days dragged past until the two weeks Christmas holidays from school arrived and they, as usual, seemed to go by in no time at all. When school resumed in early January Billy Matthews was not there. He too had died. Drowned, they said, in the sea off the coast at Blackrock. It looked like an accident. He was fully clothed when they found him with the rope from a lifebuoy caught around his throat. He must have been fooling around with the lifebuoy and slipped, they said.

Brother Laffin escorted Billy's classmates to his funeral. He offered his profound sympathy to Billy's parents on the death of their 'very spirited' young son. Mr and Mrs Matthews took this as a great compliment.

3

March 1950

'Do not be afraid of those who kill the body but cannot kill the soul; fear him rather who can kill both body and soul in Hell'. The missioner delivered these words in a booming oratorical voice.

'This text, my dear men,' he continued, in a more intimate, but no less dramatic tone, 'is taken from St Matthew's Gospel, Chapter 10, verse 28'.

The second week – men's week – of the annual Parish Retreat was drawing towards a close. The women's services had finished on the previous Sunday afternoon, and the men's had started that evening. Alan and his Dad, along with just about every other male over twelve years old in the parish, had been there every evening since.

The missioner drew himself up to his full height, adjusted the cord around the waist of his dark brown robes, paused as he slowly surveyed his audience, placed his palms on the rim of the pulpit, and launched forth into his sermon.

'Who is it, then, who can kill the soul? Who is it that we must be ever on our guard against?' another pause. 'Satan! Satan the arch killer of souls, who roams the earth night and day like a hungry lion seeking those whom he can devour. That's who. He it is that we must be ever wary of. Satan, the most powerful of the fallen angles, next only to God Himself in power and strength. So powerful in fact that we mortals have no chance of escaping his attacks upon us unless we are constantly vigilant and constantly praying for the grace to live good and pure lives. Remember, my dear men, that the Lord Jesus Christ Himself has warned us 'Many are called, but few are chosen', that we must 'Stay awake, praying at all times for the strength to survive all that is going to happen', that we must 'Strive to enter by the narrow gate, since the road that leads to perdition is wide and spacious, and many take it; but it is a narrow gate and a hard road that leads to life, and only a few take it'.

The finger he now pointed at the congregation, as his glance swept the entire church, seemed to be aimed at each person individually – 'Are you,' he asked, pausing for heightened effect, Are you,' he repeated, more emphatically and ominously, 'prepared to make the effort to be among that few?'

Remember that the Gospels tell us that Satan even had the audacity to tempt the Son of God Himself. When Jesus had spent forty days in the wilderness and was weak from fasting, Satan picked his moment. He showed Jesus in a moment in time all the kingdoms of the world, and said to Him 'I will give to you all this power and the glory of these kingdoms, for it has been committed to me and I will give it to anyone I choose. Worship me then, and it shall all be yours.

Let us contemplate these fearful words. If we were ever in doubt about the danger Satan poses to us, all we have to do is recall these words of St Luke's Gospel which tell us in the clearest language possible that this world has been committed to Satan. How else could he give it away unless it was already in his power?'

The missioner continued in this vein, and in flowing theatrical manner, for the following half hour, driving home his warnings of impending damnation and divine retribution, pointing out the evil effects of the public house and the dance hall, of immoral books and magazines and films, of bad companions and, most particularly, of company-keeping, by which he meant unmarried men and women spending time together on their own. By the time he had finished his dramatic gesticulations and pulpit-poundings most of the chastened congregation resembled an assembly of mummified downcast cadavers, each solidified in the spot where he sat.

On his way out of the church Alan overheard a man comment that he thought that what they had been listening to would make a saint uneasy. It was a sentiment Alan had no difficulty relating to. He looked up at his Dad for some reaction. He trusted him more than anyone he knew, and the half smile and wink he received was enough to take some of the heat out of what they had just been subjected to. His father, Jim, was not one for enjoying the sound of his own voice. He exuded a quiet confidence in himself and an air of contentment that suggested he was quite happy to be who he was. His ease with himself was a source of reassurance to Alan. He felt that his Dad's evident lack of alarm meant that there was no real reason to be frightened. But this did not prevent him being pursued in his dreams that night by a large, black, snarling dog that got closer and closer to his heels with every bound no matter how fast he ran.... until he realized he was looking into the startled eyes of his elder sister, who had shaken him from his nightmare. She looked startled and concerned as she stood by his bed in her long, white nightdress.

'You were shouting,' was all she said. It was more of a question than a statement.

It took a few seconds for Alan to put everything into context.

'Sorry,' he said. 'I must have been having a bad dream. I'll be all right now. Go on back to bed. Sorry I woke you.'

'That's okay. Goodnight then.'

'Goodnight Terry.'

Alan lay awake for what seemed like an age before his mind ceased racing and sleep returned.

The following night the other half of the missionary team – they always seemed to work in pairs – followed the traditional format for parish retreats by preaching on the Blessed Virgin Mary. The difference in tone and spirit from that of the previous night was such as would cause the uninitiated to wonder if both sermons could possibly have had their roots in the same religion. The dread warnings and fear that had been instilled in the congregation the previous night had now all turned to sweetness and light. This bipolar strategy - Christ and Mary gathering everyone into heaven with open arms, alternating with the virtual inevitability of all but the chosen few being on the slippery slope to hell - continued until both preachers joined forces on the Sunday evening to bring the annual moral cleansing of the parish to a close in a blaze of lighted candles and a welter of lusty, fervent hymn-singing. On Monday morning, as the dust settled behind the departing divines, the parish took a collective deep breath and returned with relief to the comfortable weaknesses of normal living for another year.

The retreat had taken place, as was usual, during the Lenten period before Easter, which meant that Alan was approaching the end of his second year with the Christian Brothers in secondary school. The curriculum, unsurprisingly, ensured that a significant emphasis was placed on the study of the Catholic religion.

This year it had been Brother Driscoll's turn to perform this particular function. Driscoll, nicknamed Drak, was a small anaemic man whose appearance suggested that he had been absent when his Creator had been dispensing his allocation of blood. Winter or summer he always wore an overcoat over his soutane. Despite his diminutive stature his presence was palpable at all times from the aura of latent anger that seemed to surround him. He was a master of the psychology of classroom tension, with an extensive and perfected repertoire of non-verbal language, guaranteed to keep every boy in the room on tenterhooks. This language consisted of finger-drummings, tappings, slow cat-like pacings back and forth at the rear of the classroom, intense glares accompanied by thin smiles that displayed more menace than mirth, more leer than laughter, and an unnerving clicking sound made between tongue and cheek which always heralded trouble for the unfortunate boy who happened to be the subject of Drak's attention at that particular moment. A favourite stratagem, when he felt the urge to beat someone, was to stand to the side of the classroom, hands clasped behind his back and instruct the victim of the impending beating to walk to his table and bring him his leather. If this operation was not performed with suitable alacrity the dilatory scholar, on arrival within Drak's firing range, might well receive a slap across the face, delivered with the speed of a flyweight boxer's left hook. Strangely, no matter how often this happened, it always seemed to catch the luckless boy, and everyone else in the class, by surprise.

The content of the religious instruction programme had moved on considerably from that of the catechism used in the National schools. For a start the subject itself was now called 'Apologetics', which seemed to Alan an odd and confusing title for something that was presented as the absolute truth regarding the most fundamental and important aspect of life.

The curriculum covered everything from the proofs of the existence of God, the reality, spirituality and immortality of the human soul, the insufficiency of other codes of belief, revelation, miracles, prophesy, the authenticity and value of the New Testament, proofs of the divinity of Jesus Christ, to the Catholic Church being the one and only true Church founded by Jesus Christ, infallibility, the institution and efficacy of the sacraments, the unique nature and position of the Mass and the Eucharist, the gift of faith, the nature of sin, an analysis of the Ten Commandments, the necessity for prayer, and the existence of heaven and hell.

Drak brought the same steely approach to his teaching of

religion as he did to his classes on geometry or Latin. In fact his attitude suggested that these subjects were all more or less one and the same in his book. They consisted of facts that were there to be presented, analysed, proved, learned and accepted.

On one memorable occasion he asked a pupil named Liam Wilson to define the Blessed Eucharist. Liam's attempt failed to satisfy Drak's formula, and resulted in him being encouraged to do better by the customary stimulant of a dose of leathering. Drak, for good measure, threatened the boy with having 'to speak to his father unless he was prepared to apply himself more diligently'. What Drak was unaware of was that Liam's father was dead. At this point Liam, smarting from the painful effects of the beating, made the disastrous mistake of muttering 'You'll have to dig him up first'. There was absolute astonishment in the classroom. Not only was this a gross insult to Drak's person, and an unprecedented challenge to his authority, but it also put him on the back foot momentarily. It was the only occasion throughout the year on which Drak was observed to lose his steely composure, however briefly. But Drak was not about to allow himself to be humiliated by a fifteen-year-old upstart without due retaliation. His initial response was a one word sibilant order to 'Sit'. For the remaining forty-five minutes of the class Drak ignored everyone else apart from Liam Wilson, who was asked a relentless succession of questions on the Trinity, the characteristics of Mercy, Justice and Charity (which seemed peculiarly ironic in the circumstances), Free Will, Transubstantiation, and a variety of similar esoteric tenets of the Catholic religion. Liam could answer none of these satisfactorily and as failure followed failure beating followed beating. Alan counted eight leatherings in all. Liam Wilson refused to break down, much to Drak's increasing frustration. When the bell mercifully sounded the end of the period the boy's hands were raw red and twice their normal size. He was marked out for special attention in Drak's classes from that day onwards.

Liam had been, by and large, as unremarkably devout, or

undevout, as the rest of his classmates up to that time. After this incident religion gradually lost all meaning for him and eventually became something to which he was happily indifference.

Indifference to the presence of the Catholic Church was not, however, something that had ever occurred to Alan. Its all-pervasive influence was everywhere, and it had been that way all his life. A violinist might just as well have a notion of indifference to music. The Church was to the way of life he saw around him as flour was to bread, or water to the ocean. It simply *was*.

At this particular time its pervasive presence was, if possible, even more evident than usual. Rome had declared 1950 as a Holy Year, and on Easter Sunday as Alan and his Dad past the newspaper seller at the church gate on their way to Mass one of the Catholic newspapers proudly headlined *Ireland The Most Catholic Country In The World*.

'Is that true, Dad?' said Alan, pointing towards the newspaper.

'Is what true, son?'

'That Ireland is the most Catholic country in the world?'

His father smiled quizzically and said, 'I don't know, son. Obviously somebody thinks so. I've never really thought about it.'

Fr Burke, the man who had replaced the late Fr Deering, was the celebrant that morning, and when he reached the point at which the parish announcements were made during Mass he referred to the fact that May was only two weeks away, so it was time to start making preparations for the procession which would take place on May 20th this year.

'The parish choir' he said, 'will meet as usual for practice on Tuesday evening, and on each Saturday morning at 10 o'clock between now and the May procession the girls from the Children of Mary will meet here in the church to practice the Marian hymns.'

Alan gave his Dad a playful nudge and whispered 'Terry'. His sister was a member of this group. Jim returned the nudge and made a small shushing sound.

Fr Burke continued his announcements by telling the

congregation that the Miraculous Medal devotions would take place as usual at 8 o'clock on Monday. The women's monthly Sodality would meet on Thursday at the usual time, and because of the week that was in it, Easter Week, there'd be a special service of the Stations of the Cross followed by the Rosary and Benediction on Wednesday at 7.30. Next Sunday the annual Forty Hours Adoration of the Blessed Sacrament would commence after last Mass and continue through Sunday night and finish at 4 a.m. on Tuesday. The Eucharist, Fr Burke emphasised, should never be left unaccompanied in the church during this time. He invited those who were prepared to spend an hour before the tabernacle, especially during the night hours, to put their names down on the roster on the notice board in the church porch on their way out. He had been asked by Fr McGarry, the Parish Priest of the neighbouring parish of Shanardin to mention that there'd be a Novena starting there on Friday next at 8 o'clock to St Teresa of Liseaux, Patroness of the Foreign Missions, to whom Shanardin church was dedicated. The Diocesan Pilgrimage to Lourdes, which would be led by His Grace Archbishop McQuaid this year, would be leaving for Lourdes on September 15th. Those who intended taking part in the pilgrimage, or who had an invalided relation whom they would like to have included should contact Fr Galvin. Anyone could become an Associate member of the pilgrimage by making a contribution, again by contacting Fr Galvin.

There were, Fr Burke continued, a number of groups meetings in the Parish Hall during the week – The Legion of Mary, The Patricians, The Saint Vincent de Paul Society and the Pioneer Total Abstinence Society among them. Details were on the notice board along with information on other events that were taking place throughout the diocese in the near future. Finally, he announced that the church gate collection next Sunday would be on behalf of Saint Joseph's Young Priests Society, who supported young men financially to fulfil their vocation to become priests if their own families were not in a position to do so.

Fr Burke closed the folder from which he'd been reading and returned from the pulpit to the centre of the altar to continue intoning the Mass in the reverential-sounding, customary Latin phrases.

A mini-crisis arose for Alan when it came to the time to receive Communion. He stood up to leave the pew along with his Dad, and then suddenly sat back down again. Jim bent down and asked him what was wrong. With a very red face he said,

'I've just remembered, I'm not fasting.'

'How do you mean your not fasting?' Jim asked his son. 'We didn't have breakfast before we left the house.'

'I just remembered, Amy gave me a bit of her Easter egg this morning, and I ate it without thinking.'

Jim gave him a slightly long suffering look, and then said, 'Okay. Stay there, and don't worry about it.'

As they left the church at the end of Mass Jim stopped at the notice board in the porch. He was one of the regular collectors for the Saint Joseph's Young Priests Society and he wanted to check which Mass he'd been scheduled for the following Sunday. As he turned to leave he was greeted by Peter Millar, little Declan's father. After exchanging a few pleasantries Peter Millar said,

'You know, Jim, it seems to me that if you were to go to half of these activities you'd end up meeting yourself coming back!'

'You could be right, Peter.'

As the two men continued to chat Alan scanned the notice board. Among the information spread about were details of a pilgrimage to Knock in County Mayo in June, an invitation to join the Third Order of Saint Francis in Merchants' Quay in Dublin city, and a reminder of the weekly devotions to Saint Jude, the patron of hopeless causes, in the Jesuit church in Dublin's Gardiner Street.

Later that year, in August, the sleepy trio of Alan, Terry and Amy, started to accompany their mother to 'the Nine First Fridays'. It was commonly believed that God had told a saint in a vision that anyone who completed this devotion was guaranteed to go to heaven and avoid hell; all you had to do was go to Mass and Communion in a state of grace on the first Friday of nine consecutive months. Alan's Mum believed August was a good month to start because both it and April were the only months starting with the letter 'A' and they were nine months apart, which made it easy to know when you'd completed the exercise.

This was the world in which Alan lived and moved and had his being. For him it was simply a fact that religion was unquestionably the dominant element in the lives of the people around him, as vital to their being as the blood that coursed through their veins. For him the Church was simply accepted as the all-knowing guardian of society in general and every individual in particular. There might be the odd little criticism from time to time but if there were seriously dissenting voices he was unaware of them. It had never really occurred to the fifteen-year-old Alan, who had been born into this culture and who had experienced its influence and acceptance for all of his young life, to think that this was anything other than the way life should be. In fact it had been inculcated into him how wonderfully fortunate and privileged he was to be born into the Catholic faith, as baptized Catholics were the only ones whose souls could enter heaven.

This particular aspect of Catholic teaching bothered Alan. He had been instructed that because Protestants were not members of the one true Church their souls must go to hell, and that it was a mortal sin for a Catholic to attend a Protestant service, such as a wedding or funeral. The seriousness with which this was taken was brought home to him the previous year when he heard his Dad comment to his Mum about how ridiculous it seemed that the Catholic dignitaries of the land refused to enter the Protestant St Patrick's Cathedral for the funeral of the first President of Ireland, Douglas Hyde, a distinguished Protestant and Gaelic scholar. The newspapers reported on how they had sat outside in their cars until the service ended and then followed the cortege to the cemetery.

Alan's particular difficulty arose because he had become

friendly with a Protestant boy named Philip Ffrench, with whom he played football for the local Glenawlin boys' soccer team, known locally as 'The Glens'. Philip's father owned the hardware store in Glenawlin, and the family lived in a big detached house and owned a car, which marked them out as well off by 1950's standards in Ireland. Despite their social and religious differences Alan and Philip formed a natural friendship. Alan became a regular visitor to Philip's home, where they especially enjoyed playing chess together. And Philip had a big collection of books which he was happy to lend to his new friend. Alan spent months engrossed in the mischievous adventures of Richmal Crompton's *William* and the ingenious crime-solving of Conan Doyle's *Sherlock Holmes*. Philip's parents were very welcoming and pleasant to Alan and, indeed, to Alan's mind they appeared to be extremely nice and good people. The idea that because such people were not Catholics they could not get into heaven was confusing and disturbing. As they became better acquainted the boys talked about what they believed and didn't believe and, all in all, it seemed to Alan that except for the fact that Protestants had Sunday Service instead of Mass and that they did not *really* believe that Jesus was present in Holy Communion, which they called the Eucharist, Alan felt that there was not that much difference between them. Yes, Prods did not have to go to confession and tell all their sins as Catholics did, and they were allowed to read the Bible, which Catholics were forbidden to do in case they took the wrong meaning from what they read, and for some odd reason Prods said 'which' instead of 'who' when saying the *Our Father*. But that seemed to be about it, and that didn't seem enough to make sense of all the hostility between Catholics and Protestants.

It was around this time also that another type of 'friendship' first attracted Alan's attention. His attitude to girls was undergoing a rapid change from one of typical boyish indifference and mild disdain to one of covert curiosity. One girl in particular, who travelled regularly on the same bus as he took to and from school, caught his fancy. She was a pupil in the nearby convent school, run by the Dominican nuns. But he had a couple of problems in getting to talk to her. Maddeningly she seemed to be inseparable from the bunch of her friends with whom she travelled. Also, for him to admit to, or be caught showing, an interest in a girl, in front of the group of lads he associated with, was to risk being labelled a sissy and suffer some merciless teasing.

The longer this situation continued the more disconcerted and abstracted he became. His schoolwork suffered. He thought about her day and night. She became the most interesting creature in the world, but also the most elusive. He planned a hundred and one ways of getting to talk to her on her own, and dismissed each one as quickly as it came to mind.

Ultimately good fortune came his way. Occasionally, after school finished at 12.30 on Saturdays, instead of going home directly, he went to Dun Laoghaire and spent a relaxing hour browsing in the bookshops. And there, in one of them, quite unexpectedly, he found her all by herself! A great 'Will I?/Won't I?/How would I?' argument suddenly consumed him. He'd never spoken to her before, and couldn't just walk up to her now and start talking. She mightn't even recognise him! As he stood drowning in indecision a minor miracle happened: she glanced in his direction and smiled. He nodded and croaked out a 'Hi'. She said 'Hi'. Now he was beside her saying he often saw her on the bus. Yes, she'd seen him too. He blushed. He asked her what she was looking for. She'd got some birthday money, and she wanted to get *Jo's Boys* by Louisa May Alcott, the 'follow-up' to *Little Men*, which she had loved. He said his name was Alan. She was June. He blushed some more. When she'd bought what she wanted they left the shop together. and got the same bus home. He had the unbelievable good fortune to sit beside her and have her all to himself. He learned that she often went to Dun Laoghaire on Saturdays after school.

When they parted he was convinced that she was everything

he thought she would be, and more. He was smitten. Visits to Dun Laoghaire on Saturday afternoons became obligatory. If he met her it made his day. If she didn't appear the bottom fell out of his world. After about two months of this bitter-sweet emotional roller-coaster he plucked up the courage to ask her if she would like to go to a film with him. What a gamble! If she said no it would probably mean the end of anything to do with her.

Incredibly, she agreed. *Harvey* starring James Stewart was showing in a cinema in Dun Laoghaire, and they made a date to see the following Sunday night's show. Such a venture would put a very large dent in his pocket-money, but there was no doubt it was worth it. He was more excited than he had ever been in his whole life. And all the admonishments he had heard from priests and Christian Brothers, about sins of impurity and temptations of the flesh, were temporarily blanked out.

When they met in the cinema foyer it was the first occasion he had seen her wearing something other than her school uniform. She looked amazing. Even more attractive than she had been before. He bought the tickets. When they got inside he asked her if they'd stay at the back, and hoped against hope that she wouldn't object. She didn't. In fact she seemed just as keen as he did to seek the relative privacy of the back seats. Within a few minutes of the film starting Alan slipped his arm around June's shoulders, as he had observed others doing in similar situations. Again, she made no resistance. On the contrary, she inclined her head closer to his. Encouraged by his success he squeezed her closer to him and took her hand in his free hand. They held this embrace for some minutes while pretending to concentrate on the film. Then, as if some involuntary force had possessed them, they were kissing. After a few tentative pecks they both went to it with a will.

Alan had never kissed a girl before. Whatever he had imagined it would be like was as far from the reality as a symphony orchestra in full flight was from a barrel-organ. He was transported to a level of pleasure the like of which until then he had no idea existed. It was so exquisite that he could not contemplate life without it in future. And so began a succession of Sunday nights at the cinema with the very kissable June.

Of course he knew what he was doing was wrong. It niggled away at the back of his mind. Going out with a girl, and kissing her, was absolutely wrong unless you could afford to marry her and intended to do so. A mortal sin probably. But it was too irresistible to stop. Apart from worrying about going to hell if he died, there was another big problem for Alan. If he was committing mortal sins then he could not go to Holy Communion at Mass on Sundays, because that would be an even bigger mortal sin. Also, his parents would notice this and probably become suspicious that something was wrong, and start asking questions. To get around this problem he contrived as far as possible to go to whatever Mass his parents were not attending.

A few weeks after his discovery of this new pleasure-ground of bliss Alan got one hell of a fright. Immediately after morning prayers in class one Monday morning, Drak launched into a tirade about the fact that it had been reported to the Brothers that one of their pupils had been seen talking with a girl – *a girl* – on the streets of Dun Laoghaire the previous Saturday afternoon. He seriously hoped it was no one in this class, because if it was and they were identified...............

Talking to a girl. God Almighty, thought Alan, his stomach suddenly as tight and hard as a golf ball, what if I'd been seen and identified in the cinema!

When Drak eventually satisfied himself that he had scared his young charges from even looking sideways at the female of the species for the foreseeable future, the class returned to their study of the seventh commandment – *Thou shalt not steal.* In order to illustrate what might constitute a mortal sin under this commandment Drak offered as an example the stealing of his last sixpence from a starving man, but if you were to steal from a rich man you would probably have to steal a pound. In any event some theologians held that if you thought you had committed a mortal sin then you had done so. The class was back to normal.

After his close encounter with Drak's retribution Alan had to find an alternative to his Saturday meetings and Sunday films in Dun Laoghaire with June. They tried meeting in the city occasionally, but it all proved too awkward and furtive. The sheer unqualified magic was gone, and when the school summer break arrived and June went with her family on a month's holidays to Wexford, their enthusiasm waned and simply petered out. Alan's first flirtation with the opposite sex was over.

Now that the delights of June's company, and the entrancing sweetness of her kisses, were no longer the predominant focus and distraction of his life, he began to worry about the inescapable fact that he had been committing sins – and what sins! From what he had been taught he imagined his soul as something like a circular piece of cloth inside his body which would be pure white if he had no sins, but when you committed sins it got stained, and if you had a mortal sin on your soul it turned black. The only way to make it white again was by making a good confession, which meant telling all your sins honestly and fully, and the number of times you committed them, to a priest in confession. Even then your soul might still have some stain that would have to be burned off in purgatory if you died, before you could be let into heaven. Purgatory was like hell except it didn't last for eternity, and you had the consolation of knowing you would get to heaven eventually, which the souls in hell knew they never could do. There was a way to get your soul 'white' again; you could get a Plenary Indulgence. Catholics could get indulgences, which reduced the sinner's time in purgatory, by following certain instructions and saying special prayers. Some indulgences were good for one hundred days, others for three hundred, and so on. To get a plenary indulgence, one that would remit all your time in purgatory if you died before you committed any more sins, you had to follow a precise formula, which meant making a good confession, receiving Holy Communion by the following day and saying the required prayers, in the proper frame of mind, for the Pope's intentions. But you could never really be sure you'd got everything quite right.

He had been avoiding confession for months – since his first real date with June in fact. Before that he used to go every week or fortnight regularly like everyone else, spending maybe an hour in the queue shuffling towards the confession box, at around noon or in the evening, on Saturdays. He knew there was no way he could face either of the priests in the parish, as they would recognize him. But he would have to face the music and clear his conscience soon or he'd get no peace of mind.

He decided on going to Clarendon Street church in the city where, he'd been told, the priests had the reputation of not being too hard on people with really serious sins. He disliked going to confession at the best of times, even when he only had the usual 'shopping list' to recite – using 'bad language', missing his prayers, calling the Holy Name in vain, being disobedient, and so on, half the time struggling to find something to say. But this was much worse altogether. This was the mental equivalent of going to the dentist.

He'd never been in Clarendon Street church before. He went in through the entrance off Grafton Street, and found himself in a spacious building shaped like a cross. It had about a dozen confession boxes arranged along the walls on each side of the main aisle and in both side chapels. When he got there on the fateful Saturday afternoon there were people outside most confession boxes waiting to rid themselves of their sins. Some of the queues were noticeably longer than others. On the assumption that the reason for some priests having more penitents waiting for them than others was that they were 'easier' to confess to, Alan took he place at the end of the longest queue. He went over in his mind again and again how he would phrase what he had to say. He'd start off with the regular stuff, and hope he could slip in the difficult bit without too much fuss. He didn't want to be kept in the box for long because when someone took more than a minute or two those waiting outside would think that person had done something seriously bad.

Having inched his way towards the confession box, through what seemed like an eternity, it was now his turn. He closed the door behind him and knelt down in the dark confined space and, again, waited. What seemed like muffled mumblings were just about audible from the other side of the panel that separated him from the priest. Then, a moment's silence. The panel slid back and the priest inclined his ear towards the grill between them, and made the sign of the cross. He had a short grey beard and seemed old to Alan, although he was probably no more than fifty. Alan would have preferred someone a bit closer to his own age. This priest looked a bit like the missioners who came to the parish each year to preach what his Dad called 'hellfire and brimstone'.

'Bless me Father for I have sinned'

'How long since your last confession?'

'About four months, Father'

No reaction. Relief. So far so good.

Alan then trotted out the usual catalogue of minor misdemeanours.

'Anything else?'

'Yes, Father. I've….. I've been going out with a girl'

'And did something wrong happen?'

'Well, eh….. we got close together and, you know, did things'

The priest straightened up a bit and turned his head towards Alan.

'Did you have intercourse with her?'

'What?' said the confused Alan.

'Did you have intercourse with this girl?'

Alan had no idea what he was talking about. He had never heard the word intercourse before.

'I kissed her, Father'. Maybe that was the right answer.

'How many times did you do this?'

'Lots of times, father'

'Were they passing kisses?'

'I, eh…..don't know what you mean, Father'

'Were they passing kisses, you know?' Alan tensed at the tone of irritation in the priest's voice. Although he'd heard the guys in school mention the words French kissing he really hadn't a clue about there being various types of kisses, except, of course, that kissing June was different from kissing his mother.

'Sorry Father, I eh, don't think so…..'

'Did you do anything else. Did you touch her?'

'Yes, Father'

'Where?'

'At the pictures, Father'

The priest gave him a sharp suspicious look, and seemed like he was about to lose his temper.

'I mean where on her person did you touch her?' The voice louder, tighter. Alan winced. Jesus, people out in the church will hear!

'Oh, on the leg, Father', hastily. Please God let me out of here!

After telling him that he should never do anything that he would be ashamed to do in front of his mother, and making him promise to amend his life, the priest told him that for his penance he was to say ten Our Fathers, ten Hail Marys and ten Glory Be to the Fathers. Usually he got one, or sometimes three, of each. So, what he had done must have been pretty bad.

As he left the box he was flushed and sweating, and reckoned that everyone around was looking at him accusingly. Still, it was over, and for that he was relieved. No more messing about with girls. Nothing was worth having to go through this for. He made his way up the centre aisle towards the altar and knelt down in a pew a few rows from the front, and tried to concentrate on saying the prayers that had been to say for his penance. He knew his sins were still not forgiven until he had 'done' his penance, so it was important to get that attended to as soon as possible. His mind wandered from the prayers to the statute of the dead Christ in the tomb that decorated the base of the church's altar. He knew from what he had been told in school that Christ had had to suffer and die because of sin, his sin included. Thinking about this he'd lost track of the number of prayers he'd said, and had to start again from the beginning. Eventually he was fairly satisfied that he had applied his mind to all the requirements of his penance, and, after saying a prayer for the priest who heard his confession, as he had been trained to do, he got up to leave, feeling as if a great weight had been lifted from his shoulders. As the church doors swished closed behind him, he was amused by the 'kissing' sound they seemed to make as the rubber-insulated edges pressed together. He wondered what you'd call that kind of 'kiss'? Swishing? Sounded messy.

On his way home on the bus he thought of the words the priest had used that he had not understood. It was as if they had been speaking different languages. It had not been the only occasion on which the inadequacy of his language, and his lack of knowledge of human behaviour, had become apparent during this period of his adolescent life. A few weeks earlier an incident had occurred which still puzzled him.

After leaving June home to her door late on that particular evening, he decided, as he often did, to try hitching a lift home. He thought he was in luck when a car, driven by a man of about forty, stopped for him. There were no other occupants, which was not unusual. The man asked him where he'd been, and Alan told him he'd been to the cinema, and started chatting about the film. The man then started asking him questions about whether or not he'd been with a girl, and did he like girls, and what he liked to do when he was with a girl, and did he like the feel of them. At this point the man dropped one hand from the steering wheel onto Alan's knee and gave it a little squeeze, as if to demonstrate what he meant by liking the 'feeling' he'd been asking about. All this was done in a suggestive leery sort of way that made Alan uneasy, even though, as Alan thought, it was just a man making conversation and giving his knee a squeeze, which seemed a bit odd as he'd only just met him, but maybe that was just his way of being friendly.

Although still some distance from home Alan decided he'd prefer to walk the rest of the way rather than be with this man any longer. He asked him to stop and let him out, fibbing that he lived nearby. The man turned the car onto a quite side road and pulled in. Alan thanked him for the lift, said goodnight, and went to open his door to get out. The door wouldn't open. He tried it a couple of times, thinking he might not be operating the handle properly. The man said that the door handle was faulty and didn't work sometimes. Then he asked Alan if he would like to sit and talk for a while, and again his hand was on Alan's leg, but much higher up than before. Alan had never been in a situation like this before. He was beginning to feel panic, and knew he wanted to get out of there as fast as he could. He lifted the man's hand from his leg and, trying to keep any sign of alarm from his voice, said he wanted to go home now, and asked him to let him out. After a long moment's silence the man reached across him and opened the 'faulty' door, without apparent difficulty. Alan was away like a shot.

When he got home his Mum and Dad were sitting at the kitchen table, chatting and having their nightly cup of cocoa before bed. His Dad noticed that he seemed agitated and asked him if something was wrong. Alan told them all about what had happened. His parents exchanged knowing glances as his Mum busied herself with clearing the table. All that was said was that he would be better off avoiding hitching lifts late at night. On his way up the stairs to his bedroom Alan thought he detected a rare note of anger in his father's voice as he overheard him, in a tight undertone, saying to his mother,

'I'll bet that was that ne'er-do-well nancy-boy son of Judge Browne'.

It would be a while yet before the word 'homosexual' would enter Alan's vocabulary.

4

Summer '51

Rumours started to circulate in early June about a funfair coming to the village that summer, but no one seemed to know for sure until a rash of posters appeared on the lampposts and in shop windows announcing that *Jewells Travelling Funfair* would be in Glenawlin for the month of August. The village had never experienced anything like it before, and excitement ran high. It set up alongside the main road in a field in Morrows' farm on the Dublin side of the village opposite the 'New Shops' that had been there since God knows when. To advertise their presence they put on a fireworks display on the first night. Some locals protested about the loud music and noise disrupting their peace and quiet, and the operators agreed to stop anything noisy by 10.30 p.m. Despite this the place was thronged every evening by people coming from all direction to have fun with the various amusements.

Within a few days of its arrival Alan had inveigled himself into a job assisting on the dodgems. It was a great opportunity to make some money while having fun at the same time. It also provided another bonus he had not anticipated. Girls loved the dodgems, teenage girls especially. Part of his job was to help people to get the cars moving and to sort them out when things got in a jamb. And the ones that had most problems were the girls, dozens of them, all laughing and happy and willing to be helped. He sat in beside them – *contact* - and showed them how to use the pedals; he balanced on the thick rubber rims surrounding the cars, guiding their bewitching little hands on the steering wheel – *contact* – until they got the hang of it. It was the best situation a guy could dream of for meeting girls. Just perfect for overcoming your inhibitions and improving your chatting skills. Perfectly legitimate. And no Drax to worry about tomorrow either. But he soon wanted more than simply to meet them. The situation was tantalizing, especially now that he knew from his experience with June just how exquisite the touch of a girl's lips could be. But there was one big problem – the girls were always in groups or in pairs. You could never get to talk to one on her own.

A few nights after he got the job a solution presented itself. He was strolling home with Joe McLoughlin, another attendant on the dodgems, after the fairground closed when the chat turned to girls. Joe had been a couple of years ahead of Alan in the local National school, and had a reputation for being pretty streetwise. He had a proposition, but he wasn't too sure about how willing Alan might be to cooperate with it. His plan was simple. If they joined forces they might have a better chance of getting somewhere with the girls than own their own. Alan was all ears. The plan was that if either of them got talking to a pair of likely looking girls in one of the cars they'd point out the other guy and suggest that the four of them meet up for a coke or whatever at the ice cream kiosk when the dodgems were finished. People always hung about for refreshments after the rides started to close for the evening.

The plan worked like a dream. Each evening for three glorious weeks the two young aspiring Casanovas succeeded in lining up a pair of girls to meet them when they finished work. Sometimes the girls wouldn't show up, or they'd stick together like Siamese twins if they did. But mostly, due to Joe's skilful ingenuity, each of them would soon have the very pleasurable delights of a girl all to himself. Sometimes the same pair returned two or three times, and the boys knew they were in business. The shadowy areas of the fairground, and the excitement of its slightly sleazy atmosphere were perfect for slipping into that fuzzy suspended state where inhibition easily succumbs to pleasure, and restraint is drowned in the moment.

Although he didn't have to worry anymore about the dreaded Drax, and managed to muffle the little voice that niggled at him about having to face the mortifying business of confession at some stage, he did have one scary moment when it seemed that his nightly amorous adventures might prove very uncomfortable.

Usually by the time he got home everyone was in bed and the house was in darkness, but one night, shortly before the fair was to end, the lights were still on in the kitchen when he got there. Alan felt a little dart of apprehension. Who was up? Had the girl he'd been with for the past couple of hours left makeup on him? His Dad was sitting at the table with the bits and pieces of a clock spread out before him. He nodded to Alan and while seeming to return his concentration to the dismembered clock said,

'Working overtime, were you?'

Jeez, what's this about?

'Eh, no Dad, not really. Just got chatting to Joe McLoughlin on the way home.'

'Joe McLoughlin? I hear you two have become very friendly.'

'Well, we work together on the dodgems.'

'Work together. Good.' After a slight pause he lifted his head and looked at Alan.

'Joe has a bit of a reputation in these parts, son. Be careful you don't do anything you'll regret later.'

'Sure, Dad.'

"Night, son.'

"Night, Dad.'

Alan figured his father knew a great deal more about what was happening at the fairground than he let on.

* * * * * * * * *

By the time summer ended and he returned to school Alan regarded himself as quite grown up by comparison with the naïve boy he'd been three months earlier. He was no longer too concerned about what his teachers thought of what he did outside school and, as was usual in this second last year at secondary school, the beatings had stopped, possibly because many of the students were by now as big or bigger than the men who taught them. Although fifth year was regarded as relatively easy, with no major exam to worry about at the end of it, he settled down to his studies willingly after his exposure to the pleasurable experiences of the summer holidays. The year went by smoothly and it was not until it was coming towards an end that another significant event occurred which was as far removed from his fairground escapades of the previous summer as he could have imagined.

It was traditional for the school to arrange for all the students to spend one week in a Jesuit Retreat House during the course of their fifth year, away from the world and all its distractions, undergoing intensive instruction in their Catholic faith – a sort of spiritual mini-finishing school. This year was chosen in preference to the final year so as not to interfere with the students' preparations for their state examinations. Alan was quite looking forward to this week for various reasons. It promised to be novel and it also meant a week off school, which was always welcome. Mostly, however, he was curious to see and listen to the Jesuits in action. On the one hand he had heard that they were more pragmatic in their approach to life and religion than the other run-of-the-mill orders of missionary monks. (Hadn't the Jesuits adopted the caste system among themselves in India in order to try to make headway converting the masses there?). On the other hand he had got hold of a clandestine copy of James Joyce's

Portrait of the Artist as a Young Man (strictly forbidden reading for all Catholics, much less a teenage boy, because of its sexual content) which contained graphic and frightening accounts of hell as preached to Joyce and his classmates by their Jesuit teachers, when they were about Alan's own age.

Upon arrival at the ivy-clad monastery-cum-castle in the verdant suburbs of west Dublin, where the week's retreat would be conducted, each boy was directed to a small sparse room containing a narrow bed, a small table, a chair and a clothes closet. This would be home from the Monday morning of arrival until the following Sunday afternoon. Alan's room was on the second floor and, when he closed the door behind him, despite its Spartan appearance he felt a surge of pleasure. He'd never had a room to himself before.

When the checking-in procedure was completed the boys were summoned to assemble in the chapel. There a sprightly young priest, Fr McAdam, outlined the rules and schedules that were to be adhered to for the coming week.

'It is of the utmost importance that strict silence be observed at all times, even at mealtimes, during which passages from the Scriptures will be read to you.'

Silence, he emphasized, was essential in order to create the right atmosphere in which to meditate and reflect on the content of the homilies they would hear, and so as not to interfere with the contemplation of anyone else.

The retreat was conducted by three priests; the young Fr McAdam, who exuded energy and enthusiasm, Fr Roberts, a man in his fifties, of rather florid, Friar Tuck, appearance, and Fr Stritch, a tall elderly man of ramrod bearing and ascetic demeanour. Fr Stritch was Retreat Director and very clearly the dominant figure and leading light in the week's events and presentations. He generated the unmistakable impression that this retreat was the most important work he had ever set his mind and heart to in his life, and, by association, it was the most significant event that would ever occur in the life of each boy who was there. By the time Alan left the confines of the retreat house the following Sunday his predominant feeling was one of fear. Everything he had been taught about the dire consequences of sinning had been brought back into sharp and graphic focus.

Each day followed a pattern of early morning assembly for morning prayers, followed by Mass, breakfast, a short break before the first sermon of the day, recreation – when the boys were permitted to walk about the grounds, dinner, another short break before the day's second sermon, which was immediately followed by Benediction, then a period devoted to contemplation or reading from a selection of books in the monastery library, a further recreational period, tea, the final sermon of the day, Night Prayers, and, for those who wanted it before going to bed, Confession or a one-to-one talk with one of the available priests, during which boys were encouraged to discuss any special problems that might be bothering them.

Each of the three priests presented one sermon each day. Every word they spoke was delivered with complete certainty and with all the accumulated authority of two thousand years of Christian wisdom, and with all the power and energy surrounding an infallible belief system. And chief among the great certainties were Death, Judgement, Hell or Heaven. These were the subjects that dominated the week's programme and, of them, the main focus was on Hell, about which they seemed to know a great deal. The three preachers seemed to be of one mind in believing that engendering a Fear of Hell in their listeners was the most effective way of ensuring the salvation of their souls.

Hell, or heaven, was the ultimate end for everyone, but before having to face that perilous eventuality there were other portentous matters to be considered.

'There are, my dear boys,' the cultured melliferous tones of Fr Stritch's voice, as he delivered his first sermon, resonated throughout the chapel, 'few things that are certainties. But of one thing we can all be absolutely certain, and that is, once having been born, each and every one of us will die. Death, like God, Judgement, Hell and Heaven, is one of the great certainties.'

It was his habit, as he spoke, to stand directly in the centre of the elevated area in front of the altar. Occasionally he would bow his head, close his eyes and, making a steeple of his forefingers, place their tips on his lips, and pause, so as to let a point sink in, or to gather his thoughts before continuing with his oration.

Death, he emphasized, would come unannounced, like a thief in the night. No one knew the hour or the day when they would breathe their last.

'Only a few weeks ago, a man who was attending a week-end retreat in this very retreat house retired to bed having taken his supper on Saturday evening, only to be found dead in his bed the following morning. God grant that his soul was prepared to meet its Maker.'

Would our souls be ready if Death came for us so unexpectedly, he asked? There was nothing more important than to be properly prepared for that moment, to be in a state of grace, to be pleasing and wholesome in the sight of God, for on this depended our eternal destiny – bliss in heaven, or most dreadful punishment in hell.

'You may elude Death once, twice, three times, but you cannot keep it at bay forever. Surgery, medical skill, care of your health, a warm sunny climate, may prolong life, but not forever! You will not escape; no one escapes. Imagine that dreadful moment. Your strength is failing, your senses dulling. The cold hand of Death is upon you and will not be removed. Imagine the anguish you will feel if your soul is stained with mortal sin and you have no opportunity to repent. Remember, you do not know at what hour Death will come. Our Lord, in Chapter 24, verse 44, of St Matthew's gospel, warns us of this: 'Therefore you must stand ready because the Son of Man is coming at an hour you do not expect', and again, St Paul warns us in his first letter to the Thessalonians: 'The day of the Lord is going to come like a thief in the night'. Does a thief who intends to rob you send you a warning? Does he let you know the time of his coming? No, he comes in the night when you are asleep and off guard, at a moment you least expect. So it is with Death. It comes unexpectedly: Some drop dead suddenly at work, or in the street; some are found dead in bed; others die on the spot in a motor accident.'

Alan and his companions were exhorted to meditate on these truths frequently, and especially on whether or not at the moment of death each one would be judged a friend of God or His enemy. On this depended where each one would spend eternity. With this truly awesome prospect in mind St Paul, when writing to the Philippians, had wisely warned us to 'work out our salvation in fear and trembling.'

'Not only does the great apostle Paul caution us in this context, but in St Matthew's gospel we hear the words of Jesus Christ Himself: 'If your eye should cause you to sin, tear it out and throw it away; it is better for you to enter into life with one eye than to have two eyes and be thrown into the hell of fire.' What is more precious to a man than his eyes? Yet our Lord, who knows what hell's sufferings are like, warns us sternly: 'Lose everything rather than be cast into hell.'

Fr Stritch spoke in vivid terms of how, at the moment of death, the soul, still in the presence of the body from which it has just departed forever, assumes its own brilliant consciousness and sees before it in graphic and uncompromising detail the scenes of its life. Every sin is exposed, every guilty word, thought, deed and omission, every offence against and rejection of God's grace will be seen in all its foulness, and, most frighteningly of all, the awesome irreversible decision will be made regarding each soul's eternal destiny. In that moment either the indescribable glories of heaven, or the never ending torments of hell will open to receive the soul.

If Fr Stritch's emphasis was on death then the younger, brisk

Fr McAdam's special area of focus was Satan. In contrast to Fr Stritch's statue-like stillness as he spoke, Fr McAdam's preferred method of emphasis, as he made each salient point, was to pace a few steps from, and then return to, his chosen rostrum.

Satan, he informed the callow gathering before him, was our most formidable enemy. He was next only to God Himself in intelligence. He made it his business to know each one of us intimately, to know our weaknesses, our 'predominant passion' – that vice which we were most attracted by and most likely to succumb to. He would stalk us and tempt us relentlessly throughout our entire lives, especially in those areas where our fallen and essentially depraved nature was most vulnerable.

'He is clever and cunning beyond description, and without the aid of Holy Mother Church our puny intelligence is no match for his wiles.'

In case anyone should be in any doubt about the reality of Satan's presence among us, Fr McAdam could confirm, from his own personal experience, visiting a Dublin hospital where, from the moment a particular man was admitted to a ward where six other patients were receiving treatment, no one among them made any progress towards recovery. From the time of his admission the ward had been filled with a foul odour. When the other six occupants of the ward were removed to other wards, their natural recovery resumed immediately. The man, who was undoubtedly at the heart of the problem, was observed conversing with an unseen presence that seemed to hover near his bed. There could be no other explanation but that this man was in league with Satan, whose evil and foul presence pervaded everything around it. Yes, Satan was very real and we should fear him constantly. One consolation we had was that, whereas God, because He was Our Creator, could enter freely into our being at any time, Satan needed to be invited in.

'Each time we sin is like issuing an invitation to Satan to come and join us, and he will not be slow to accept that invitation.'

Fr McAdam was keen to emphasize that Satan, in his insidious and devious way, loves to dupe evil-doers into thinking that, come the hour of death, they will be annihilated. He would like us to think and act as if there would be no retribution for the wrongs we were responsible for in this life. In this way we are seduced into lowering our guard and into making his demonic task all the easier. But we know from our catechism, and from Scripture that the soul will live forever, and the damned will suffer in eternal flames. Furthermore, we should be most wary when we hear someone treat Satan as a subject for levity.

'There is nothing he loves better than to hear people make jokes about him, and laugh at him, because this is the surest way to make men cease to fear him and cease to believe in his existence.'

These weighty sermons were, of course, interspersed with less terror-inducing subjects - the importance of the Mass, sacraments and prayer in the Christian life; the role of the Blessed Virgin as the great mediator between us and Her Son, Jesus; the inspiration to be gained from the lives of the saints; the gift of faith; the necessity for charitable works; the benefits to the character of self-denial; and the avoidance of 'bad companions'.

Despite these relatively lighter interludes, it was the recurring emphasis on death, sin, hellfire and damnation that excited and agitated Alan's imagination most. Instead of enjoying seven or eight hours unbroken sleep, which was his normal pattern, he now found that scarcely an hour passed before he woke from one disturbing nightmare or another. In one vision he saw himself awake staring at a snake that had coiled itself up on the foot of his bed. When he tried to kick it away it slithered onto the floor and out of sight. Roused by panic he was half afraid to put his feet on the floor to check that the only snake in the room was the insubstantial one in his distressing dream.

Another night, in his fitfulness, he stood in a narrow, derelict, high-walled chapel with only one tiny window high above a crumbling altar. Philip Ffrench beckoned to him from a narrow doorway, which appeared to be the only way out; but as he approached them both Philip and the door disappeared. He was trapped inside. He pounded his fists on the wall where the door had been. When he eventually awoke he could not recall how, or if, he had escaped. The experience left him with a vague feeling of irritation and uneasiness. As he lay there he remembered that he had the luxury of having a room to himself and, free from having to be concerned about disturbing anyone else, he switched on the bedside lamp. The corners of the room remained in virtual darkness, as the lampshade cast wavy shadows around the walls. From the small cocoon of light left surrounding him, he decided to try reading some of the Catholic Truth Society pamphlets that had been left on the table in the room, but was either too tired or too uneasy to concentrate for long. He got out of bed and stood by the window, watching the moonlight glisten on the lake below. This was the lake he had read about in one of the pamphlets in which, not all that long ago, a saintly young priest, whose cause for canonization had already been commenced, would stand up to his neck for hours on winter nights, in penance for sin.

His contemplation of this extraordinary act of atonement was interrupted by what sounded like a commotion in the corridor outside his room. He could not make out what was being said, but the voices seemed both muffled and angry. Alan opened his door slightly to see what was happening. He could see Fr McAdam outside the room next to his own, gesticulating angrily. Alan knew it was Maurice Kennedy's room. 'Keno' was the school's star rugby player – the only one from the school to be selected for the schoolboys' international rugby team in years – and had the reputation of being 'a bit of a hard case'. As he watched, two other boys emerged sheepishly from Keno's room. Alan closed his own door softly, figuring that it was best not to get involved in this situation.

On his way to breakfast the following morning, Alan saw the three offenders standing, bags packed, in the entrance hall, waiting to be escorted home.

The news was that 'Keno', and two of his pals from the school rugby team, had been discovered, at two o'clock in the morning, in his room playing cards, and drinking bottles of Guinness that Maurice had smuggled into the retreat house in his suitcase.

The sobering effect of these expulsions on the remaining retreatants, and the sight of the three vacant spaces at the breakfast table, did not last very long.

Fr Roberts, the bald, Friar Tuck look-alike and third member of the retreat's presenters, usually gave the first sermon each day. He always processed from the chapel door to the altar steps with a noiseless, flowing, undulating motion, the grace of which defied his bulk. Typically, he stood with his head tilted slightly backwards, chin elevated, and hands clasped behind his back. Occasionally, to underscore his thoughts, he raised his considerable bulk on the balls of his feet and held that position for a few moments, before lowering his heels to the marble floor. Alan was always slightly distracted by this mild form of callisthenics, thinking to himself how strenuous it must be for such a rotund man.

His voice, like his gait, had a smooth modulating flow to it, measured, mellow and hypnotic. On one occasion he commenced by inviting the boys to consider the fact that each of them was blessed with one great gift that he no longer had.

'And what might this gift be?' he asked rhetorically.

'Hair,' came the muffled 'answer' from Kevin Kenny, the class clown, sitting in the pew furthest from the altar. Alan, who was sitting directly in front of him, along with half a dozen others within earshot, doubled up in constricted laughter. Fr Roberts did not seem to notice this breach of the rule of silence as he announced the solution to the mystery,

'It is, of course, the gift of youth.'

However, from among his various topics the one that left the most lasting impression on Alan's psyche was his thoughts on sin.

In the course of this sermon, he reminded his juvenile audience of what they had been taught in their catechism: sin was any wilful word, deed, thought or omission contrary to the law of God, and mortal sin killed the soul by depriving it of its true life, which was sanctifying grace, and brought with it death and everlasting damnation. If one wanted to realize just how horrible sin was in the sight of God all one had to do was picture the passion and death of Jesus on the first Good Friday. It was sin that caused Him to suffer the agony of each thorn being driven into His head, each lash at His scourging, each painful step as He dragged His cross along the road to Calvary, each nail through His sacred hands and feet, the slow ghastly agony as His body hung, bleeding and covered in wounds, for three long hours until the end came. Sins – our sins – caused this.

Whenever Fr Roberts paused in his homily a look of profound sadness, or the merest indication of a tragic smile, passed over his countenance.

'But,' he reassured his chastened listeners, 'as Catholics, we have the great consolation of the sacrament of Confession.' He went on to emphasise that no matter how heinous or profligate our lives had been in the past, no matter how addicted we had become to any particular sin, we could regain God's love and restore our souls to life. All that was required was to examine one's conscience and approach a priest, who was God's own representative, with a sincere heart and a desire to make a good confession, and all would be well.

Not surprisingly Fr Roberts popularity at confession time was unrivalled.

Perhaps the most fear-inducing contribution of the week came from the intense Fr McAdam. Having already impressed on his young listeners the terrifying power and ever-present reality of Satan, he proceeded to enlighten them about the horrors awaiting those who were damned to hell.

No one, he asserted, could be in the slightest doubt about the existence of hell. There was no escaping the certitude of this fact based on the numerous references to it in both the Old and New Testaments. He quoted from *Daniel* – a furnace of blazing fire, from *Revelations* - a lake of fire burning with brimstone, and, from Jesus Christ Himself in *Matthew's* gospel – a furnace of fire. Not only is hell a 'lake of fire' but this fire is everlasting, where the damned will be tormented in both body and mind for all eternity without respite. In fact the most terrifying aspect of all about hell is its length or duration. Sceptics throughout the ages have scorned the eternal nature of hell, substituting in its place notions like the destruction of the damned. But, Fr McAdam, now in full flow, asserted, the reality could not be clearer when we examine the Gospels. *Revelations* spelt it out: 'And the devil who deceived them was thrown into the lake of fire and brimstone, where the beast and the false prophet are also; and they will be tormented *day and night forever and ever*'.

'This verse,' he asserted, 'makes it crystal clear: *Hell is forever and ever*. How could a stronger, more certain message be used? If God wanted to communicate the eternal nature of hell to us, how could He communicate it more clearly than by using the expression 'forever and ever'?'

The young priest invited his already petrified listeners to remember what it felt like to be touched momentarily by a flame, perhaps on the tip of the finger, from which it was possible to instantly withdraw.

'Now imagine' he continued 'the pain you would suffer if your entire body was thrown into a furnace where you would survive for a matter of seconds before physical death brought merciful relief. Now imagine that your body had to lie in that furnace for fifteen minutes in your full senses. Imagine the terror you would feel at the entrance to that furnace! And how long that fifteen minutes would seem to you. Each minute would in itself feel like an eternity. Now imagine that you had to endure that condition for a full twenty-four hours, for a year, for a hundred years! Imagine, then, the utter anguish of the soul condemned to hell when it learns that the fire it finds itself immersed in, a fire far more intense that the fire we experience here on earth, must be endured *forever and ever!* After millions and millions of years hell's torments would be no nearer to an end. If we were to count each drop of water in all the earth's oceans, and every grain of sand on every beach, every blade of grass in every meadow, and every star in the heavens as a million years, eternity would not even have begun.'

He made it clear that to comfort ourselves by thinking that the souls of the damned were destroyed, was to delude ourselves and mock God's irrevocable justice. Annihilation was no punishment at all, and to think so was to fool ourselves in the most self-deceiving way, which, of course, Satan rejoiced at.

'Let me' he continued 'read for you a passage from our own archbishop's pamphlet entitled *The Life of the World to Come: HELL:* Archbishop McQuaid explains that

> The fire of Hell is indeed terrifying because it is an instrument of pain specially fashioned by God. Our earthly fire can reach the soul only because it burns our body. This fire directly afflicts the soul. Our fire is sooner or later quenched; this fire will never be extinguished. Our fire gives light; this fire is darkness. Our fire consumes all that it burns; this fire burns but does not destroy. It is the very substance of the soul that this fire imprisons and afflicts. It is the spiritual powers of intellect and will that it holds captive in its grasp. It is the body too that, after the General Judgement, it will torture without consuming, for this fire of Hell is the instrument of God's power and the agent of His justice.

This was what awaited those who die in mortal sin without repenting and accepting God's merciful love. And how easy it was to be caught in a state of mortal sin at the moment of death. Only a few days previously he had read in the newspaper of a young unmarried pair who had been killed instantly when they plunged through the roof of a dance hall in London, to which they had somehow gained access. They had clearly been engaged in a grossly impure act together, and presumably, having no time to repent, must find themselves immediately in hell.

There was much more in the same vein before the welcome sound of a bell tinkling in the recesses of the building signalled the end of this particular session. The bell seemed to catch Fr McAdam by surprise. He glanced briefly at his wristwatch to make sure there was no mistake and, with apparent reluctance, brought his delivery to a close, turned and knelt before the altar, led the boys in some appropriate prayers, and made his way briskly from the chapel.

The assembled classmates seemed, as one, to heave a collective sigh of relief as they rose slowly from their places and filtered through the sombre atmosphere towards the chapel doors. Once outside they dispersed in various directions throughout the less oppressive surroundings awaiting them. Alan felt the need for fresh air and made his way outside. It was late afternoon and the western sky was a blaze of fiery red clouds. He decided to take a walk along the pathway encircling the lake. Proximity to the placid water might help to restore some calmness to his frazzled senses.

It had never previously crossed Alan's mind to question anything he had been taught concerning his religion. His Church was the one, true Church, founded by the Son of God; it had the weight and the wisdom of the ages behind it; it had the learning of its clergy, who were undoubtedly people of the highest integrity, called by God to spread his word on earth. Yes, some religious he had encountered had left something to be desired in their behaviour, but that could always be accounted for as simple human weakness. On this afternoon, however, a small nagging doubt began for the first time to form in the back of his mind. That he should even admit to himself that he could possibly think that anything within the teachings of the Church, or its teaching methods, might be less than perfect, was very scary. Wasn't indulging in such notions arrogant to the point of sinfulness? He had been inculcated with the belief that the Church could not be questioned, or be considered wrong, in any way, shape or form.

But Alan's uneasiness persisted throughout the remainder of the day, and was still with him when he went to bed. His sleep was fitful and filled with dark and shadowy images of whispering forests from where the sound of eerie hollow laughter swelled and faded like some demented banshee.

The following morning, Saturday, Alan was cheered by the realization that this was the last full day of the retreat. Over breakfast it was announced that two more boys had 'gone home' the previous evening. They had, it was explained, been suffering from 'flu-like systems and it was thought best that, rather than risk others becoming infected, they should curtail their involvement in the retreat and return home where they could receive proper care and attention. As it transpired both boys turned up for school on the following Monday morning, looking very fit and healthy. They had, according to themselves, gone for a midnight swim in the monastery lake, and their protestations that they had done it for penance didn't wash.

In this last full day of their insular confinement behind the monastery walls, the statuesque Fr Stritch returned to centre stage to deliver his final words of guidance to Alan and his young colleagues. His chosen topic was Judgement.

By this stage Alan's brain was like a sponge that had been saturated with so much about sin, death, hell and Satan, that he was virtually incapable of absorbing anything else that might be said about them. He felt tired, restless and slightly claustrophobic. It became progressively more difficult to keep dragging his wandering mind back to listening to what the earnest priest had to say.

He was vaguely conscious of being made aware - again - of how.... *every idle word that men shall speak, they shall render an account of it at the day of judgement....* Of....*Depart from Me, you cursed, into everlasting flames....*of....His mind came back into focus to hear the priest say something about the eternal clock ticking relentlessly in our ears to the sound of 'Ever/ Never' – How long will I be here? Ever. When will this torture end? Never.

'The eternal clock, boys. Can you hear it ticking, even now? Ever...never, ...tick...tock,...ever...never...

Again the priest's voice gradually became a background drone as Alan's thoughts drifted from trying to visualize his own judgement to remembering those he had known who had died. The grandfather whom he had spent happy holidays with when he was small, and the uncle who had died quite young and who loved to play football with him. He was thinking about whether or not he would be picked to play for his soccer team on Sunday afternoon when everyone began shuffling to their knees for prayers to end this final sermon....*forever and ever, Amen.*

After breakfast the following morning he and his classmates were free to leave. Silence was no longer required, but the boys seemed generally more inclined to pack their belongings and be off than to hang about talking.

Once beyond the monastery's massive entrance, Alan began to experience a sense of relief. He hoped he'd get a game of football that afternoon; he needed it to relax his body and clear his head. Whatever vague expectations he had harboured before participating in this event, he knew he felt disappointed. What he had listened to was simply the same as he had been hearing for as long as he could remember. And why should he have expected it to be any different? It was the same old story of fear, restriction and control. The only difference during the past week was the intensity and the relentless reinforcing of the message in such a compressed period. The world, as seen behind those walls, was a place of many tripwires just waiting to cause you to stumble and fall.

The only thing he'd miss was having a room all to himself.

5

September 1952

'Good morning, Gentlemen.'
It was the first morning of Alan's final year in secondary school, and the greeting he had just heard was nothing short of an amazement to him. They were the first words on entering the classroom by the Christian Brother whom he would have for most subjects during this academic following year. The greeting was so contrary to what he had been accustomed to in previous years that Alan's first reaction was to think it must be facetious or sarcastic. He was wrong. The teacher in question was Brother Synnott, and like all teachers he had a nickname that was passed down class by class, year by year. His was 'Pope'.

Alan had had no dealings with him in previous years but, from seeing him about the corridors from time to time, thought he seemed to be a fairly congenial type of person. But you could never tell for sure with any teacher until you experienced at first-hand how they behaved in the confines of the classroom.

As it turned out Alan quickly realized that the tension that had been the hallmark of his classroom experiences previously was absent during Brother Synnott's classes. Gradually Alan's attitude to learning changed from that of being a chore and a necessary, inescapable, boring activity to something which was exciting and interesting, and had a real relevance to life. Instead of putting the minimum effort into studying and homework, so as to avoid the wrath of his various teachers descending on him, he now pursued these activities with a will. He developed a sense of never wanting to let this teacher down, and strove to produce the very best results he could achieve. His efforts were acknowledged and encouraged, as were those of his fellow students. The overall outcome was that, in general, the class became more positive, hardworking and cheerful. Brother 'Pope' Synnott was the first educator to appeal to the better nature of this group, an approach that yielded very beneficial academic, and psychological, results.

His Religious Education classes, instead of concentrating on the more esoteric aspects of the subject, like consubstantiation and transubstantiation, the signs of revelation, causality, the various types of grace – actual, habitual, sanctifying, sacramental – and their characteristics and specific functions, the ecclesial dimensions of the sacraments, relics, miracles and prophesy, and so on, tended towards discussions on the practical application and necessity of good moral standards in promoting a just society. In an Irish context where, for example, to steal money from the church collection plate or from your employer's till was unquestionably wrong, whereas tax evasion was a national game, he would argue and explain that both actions were exactly of the same nature. He challenged the class with questions about the balance between spirituality and physicality that should be present in a decent person's life. He was clearly of the view that we were not angels, and for anyone to try to be one by over emphasizing the spiritual dimension in our daily existence was folly.

Strangely, although the class thrived academically under his guidance, a remarkable amount of time seemed to be spent engaged in exploring all sorts of topics that had little, if any, connection to the course material. An analysis of Hamlet's psychological make-up might divert into a discussion about why the Irish seemed to be psychologically inclined to prefer fast scoring games, like Gaelic football and hurling, rather than soccer, and why the English, for example, seemed to be quite the opposite? The class would be returned to order with a remark like,

'A digression, Gentleman. Let us get back to Elsinore, and the troubled Prince of Denmark. But, remember, enthusiasm and an enquiring mind are great gifts. They will not make life easy, but they will make it interesting.'

Beyond the classroom, the major news, during the first couple of weeks of the new term, was that it had been decided to break with tradition this year, and to present a Gilbert and Sullivan operetta, *The Pirates of Penzance*, in place of the usual annual school concert.

It would be performed in the school assembly hall in late November, and would, like the concert in previous years, be open to the parents and relations of the students. This event was, in fact, about the only regular contact between the school authorities and the parents, as any form of attempted involvement by parents in the running of the school was regarded by the Brothers as interference in what did not concern them, and was strictly discouraged and resisted.

Preparation for the operetta began towards the end of September, with auditions and selection of the cast. Mr Edmund Madden, a heavily built, pale, moonfaced man of about sixty, with some directorial experience at the Abbey Theatre, was hired to take charge of the production. Alan, being one of the taller students in his class, and not being possessed of a particularly remarkable singing voice, was assigned to the Policemen's chorus, which was not too demanding and would not interfere with his studies before the all-important Leaving Certificate Examination, the benchmark for students in relation to such vital matters as further education and employment.

One rather bizarre aspect of the production was the casting of younger boys to fulfil the roles of 'The Bevy of Rapturous Maidens' that made up a very significant element of the operetta's storyline. This feature of the event almost caused the entire abandonment of the production when a couple of the parents, who had sons in the cast and daughters in the local convent school, suggested that it would be far more sensible and seemly for the two schools to present a joint production in which boys and girls could take the respective male and female parts. It was made uncompromisingly clear by the Brothers that any proposal that involved the intermingling of their students with the girls from the convent school, was absolutely anathema to them, and that the entire project would be abandoned rather than countenance such a potentially temptation-laden scheme. On no account could they be responsible for the perverse dangers to sexual immorality that would be opened up in such circumstances. They appeared to see nothing at all perverse in dressing teenage boys up as pretty girls.

The connotations of this arrangement became very apparent when, on the evening of the first dress rehearsal, these 'maidens' eventually appeared in rouged faces, ringlets and long shapely gowns. Alan could not help thinking that, made up like this, these boys made better looking 'girls' than most of the girls he knew.

Brother Dunne, a burly science teacher, who had been assigned to assist Mr Madden, the director, lined up the 'rapturous maidens' and the 'policemen' in their separate groups in the wings of the school stage, and left to join the director out front. Once the coast was clear, Kevin Kenny, the class joker, and tallest of the 'policemen', tipped the wink to his co-defenders of the law, and said,

'Watch this, guys.'

He turned to the 'maidens' and, picking on the most ravishing-looking one, said,

'Hey, Maureen, show us your knickers,' with a broad smirk on his face.

The embarrassed victim, with cheeks flaming, said,

'I'm not wearing knickers.'

'My God! No knickers! Did your mother never tell you that nice girls never go out without their knickers?'

'I didn't mean I wasn't wearing…..'

Other voices, brimming with anger and humiliation, started to ring out among the 'maidens'…

'Get lost, Kenny, leave him alone, you big eegit.'

'Yeh, fuck off, Kenny.'

Wide-eyed mock horror from Kenny –

'Such language from nice young ladies!'

He looked around the exotic group, with their ringlets and billowing gowns, and, putting on a serious face, said,

'By the way, any of you girls fancy a snog later?'

A stunning redhead charged head first into Kenny's midriff, followed instantly by the rest of the 'rapturous maidens'. The 'policemen' immediately pitched in to Kenny's defence. Mayhem ensued.

Within half a minute wigs were askew, helmets rolled around the floor, and some of the 'maidens' hooped gowns were in the oddest, and very unmaidenly, positions; and the only one standing aside from the melee was Kevin Kenny.

A roar, the like of which a wild bull would have been proud, brought the fracas to a skittering halt.

'What the hell is going on here?' A puce-faced Brother Dunne, seemingly inflated to twice his normal size with rage, waded in and separated the bizarre scrummage by, literally, lifting one boy at a time, and throwing him in the general direction of the group he belonged to. When he had cleared a space between the warring factions, he levelled a stare at Kenny.

'You, Kenny, I'll bet you're responsible for this?'

'Me, Sir? No, Sir.'

'Me, Sir. No, Sir. By God, Kenny, if I….Logan, who started this?'

'Eh, I don't know, Sir. I just saw the fighting going on and tried to break it up.'

'I'll do some breaking up of my own if there's any more of this,' fumed Dunne in impotent rage, as he took in both sets of protagonists with one sweeping glance.

'You've got two minutes to sort yourselves before the rehearsal starts. And you lot, pointing to the 'maidens', 'try to give the impression that you know what the word 'decorum' means, when you go on stage. I'm going back out front now.'

With that he turned on his heel and, waving his arms about despairingly, disappeared like a great black bat. He was barely out of earshot when the 'policemen' doubled up in a fit of laughing, while the 'maidens' seethed.

The cue for one minute restored some order, but as the 'maidens' started 'tripping', none too lightly, towards the stage, the silence behind them was broken by the word – *'Knickers'.*

The rehearsal was not reassuring. The director sat trying to figure out why the 'policemen' appeared so wonderfully pleased with themselves, while the 'maidens' were so murderous-looking. Brother Dunne slumped in his seat in smouldering desperation.

By the time the show was presented publicly the 'maidens' had recovered their sparkle, and the entire production was regarded as a great success.

Another feature, unique to this final year, was the constant succession of priests and brothers from various religious orders who turned up to try to recruit students for their particular communities. This was known as discovering if you had a vocation – a call from God to the religious life. The conventional wisdom was that such a calling should be esteemed as the most wonderful honour that God could bestow on a boy, but if you felt you did not have a vocation that was alright too, as the secular world needed good people also to carry out all the worldly activities that the good ordering of society required. Choosing the 'world' rather than the religious life was a rather sad second option, but you shouldn't be too upset about it.

Five boys, out of a total of sixty at final year level, opted to train as priests. One of them, Bobby Hagan, confessed quite openly to Alan that he was motivated by the fact that he had been told he would have access to books on sex which the public were prohibited from reading. Young Hagan was obviously excited and obsessed by this prospect, and told Alan that he believed that the Church's training programme for seminarians required them to learn in detail every aspect of sex, so that they could competently, and in a fully informed manner, deal with the sins relating to sex that would eventually be confessed to them as priests in confession. Alan was envious, and felt guilty at being envious.

Alan had no difficulty in feeling some sympathy for such a tainted reason for entering a seminary at that time, as the entire subject of sex was such a taboo topic. A desperate curiosity was met with a virtual absence of information. He was by now so familiar with the Church's dire warnings about the evils of sex that even to mention the subject seemed like virtually 'supping with the Devil'. It was avoided by parents, ignored by teachers, and banned from distribution in publications of any sort. Scraps of information were picked up in the most haphazard, ill-informed ways, usually by way of the school playground, or the films.

Apparently Bobby Hagan fared no better in his search to satisfy his curiosity about sex; Alan heard later that he had abandoned the seminary within six months. The library there, it seems, did not live up to his expectations.

Of course Alan knew since he was ten, when Barry had been 'brought home from the hospital', that babies came from inside women's bodies; but at seventeen he, typically, still didn't know how they got in there, or, indeed, how they got out. Those who possessed this mysterious information guarded it maddeningly with Masonic secrecy. The clear impression was that should teenage boys and girls learn too much too soon they, and humanity, would be doomed to moral havoc. The message being generated by those whom Alan looked to naturally for guidance seemed to indicate that everything in this area should be viewed with the type of suspicion and vigilance more appropriate to preventing the spread of an infectious disease.

This pervasive regime of general odium and abhorrence towards anything to do with sex meant that the entire subject was shrouded in the garb of something dark and dangerous. With complete authority and conviction, the powers-that-be projected the concept that sex was naturally evil. Although Alan was as stamped with this ideology as everyone else, he began to harbour vague misgivings. But even to think that the Church, which he knew as the rock and fountain of all wisdom and right living, might be mistaken, even in the smallest degree, seemed absurd, and so his incipient doubts about the truth of the Church's attitude on this subject remained bottled up and unexplored. The Church knew best. Despite his ardent fairground adventures of the previous summer he knew from his religious instruction that all one was entitled to do was associate with girls in groups and in mixed company, and if you found one you genuinely thought you might marry you could enter into a chaste relationship with her, but always in the company of other good companions, or of each other's families or friends. Anything beyond these well-defined boundaries was 'an occasion of sin' and 'a cause for confession'. And that was that.

But there were other influences creeping into society that were not easily controlled. The two that were of most relevance to Alan were the cinema and 'foreign' radio. Cinema was almost entirely dominated by Hollywood productions, and these were not simply Westerns, Biblical Epics and Crime Thrillers; there were Love Stories too, with beautiful looking, sweet-natured girls who got kissed, and married the hero in the end. However, by now Alan was well aware of the State's restrictive film censorship laws that were rigidly enforced under the ever-vigilant eye of the Church authorities. The nation's moral standards could not be placed at risk by releasing anything that had not been carefully approved of. The people needed to be protected from viewing foreign, pagan behaviour. Mingling the influences of the Church and Hollywood meant that for Alan, and many young fellows like him, the image of the ideal girl was something of a cross between a Hollywood pin-up and the Virgin Mary – sexually alluring and spotlessly virtuous.

Alan's first realization of the thoroughness of the censorship alliance that held Irish society in its grip, came about when he read that the film *Jolson Sings Again* had been banned. He had seen and, like millions of cinemagoers the world over, enjoyed *The Jolson Story*, and looked forward to the sequel. It emerged that the basis for the banning of *Jolson Sings Again* was that, in showing the life story of Al Jolson, the film recorded his divorce from his first wife and, even worse, that he had remarried and was portrayed as being happy in that new relationship. The fact that Jolson was not a Catholic but a Jew, and therefore free according to his own traditions to divorce and remarry, did not seem to cut any ice with those who held the moral reins, or indeed that the film was about how an artist, who was commonly regarded as the greatest entertainer of his day, performed.

Around this time Alan experienced at first hand another example of the seriousness with which the moral vigilantes took their stewardship of the nation's conscience. One evening while viewing the biblical epic, *The Robe*, with Philip Ffrench, with whom Alan had become firm friends, a commotion occurred in the cinema. In the way in which Hollywood is never inhibited by the facts, there is a scene in which Judas, played by Victor Mature, who could ham it up with the best of them, is depicted standing at the foot of the cross, full of remorse at his betrayal of Jesus. Mature, with trembling lips and dewy eyes, blubbers

'This man loved me. He loooovvved me!'

A voice from the auditorium boomed out

'Yeah, he's a homo.'

Gasps, sniggers, stifled laughter rippled through the cinema;

and then, very clearly, a number of scandalized voices dominated everything else.

'I protest! I protest! Disgraceful! Shame!'

Alan was completely confused by what was happening because, although he was now seventeen he had never heard the word 'homo', and had no idea what it meant.

With that the projection stopped, abruptly, and the lights went up. Ushers appeared from various directions and four young men were identified as the culprits, and were unceremoniously bustled from the precincts. The lights were lowered and the show resumed in the now purified atmosphere.

Later, when they were outside the cinema, he asked Philip if he knew why the guys had been thrown out. Philip explained that 'homo' was short for homosexual, which was a man who, instead of finding girls attractive, actually was attracted to men. Alan was astonished, even repulsed by the very notion. The thought of two men kissing each other, and finding pleasure in it, almost turned his stomach. It had never even occurred to him that nature could produce people who could feel like that. It was then that he recalled the incident with the man who had given him the late-night lift a couple of years previously. For some strange irrational reason he felt a surge of guilt about that incident.

The other source of influence that was starting to make its presence felt in Alan's world at this time, and that could not be censored or controlled by Church or State, was the airwaves that carried radio broadcasts from abroad. Occasionally Alan's Dad would express his amusement at reports in the newspaper about the banning by Radio Eireann, the national broadcaster, of such songs as *Young and Foolish* ('I wonder what they think the 'foolish' means, Annie?', or *I'm Always True to You Darling, in my Fashion*, or *My Resistance is Low*, where vice was depicted as winning out over virtue. Letters appeared in the newspapers from concerned priests about the 'unmistakable suggestiveness' of such songs that were 'alarmingly preoccupied with the sensuous delights of love'.

Radio Eireann might cease to broadcast such morally suspect material but it took only the adjustment of a dial on the radio to receive all sorts of broadcasts from abroad. Although Radio Luxemburg became the most popular of these foreign stations, the ones that Alan, and many of his pals, 'discovered' and liked best were the late-night broadcasts from the American Forces Network in Germany. The deep dark-chocolate, laid-back American voices of the 'DJ's' who presented such nightly programmes as *The Munich Night Train* conjured up an exotic world that was quite irresistible in its contrast to the sanitized fare being broadcast locally. The alluring decadence, the free irrepressible joyfulness, the haunting, aching anguish of the great swing bands and jazz singers of the age, became Alan's nightly escape from the repressed culture in which he increasingly felt himself immersed. The age of 'cool' was starting to infiltrate and circumvent the zealously guarded bulwarks of Church and State. For Alan, the much-recited Litany of the Saints, each one of whom was invoked to 'pray for us' nightly at the end of the family rosary, lost much of its allure in favour of an altogether more appealing litany of renowned jazz luminaries – Armstrong, Basie, Bechet, Brubeck, Davis, Ellington, Goodman, Grappelli, Halliday, Reinhardt et al. In his growing realization of the narrowness of the society that had shaped him, it was to the revered of the jazz world, and the joyous sense of freedom they represented, that Alan increasingly paid homage.

Predictably, jazz was quickly denounced as the devil's music by those who felt that it was their inalienable right, and responsibility, to do everyone else's thinking for them in order to preserve the moral integrity of the State. But, despite the sombre dead hand of officialdom, a jazz scene took root and prospered in Dublin and, in so doing, helped to provide Alan with a measure of independence of thought and individuality of expression which he felt an innate need to possess and demonstrate, but which would mark him out, together with his fellow-enthusiasts, as dubious types.

Despite the fact that for Alan an interest in jazz represented a psychological safety-valve against the repressive ethos of the times, it was in reality nothing more than the merest blip on his consciousness by contrast with the effect that the seemingly infallible, and inescapable, conditioning he had received, continued to exercise over him. He was still typical of the times insofar as he was programmed to reflexively weigh every thought and action for its moral susceptibility against the guilt-laden tenets of his Catholic upbringing

PART TWO

The Aftermath

6

July 1953

At the time Alan, now eighteen, completed his formal education, and finally walked free from the commanding ministrations of the Christian Brothers, the concept of choosing a career, or of finding what one would be best suited to do, or would like to do, hardly existed for all but the very privileged. For most of those who could not afford to enter university, or those who did not wish to do so, the priority was to find a job. In the event one in three of Alan's classmates had emigrated within six months of leaving school, to seek employment abroad.

While considering the emigration options himself, – England, Australia, America, South Africa – Alan continued to scan the newspapers and apply for every job that seemed remotely suitable. Eventually, after about three months of fruitless effort, Philip Ffrench's father recommended him for interview to a friend of his, whose family owned, and managed, a glassware factory in Dublin's south city. Three days after the interview he received a letter offering him a position in the firm's office. Alan had his first job.

The company, Dublin Glassware Ltd., which employed about one hundred and fifty people – exclusively male except for a few female office staff – manufactured drinking glasses, and glass jars and containers of many shapes and sizes. It was owned by the Lattimore family, Protestants, who were well known in Dublin business circles for generations. William Lattimore F.C.A., the incumbent managing director, who had interviewed Alan personally, was a tall, rather austere grey-haired man in his late fifties. He took a reserved paternalistic interest in Alan's progress, always encouraging him to 'get a qualification'. He also had the rather unnerving practice of always addressing Alan as 'Mr. Logan'.

One of Alan's duties was to collect time sheets from the various foremen throughout the factory each Friday. This brought him into contact with the manufacturing process, the core of which was the factory's enormous furnace. The temperature within this furnace had to be maintained at a minimum of 1700 degrees Celsius at all times, in order to keep the molten glass in liquid form. As a spectacle it was unlike anything Alan had seen previously. It glowed permanently with a white-hot heat. Around its three maw-like apertures, three teams, each of six men, laboured to produce the product from which the country's drinkers swallowed their pints of stout and glasses of whiskey. The factory operated three eight-hour shifts every day, except from 4 a.m. to noon each Sunday, when routine maintenance was carried out. Even during this period the temperature was never allowed to drop below the 1700 degrees mark. On seeing the furnace for the first time Alan was awestruck, so much so that it took a shout from the shift's foreman to 'Get a move on, sonny. You shouldn't be hanging about there.' to bring him back to reality.

It seemed to him to resemble the very gateway to hell itself. As he walked away it occurred to him how surprising it was that the Archbishop had not decreed that all school children in his flock be brought on tour here; perhaps he was unaware of the opportunity he had available on his doorstep to frighten them into conformity by exposing them at first hand to this rivetingly graphic, readymade vision of what awaited them if they did not conform to the Church's teachings, and his decrees.

Alan enjoyed the sense of independence that came with having a job and earning money, and although the relentless religious conditioning he had received at the hands of the Christian Brothers, and society in general, still resulted in everything he did being automatically assessed for its guilt content, there was a growing sense within him of relief as the feeling of repression, which had been his constant condition, started to lift.

Socially, Philip Ffrench and Alan had remained close friends. Philip was studying medicine at the Royal College of Surgeons on Dublin's St. Stephen's Green. Adjacent to this renowned seat of learning lay another establishment which was becoming renowned for an altogether different reason - the rather less august Green Lounge, which by the mid 1950's was at the centre of Dublin's jazz scene. It was here that Alan and Philip met regularly for the Friday night jazz session. Like jazz clubs everywhere, the Green Lounge provided a space not only for those who liked the music to enjoy it, but also an atmosphere where those who otherwise remained within the bounds of perceived respectability could rub shoulders with a rather *risque* decadence, without ever quite embracing it with open arms. There was an indefinable sense of camaraderie among both clientele and performers, as if they intuitively agreed that they represented an alternative, daring view of life to that of the establishment. The very word 'jazz' was redolent with the glamour of the exotic, the international and the subversive.

At that time Alan's world consisted of two entirely distinct areas – the world outside the club, and the world behind its doors. The atmosphere inside was like a personality transforming drug to him. From the moment he arrived he sucked it in and soaked it up. Inside everything and everybody was different from what passed for life outside. Outside was rigid censored Roman Catholic Ireland, to which Alan was umbillically linked; inside was an exotic, wonderfully alien atmosphere. Whether it was the exhilarating quick tempo stomps, rags and marches, or the soulful blues, the music had an appeal that he found virtually intoxicating beyond prosaic explanation. Jazz music seemed to him to engage the essence of human experience in ways that Irish cultural mores shunned. It filled a reality gap which, until now, he only vaguely felt, was missing. From the pure joy of celebrating the energy, exuberance and inhibition of youth, to lamenting the darkest and most tragic deeds of human behaviour, the music immersed itself - rich and raw - in every crevice of life. It sang of good and bad behaviour, of loss and courage, of friendship and betrayal, of hardship and weakness, of enthusiasm and the will to overcome. It sang of sex. It sang of blindness and meanness and death and hope. It sang of booze – booze to make you happy and booze that left you in the gutter. It sang of earthy reality. No matter how many times the same tunes were played the repetition never palled because, although the titles might be the same, the content was always varied. The title was merely a rough guide, as it were, to the topic to be discussed. Like an animated conversation at a dinner party, the improvisations that each musician in the ensemble offered were fresh and varied from one performance to the next, their contributions often being moulded as a spontaneous response to the previous player's musical statements.

Apart from the music everything about the club fascinated Alan - the musicians, the clientele, the atmosphere. The leader of the group was known simply as Atom. Whether he had acquired this nickname due to his diminutive stature, or through his dynamic style of trumpet-playing, Alan never discovered. Atom's tone was full and smooth and rounded, and his ability to produce inventive improvisations seemed to know no limits. When he played a muted blues no words were needed to convey the meaning.

The club itself was small ('intimate' was the 'in' word), and always packed by 10 p.m. As the sessions progressed the place grew warmer and the inevitable cloud of cigarette smoke curled below the low ceiling. Beer was the only alcohol served, and the bar closed at 11.30 p.m., the legal time limit for serving alcohol. Although a small number among the clientele were 'fond of their drink', the emphasis in the club was decidedly on the music and the socializing, rather than the alcohol.

The club, of course, had girls. And some of these girls were quite unlike what Alan had been raised to expect girls to be – demure, modest, reserved, coy. These were the girls of the fairground in a similarly *risqué* situation. In this atmosphere it was not unusual, as the music grew hot, and inhibitions relaxed as the night advanced, to catch a glimpse of a suspendered thigh between nylon-top and knickers as skirts swung high on the thronged dance-floor. Alan always felt that it was wrong not to look away, but this rare and exquisitely mischievous sight made that quite impossible. And look he did, week after week, and took pleasure in the looking.

But his fine-tuned conscience would not permit him to enjoy his prurient pleasure for long. Like cold water on warm skin on a winter's morning, he would awake in the cold light of day to the realization that it was sinful to indulge himself as he had done, and he would have no peace of mind until he had been to confession.

'Bless me Father.......'

'I've been looking at girls' underclothes when I shouldn't have.'

'In what circumstances?'

'At a dance, Father.'

'Was there physical contact?'

'No, Father.'

'Did you indulge in immoral acts ….',

When the whole dismal business of confession was over the priest said,

'You must avoid such places, my son. They are occasions of sin. Now, for your penance say……'

Penance said. The 'slate cleaned'. Relief. Problem forgotten. Until the following Friday night, when the magic of the music and the lure of the atmosphere would draw him once more to the Green Lounge.

Occasionally, when this salving of his troubled conscience by futile confessions struck him as loathsome and hypocritical, he would avoid the confession box for months. The enticing music, the alternative *milieu* to the Ireland that lay outside 'The Lounge' doors, and the lustful stirrings that the club's unwitting 'leg show' presented were too great a magnet to resist. Inevitably as the weeks passed and the guilt increased, the worries regarding his moral state would mount, resulting in fitful guilt-pricked nights, – and more confessional promises to improve. And he would start over – loving the music, and trying to avoid the lust each Friday.

On one occasion when he asked Philip if he felt it was wrong to stare at the girls as they swirled about the dance-floor displaying themselves, Philip, who was as committed a Christian as anyone Alan knew, laughed and said he thought it was the most natural thing in the world for a young man to be attracted to looking at young women, especially when they had gone to the trouble of glamorising themselves.

'Alan,' he joked, 'the beer may be a little too warm, but the music is great, and if you weren't tempted to look at the incidental floor-show I'd be decidedly worried about you. For God's sake, sit back and enjoy yourself.'

Philip's family, the Ffrenchs, and the Lattimores, for whom Alan now worked, moved in the same social circle. It was through this connection that Alan first set eyes on Heather Lattimore. Heather was about two years younger than Alan, and had attended the same school as Philip. Whereas the Catholic hierarchy objected to teenage boys and girls sharing the same classroom, and enforced a strict policy of segregation, Protestants had no problem with co-education. Alan was introduced to Heather at a party in Ffrench's house to celebrate Philip's twentieth birthday, in October 1954, about a year after he had started working for her father. Alan was immediately smitten. She had the clearest pale-blue eyes he had ever seen, and her long blond hair flowed over her shoulders like silk. Her smile and her voice were captivating. The fact that he worked in her father's business broke the ice in terms of conversation. They spent much of the evening in each other's company, and Alan found her the easiest girl in the world to talk to.

Heather and Alan saw quite a lot of each other during the following weeks, and Alan became convinced that he had met the love of his life. Heather's feelings appeared equally strong. They went to the cinema. They took long walks in the scenic foothills of the Dublin Mountains. They sat in cafes and drank coffee for hours. When Alan invited Heather to one of the few up-market restaurants in Dublin's centre city, it was a very special occasion. That evening, as he kissed her goodnight at her hall-door, he told her, for the first time, that he was in love with her. She returned his kiss, pressed him to her, and whispered 'You know I love you too.' By then they had been seeing each other for about three months.

During the following couple of months, as Heather and Alan continued to see each other regularly, Alan sensed an almost imperceptible change in the work environment between William Lattimore and himself. Mr Lattimore seemed to be initiating fewer voluntary contacts, and his customary enquiries regarding Alan's academic progress virtually ceased. Alan became concerned that the quality of his work was in question. He asked Heather if her father had said anything about this. Heather told him her father never talked to the family about personnel issues in the business, but she did say that her father had questioned her, very specifically, about how serious her relationship was with Alan. He had offered no response when she told him she believed it was quite serious as far as she was concerned, and she believed Alan felt the same way.

At about 10.30.a.m. one Monday morning in early April, Alan answered the phone on his desk. It was an internal call from William Lattimore, asking him to come to his office. Alan's heart skipped a beat as he replaced the receiver.

Alan knocked nervously on Mr Lattimore's door and was invited to 'Come in.'

'Good morning Alan.'

'Good morning Mr Lattimore.'

'Please sit down.'

'Thank you.'

'Alan, I have a matter of a rather delicate and personal nature to discuss with you.'

He had never been addressed as 'Alan' by Mr Lattimore before.

'Yes, Mr Lattimore.'

'I hope you will not be offended by what I feel I have to say.'

Puzzlement.

'Is there a problem with my work, Mr Lattimore?'

'Absolutely not, Alan; absolutely not. This has nothing to do with business. It involves a matter of a personal nature that is of concern to me. I want to speak to you about Heather.'

'Oh!'

'Yes. She tells me that you have been seeing each other regularly for three or four months now, and that the relationship is, too use her words 'Quite serious'. Is that how you see it?

'Yes, I'm very serious about Heather. To be honest, I think she's …… she's the most wonderful person I've ever met.'

'Thank you, Alan. I think she is a very special person too. But, regrettably, this presents me…us….with a difficult situation.'

'How do you mean, Mr Lattimore?'

'I believe that it is better to explain my position to you now, while the relationship is still in its early stages. Sooner rather than later, as it were.'

Alan raised his eyebrows to indicate his lack of comprehension.

'Both of you are still very young. She's eighteen, and you're ……..not quite twenty yet?'

Alan nodded.

'It may seem premature to even think of the possibility of the relationship reaching the point where marriage becomes an issue, much less talk about it. But, in the circumstances it is better to do so now rather than wait until the issues involved might result in a far more painful situation. What I'm driving at, Alan, is that you and Heather are of different religions. She, as you know is Church of Ireland…Protestant. You are Roman Catholic. As you probably are aware the Roman Catholic authorities in this country will only sanction marriage between a Roman Catholic and a Protestant provided they are married by a Roman Catholic priest in a Roman Catholic church, and provided that the Protestant party contracts to bring up any children of the marriage as Roman Catholics, and, indeed, undertakes to try to convert his, or her, Protestant partner to Roman Catholicism. This they refer to as the *Ne Temere* decree.' Lattimore paused.

'I hadn't really thought about it.'

'Well, I believe it must be thought about. It must be addressed, and positions made clear. The Protestant community regards this imposition as a blatant attempt to eliminate Protestantism entirely from Ireland. Furthermore, if a Roman Catholic were to marry other than in a Roman Catholic church the marriage would not be recognized by that Church, and if the Catholic party walked away from the marriage at a latter date neither Church nor State, which is dominated by the Roman Catholic Church in these matters, would raise the slightest objection, and would even sanction as legitimate a subsequent marriage, if I can call it that, by the Roman Catholic party, provided the so-called marriage takes place in a Roman Catholic church. I hope you will understand when I say that under no circumstances could I give my consent to such a situation. Do you understand?'

Alan was almost overcome with frustration and anger, but managed to force himself to indicate that he could see the older man's point of view.

'Good,' Lattimore resumed. 'I'm glad you appreciate my position. In the circumstances I must ask you to cease this relationship, at least for now. I will speak to Heather this evening and tell her the same as I've told you. I trust both she and you will respect my position and my wishes. I believe what I'm proposing is for the best for all concerned. It may not seem that way at the moment, but I'm sure I'm right. I regret any hurt to your feelings, and I sincerely hope that our working relationship will be unaffected.'

Alan understood these words to terminate the interview and exited Mr Lattimore's office in something of a daze.

As he went about his duties during the day his mind was in turmoil. How could this happen? What could be done about it? Who was to blame? Mr Lattimore? Society? The State? The Church? The Church! The more he thought about it the more the finger seemed to point in that direction. But why? Two young people loved and respected each other, enjoyed each other's company, wanted to be together and fulfil each other's lives. They were single, unattached, uncommitted to anyone else. What could be more 'Christian' than that they should be together? But here were these 'rules' and conditions and difficulties that the Church put in the way. Alan had never considered the Church in such negative terms before. He had been fully conditioned, and convinced, that it was a great and lucky privilege to be born and raised in the Catholic faith. Even if the Church made these rules, how could intelligent people allow them to be enforced? After all, the Church was only a group of men who claimed to have the authority to tell everyone else what was right and wrong. Was it wrong for an unattached young couple to share their lives and loves exclusively with each other? The more he wrestled with these thoughts the clearer it became to him that the reason the 'Church' – essentially a group of men claiming to have a unique insight into the mind of God – got away with enforcing these imposed regulations, was because they simply had to declare that to disobey them was a mortal sin, and a mortal sin meant hell for all eternity when the sinner died. It was really as simple as that. And because the

Church was regarded with such awe and deference, the vast majority of its members were too fearful to object to, or question, its impositions.

Alan fretted and fumed inside himself all through the rest of a seemingly endless working day. He figured it was best to avoid contacting Heather until her father had had time to speak to her that evening, reasoning that if he did so earlier it might be viewed badly by Mr Lattimore.

When he did phone Heather late that evening he was relieved that she answered the phone herself, although she was clearly in a tearful state. It became clear that her father had spoken to her along the same lines as he had spoken to Alan that morning.

Through her sniffles Heather told him that 'Dad's view is that the Catholic Church is engaged in, what he calls, an arrogant numbers' game that is intended to turn Ireland into an exclusively Roman Catholic country. He asked me to promise not to see you for the next month, and he'd talk to me again about us then.'

'What did you say to that?'

'Well, I had to agree. He is very resolute and adamant in his views.'

They agreed not to meet but to keep in touch by phone. They would not make contact while he was at work and, as he felt it could be awkward phoning her at home, they would leave it to her to phone him when the circumstances allowed.

Alan was now in the worst dilemma of his life. He had difficulty concentrating on his work, and the atmosphere between himself and his boss was becoming more and more strained. He began to feel depressed and to hate having to face the factory each day. He seemed to be constantly preoccupied waiting for Heather's phone calls, but there could be three or four days between these, and they increasingly left him feeling frustrated and helpless.

Three weeks after his summons to Mr Lattimore's office he was surprised to receive a letter from the Imperial Bank referring to an interview he had had over a year previously, and which he had entirely forgotten about. He was being offered a clerical position, subject to the usual conditions, which meant he could be sent to any branch in Ireland at the bank's behest. To be offered such an opportunity in the depressed economic morass that Ireland had sunk into was considered most fortunate. Having discussed it briefly with his family – there really was little to discuss, as his parents were overjoyed at what they saw as a true godsend – he promptly accepted the job and gave in his notice to Dublin Glassware.

The same day, feeling less restrained by Mr Lattimore's influence, he phoned Heather to tell her the news. Her reaction seemed rather vague and guarded, and left him confused. Having spent a restless night he contacted her again the following day and urged her to meet him and, after some considerable encouragement, she agreed to see him briefly that evening, explaining that she did not want to go against her father's wishes or her promise to him.

When they did meet over coffee she told him that her father had been on to her again, and was dead set against the relationship continuing. She suggested that they could keep in touch but they would really have to wait – until they were both over twenty-one, and adults, and free to make their own decisions – to resume their relationship. Alan was devastated but, on the basis that they would stay in touch as best they could, without actually dating, he agreed. Before parting she told Alan that it had been arranged by her family that she spend the next couple of weeks with her aunt – her mother's sister, who was married to a farmer who had a large farm near Bandon in Co. Cork. She would be leaving for Cork the following weekend.

The following Monday Alan joined the Imperial Bank, and spent a hectic week being put through an induction programme. At the end of that week he was informed that he was being assigned to the bank's branch in the town of Wexford, starting the following Monday morning. Temporary accommodation would be arranged until he found himself a place to lodge. As Wexford was reputed to be the sunniest place in Ireland, Alan figured he had done rather well.

During the week he spent training in Dublin he heard nothing from Heather, which did not surprise him too much, bearing in mind that she was now in the depths of rural Ireland. The following week – his first in Wexford – passed quickly. When the bank closed at 12.30 p.m. on Saturday he went straight to the railway station, and caught a train for Dublin. When he arrived home in mid-afternoon, there was, as he had hoped, a letter from Heather awaiting him. It was disappointingly short, and told mostly of how quiet it was in the Cork countryside by comparison with Dublin.

Two weeks later, on his next trip back to Dublin, another letter had arrived for him. This one was postmarked 'Southampton'. It read

May 28th 1955
Dear Alan,

You will be surprised to see that I am now in Southampton. I want to explain to you that when I went to my aunt's place in Cork it was to do some serious thinking about my future. During the previous month, when we were not seeing each other, my parents (especially my father) had kept on at me about this, time and time again. As you know I have said in the past that I would like to be a teacher, but because my Irish is so poor I could not get into a teacher training college in Ireland. My father checked out the situation here in England and discovered that I would qualify to enter the British teacher-training programme. When I went to Bandon it was really to think about all this and make a decision, and I have decided that the best thing in the circumstances is to try this teaching course.

I've now been accepted by a college here in Southampton, and, for the moment, I'll be staying with some family friends who live here.

I'm sorry, Alan, if this news upsets you but, as I've said, I think it is really the best thing to do at this time.

Please write soon and tell me all about your new job and Wexford. I hope you are settling down well.

Love,

Heather.

Alan felt as if a door had been slammed in his face. He recognized it for what it was – a 'Dear John' letter. It was over. He folded the letter and put it in his pocket. Without saying a word to anyone he headed up the stairs to the room he now shared with Barry, closed the door behind him, lay down on his bed and stared blankly at the ceiling. His Dad, who was 'good with his hands', had renovated the upstairs area of the house some years earlier so that, as the children were getting older, the boys and girls could have separate bedrooms.

An hour later, when his mother knocked and entered the room, he was still lying there.

'Is something wrong, Alan?'

'That letter was from Heather. She's gone to England to train as a teacher.'

His mother sat down on the chair beside his bed.

'How long will that take?'

'Four years probably. But that's not the point. If she trains there she'll have to teach there. Even if she wanted to she couldn't teach here without a qualification in Irish. Which means she's gone for good.' He paused, and with a mixture of anger and bitterness he continued, 'This is all her father's doing, you know.'

'Alan,' his mother said softly, 'I don't want to say the wrong thing here. I've always liked Heather. She's a very nice girl. But if you're going to get involved with people who are not your own kind you may have to suffer the consequences.'

Alan sat up and looked at his mother intently.

'How do you mean 'your own kind'?'

'Please don't get upset, Alan. I mean people of a different religion. Protestants are different to us. They see things their own way, just as we see ours our way. Catholics and Protestants don't mix easily.'

Alan lay back on the bed again.

'Religion!' he hissed, 'It seems to me to create more divisions among people than anything else.'

'Alan, that's an awful thing to say. You mustn't say things like that.' There was an element of alarm and fearfulness in her tone.

'Mustn't,' thought Alan to himself. 'Why 'mustn't' I say what I feel?' His mother, now in her fifties, had become much more conservative than the young woman who years earlier had threatened to stop attending Sunday Mass. He saw no point in upsetting her by getting into an argument.

After a brief, awkward silence she asked him if he would like her to bring him up a cup of tea and a piece of chocolate cake she had just made. He thanked her, but said he didn't need anything just then.

A few minutes later another, gentle, knock came to his door. He would have preferred to have been left alone, but he swung himself off the bed and opened the door. Mimi, now fourteen, stood there, looking concerned. No one he knew had a softer heart than Mimi. Although of a naturally happy and contented disposition, she seemed to feel everyone else's sadnesses almost as keenly as they did themselves. She had a strikingly pretty face, with large, doe-like, beautiful blue eyes, and natural ash-blonde hair that flowed beyond her shoulders. She and her father had been in the sitting room when her mother had come in to tell them about Heather's letter.

'Come in, sis,' Alan invited her.

'You probably just want to be by yourself, but I just wanted to say, you know, I think it must be awful for you…..'

Alan put his arms around her.

'Thanks, Mimi. Don't be upset, now. It's just one of those things, I guess. I think I'm very lucky to have a family, and a sister like you, to be concerned about me.'

She gave him a tight hug. When they eased away from each other he asked her if Terry was around?

'No,' Mimi replied, 'she went out to the pictures with Gale Millar before you arrived home.'

'I think I should go out for a while myself,' said Alan, as if the idea had just occurred to him.

'Yes, that's a good idea. I think you should do that,' Mimi encouraged him. 'I'll see you later, Alan.'

As he was freshening up in the bathroom a few minutes later he heard young Barry's noisy arrival at the hall door.

'Is Alan home yet?' rang out.

'And hello to you too, Barry,' replied his mother with a touch of irony. 'Yes, he's upstairs, but he might like a bit of peace and quite at the moment.'

Ignored, totally.

'Hi, Alan!' yelled the ten year old.

'Hi, Barry.'

'Where are you?'

'In the bathroom.'

'Oh,' a note of disappointment sounded in the youngster's voice.

'What's wrong?'

'You're going out?' a bit dejectedly.

'Yes, why?'

'Nothin'.' Silence.

'Nothing?'

'Well, eh, I thought you might play a game of chess with me.'

Alan thought for a moment.

'Tell you what, pal, could we have a game tomorrow?'

'That'd be great, Alan,' enthusiastically. Barry loved it when he had his big brother's attention all to himself.

'Bye the way, buddy, there's a 'g' at the end of 'nothin','' Alan called after him as he disappeared downstairs.

'Yeh, Okay,' and then 'you're worse than the teachers in school!'

Alan smiled to himself. There was nothing as good as family to comfort you. But he needed to seek additional comfort, or escape, from another source that evening. A visit to the Green Lounge and 'Doctor' Jazz – *When I'm worried and I feel blue, He's the one that I talk to* - the familiar words of Jelly Roll Morton's classic ran through his head. He phoned to check if Philip Ffrench was free, but was told that Philip had already gone out for the evening.

As he popped his head around the sitting room door to tell his folks that he was going out for the evening, his Dad lowered his newspaper and, with a wry look to accompany his dry humour said,

'Remember, son, girls are like trains; there's always another one coming behind.'

He knew it was his Dad's way of showing his concern, and of trying to cheer him up.

'Thanks, Dad. I'm sure that will be very helpful.' There was only a slight touch of sarcasm in his voice. And with that he was gone out the hall door.

He took a bus to the city and headed for The Lounge. As he approached the entrance he could hear, and feel, the rasping guttural sound of Stan Bradshaw's trombone tearing through the fabric of the blues number *Black and Blue*. Alan was mildly amused at how appropriate it seemed to his present situation. Stan was around thirty and stood about six feet two. His ginger hair and beard encased his head in a mass of tiny curls, giving him the appearance of the quintessential Celtic warrior. In the few years that Alan had been attending these sessions, he had never seen Stan dressed in anything else but the wheat coloured jacket and dark chocolate brown, baggy, corduroy pants he was wearing this evening. But it wasn't the fashion ensemble that was of interest to the patrons. It was the music. And when Stan took centre stage to perform a solo, and his booming improvisations filled the hall, everyone's eyes were fixed on one spot, and all ears were cocked in one direction.

Alan spotted Philip and some other friends at the rear of the room, and joined them. There were four of them in the group, all drinking pints of Guinness.

'Hello, Alan,' Philip greeted him. 'I didn't expect that you'd be here tonight.'

Alan explained that he had got home from Wexford fairly early and 'felt like getting a fix from Doctor Jazz.'

Philip quizzed him about his new job, and what he thought living in Wexford would be like. Alan filled him in briefly, above the noise of the music. He excused himself, saying he was going to get himself a drink, and asked if anyone else in the group was ready for another. No one was. When he returned he sat engrossed in the music

The band finished playing the lively *South Rampart Street Parade* with their customary, tight flourish, and Atom, the bandleader, stepped to the microphone. He nodded to the drummer, Jimmy Wilkins, to roll the drums to get the crowd's attention. When the conversation level died down, he said he was delighted to announce that they had a celebrity with them in the hall this evening - Miss Jilly Peters - and she had agreed to join them on stage. Jilly Peters, who hailed from Belfast originally, had carved out a reputation for herself on the British jazz scene, as a truly exceptional talent. Her voice and interpretations were, it was said, indistinguishable from the great black female performers in the United States.

Amid an enthusiastic round of applause she joined the band on the stage and consulted briefly with Atom. The chosen number was a blues, *The Longest Street in Town*. After a brief ensemble lead-in she launched into the vocals of the traditional twelve bar song, filling the hall with her power and passion –

I'm walkin' down the longest street in town,
Just walkin' on down the longest street in town,
It's sure a long lonesome street, since you ain't been around.

I'm walkin' down the longest street in town,
Yes, walkin' down the longest street in town,
And if you see me baby, I'll be wearin' a frown.

Each Saturday evening on the corner we'd meet,
Each Saturday evening on the corner we'd meet.
Now on Saturday evening – it's just a long lonesome street.

I'm walkin' down the longest street in town,
Just walkin' down the longest street in town,
Kinda hopin' baby I'll find you hanging around.

The song's sentiments chafed against Alan's fragile emotional state. He sipped his beer and listened while Jilly performed two or three more numbers, ending with a tremendously soulful interpretation of the ever-popular *Careless Love*. Alan, already uncharacteristically slightly maudlin, felt that someone was reading his thoughts that evening.

'You seem very quiet tonight, Alan?' It was Philip's query that roused him from his self-indulgent reverie.

Alan wanted to tell his friend what had happened, but didn't want to get into it in this atmosphere, and among this group.

'A bit tired I guess; it's been a pretty hectic week,' was all he said. But when the session finished and they were on their way home together he filled Philip in on all that had happened.

'It's a tough break, my friend,' Philip said by way of trying to console him as they parted, 'but who knows how things may work out eventually.'

* * * * * * * * *

The following morning, Sunday, Alan slept late. He was woken by the sound of the rest of the family returning from 8.30 mass. When he arrived downstairs his mother greeted him with,

'Good morning, sleepyhead. You must have an easy conscience to be able to sleep till this hour of the day.'

He gave her a kiss on the cheek, and said,

'Morning, Mum. I'm off to 10 o'clock Mass.'

'What are your plans for the day? Dinner will be about one o'clock. Will you be here?'

'Oh yes, I'll be here. I'll probably go to see 'The Glens' playing this afternoon. I'll take Barry if he's interested. There's a train for Wexford at 6.30, so I'll have to leave here around half five.'

'Okay then. We'll see you later.'

The minute Alan arrived back from Mass Barry was waiting for him at the front door.

'Hi, Alan. Can we play chess now?'

Barry had already set out the chessboard on the sitting room table.

As they played, Alan quizzed his young brother about school, and his pals, and what he was reading.

'So, tell me, what would you like to be when you grow up?'

'I think I'll be an actor.'

'An actor, humm…, Very interesting,' said Alan, trying to keep a straight face.

'But I wouldn't like to have to kiss girls.'

'Well, who knows? You might change your mind on that.'

Barry 'won' the game just in time to hear their Mum call them for dinner. The roast beef, mashed potatoes, cauliflower and Brussels sprouts served up by his mother, followed by her own homemade apple tart and custard, was the best meal Alan had eaten since he'd last been in Dublin. As they ate, his Dad had a hundred and one questions about Wexford, a place he knew quite well from his job as a train driver.

'You know, there's a statue of a famous Wexfordman on the quays there. I've passed it a thousand times on the train. His name was Commodore John Barry,' - here Jim Logan looked towards his younger son, - 'a good name, aye son? He is known as The Father of the American Navy.'

When the meal finished, Jim Logan joined his two sons as they set off to watch the team that Alan and Phillip Ffrench played for as boys. As they stood on the touchline, waiting for the kick-off, Alan asked Barry why he wasn't out there playing for the team.

'I'm no good at football.'

'But he can run like the wind,' said Jim.

By the time they arrived home from the match, it was time for Alan to say his goodbyes and leave. Once he was on his own on the train back to Wexford his mind drifted to imagining what Heather was doing at that moment in Southampton, and a vague sense of sourness settled on him. A few days later he wrote to Heather voicing his anger and frustration at the fact that she had not given him the opportunity to speak to her in person and put his point of view and, perhaps, persuade her to come to a different decision about her future. He got no response from her.

He immersed himself in his new employment, but his attitude to people in general, and young women in particular, was, if not quite cynical, then sceptical. Whereas previously his natural reaction to people was to regard them as basically decent until they proved otherwise, he now viewed everyone he met with a jaundiced mistrust until they showed themselves worthy of his better opinion.

His trips home to Dublin became irregular and infrequent. On Saturdays, if there was a horserace meeting or other social event of any significance in the vicinity of Wexford, bank staff was expected to attend and rub shoulders with the bank's clientele, who inevitably attended such events in large numbers. Getting to Dublin late on Saturday by train and having to return to Wexford on Sunday afternoon did not leave much time to do very much at all. His life gradually became more centred round the local social activities in Wexford itself. The locals reacted to him in two quite distinct ways. Some regarded him as 'a Jackeen', a Dubliner, an outsider and a 'runner-in' to the 'country' way of life, which Dubliners were believed to look down their noses at, and not understand. Others afforded him a certain degree of deference and prestige due, as they saw it, to his status as a 'Bank Official'. This Alan found quite amusing, but did nothing to dissipate. It gave him an element of insulation against the more overtly prejudiced among the local community.

7

May 1955

'Did you have a disturbed night, Mr Logan?'
It was breakfast-time – porridge, bread and a boiled egg – and the questioner was Mrs Furlong, the woman whom Alan had taken lodgings with in Wexford town. She was a widow in her mid-forties whose husband had died from tuberculosis within a few years of them marrying twenty years earlier. She had two children in their late teens, a girl and a boy. She needed the income to support the family.

'What makes you think so, Mrs Furlong?' asked Alan, concern growing inside him.

'Oh, it's just that I thought I heard noises.'

'I'm sorry if I disturbed your sleep, Mrs Furlong.'

'Oh, I wasn't disturbed at all, Mr Logan. I just thought that perhaps you weren't well.'

'No. I'm fine. I might have had a bit of a nightmare. I do sometimes. Sorry if I woke you up.'

'No need to be sorry at all, Mr Logan. I'm sure we all have bad dreams from time to time.'

He remembered now. It was dark. There had been a high granite wall and a solid wooden gate that he had been frantically trying to push open. Again and again he pushed without any effect, except to make himself more desperate to get through it. There was something on the other side he needed to get to urgently. He had no idea what it was. He heard what sounded like high-pitched laughter behind him and looked around to see who was there. A policeman waved to him in slow motion from the end of a row of terraced houses and then turned and disappeared around a corner. He turned back to the gate, but it and the wall were gone, and he was standing on the edge of a cliff. As he bent to look over, he woke up with a jolt. He was perspiring profusely.

As he had told his landlady, he had been having similar 'bad dreams', as she had called them, quite a lot in recent weeks.

On his first Sunday in Wexford he asked Mrs Furlong for directions to the nearest Catholic church, and set off giving himself plenty of time to find it before Mass started. He was about ten minutes early, so the church was more or less deserted when he got there. This was not surprising as, in his experience, congregations anywhere he'd been in Ireland seemed to have exquisite timing when it came to arriving for Mass at the last second. He took his place, as he habitually did in any church he attended, about half way up the aisle on the left-hand side. As the church filled up he sensed he was being looked at rather quizzically by those around him, and that some of the children near him seemed to be finding something very amusing, as they giggled with their hands covering their mouths. Suddenly it occurred to him that he was surrounded by women and girls, and that all the men and boys were on the right-hand side of the aisle. This, he discovered later, was the local, and to his mind bewildering, custom. Males and females, even of the same family, did not mix at Mass. With considerable embarrassment he removed himself to the other side of the church. Calm was restored all round.

One evening during the following week, when he had finished

his evening meal in Mrs Furlong's kitchen, she invited him, 'if he would like to' to join herself and the children for the rosary, which they recited each evening at 'a quarter to seven, before the good programmes come on the radio'. He thanked her, but declined, saying he liked to do his praying alone. Mrs Furlong had resisted making this suggestion until, having seen him going to Mass the previous Sunday, she was sure he was a Catholic. You could never be sure about the religion of people who worked in banks, and with a name like 'Logan' you wouldn't know either.

A few Sundays later an incident occurred that caused him to seriously reassess his attitude to his religious beliefs in general, and to Sunday Mass in particular. The parish was administered by two priests: a curate whom Alan judged to be in his early thirties, and whose homilies Alan found practical and interesting, and a parish priest in his sixties who seemed to be of a rather autocratic disposition, and whose main focus of attention appeared to be collecting money. One could never be sure which priest would officiate at which Mass, and on this particular morning the celebrant happened to be Fr Ford, the parish priest. Once again, his topic concerned collecting money for something or other in the parish. There had, he told the congregation in forthright terms, been posters all around the parish for the past two weeks asking for funds, but there had been an abysmal response so-

'Now that the blind have had their opportunity to ignore me, I'll give the deaf the chance to do the same…..'

Alan could hardly belief his ears. Whatever else he had heard from pulpits, he had never before witnessed people being subjected to sarcasm. Where was the message of Jesus Christ in this? Where was 'Do unto others as you would have them do unto you?' And the assembled mass-goers just sat there like robots without the slightest murmur of objection. Alan stood up, left the pew, and walked from the church. There was a general stirring and turning of heads, but Fr Ford didn't miss a beat as he continued his harangue.

Alan walked back to his lodgings in a high state of mixed emotions. He was angry at the apparent casualness of the priest's insulting behaviour, and appalled with himself for leaving Mass before the consecration. Clearly this meant that he had not fulfilled his religious duty to attend Sunday Mass, and to miss Mass was a mortal sin. He had never before missed Mass deliberately on a Sunday or Holy Day of Obligation. It had never seriously occurred to him to do otherwise. He was convinced that every thing he had been taught since the day he was born about the Catholic Church was correct. It had the unbroken wisdom and tradition of two thousand years behind it. He had learned about its numerous saints, who had seen apparitions and worked miracles through the ages. He knew that here in Ireland, despite hundreds of years of persecution of the Catholic Church by the English, the Irish people had resolutely remained faithful to their traditional Catholicism. There was no question in his mind but that he too wanted to remain faithful. This was *the* most important purpose of life for anyone fortunate enough to be born into the Catholic faith. If one came across the odd violent or sadistic Christian Brother or a misogynistic, cantankerous, ill-mannered or arrogant priest, one had to make allowances. Despite their calling, and their superior position regarding their nearness to God and the sources of sanctifying grace, which inevitably meant they were better than ordinary lay people, it was only human nature that there would be the odd few among them whose behaviour was less than exemplary.

When he arrived for work a few minutes before 9 a.m. the following morning the bank manager, Mr Grant, opened the door to him as usual, and they exchanged the customary greetings. As he was on his way to his desk the manager said,

'I thought we might not be seeing you this morning, Mr Logan.'

Alan felt his stomach tighten. He had no idea what was behind this comment.

'Why was that, Mr Grant?'

'Oh, I noticed you leaving Mass early yesterday. I thought you might be ill.'

Alan's stomach did a somersault. He realized that his pointed departure from the church had wider implications than a private and personal protest. If his action was interpreted in the local community as belittling the Church, it could have implications for the bank's business, especially among the local Catholic business fraternity. Thinking quickly Alan fibbed,

'Eh, yes, I didn't feel well – stomach bug. I needed to get home quickly.'

After a moment he added,

'It was very embarrassing having to leave the church like that.'

'You're recovered, then?' Mr Grant queried with raised eyebrows.

'Oh yes, it cleared up quickly, thank goodness.'

'Good, good. I'm glad to hear that,' the manager commented, less than convincingly.

Alan had no doubt that his behaviour had been noted, and his card marked.

As the days passed he became increasingly troubled by the thought that he was probably living in mortal sin because he hadn't fulfilled his obligation to attend Mass by leaving so early, and could go to hell forever if he died. He had no peace of mind until he got to confession the following Saturday evening. Even then he was concerned about being tempted to question, or even lapse, in his religious duties. After all, he had heard many stories about young people giving up on their religion once they were away from the influences of their families and local community.

Socially there was no lack of variety of things to amuse himself with in Wexford but, apart from having a couple of beers with his male colleagues after work on Friday evenings, and attending the local race meetings on Saturday afternoons, he confined himself to joining the local athletics club. He liked to run, and his way of staying reasonably physically fit was to train at the club on a couple of evenings each week. Apart from that he attended the cinema regularly, joined the local public library, and enjoyed the luxury of having his own room, where he could read to his heart's content. He also became a member of the local Saint Vincent de Paul Society, a Catholic charity which, among many other activities directed towards helping the less well-off in society, provided contact between the Society's members and individuals and families in need. One positive aspect of his religious upbringing was the emphasis laid on voluntarily helping those less fortunate and needy people in the community.

However, reading was his main leisure activity. The local library was quite well stocked with books on travel, history (although works on Irish history post 1916 were almost impossible to find), and pastimes and hobbies. Biographies also abounded, many of them on Christian saints, although these were usually to be found in the large section devoted to religion. Among the fictional selections, thrillers, crime novels and the classics interested him most. He went through a phase of reading the crime novels of the American author James Hedley Chase and was surprised to discover that, when he sought some of his listed titles, they were banned. It was the first time he began to realize the extent to which the censorship of books applied in Ireland.

Time and again, however, his interest was drawn to those works in the religion section on interpreting Catholic Church teachings. He constantly sought for indications of some 'softening' of the harsh teachings that had been the staple diet of his life till that time. He sought a system of belief that he could respond to in a more convinced and enthusiastic manner. Frequently, however, the material he came across had the opposite effect. In a book entitled *A Sight of Hell*, written 'for the instruction of children' by an extraordinarily appropriately named Father Furniss, a Redemptorist Catholic priest, he read the good priest's thoughts on an extract from Psalm xx, *Thou shall make him an oven of fire in the time of thy anger-*

'You are going to see again the child about which (sic) you read in *The Terrible Judgment*, that it was condemned to Hell. See! It is a pitiful sight. The little child is in this red-hot oven. Hear how it screams to come out. See how it turns and twists itself about in the fire. It beats its head against the roof of the oven. It stamps its little feet on the floor of the oven. You can see on the face of this little child what you see on the faces of all in Hell – despair, desperate and horrible!'

Alan took some small consolation from the fact that this damnatory polemic was penned by a Redemptorist, a member of an order of Catholic priests who were starting to be regarded, among the better educated among Catholic congregations, in the same light as the holy rollers of other religious denominations.

When he tired of finding anything inspiring or to his satisfaction among the selection of books on religion he found himself more and more inclined to favour the novels of the world's most renowned authors. It did not take him long to discover that a significant number of the works he found references to, and consequently wished to read, were not available. This situation, he quickly learned, was not primarily to do with any inadequacy on the part of the library, but due to the highly restrictive nature of Ireland's laws on the censorship of books. He sought in vain Aldous Huxley's *Point Counter Point*, John Steinbeck's *Tortilla Flat*, Graham Greene's *The Power and the Glory*, Kate O'Brien's *Land of Spices*, Henry's Millar's *Tropic of Cancer*, James Jones's *From Here to Eternity*, Thomas Hardy's *Jude the Obscure*, Walter Macken's *Sunset on the Window Panes*, and various other works by authors such as Frank O'Connor, Sean O'Faolain, Hemingway, and Swift. Even Goldsmith and Milton had not escaped the censor's shears. When he looked for any of these books he was invariably informed that they 'were on the Index', meaning The Vatican's Index of Banned Books. If a book appeared on 'The Index' it was virtually certain to be banned in Ireland, such was the influence of the Roman Catholic authorities over what the State's citizens were allowed to get their hands on. The Church's all-seeing censure was enforced not only by the police but, much more powerfully, by the Vatican's edict declaring that a Catholic could only read the proscribed works under pain of mortal sin, unless dispensation had been obtained from a bishop. Alan later discovered that even the Archbishop of Dublin felt obliged to obtain a dispensation from his own confessor, a Fr Bernard Fennelly, before taking it upon himself to read Dr Marie Carmichael Stopes' *'A Letter to Working Mothers'*, a manual on sexology, banned in Ireland since its publication in 1935. Fr Fennelly generously cleared the Archbishop to read 'dirty' literature *carte blanche*, including works considered deviant or pornographic, in view of the necessity for him to be familiar with such material when dealing with Catholic doctors, priests and the legal profession.

The longer the list of banned books he could not access grew, the more determined Alan became to locate them, despite the conscience-afflicting strictures that resulted. It was not, in fact, all that difficult to acquire banned books in Wexford if, as Alan soon did, one got to know the local ways of doing things. The fairly easy availability of the banned material was probably due to the proximity of Rosslare Harbour, which was a major trading port with Britain. Regrettably most of what came through this source was of a genuinely salacious and brain-fevering content, but the more worthwhile and serious material was also there to be found. Alan enjoyed the reading, suffered the pangs of conscience, worried about hell, confessed, and continued to read what he wanted to read anyway. In any event some of the individual priests he spoke to didn't seem too convinced about the harmfulness of the books in question.

Worry about the eternal effects of viewing forbidden material came to Alan's attention in an entirely different, and quite pathetic, manner a few months after his arrival in Wexford. As a result of his voluntary work with the Saint Vincent de Paul Society he had become acquainted with a few elderly bachelors and widowers in Wexford town, and called on them regularly, just to make sure they were managing all right. One evening when he called on an old bachelor, Jack Fitzpatrick, who lived alone in a tiny cottage on the outskirts of the town, he got no answer to his knocking, but thought he heard noises from inside. Out of concern, and conscious of trying to preserve Mr Fitzpatrick's privacy, he went around to the rear of the little house and peered in through the kitchen window. Alan was shocked to see the old man lying face down on the floor. He was groaning loudly. Alan tried the backdoor. It was unlocked. He entered quickly and tried to make out what had happened. The old man was conscious, but blood had pooled on the floor about his head where he appeared to have struck it when he fell. He kept moaning to Alan about not being able to move his leg.

Alan remembered that it was recommended not to move someone in this type of situation, until his injuries were fully known. He hurried to get blankets to throw over the injured man, cleaned the blood from around his head, and tied a towel around his forehead, although the gash seemed to have stopped bleeding. He then ran to the nearest telephone box and rang for an ambulance.

When Alan returned Mr Fitzpatick seemed to have regained his senses more fully.

'Don't try moving, Mr Fitzpatrick. You might only do yourself more damage. The ambulance will be here soon.'

The old man suddenly seemed very agitated.

'Alan, I want you to do something for me quickly!'

'What is it, Mr Fitzpatrick?'

'Under the mattress in the bedroom there,' he said, pointing as best he could towards the bedroom door, 'there's a book I want you to get rid of before anyone else comes.'

Alan was nonplussed.

'Okay, Mr Fitzpatrick.'

Alan rooted around under the mattress until he found what he was searching for. It was a small magazine entitled 'Men Only', which was one of the innumerable publications banned from sale in Ireland. Alan flicked through it. It consisted mostly of what seemed to be short stories and features to do with sex, and a few pictures of girls with bare breasts. Alan stuffed it in his pocket and returned to the patient, assuring him with a nod that the matter had been taken care of.

'You won't be telling anyone about this, will you Alan?'

'No, Mr Fitzpatrick. Don't worry about that.'

'Another thing, Alan. I wouldn't want to meet me Maker without seeing a priest. You understand?'

'You're not going to die, Mr Fitzpatrick, but I'll look after that for you.'

'Thanks. That'd be a great relief to me. You're a good lad.'

The ambulance crew arrived shortly afterwards. They discovered that, apart from the gash and a nasty bump on his head, the old man had fractured his femur, which, clearly, was why he was unable to move.

When Mr Fitzpatrick was safely stretchered into the ambulance and on his way to hospital, Alan straightaway arranged for a priest to visit him that same evening, knowing that the old man would not rest easy until he confessed his sins and received absolution. That a harmless old man should be suffering the mental anguish of possibly spending eternity in hell for disobeying the Church's moral strictures by looking at a few pictures of bare-breasted girls, the like of which could be viewed in any art gallery in the world, including the Vatican, struck Alan as little short of spiritual terrorism.

The longer he lived and the more he saw of life in Ireland, the more it seemed clear to him that the fear of hell was an endemic and all-pervasive force that reduced old and young alike to conditioned and mind-controlled bundles of latent anxiety. The sacred right to think – even to dare to think – had been stolen from them and replaced by an imposed theologically-centred despotism. It was around this time that Alan really began to ask himself if this was truly what Christianity in general, and Catholicism in particular, was meant to contribute to human life and dignity.

Alan was well aware that these were not the types of misgivings that could be voiced indiscriminately without risking hostile reaction. There was, however, one person to whom he could always speak freely on any matter - his friend Philip Ffrench, whom he always tried to meet up with on his trips to Dublin. Philip was progressing well with his arduous medical training. He hoped to eventually specialize in psychiatry, but that was still a long way off. When Alan told him of the pathetic episode with the elderly Jack Fitzpatrick, and of how it had caused him to think about the incongruity of the Christian concept of an all-loving God creating a place of eternal flames, Philip's reaction was to say that although he had listened to clergymen of his own denomination fulminating about how most of us were hell bound, he personally could not take it too seriously. What did concern him was the disturbing effects such beliefs had on the mental health of people of a psychologically fragile or scrupulous nature, or on the many ordinary folk whose lives were lived constantly by reference to a sort of 'guilt barometer', due to their religious conditioning in childhood.

Inevitably in these meetings with Philip the subject of Heather would be mentioned. During his early months in Wexford Alan had heard nothing from her, but she was still very much on his mind. Any news he got about her came through Philip, as the Ffrenchs and Lattimores were still in regular contact and, naturally, the subject of Heather's life in England would be talked about when they met. Alan never enquired about her specifically, but Philip would always find an opportunity to fill him in briefly. For the first few years there was nothing much to report, other than that she seemed to be settling into her studies. Any mention of her still unsettled him so much that he was never quite sure whether he wanted to hear anything about her or not.

After she'd left for England it had taken many months before his anger and frustration started to abate, and when eventually he did venture into the world of dates and relationships, they never amounted to anything serious or remotely enduring. His underlying feeling was one of marking time until his *real* life began. His life in Wexford, although generally agreeable, was also tempered with a sense of impermanence. It was customary for the bank to require staff to spend at least five years in a posting. By the time he'd completed his basic stint in Wexford he was restless to return to Dublin. He missed his family and friends. He missed The Lounge. He asked the bank for a transfer back to Dublin and a few months later his request was granted.

8

July 1961

Lucy O'Connell was almost three years Alan's senior, which meant she was approaching her thirtieth birthday by the time Alan was granted his transfer back to Dublin. Lucy was from Galway and, like most middle-class girls of her time, she'd been educated in a convent school, in her case the Sisters of Mercy. Her experience of the nuns who taught her was much the same as Alan's had been of the Christian Brothers, which meant it ranged from the worthy to the venomous. Whereas the Brothers favoured physical beatings as a method of instilling virtue, the Sisters, although no shirkers in applying the strap and the cane, tended to specialize in those more subtle forms of Christian correctives (for which the Gospels missed providing any examples) – ridicule, sarcasm, derision and invective. Lucy escaped the worst of this treatment, probably because her family were influential shopkeepers in the community. Despite this, on one occasion, when she was eleven years of age, she was made to stand on a chair in front of the class, while the good Sister proceeded to pin newspaper around the hem of her skirt, because it did not reach far enough below

Lucy's knees to satisfy the reverend lady's sense of modesty. That evening when Lucy announced that she wouldn't go to school until she got a new skirt the whole episode came out. Her father was furious. The following morning he appeared, with Lucy by the hand, at the Principal's office, and told her in very forthright terms what he thought of the humiliating manner in which his daughter had been treated.

'If the school has a problem with the child's attire the civilized way to deal with that would be to contact her parents instead of embarrassing her in front of her classmates,' he fumed.

The Principal, unused to being confronted by parents on any subject, undertook to speak to her zealous colleague. Lucy had no further problems.

When she finished her schooling Lucy worked in her father's hardware store in Galway for two years before getting an appointment to the Civil Service. She was assigned to the Department of Social Welfare, which meant moving to Dublin. Initially she found accommodation in a hostel run, and tightly supervised by a French order of nuns, who had been granted permission by the Archbishop to set up a ministry in Dublin especially to cater for young country girls, until they learned to cope with the difficulties and dangers of city life. Lucy spent six months in the hostel before finding a 'bedsit' in Dublin's inner south city area. The 'bedsit' was typical of its type; consisting of one room which contained a bed, a small cooker, a wash-hand basin, a table and a couple of chairs. She shared a bathroom with three other residents of the house. It was warm and comfortable, and she remained there for the next seven years. Now in her mid-twenties, and with no signs of marriage on the horizon, she decided to invest, with her father's assistance, in a small three-roomed cottage within walking distance of the city centre. The accommodation consisted of a living room, kitchen, bedroom and bathroom, with a small front garden and a much larger garden to the rear.

Initially she had continued to return to her family home in Galway on most weekends, leaving Dublin by train on Friday evenings, and returning by the first train from Galway on Monday mornings. As the years passed these trips tended to become fewer and fewer until they became monthly events at most.

On the last Sunday in July 1961 Lucy set off by train for the west of Ireland, but on this occasion her destination was not Galway. The train was bound for Westport, on Ireland's Atlantic coast, and on board were a few hundred others who, like Lucy, intended to climb to the summit of Croagh Patrick – St Patrick's 'steep-sided mountain', that had been a place of pilgrimage for over 1500 years, ever since St Patrick was reputed to have spent forty days and nights in prayer and fasting on its bleak summit imploring God to grant him success in converting the pagan Celts of Ireland to Christianity. Lucy's appeal to God was on a far less grand scale, but nonetheless of prime importance in her life. She was rapidly approaching thirty, she was unmarried, and she was a virgin. And, as she had confided to her sister recently with vodka-fuelled uncharacteristic frankness, she did not wish to 'die wondering'. For Lucy, who was devoted to her Catholic religion, that meant finding a husband.

When she dismounted from the bus that conveyed her from the railway station in Westport to the foot of the mountain, she set off resolutely by herself along the pilgrim path. She did not wish to be distracted by the conversation of others. The first 2000 feet were relatively easy climbing, but the final five hundred feet were steep and covered in loose shale that made progress difficult and hazardous. Her flat, leather-soled, laced shoes, although sturdy, were quite unsuitable for this particular purpose. She saw others climbing in their bare feet and was tempted to do so herself. She quickly thought better of it. Eventually, with much slipping and stumbling, she arrived at the mist-covered summit, on which stood a small chapel where priests took it in turn to say Mass, and around about which they heard the confessions of those who wished to be absolved of their sins. Lucy went to confession, attended Mass, and spent about twenty minutes gazing out over the magnificent Clew Bay before starting her descent.

She soon realized that keeping her footing on the way down was much more difficult than on the ascent. She wished she had had the foresight to arm herself with a staff or walking stick of some sort, as many about her had done. She had scarcely descended one hundred feet when her feet went completely from under her and she fell heavily. She tore her stockings and grazed her hands and knees. Her feelings of stupidity and embarrassment and frustration brought her close to tears as she tried to regain her feet. How could she face the long journey back to Dublin in such a dishevelled state?

It was at that moment that she felt a hand on her shoulder and a voice above her saying,

'May I help you?'

The voice she heard, and the face she saw through her incipient tears, was that of Alan Logan. She had, quite literally, fallen at his feet.

Alan had been based back in Dublin since the beginning of 1961, after spending almost six years in Wexford. He had done well in the Institute of Bankers examinations, which he had taken over the years and had been invited to join the bank's Internal Audit and Branch Inspection team. This was a three-man group charged with visiting the bank's branch offices regularly to check that everything was as it should be. As the job entailed travelling outside Dublin about every second week Alan was provided with a company car, a major 'perk' of the position.

At the time of his visit to Croagh Patrick he and his two colleagues had spent the previous week auditing procedures in the bank's branch in Tuam, County Galway, and instead of returning to Dublin on Friday evening as he would have done in normal circumstances, he decided to remain in the west of Ireland and see Croagh Patrick for himself on the following pilgrimage

Sunday. It was one of those things that he had wanted to do for a long time but never quite got around to, so this seemed like the ideal opportunity.

'Thank you. I feel so silly,' Lucy answered as she scrambled to her feet with his assistance.

As she started to brush her knees he offered her a handkerchief, and suggested they find one of the first-aid stations located at regular intervals on the mountainside.

By the time she had been patched up and they had reached the bottom of the mountain she had agreed to his offer to accompany him back to Dublin in his car, rather than take the train. She had never felt more confused and agitated in her life. Never had she wanted more to look her best, and all she could think of was what an absolute wreck she must appear. Although, as an act of self-denial to coincide with her pilgrimage to Croagh Patrick, she had decided not to smoke on this particular day, they had barely started on their journey home when she felt she needed a cigarette to calm herself down. She asked Alan if he would like one. He told her he didn't smoke.

'No vices, then?' she tried to joke.

'I wouldn't say that exactly,' he responded.

The journey would take about six hours, which meant they would not reach Dublin until quite late. By the time they had covered about half the distance she was out of cigarettes. Alan suggested that they stop for something to eat, and to let her get more cigarettes. Although she was hungry and felt like stretching her legs, she was reluctant to appear in public in her dishevelled and patched up state. Eventually convenience overcame vanity, and she agreed. Alan pulled into the car park of a hotel he was acquainted with from his work travels. She headed straight for the ladies room and returned ten minutes later, tattered stockings removed, hair combed, make-up reapplied, and looking altogether better than she had done on arrival.

They chatted as they had their refreshments, and generally

filled each other in on their backgrounds. When they had finished he asked her what brand of cigarette she smoked. He would get her some before they resumed their journey.

'Gold Flake. Thank you. I'd feel like a ten year old tomboy going into a shop with these cut knees.'

Alan drove her to her door. She had reconciled herself to the fact that the events of the day were nothing more than a chance encounter when, as she was exiting the car, Alan hesitatingly asked her if she would like them to see each other again. She was so surprised that she almost tripped again. She said she thought that that would be nice. They exchanged phone numbers and he said he'd be in touch shortly.

The following week was one of those alternate weeks that Alan spent at the bank's head office in Dublin, sifting through and reporting on the previous week's findings. On the Tuesday evening he rang Lucy's number. She answered promptly.

'Hello.'

'Lucy?'

'Yes'

'Alan here, you know, from Croagh Patrick?'

'Hello, Alan. Yes, I recognize your voice.'

'I said I'd give you a call. I was wondering if you'd be interested in going to a film some evening this week?'

'I'd love to.'

'How about tomorrow night?'

'That would be fine.'

They chatted for a few minutes about their weekend adventure, and agreed to meet in the city the following evening at the Metropole cinema.

At 7 p.m. the next day he was waiting for her in the cinema's foyer. When he spotted her coming through the doors he was surprised at how attractive she appeared. She was petite – no taller than five feet four and probably about one hundred and twenty pounds. Her hair and eyes were dark and her skin olive. There was an Italianate quality about her that he found very attractive. As they greeted each other and discussed whether to remain where they were or go to another cinema Alan became more aware of her soft west of Ireland accent, and of how pleasant it sounded to him. They stayed where they were. As they queued at the box-office she offered him a cigarette, forgetting he had told her he didn't smoke. She lit one for herself as they chatted about the films they liked, and laughed at the unusual way they had met.

After the show they had coffee and a late night snack together, and her drove her home. As they parted they shared their first kiss. It was also the first time Alan had kissed a girl without feeling the shadowy presence of Heather Lattimore at such a moment, since her sudden departure to England years previously. The evening seemed to have been a success for both of them.

And so began the courtship of Lucy and Alan.

They gradually became acquainted, and socialized, with each other's friends but, although Alan still kept up his contact with Philip Ffrench, he saw less of him than he had done in the past. Over the years Philip and himself had continued to meet regularly at the jazz sessions on Friday evenings. But, as Lucy found jazz incomprehensible - 'It all sounds the same to me' -, Alan had given up his long established Friday night routine in favour of activities more to Lucy's taste.

Eighteen months after their providential meeting on Croagh Patrick they became engaged, and were married a year later. Lucy had got her wish; she would not 'die wondering'.

As was the rule in Ireland at that time Lucy was obliged, now that she had married, to give up her Civil Service job. All women in the public service sector, and in many private employments also, were subjected to this restriction.

As Lucy wanted to start a family straight away they decided that there was no point in her trying to find another job and, as it happened, she became pregnant within a few weeks of the wedding. Initially Alan had moved into Lucy's small home, but with the prospect of children arriving they set about selling her place and finding a larger house. They found what they wanted, and could afford, in the rapidly developing suburbs of Dublin's south city, and the months of Lucy's pregnancy passed quickly, as they set about transforming their new house into a comfortable home. Alan's job still meant he had to travel from home every alternate week and although he spent only four nights away in each two week period he found himself being more and more resentful of the period he had to be away from home.

At about 5 a.m. on Sunday morning February 23rd 1965 Lucy woke Alan to tell him that she thought that she was starting to have labour pains. They got dressed quickly, put the suitcase she had prepared into the car, and drove to the maternity hospital. They were excited and, naturally, apprehensive, as this was their first child. On their arrival they were told that it would take some hours before there'd be any significant development and that there was no point in Alan waiting about. He spent the day going backwards and forwards between the hospital and his own family. During the afternoon he picked up Lucy's mother, who had travelled up from Galway, at the railway station and brought her to his own mother's home to await news from the hospital.

The delivery was long and difficult. When Alan returned for the umpteenth time to the hospital around 5 p.m. he was told that judging by Lucy's contractions the baby should be born within an hour or two. It was 7.30 that evening before the baby – a girl – was eventually delivered. The attending nurse wrapped her in a blanket, held her up briefly in Lucy's direction and said,

'Here's your baby, Mrs Logan – a little girl.'

The nurse then quickly whisked the baby away to the neonatal intensive care unit. It was immediately obvious that all was not well.

Throughout these dramatic developments Alan had been pacing the waiting room floor, drinking coffee, or trying to read the Sunday newspapers. When the solemn-faced attending gynaecologist, a Dr Woods, appeared in the waiting area a few minutes later, and invited Alan to his room, Alan sensed that something was wrong. The doctor, a fit-looking man in his forties, signalled to Alan to be seated.

'Mr Logan, your wife has had a baby daughter. It was a difficult birth but Mrs Logan is fine. However, and there is no easy way to tell you this - the baby is very weak and frail, and appears to have severe problems. She is in intensive care right now.'

Alan was stunned. This was the most dreadful shock of his life. What was to have been a day of great joy had turned into an ordeal of anguish and desolation. After a few moments Alan asked if Lucy was definitely all right.

'Mrs Logan will be fine. We have made her as comfortable as possible.'

'What do you think is wrong with the baby?' Alan ventured to ask.

'I can't say for sure yet, but it seems to me to be a condition known as Edwards' Syndrome, which is a severe form of Down's syndrome and very rare,' the doctor explained.

'Will the baby live?' Alan wanted to know.

'The prognosis is not encouraging if it is Edwards' syndrome. To be frank with you, Mr Logan - and you understand we do not have any test results to go on at this stage – very few babies with that condition survive till their first birthday.'

'Does Lucy – does my wife know yet that there's something wrong?' Alan asked.

'Apart from the fact that the she's been told that the baby needs special attention, no.'

'Do you want me to tell her?'

'I intended to see her myself, after speaking to you.'

'Could I go with you, you know, be there when this news is broken to her? I'd like to be with her then.'

'I'd appreciate if you would.'

Alan bowed his head for a moment, and then looking at the doctor, said,

'I guess there's no way to avoid telling her what's happened, and delaying isn't going to make things any better. So, I guess we should go to her now.'

'Yes' said the doctor, 'but just bear in mind Lucy may be a little drowsy. She's been given painkillers and some medication to help her relax.'

When they arrived at her bedside, Lucy, despite the sedatives she'd been given, seemed alert and agitated. Her first words were,

'What's wrong with my baby?'

Dr Woods did not elaborate beyond saying that the baby was physically weak, and tests were being carried out to try to determine the cause. He told her these would be available the following day, but in the meantime it was best to monitor the baby in the Intensive Care Unit. He then left Alan and Lucy alone.

'Have you seen the baby?' she asked Alan.

'Not yet.'

'Did he tell you anymore than he told me just now?'

Alan was in a dilemma. Should he follow the doctor's lead, and say very little, or tell her everything he'd been told? He took hold of her hand, and said,

'Lucy, it seems that they don't know the extent of the problem, but they seem to think it could be pretty bad.'

Lucy started sobbing – an almost silent, heaving sound from so deep within her that it seemed to come from somewhere beyond her body. Alan took her in his arms, and held her for what seemed like an age, until she became calmer.

When he eventually left Lucy's room, he became keenly aware of the cries of lusty, newborn babies ringing through the corridors; this joyful, belligerent chorus to new life gave him a singularly profound feeling of rejection. He was filled with a sense of hollowness, emptiness, and unfathomable loneliness.

Alan had kept in touch by telephone with his family throughout the day, and now, before leaving the hospital, he made one final call to tell them the shattering news. His mother insisted that, instead of going home alone to his own house, he should come and spend the night with them. This he agreed to do. When he reached his old home the door was opened by Terry, his elder sister, who, like himself was quite tall and dark, and already married and the mother of a two year old girl. She embraced him consolingly. His Mum, who obviously had been crying, appeared behind Terry, and put her arms out to him, and then made way for the equally tearful Mrs O'Connell to embrace him. As they moved towards the sitting room, the blond and shapely figure of the ever soft-hearted Mimi descended the stairs, her eyes full of concern and sympathy. Alan held her for a long moment before turning to acknowledge the greeting of his Dad. Finally, the other blond member of the family, Barry, uncoiled his six foot two inch frame from the sofa where he'd been sitting and squeezed Alan's hand in both of his.

Alan related all the details he knew about the birth, and the conversation drifted back and forth between this harrowing subject and various others before they all eventually retired to bed in the small hours of the morning.

The following day Alan made contact with the priest who acted as the hospital chaplain, and arranged to have the baby baptized without delay. They named her Christine.

During the following days Alan learned, from the various meetings he had with the hospital personnel, that Edwards' syndrome occurred in about one in every three thousand births and was more common among girls than boys. A significant numbers of mothers of affected infants were in their thirties. It was caused by a rare chromosomal disorder and, in the gynaecologist opinion 'was not compatible with life'.

Many tests were carried out, at the end of which the doctor explained to the distraught and frantic young parents that to attempt to correct or improve little Christine's various problems would require extremely invasive surgical procedures, which might not be in the baby's best interests, and that his recommendation was to simply make her as comfortable as possible while she lived.

The gynaecologist's supposition proved correct. In the event the baby never left the hospital. She survived for less than three weeks. She had serious physical defects and, had she survived, would certainly have had severe mental disabilities also.

During the three-week period between the arrival and the passing of the tiny struggling bundle of humanity that was their firstborn, Lucy and Alan existed in a state of stunned confusion and disbelief that was close to the unreal world of a nightmare from which there was no escape. Lucy's smoking increased to the point where she never seemed to be without a cigarette at her lips.

In the weeks following Christine's death Alan was filled with a sullen rage. When good-intentioned friends and well-wishers offered consoling comments like 'It is God's will', he found them almost blasphemous. How could such a birth and death, or such suffering and heartbreak by two young people who had looked forward with delighted anticipation to the pleasure of nurturing their new arrival, be the 'will' of a loving God?

The affect on Lucy was catastrophic. What had happened was incomprehensible to her. Each time the reality of what had occurred exploded in her mind, she shrank form it instantly. Initially she kept feeling that it must be some sort of very bad mistake. As the reality of the situation took hold her psychological stress became increasingly volatile. Suddenly she would find herself uncontrollably tearful, or being overwhelmed by waves of sadness, emptiness and loss. These emotions would in turn give way to feelings of searing anger against an ever-shifting spectrum of targets; against the maternity hospital and the doctor; against Alan, for no definable reason whatever, other than he must be responsible in some way and should have prevented it; against God – 'Why do this to me?' – but blaming God immediately brought on bouts of guilt. She became angry when people told her, intending to comfort her, that she could always have more babies, which seemed to her to diminish the individual worth of the child she had lost, as if you could replace one baby with another, like you were replacing a light bulb. And then there was the anger against herself, at what she felt instinctively must be her defectiveness, her inadequacy. All of these reactions merged into one enormous, smothering sense of guilt. She kept asking herself what she had done wrong. She became immersed in feelings of worthlessness, and even wickedness, and worried that everyone would see her in that light. She lost her appetite, and seemed to live on nothing but cigarettes during each day, while spending her nights lying awake in sleepless agitation. She had little energy or initiative, and virtually no interest in anything outside herself. She was locked in a dungeon of emotional misery.

During the following months, despite the fact that nightly he would hold her in his arms in bed, Alan felt as if he was living with a stranger. He felt excluded, locked out. His efforts at consoling Lucy, or even at communicating with her in any way, beyond the most mundane level were received with an indifference and unresponsiveness that left him crushed and even frightened. Reluctantly he began to realize that he found himself looking forward to those few days, every alternate week, when his job took him away from home.

The most worrying manifestation of Lucy's condition was her obvious loss of weight, simply because it was the most visible aspect of the change which little Christine's birth and death had brought about in her. Thin as she had been to begin with, within six months she had become gaunt and haggard-looking. Alan observed her deterioration with a mixture of alarm and vexation at his inability to help her to recover.

The other person who was sorely worried by Lucy's condition was her mother. She made several trips to Dublin during this period to be with her grieving daughter. Eventually it was decided that a change of location might help Lucy to recuperate physically and regain her former perspective on life, and with this objective in mind Lucy returned with her mother in mid-September to her family home in Galway, on the understanding that she would spend a couple of weeks there. When Alan visited in early October everyone agreed that there were signs of improvement in Lucy's appearance and responsiveness to the normal affairs of life. In view of this it was generally thought best that she remain in Galway for a while longer. In the event the weeks slipped past until it was so close to Christmas that it was decided that they would all spend the holiday period in Galway, and that Lucy, who was improving steadily, would return to Dublin in the new year.

By the time Lucy and Alan resumed their life together in Dublin, a year had almost elapsed since Christine's birth. During that time they had not been intimate. Alan felt that the questions surrounding their relationship as man and wife, and of having more children needed to be addressed. Although Lucy appeared to be recovering well physically and temperamentally she had shown complete indifference to having sex, or any kind of intimacy.

When Alan broached the subject over dinner one evening in late January it quickly became clear that he had hit a raw nerve. Lucy became troubled and defensive. She accused him of being insensitive and left the table in tears. He bottled his frustrations, and felt ashamed of having reduced her to crying.

The following weeks were filled with an uneasy and mounting tension as they both pretended to ignore the very subject that was most vital to their future. It was April before the ice was broken and when it happened it came as a surprise to Alan. He arrived home from a business trip one Friday evening, to be greeted more warmly by Lucy than he had been in what seemed like an age. She had clearly made a particular effort to make herself look well. She chatted and asked him about his week as she prepared dinner, but Alan sensed that there was something more to her manner then met the eye.

They had scarcely sat down when she said,

'Alan, I've been thinking about what you wanted to talk about a few weeks ago, about us having sex, and maybe another baby. I'm sorry I reacted the way I did, but I just wasn't ready to think, or talk, about all that.'

'I understand. You were right. I was probably very insensitive,' Alan replied.

'No, I don't think that's really true. I think I was afraid – am afraid – of the implications.'

Lucy had now placed her knife and fork alongside her plate, at which see seemed to be staring intently.

'What implications?' asked Alan, who had also abandoned eating.

'Well, mostly I'm afraid that if we have another baby it might be the same as...,' Lucy was now looking directly at Alan's face.

'I've thought about that too, Lucy,' Alan responded. 'I'm sure you remember as well as I do that one of the things the gynaecologist mentioned was that, although research was very limited at this stage, it seemed that there was good reason to believe that there's about a one in four chance of any future baby being affected in the same way.'

'I remember that very clearly,' Lucy confirmed animatedly.

'Well then, we have to think about whether or not it's worth the risk, don't we?' said Alan.

'That's what I have been thinking about,' replied Lucy. 'I don't think I could bear to go through that again. I can't imagine what it would be like to spend nine months carrying a baby and wondering all the time if it was all right. I don't think I'd be able for that, Alan.'

'I understand that. Perhaps we'll just have to make our minds up to the fact that it would be best for us not to have a family.'

The expression on Lucy's face said it all about her relief.

'Thanks, Alan. You don't know how good it is to hear you say that.'

'Good,' said Alan,' but we still have to figure out how you and I are going to have a normal relationship as a married couple.'

'You mean having sex?'

'Yes, of course.'

Both of them were silent for a few minutes. Alan felt that the tension that had so recently started to ease was beginning to build up again, something he acutely wanted to avoid. He reached across the table and took hold of Lucy's hand.

'We don't have to talk about this now. Think about it and we'll talk about it when you're ready.'

She nodded her agreement, and they resumed their meal. But the latent tension was back in the air.

As the weeks passed without any return to the subject, a vague sense of depression started to grow inside Alan. He became increasingly quiet and introspective. He began to feel trapped in an oppressive and soul-destroying predicament that was not of his own making and to which there seemed to be no solution. He felt as though he was gradually sinking in a mire of dispiriting quicksand. Eventually his evenings sank into periods of apathetic torpor, as he sat watching whatever appeared on the television screen before him. As time passed he simply exchanged habitual 'goodnights' with Lucy as she retired to bed, while he remained sprawled on the sofa until the TV went blank around midnight. He would then coil up and sleep where he was, rather than go to bed beside her. He found it easier to drift off to sleep like that rather than to spend hours ill at ease and miserable, lying beside a wife who seemed to have lost all interest in his presence at her side. Never since his schooldays had he experienced such negative feelings towards facing each new day. Now similar feelings had re-emerged, but these were more of apathy than fear. He began to imagine a black hole inside himself into which everything that was 'him' – his spirit, his energy, his will to engage with life at any level – start to drain away. It became increasingly difficult to feel that there was any point to his existence. Thoughts of being free from life began to waft through the corners and corridors of his mind.

For her part Lucy was not unaware of the artificial and unconscionable nature of their life together, but the profound fear of becoming pregnant, and enduring another such birth, caused her to push it as far from her mind as she could for as long as she could. As the months passed her conscience became increasingly troubled. As a born and raised Catholic she had been taught that marriage brought with it duties and obligations to God and to one's partner, and she knew that these were not being fulfilled. Fully eighteen months had elapsed since Christine's birth and death before she found the resolve to confront the situation. She decided that she would go to confession and ask guidance from a priest.

The priest was sympathetic towards her and commiserated on the tragedy of losing her baby. But, he explained, as a married woman it was wrong for her to deny her husband his 'conjugal rights' – his moral rights to an unfettered sexual relationship with his wife.

'You may in conscience consider using the rhythm method which is permitted by the Church in certain circumstances in order to limit the size of families,' He added.

'But,' pleaded Lucy 'I am afraid of becoming pregnant and having….well, having another handicapped baby. The rhythm system is not reliable. Friends of mine have tried it and it failed.'

'These matters are in the hands of God. God loves every newborn baby equally, whether it is born in perfect health or otherwise. We must trust in God and know that to Him it is the creation of a soul that is truly important,' the priest offered.

'Your duty now is to your marriage and your husband. You must leave the future in God's hands and accept His will. As a Christian, to do otherwise would be sinful. You must pray for the strength and courage and enlightenment to accept the cross Jesus has called on you to bear, ' he added.

This was of no help or consolation to Lucy. It simply served to deepen her dilemma and make her even more wracked with anxiety than she had previously been.

The following morning, Alan and Lucy attended Mass together as they habitually did on every Sunday morning of their lives. The priest chose to talk about ecumenism in his homily, a subject on which there was much confusion in the minds of lay Catholics at the time, especially as the views being expressed by the Irish bishops seemed to differ widely in tone and interpretation. The priest, despite being under the jurisdiction of the arch-conservative Archbishop of Dublin, John Charles McQuaid, based his comments on the writings of the recently appointed Archbishop of Armagh, and most senior Irish cleric, William Conway. Archbishop Conway had drawn attention to 'the unity of all Christians', and to the fact that relations between Catholics and other Christians had 'grown markedly warmer'. He also quoted Pope John XXIII's own statement that 'Christians separated from us possess much that is true, good, Christian and holy.' The priest reminded his congregation that the Pope had encouraged all Christian to meet together 'as brothers'. He went on to explain that many Catholics were, understandably, confused and in doubt about whether or not they were morally entitled to attend such events as the weddings and funerals of Protestant friends and acquaintances. The priest explained that there was the world of difference between attending such functions as an act of courtesy or civil duty, as against participation in an act of worship, which would be wrong.

'Interesting homily,' Alan commented idly as they drove away from the church.

'How do you mean?' asked Lucy as she flicked the ash from the cigarette she had lit on leaving the church out the car window. Alan hadn't expected a response from Lucy, who usually remained closed away in her own world. He glanced at her and, sensing that she was actually interested, explained to her what had been going through his mind as the priest spoke-

'Well, when you think about it, a few years ago we were being warned that anyone who went to a non-Catholic service was committing a mortal sin. In other words they'd be damned to hell for all eternity if they died after attending a Protestant service and before they confessed it in confession, and now we are being told to fraternize with our fellow-Christians and treat them as brothers, which, I have to say, seems eminently sensible to me. I just wonder if those people who died after defying the previous regulations are now in hell forever, bearing in mind that what they did then was a mortal sin. Pretty tough on them, wouldn't you say?'

'You shouldn't make a mockery of the Church like that,' said Lucy sullenly, as if she had taken his remarks as a personal accusation. Alan became a little heated-

'Who's making a mockery of the Church? It seems like a very fair question to me. What was labelled a mortal sin a little while ago is now being dressed up as a charitable act. That's some change to make in the Church's thinking. If the Church has decided it was wrong then why not come out clearly and say so, and explain to us how something can be a mortal sin one day and not the next. Do the Church authorities simply expect intelligent people, who take their religion seriously and rely on them for clear guidance, to do mental somersaults without asking straightforward questions out of genuine interest and concern? Are we not entitled to expect plain, straightforward explanations and answers? If they were wrong why not say so without pretending it was some sort of little mistake that there's no need to even mention. Think of the anguish they've caused to God knows how many conscientious people over the years.'

'I don't like this conversation,' Lucy responded dismissively, as she turned away to tap more ash out the side window, through which she continued to gaze at nothing in particular.

'Actually,' Alan gibed angrily, 'this isn't a conversation. In order for it to be a conversation two people would have to take part.'

'That's a nasty thing to say,' said Lucy, now on the edge of tears. 'What's the matter with you?'

Alan's latent anger and frustration surged to the surface.

'I think you have a damn good idea of what's the matter with me.'

He had never addressed her in such terms previously. He swung the car into their driveway and stormed off into the house with the Sunday newspapers under his arm. She followed silently, but the shock and tension she was feeling was palpable.

A few minutes later she entered the sitting room where Alan now sat sullenly looking at a newspaper without a word he saw registering. She sat down and said,

'Alan, would you put the newspaper down for a minute, please. I have something I want to tell you.'

Alan lowered the newspaper and looked towards Lucy, who had sat down almost on the edge of the seat of an armchair opposite to him. She was staring at a spot on the floor between them. He felt guilty for what he had said. He spoke before she could continue.

'Look,' he said, 'I'm sorry I spoke to you like that. I know what you've been through and I don't want to cause you any more suffering. It's just that I get frustrated and depressed at what our lives – my life – has turned into. It's unnatural. Frankly it's becoming unendurable.'

'I know, I know,' she responded forcefully, as if she couldn't wait to let him know she agreed with him, in case the moment might be lost. Her reaction took Alan by surprise.

'What I wanted to tell you was that I have been very worried for quite a while about the way we are living. My conscience has been bothering me, but I wasn't able to face the fear I have of becoming pregnant. Yesterday I spoke about it all to a priest in confession for the first time.'

By now Alan had dropped the newspaper on the floor, and was intent on what Lucy was saying. She recounted all that had passed between the priest and herself in confession the previous day. When Lucy related the priest's comments on conjugal rights within marriage, Alan interjected -

'I've always hated the sounds of those words 'conjugal rights', much less the idea of one person insisting on forcing themselves on another against their will. It makes lovemaking sound so animalistic. To be honest it seems to me to be as near to rape as 'damn it' is to swearing.'

Alan's outburst seemed to encourage Lucy to press on.

'So, what do you feel we should do now,' she asked.

'Well, the way I see it, you are frightened to become pregnant again and I agree that in view of the very real risk of another pregnancy resulting in another handicapped baby it would be better if we avoided having more children, despite what the Church says about our duty to have children, and trusting everything to God's will. And that seems to leave us with contraception as the only way to have an intimate relationship without risking pregnancy.' Alan paused here. He could see from Lucy's discomfort that he had touched a sensitive area. After a few moments silence she said,

'I've thought about that, but the only method of birth control which the Church says is not a mortal sin is the rhythm system, and it's unreliable.'

Despite Alan's frustrations and Lucy's worries they continued to discuss their problem in a calmer atmosphere than when they had started. Eventually they decided that they needed to find out more about both the medical and ethical issues involved before making up their minds about what was best and right to do.

During the days and weeks that followed their Sunday morning talk, they both made efforts to seek information and advice on the medical and moral implications of their dilemma, to – as the Church described it - 'inform their conscience'. What they discovered was really what they knew already; to stay within the moral law it was either give up sex or use the hit-and-miss rhythm system

On the subject of 'total abstinence' Lucy brought home a pamphlet she found on sale in their local church entitled *The*

Young Husband, bearing the *imprimatur* of Archbishop John Charles McQuaid, Primate of Ireland. It advised young married Catholics to keep their lives unstained from the crime of birth-prevention, and warned that 'The one who desires to limit the number of his children will come under God's anger. There may be very serious reasons for limiting the number of children – illness, great dangers to health, and so on. In such a case, the married pair must use their willpower and prudence and live as brother and sister. Such abstinence is difficult, but possible. And there is no other way.' The reference to 'God's anger' could not be interpreted otherwise than to mean mortal sin. The word 'health' referred specifically to physical health only (the damage to someone's psychological health was simply not an issue), and as it was not Lucy's own health that was in danger but only the possible health of any baby she might have, there was no comfort to be discovered in that direction. The Archbishop's views did not appear to regard abstinence in her situation as a valid moral option, and his reference to desiring to limit the number of children causing God's anger' seemed to clearly rule out even the unreliable rhythm system. Her options were to live so as to have children, regardless of their possible handicaps, or live a life of sin.

However, other influential voices in the Church did not share the Archbishop's view on the rhythm system. Although, according to those voices, it was immoral for a couple to do anything 'to deliberately frustrate that act in its natural power to generate life', and declared that contraception was an offence against the law of God and nature, the rhythm system was permissible because it was 'natural'. Everything else was 'unnatural' and therefore sinful.

The 'pill' had also been much in the news recently, but the Church had made it clear that it could only be used, in good conscience, for health reasons to regulate a woman's menstrual cycle. As there was nothing amiss with Lucy's periods, there was no moral basis, according to Church law, for considering the contraceptive pill as an option. The pill was available only on prescription, and there were doctors about who dispensed prescriptions for its use without any fuss, but, although she might easily find a cooperative doctor, Lucy knew she could not fool God by using 'health' as a reason for using the pill. In any event there were questions about its reliability as a contraceptive apart from concerns about possible detrimental side effects on the health of those women who used it, especially over an extended period. All in all, the pill was not the answer for Lucy.

Apart from the moral and medical issues, Alan discovered that under various laws enacted between 1929 and 1935, it was actually illegal in Ireland to advocate contraption. The primary target of these laws was the condom. These laws, like many other secular laws, didn't bother the Irish psyche in general to any great extent. What was much more influential for Catholics were the diktats of their Church. The most relevant of these for Lucy and Alan was Pope Pius X1's pronouncement of December 1930, stating that since 'the conjugal act is destined primarily from nature for the begetting of children, those who….deliberately frustrate its….purpose sin against nature and commit a deed which is…. intrinsically vicious.'

By using words like 'intrinsic' and 'vicious', which, to traditionally conscientious Catholics like Lucy and Alan, could mean only one thing – mortal sin and punishment in hell fire for eternity - the Church made certain to frighten believers away from using condoms. Up to this time Catholics had been conditioned to let the Church do their thinking for them in all matters relating to morality. The Pope was Christ's representative on Earth, and as such Catholics were conditioned to accept that he must have the correct answers to all such matters. Catholics were relieved of the need to think. Like obedient children, they were given directions and answers; they were spoken to, and were expected to accept and follow what they were told.

This was the milieu against which the troubled young married couple struggled to try to work out their relationship. The Church was the dominant force in Irish society. This dominance went all the way through to every level of government. For the government to cross swords with the Church was synonymous with crossing swords with the people, which would inevitably cost them votes. And so the politicians of the day acquiesced and deferred to the views of the Catholic Church, for which they could hardly be blamed, if they wished to stay in power. When Archbishop John Charles McQuaid, made his position clear in a letter read at all Masses in his diocese, which stated that contraception was 'evil, and there cannot be on the part of any person a right to do what is evil', and described it as 'a curse upon the country', 'a right that cannot even exist', and as 'wrong in itself', who would argue?.

But the situation was not quite that clear cut. From following what was happening at the Second Vatican Council Alan was aware that the Pope had set up 'a special commission' to study 'birth control and related themes'. This commission consisted not only of clergymen but also included members of the laity, both male and female. This represented a huge departure from the Church's traditional, ultra-paternalistic stance towards decision-making. Despite teaching that the Holy Spirit worked through every Catholic, the hierarchy was not in the habit of consulting anyone outside their own ranks or of paying any attention to the insights that the laity might have to offer no matter how overwhelming, strong or well researched those insights might be. This new attitude to apparent inclusiveness by the Vatican was, therefore, met with surprise, enthusiasm, hope and intense interest in the lay Catholic world. The 'birth control' commission became the focus of much media attention and articles, features, reports, speculations. Much space in the letters columns of the national newspapers was devoted to the subject. Among the earliest contributions that Alan noticed was a letter from a Jesuit theologian stating that in his opinion the Church 'would be well advised to stay out of the bedrooms of married couples'.

At this point Alan and Lucy decided that, while awaiting the outcome of the birth control Commission, their only option, in relatively good conscience, was to use the rhythm system for the time being.

Despite agreeing to acquaint herself with the workings of the rhythm system Lucy was struggling to mask the huge anxieties she was experiencing within herself. She agreed to Alan's suggestion that they should spend a long weekend in a quiet location away from the city, and let things take their course. She calculated a 'safe period', and he made the travel arrangements. In the days prior to their departure Lucy prayed that all would go well, and that she could manage to get through it without mishap.

In the event - despite the tranquillity of their surroundings in the comfortably converted Georgian mansion they had selected for their little sojourn - between consulting thermometers and filling-in charts, the weekend had more to do with mechanics and mathematics than with providing an atmosphere conducive to intimacy. They 'had sex' rather than made love on a couple of occasions. The spectre of pregnancy, and all that this might entail, filled Lucy with tension and apprehension. Her inability to respond to Alan left them both with a deep sense of lassitude and despair. By the time the weekend was over their relationship was struggling through an emotional wasteland, and they both knew it. Alan's sense of finality and loss was profound. He knew he could never approach her again; he realized that to do so, apart from the obvious stress it would cause to Lucy, would be like a virtual violation of her being, and would demean his own self-worth. When they got home she was relieved when he told her that he would sleep in the spare bedroom for the time being.

During the following weeks Lucy was constantly consumed with anxiety about the possibility that despite their precautions she might have become pregnant. She was by now chain-smoking in her effort to keep her anxieties in check. To her great relief, nature confirmed in due course that she was not expecting a baby.

9

August 1968

By the time Pope Paul V1 promulgated his long-awaited encyclical *Humanae Vitae* in July 1968, denying the use of contraception to Catholics under the Church's traditional stricture of grave sin, Alan had lost all interest in the sexual element of his marriage. The Commission that the Pope had appointed to deliberate on the issue of the morality of contraception had not produced the result that Pius VI had wanted, and which he could have hidden behind, and which would have enabled him to appear to be merely endorsing an independent Papal Commission's findings, in a new spirit of inclusiveness. At the press conference in Dublin to announce Rome's decision, the spokesman for the Irish hierarchy, with the Archbishop of Dublin by his side, declared that he 'had never received a better piece of news'. In the event it was a piece of news which quickly resulted, initially, in women turning their backs on the Church's many non-compulsory activities – sodalities, devotions, prayer groups – and once the women had taken the lead the men soon followed. The churches, which traditionally had been thronged on many nights of the week, were now more or less deserted from one Sunday to the next.

For her part Lucy received the pronouncement from Rome, and its ringing endorsement by the clerical powers in Ireland, as a sort of comforting sign of approval for her own willingness to avoid sex. She had taken up a job as a receptionist in a firm of solicitors, as a way of filling her time. Outside her work she immersed herself in various charitable activities in the community, and smoked her way through magazines and bestsellers.

Gradually over the previous couple of years Alan feelings towards his relationship with Lucy had drifted from hope to frustration to anger to indifference. Between them they maintained a façade of harmony and respectability, but this was based on a sullen truce. While they lacked for nothing materially, they lived a life of emotional destitution.

Alan's career in the bank had progressed steadily. As a consequence of the frenzy of mergers and takeovers which the Irish banking industry started to experience from the late 1960's, the Imperial Bank, where Alan now held the title 'Manager Internal Audit Department', had been absorbed into one of the nation's major banking groupings. In the resulting restructuring Alan was appointed Assistant Manager in a branch office in Dublin's city centre. One benefit that derived from his new status was that he could borrow money from the bank, within defined limits, at very favourable rates. He took advantage of this perquisite to purchase a small residential property overlooking the Grand Canal on Dublin's south side. He rented this out to young bank officials who were, from time to time, transferred to Dublin from rural areas. In time, encouraged by the success of this first venture, as a way of keeping busy, and of taking his mind off the barrenness of his home life, he invested in more properties to rent out to young bank staff. As a substitute for intimacy this activity was not ideal, but it did provide a measure of diversion and a focus for his energy.

He rediscovered his interest in the Dublin jazz scene, and

started to attend the various regular sessions around the city, especially at weekends. He also found more and more reasons to 'entertain' bank clients, which meant drinking more than was good for him.

Between these activities and his role within the bank, he was just about able to keep his mind from dwelling for too long, or too frequently, on his impoverished domestic situation. But, except for the music, it was a routine, mechanical existence, underlying which there simmered a sense of waste, of being cheated by life, of something lost or missing, of *ennui*. In his quieter moments visions of what he had imagined his life would be like, of what he had wished for before he married, pressed in upon him. He recalled how he had pictured himself in a fulfilling relationship with a wife, surrounded by a family to whom they both would devote themselves to happily rearing. By comparison with this vision, his domestic life was a lifeless, depressing inversion. It seemed that whenever such musings took hold of him they almost inevitably centred round the image of Heather Lattimore, and the vague, haunting question of what might have been.

Over the years he had heard, through Philip, that Heather had married a naval officer shortly after she had graduated, and that they were living in Portsmouth where she was working as a teacher. About a year after marrying she had a baby girl, and a boy was born about two years later. In early 1970, her father, William Lattimore, Alan's former employer, died. Alan considered going to the funeral, not out of any respect for his late employer but in the hope of seeing Heather, but thought better of it. Philip told him afterwards that he had met her at the church along with her two children, but that her husband had been unable to make the trip. She was staying with her mother and Philip had visited them a couple of times during the few days she remained in Dublin, before she returned home to Portsmouth. She looked well and had enquired, with what certainly appeared like genuine interest, about Alan.

Around this time Alan noticed that Lucy, who was approaching her fortieth birthday, and who was never one to complain much about physical ailments, was retiring to bed earlier than had been her habit. When he asked her if there was some reason for her change of routine, she simply said that she felt increasingly tired. He suggested that she have a check-up, which she did, but nothing amiss was discovered. The tiredness was simply attributed to her age and, apart from recommending that she cut down her smoking and take a holiday, the only other treatment was the prescription of a tonic. She ignored the advice about smoking, and went to stay with her family in Galway for a couple of weeks. But the fatigue persisted. Alan suggested that she cease working, at least for the time being, but she was reluctant to do this. As the weeks and months passed, instead of feeling any better, each evening when she got back from work she seemed to be more exhausted than ever. She also developed a persistent cough, and complained of pains in her back and across her shoulders.

About three months after her check-up a call came through to Alan's desk from one of the partners in the firm of solicitors where Lucy worked, to say that she had been taken ill and was being driven by one of his colleagues to the local hospital. Alan wanted to know exactly what had happened to her.

'Mrs Logan,' said the caller, 'seemed to be having difficulty breathing, and said she was having some pain in her chest.'

Alan thanked the solicitor and left for the hospital immediately.

When he made himself known at the hospital's Accident and Emergency Unit the doctor in charge appeared beside him without delay.

'Mr Logan?' he asked, extending his hand.

'Yes, Doctor. Tell me, has my wife had a heart attack?' Alan's tone was urgent.

'No. No. Mrs Logan was experiencing severe difficulty in her breathing. She has been given an injection to ease that condition, and she is breathing normally now, and she's resting. We are arranging to have her admitted straightaway for some tests which we'd like to carry out.'

'Can you say what caused this to happen?'

'Not at the moment. Not until we have the results of the tests I've mentioned.'

The doctor paused for a moment, and then continued.

'I'm sure it's nothing too serious, Mr Logan. She is in very good hands now'

'May I see her?'

'She's here in Casualty right now, but we'll be transferring her to the main hospital shortly. I'll take you to see her now, but we've given her something to help her relax, so she may be asleep or drowsy. Before I take you to her, could I ask you to take this form with you and to fill it in before you leave the hospital? We'd appreciate it. It's intended to give us some background on Mrs Logan's medical history. I know this is a stressful time for you, but it could be very helpful to us if you can manage to do it as soon as possible.'

'Certainly, Doctor.'

When he entered the cubicle where Lucy was being attended to, Alan was startled by her appearance. She was deathly pale and had an oxygen mask over her mouth, and appeared to be asleep. When he touched her hand she opened her eyes. The attending nurse removed the oxygen mask.

'Alan,' she murmured, distress written all over her face. She raised her arm towards him weakly, as he bent to kiss her.

'Don't try to talk now, Lucy. These people will take good care of you,' he tried to assure her.

'Alan, I'm frightened,' she whispered. 'I took a fit of coughing and couldn't breathe.'

'I know. I've been speaking with the doctor.'

Tears appeared at the corners of her eyes as she struggled to say, 'There was blood when I coughed.'

At this point the nurse intervened.

'I think Mrs Logan should rest now. We need to replace the oxygen to help her with her breathing.'

'Okay nurse,' Alan agreed. 'Lucy, I'll go and wait outside for the moment,' he said as he gave her hand a squeeze and rose to leave.

Three days later it was confirmed that Lucy had lung cancer.

The realization that Lucy was suffering from a life threatening illness affected Alan in various, and totally unexpected, ways. After the initial phase of trying to convince himself that it could not be true, he began to feel a huge sense of guilt, as if he was in some way responsible for what had happened to her, or that God was punishing him for not being a better and more understanding husband over the years.

He saw to it that Lucy was placed under the care of an eminent cancer specialist who, having discussed with Lucy and Alan the various treatments available, based on the degree of severity of Lucy's condition – surgery, radiation therapy, chemotherapy – recommended immediate surgery, followed by a course of radiation therapy. Lucy's lungs, he explained, showed considerable bronchial damage, probably due to her smoking habit.

During the following month Lucy underwent the surgery, which left her initially with severe residual pain, and started her radiation treatment, before being discharged and reassigned for continuing outpatient care. In the months that followed, the main focus of their lives, during this harrowing time, centred on Lucy's regular trips to the treatment clinic, and the inevitable nausea and fatigue that resulted from each visit. Once again Lucy's mother came to their aid, spending as much time as she could in Dublin with her ailing daughter.

During this period, as the reality of her condition sank in, apart from the trauma of trying to deal with the physical aspects of her illness, Lucy's distress at the thought of her prospective death became intense. Also, with the strange unpredictability that fashions human emotions, it was during this most traumatic time that Alan and Lucy rediscovered the feelings for each other that had brought them together initially. He devoted all his time outside the office to doing whatever he could to look after her, and to make sure that everything possible was done for her comfort. On many occasions when he asked her if there was anything that she needed or would like, she would simply reply,

'Yes, I'd just like you to hold me.'

This simple request, which Alan was happy to willingly fulfil, also created in him a feeling of deep remorse. He did not know how things could have been different, but he could not escape feeling that they should have been, and that it was his fault. Guilt sat on his shoulder day and night.

Despite the past, and the regrets, they found a pleasure in each other's company that they had not felt in years, an experience that frequently brought tears to both their eyes. The irony of the fact that the tears they shed now where tears of joy at their rediscovered closeness, rather than tears of grief in the face of Lucy's precarious health, was not lost on either of them.

Lucy's treatment lasted for six months, after which she gradually showed signs of physical improvement. She regained some of the weight she had lost during the previous months, and with Alan's assistance started to build up her strength again by taking walks in the neighbourhood each evening. But the fear of relapse was never far away, and barely four months had elapsed since her treatment had ended, when the illness struck again.

Examination confirmed that the cancer had spread to her diaphragm and was inoperable. The choice facing Lucy was between reintroducing radiation therapy treatment, and suffering the dreadful, nauseous side effects, or confining herself to medication that would alleviate rather than cure her condition. As the chances of the radiation treatment achieving anything beyond a short extension of her life were negligible, she decided that there was nothing to be gained from putting herself through the physical distress and false hope that it would entail.

Lucy spent the following six months at home being cared

for by her mother and Alan, apart from a nurse whom Alan had arranged to attend her regularly. As her physical condition deteriorated, another distressing situation emerged. Lucy became increasingly preoccupied and anxious about what would happen to her soul when she died. When she stood before God to be judged would she be sent to hell because of the way she had disobeyed the Church? Had she been a bad wife?

These were the fears and doubts that she repeatedly expressed to Alan as her health worsened. Inevitably it became impossible to nurse her properly at home. After much discussion, and based on her own realization and acceptance of the fact that she could not survive for very much longer, it was decided that she would spend the time remaining to her in a Dublin hospice renowned for its caring ethos and expert attention in dealing with this most sensitive and traumatic time in peoples' lives. Despite living up to everything that could be expected of the hospice as a haven of tranquillity and physical easement, Lucy's final weeks there were plagued and afflicted with the obsession that her soul might go to hell. Every minor transgression of her life took on the dimension of a serious failing, and all the religious teachings of her youth, and the constant sermons she had heard throughout her life on hell and damnation and suffering in eternal flames, haunted her continuously. Alan was distraught to witness the trauma of Lucy's physical deterioration being compounded by the addition of this mental anguish. As he was leaving her room, after one particularly distressing visit, he bumped into the elderly Catholic chaplain, who was assigned to the hospice, in the hallway outside Lucy's door. The chaplain visited Lucy on a regular basis and on many occasions had tried to comfort and reassure her, telling her that she should have no fears about saving her soul. She, he told her, had confessed her sins sincerely and should trust entirely in God's love.

The old priest nodded a tentative greeting in Alan's direction. Alan, in his distressed frame of mind, could not restrain himself from commenting,

'I'm Lucy Logan's husband, Father, and right now I feel bound to say that the Church has a lot to answer for!'

The priest, an inoffensive kindly man, was taken aback. Recovering himself, he spoke gently to Alan.

'I'm sorry to hear that you feel like that, Mr Logan. Is there something in particular you're referring to?'

'What I'm referring to is the fact that my wife is dying, and all she can think of is the idea that she might go to hell. It seems to me that frightening people with the notion that they could burn in red-hot flames for eternity, which is what Lucy is severely agitated about right now, is unspeakably cruel.'

'I have tried to reassure Lucy time and again that she has nothing to fear,' the chaplain pleaded.

'Father, my comments were not directed at you personally. I know you've been genuinely caring towards Lucy, and I thank you for that. But the point is that she, like millions of others, myself included, have being indoctrinated by the Church, since we were children, into believing that all of us are virtually hell bound.'

The priest was discomfited and Alan, not wishing to carry the argument any further, excused himself and went on his way.

That night Alan lay awake, his mind tossing and turning between his exchange with the old chaplain, which he felt sorry about, and imagining the pain and anguish Lucy was suffering. For her sake, it must end soon.

A few days later Alan received a call from the hospice to say that Lucy's condition had worsened, and asking him to come in as soon as he could. He hung up the receiver, told his secretary that he was leaving the office, and would not be available for the remainder of the day, and left for the hospice immediately.

When he arrived at her bedside Lucy seemed somewhere between consciousness and coma. She looked flushed, and was experiencing great difficulty breathing, each breath a long slow gasp. When he took her hand she turned her head towards him and, struggling with the effort, uttered the one word 'Water'.

Alan went directly to the nurses' station and explained that his wife needed a drink urgently. The attending doctor appeared on the scene and, taking Alan to one side, tried to explain to him that Lucy's system was no longer capable of controlling her temperature and that she was likely to become increasingly hotter as her system broke down. Alan was dumbstruck. The doctor suggested that the best thing to do now was to arrange with the nurse to provide him with a bowl of water and a spoon, and for Alan to sit by Lucy's bedside and spoon the water to her as best he could. It gave him something to do, and provided Lucy with some small respite.

Lucy's condition became increasingly harrowing. Her eyes were like burning coals, each a red circle around a shining black centre; her face resembled a piece of raw meat from which rivulets of perspiration streamed; her pencil-thin lips appeared as brittle as parched kindling wood. Hour after hour as Alan sat by her she drifted in and out of consciousness. She was no longer capable of taking water and, as her breathing had become more laboured she was now provided with an oxygen mask. Her condition was utterly distressing, and on those occasions when she opened her eyes she seemed to plead for final respite. Around 1 a.m. she lapsed into unconsciousness and her gasping became even more markedly louder and more desperate. Alan went in search of the attending nurse and asked her if anything more could be done to help Lucy. The nurse returned with him to the bedside and while he stood by she felt Lucy's forehead, straightened the bedclothes, checked the oxygen supply and mask, and told Alan that there really was nothing more that could be done at that time. She suggested that she leave Alan alone with Lucy for now, and told him to be sure to call immediately if he needed her for any reason.

When she closed the door behind him as she left the room he remained standing beside the bed gazing at the struggling figure of his wife. Lucy was literally burning up before his eyes, and clearly on the point of death. He sat down and buried his face in his hands, and came to a decision that would haunt him for the remainder of his life. He stood up and with trembling hands he lifted the oxygen mask from Lucy's face. Lucy made a few final harrowing efforts to breath and then was still. With hands still shaking he replaced the mask. After the agonizing drama of the previous few hours the silence that followed was eerie. It seemed to consume everything around it into a sort of sacred stillness. He bent over her and kissed her forehead and sat down again. He remained sitting motionless for what seemed like an age, before pressing the call button for the nurse. The stillness and eeriness and numbness were broken by her arrival. Within minutes he was vaguely aware of the presence of the kindly old chaplain offering his gentle prayers and ministrations for Lucy's departed soul. It was the last day of March 1972, barely three weeks after her fortieth birthday.

10

April 1972

'Angry!' It was Alan's terse response to his friend Philip's 'How are you?'

It was evening time, about ten days after the funeral and Alan had been at home alone when he heard the front doorbell ring. The one person he was glad to see was standing there when he opened the door - his old pal Philip. Although everyone had been very solicitous towards him during the previous difficult days he was not in the mood for consoling company.

Philip put his hand on Alan's shoulder and gave him a wry, sympathetic smile.

'Come in,' said Alan. 'Sorry to be so direct, but answering the 'How are you' question can be difficult. I think when people ask that they don't expect you to bare your soul, so generally it's easier just to say 'I'm fine', or 'Not bad', or some suchlike facile, dishonest reply. But I know you don't want that sort of superficiality, and I wouldn't insult you with it.'

They went through to the sitting room and Alan invited his friend to take a seat. He located a bottle of Jameson whiskey in the drinks cabinet and poured them each a glass.

He handed one to Philip and took a seat himself.

'So,' said Philip, 'do you want to talk about the anger?'

Alan didn't need a second invitation to launch into what had been going round in his head in the previous days

'Well, I'll tell you this Philip,' he said, 'the more I think about it the more it seems to me that the last few months of Lucy's life were blighted by an enormous amount of pointless suffering. I'm not talking about the awful physical suffering she went through. As a doctor you know very well that as flesh-and-blood human beings we're all subject to physical pain. That's very distressing in itself. But in a sense it's natural, and mercifully the medical profession does a great deal to alleviate that sort of suffering. That's not what I'm referring to. It's the mental suffering that Lucy endured, her fear of facing God's judgment, and being sent to hell, that makes me angry now. She was so indoctrinated with how she could have committed mortal sins that there was no way to convince her to stop worrying. Hell was as real to her as the glass of whiskey in your hand. Flames and devils and all the other horrors we were taught. And you have to wonder how much of it could be true. Could an all-loving God really create such unspeakably horrific punishments? I don't know. I do know that the idea of it caused Lucy to live in terror during her final months, and I'm sure it does the same to many others.' Here Alan paused and looked at Philip as if inviting a response.

'Personally' said Philip, taking his cue and hoping to think of something that would help his friend, 'I have no idea what the afterlife is like, or even if there is one, but I do know from my own work as a psychiatrist that people have all sorts of hang ups, usually related to their childhood experiences. If you get a child early enough it's possible to convince it to believe just about anything, and for the vast majority of people it will be impossible for them to be unaffected for the rest of their lives by what's been instilled into them as kids, especially about religion and morality, for better or worse.'

'I can relate to that,' interjected Alan, who was pretty worked up by now, 'especially when it comes to what was drummed into me about sin and punishment and hell when I was growing up.'

At that moment Alan considered telling Philip about removing Lucy's oxygen mask and of how, day by day, ever since he had taken that fateful decision, waves of guilt were flooding over him. But he could not bring himself to reveal what he'd done.

They were silent for a few moments.

'Are you worried about Lucy, I mean about her soul going to heaven and all that?' Philip asked.

'No, not in the slightest.' Alan replied without hesitation. He had already asked himself that question and had assured himself that, although clearly Lucy had wanted an end to her suffering, she had in no way influenced him to assist her in ending her life, and as she had in fact been unconscious at the end, she could not be held morally accountable in any way for terminating her life. Any guilt there was sat squarely on his shoulders alone.

'Are you worried about yourself?' Philip asked, perceptively.

'How do you mean?' Alan was surprised by Philip's question, and the note of alarm was evident in his response. Had his friend picked up on his thought sequence somehow?

Philip sensed Alan's anxiety and, trying to reassure him quickly, said, 'Well, all I meant was that I know you take your religion seriously, and although you've never said much I know your relationship with Lucy had its problems, and I just wondered if you might be experiencing some measure of remorse or guilt yourself, which, I might add, would not be uncommon.'

Alan was relieved that Philip's observations were no nearer the root cause of his anxieties. He paused to considered what Philip had said before saying,

'You are a good friend, Philip, and you know me well. Yes, I guess it's true to say that guilt is never far from the surface with me, or the thought of the possibility of the dreadful consequences that might have to be suffered according to what the Church expounds.'

'You're referring to hell? ' Philip observed.

'In a nutshell,' Alan readily confirmed.

'Have you ever tried to do anything about relieving your fears?'

'Well, as Catholics we have confession, which is supposed to give us peace of mind when we've done wrong and promise to improve. But for me the problem is much deeper than that. The whole concept of an all-loving Divinity creating spirits or souls on the one hand and then creating a place of eternal suffering to frighten them with in this life and punish them with in the next, seems utterly incompatible, seems more sadistic than divine, and the practice of frightening small children, from the time they can begin to imagine or relate to such ideas, with such a concept seems to me unspeakably cruel and inhuman, and not what an all-loving fatherly God should be about.' Here he paused for a moment before adding in a slightly hopeless tone, 'But as regards what else can be done to relieve one's fears, I don't know.'

'Some people find writing a help,' Philip suggested.

'Writing?' Alan queried.

'Well, sometimes it helps to tackle an issue squarely – to write down what you feel, or believe, or doubt, or wish for. It might help if you were to learn more about the background history to what's troubling you, and the current thinking in the Church. It's just a thought.'

'Yes, it's a thought,' Alan said reflectively.

Philip took the loll in the conversation that followed this comment to try to steer his friend's attention in another direction. He mentioned that his mother had phoned him a few days earlier to say that Heather had phoned her from England looking for Alan's address as she had heard about Lucy's death through her own family.

'I gave my mother your address to pass on to Heather. I hope that's all right with you?'

'Yes, that's okay,' Alan nodded.

It was around midnight before Philip left. Although he felt very tired Alan was reluctant to go to bed, knowing that despite his physical weariness his mind would not switch off. Night after night he relived those final moments of Lucy's life. Each time he drifted into sleep it seemed that he had no sooner closed his eyes than he woke up again in a state of panic at the thought that he had ended Lucy's life prematurely. He would then find himself on a pointless, exhausting, mental treadmill, trying to rationalize that the action he had taken was the humane and compassionate thing to do, only to have another voice telling him that he had 'played God', that he had committed the heinous and culpable crime of taking a life.

In an effort to distract himself he started to look through the bundles of Mass cards and the letters and cards he had received, offering him sympathy and condolences on Lucy's death. As he went through this sad correspondence – much of it from people he barely knew - he was struck by the thought that there was such a tremendous amount of goodness in people. With this consoling thought in mind he went to bed to sleep his fitful sleep.

A few days later he received a letter postmarked 'Portsmouth'. It read: -

>Dear Alan,
>I was so sorry to hear of your wife Lucy's death. No doubt this is a very difficult time for you, and I'd like you to know that you have my heartfelt condolences. I believe that she was very ill for quite some time. Perhaps it will be of some small consolation to you to know that she is no longer suffering.
>
>I hope that you will find the strength and courage to cope with such an awful, personal tragedy. I'm sure you will.
>
>Yours very sincerely, with love,
>Heather.

Alan read it over a couple of times before replacing it in its envelope and putting it down beside the rest of the cards and letters, all of which he would have to respond to in due course.

But for now he was in no fit state to put his mind to that particular task. The one thing that he was singularly failing to do was to cope. His anxieties concerning his part in Lucy's death continued to play on his mind and grow more vivid as the days, and more especially the nights, passed. His Catholic conscience kept pounding away telling him that what he had done was gravely wrong and that retribution would inevitably have to be suffered. He became increasingly reluctant to go to bed each night, and even more reluctant to get up each morning. The nights brought with them dark musings and freakish dreams and nightmares. But these were mild by comparison with trying to maintain an air of normally in his everyday activities, as depression grew inside him like a black hole. Since he had been a child he had always imagined the soul to be something like a white, round object somewhere in the middle of his body, and if you committed sins, black spots appeared on it. But what he imagined now was not an object; it was more like a black hole or a void deep inside him. The most frightening thing about this was that each morning this black hole seemed to grow bigger, as if it was gradually drawing everything that was 'him' into it. The round, black cavern expanded and expanded so much that he became alarmed that he would be devoured entirely into it, and have no identity anymore. He would be lost somewhere inside a black void where he could not be seen or heard, and simply cease to have any contact with any other entity. He feared falling into a deep black aloneness. He was caught in the paradoxical position of no longer wishing to live, no longer wishing to exist, but not wanting to die for fear of being punished in hell by God.

He managed to keep these anxieties and apprehensions to himself until one morning about two months after Lucy's death. As he was sitting at a meeting in the office, with six other colleagues, he became alarmingly aware of a mounting sense of increasingly uncontrollable turmoil storming about his mind. As the chaos and conflict inside him rose in waves he struggled to keep his concentration until the most frightening incident of his life occurred. His mind seemed to close down. It was as if his mind was quite independent of the rest of him, and decided that it could no longer cope and, despite his desperate efforts to arrest the process, it closed down. He knew he was sitting in a room with other people at a meeting, but could get no control of his mind. He wanted to leave but was incapable of any movement or utterance. He feared making a fool of himself, like falling down or crying out. His mind seemed to be sinking further and further beyond all control. The warring factions in his head seemed to have broken through the mind's natural defences and were furiously flaying and slashing all about them. Simultaneously, he was also aware that, somewhere deep inside him, another struggle was being fought to get his mind and body back into some form of coordination and equilibrium. By the time he started to relate again in something like a normal way to his surroundings he realized that, although it seemed like the episode had lasted for minutes, it could not have taken more than twenty or thirty seconds to pass. Fortunately no one around the table seemed to have noticed.

That evening he attended his doctor and recounted what had happened. The doctor told him he appeared to have suffered a panic attack, and needed to rest completely for at least a week away from everyone and everything connected with work. He persuaded Alan to book into a private nursing home immediately, and prescribed medication to help him to relax and to assist with his stress and depression. The following day Alan arranged with the bank to take some holidays that were due to him, cleared his desk of anything requiring urgent attention, and checked into the nursing home.

His recollection of the week he spent in the nursing home was of time passing in a kind of rapid blur. It seemed to him that he had slept through most of his stay due, presumably, to the copious quantity of potent sleeping pills he'd been given. He remembered that he had no sooner requested a writing pad and pen than the ever-helpful nursing staff had found one for him. It had occurred to him that it might do him good to write down his thoughts and feelings, as Philip had suggested. One afternoon, about four or five days into his stay, he dozed off just as he had finished reading *Madame Bovary*. When he emerged from his dreamed-laced sleep about an hour later he had, what seemed to him at the time, a fanciful, yet irresistible, urge to write a poem. He sat up and reached for the pen and pad and became absorbed in this novel endeavour. Before he switched off his bedside reading lamp at 11.25 that night he had written:

> 'To seek the deep beneath the deep,
> And sleep the sleep beyond all sleep;
> To fade from fickle light of day,
> From mind-blind senselessness away.
> Into the quiet darkness drown,
> And know at last oblivion,
> Or spirit blest, or lost soul pain,
> Thus meaning's vexing quest distain.
> In dusty timeless time defused,
> Through spaceless space, no more bemused.
> Beyond this starry speckled arc,
> Into a gentle, harmless dark.'

In the course of conversation with Amy the following afternoon when she asked what he was doing to pass the time, he sheepishly mentioned that he'd been trying to write a few lines of poetry.

'May I see it?' she asked.

He reached into the drawer of his bedside locker where he'd been keeping it out of sight and handed her the pad.

As she read it her big eyes clouded over and, sounding a little apprehensive, said,

'I'm not sure I understand it.'

'I'm not sure I understand it myself,' Alan replied. 'I think it's more about a feeling than about something that can be explained.'

After a moment, sensing that she was still concerned he took her hand and added,

'In case you might think otherwise, I have no intention of jumping of a roof.'

'God forbid that you should even think of such a thing,' she said with feeling.

She glanced over the lines again and said,

'I never knew you wrote poetry.'

'I don't. At least I never did before.'

'How did you think of this then?'

'Well, to tell the truth the urge to write this sort of came at me out of the blue.' He smiled at her reassuringly before adding, 'I think it must be a side effect of all the drugs they've been giving me. It reminds me of Coleridge's story about writing Kubla Khan. He claimed that the words came to him in a rush after he'd taken opium when he'd been ill.'

Her eyes brightened, and she smiled and said,

'A likely story. Are you going to give it a title?'

'I hadn't thought of one. Maybe I should call it *Side Effect*. What do you think?'

They both laughed.

Although he remembered Amy's visit quite clearly he was perturbed to discover later that he had no recollection of some of those who had come to visit him during his stay in the nursing home. He found this scary, but, on checking with his doctor later, was assured that this was not unusual in his circumstances and was really nothing to be worried about.

He returned to work but, as the comfortable zombie-like condition induced by his treatment in the nursing home wore off and the realities of life reasserted themselves, he realized that the root causes of his anxieties were unresolved. The fitful sleep and nightmarish dreams persisted by night, and the treadmill of perplexity continued to run in his head by day. But, in general, life was more manageable than it had been previously. On the positive side he had discovered that putting his thoughts down on paper seemed to help. Writing in this way was like talking to a good listener, and it made you think and find things out. It prompted you to be more considered and measured in your conclusions.

As a way of keeping a tidy record he bought himself a leather-bound journal. He made his first entry in September 1972. It read:-

> Dear Journal,
> Some things you should know. I'm 37 years old – which means I'm past the half way mark by the 'three score and ten' reckoning. As I'm Irish and a Catholic it also means that I have spent all my life under a civil and religious system dominated by the Catholic Church. It is important to know that my objective here is not to undermine Christianity, which, I believe, has probably been responsible for more positive influences in the world than any other ideology. But, rightly or wrongly, although my Church preaches love, it thrives on fear. And I must search out why this is so, and if it should be so. I have seen the malign effects of this indoctrination of fear and guilt on others, and I know that in my own case the predominant effects of the religious culture in which I was immersed, contrary to filling me with a sense of joy and peace (which might be hoped for and even expected), have been to saddle me with fear and anxiety. Most especially I am haunted by my part in Lucy's death. Did I do something very bad? Or was my action a true kindness, and therefore good? Will I be damned for

taking over God's role in deciding when a life should end? Or will a kindly God be pleased that a rational and humane act was performed to relieve one of His creatures of further needless suffering?

Two weeks later, after experiencing a particularly vivid nightmare the previous night, he made another entry: -

Dear Journal,

When does a dream become a nightmare? Does every nightmare start as a dream? Mine seem to. They seem to drift in through a shadowy mist floating around a sort of jumbled archive, accessible only during sleep. Gradually the wispy mist dissolves or wanders away, leaving the sleep-locked imaginations of the mind to reveal some surreal event or drama. Of course, every dream does not have to become a nightmare. I've seen my father wave as he rides off on a motorcycle, even though, as far as I'm aware, he has never been on a motorcycle in his life. Or I'm wandering in a tunnel or around a cave with a torch looking at some incomprehensible carvings on the walls. Or someone I haven't seen for ten years is sitting in an armchair in a room with me, nodding and smiling at some gibberish that my dream-self seems very pleased to have thought of.

And then there are those dreams that seem to survive on a current of latent anxiety. They start in the middle and strain to achieve some coherence, only to peter out in a sort of flapping exhaustion of mounting bafflement. Why doesn't that huddle of people know that they must let me through to see what they are looking at? And why are there just as many still standing there no matter how many walk away? Why, when I open that door to that building, is there a gaping hole where the hall floor should be? How am I to get across? And why is that black woman, whose face looks like an over-ripe fruit, waving at me with slow windmill arms? And where did she vanish to when I needed to speak to her, to ask her....what?

But nightmares are different. They erupt from a more primeval pit, bearing the armour of terror. Last night I felt the heat from a blazing bonfire, twice my own height, and, as little knots of people stood about obliviously, I see that there is a baby in the flames, and it is screaming, trying to get the people's attention, but they just look at me strangely and carry on as they are while the baby screams and I scream more... and more... and convulse myself awake, streaming with perspiration.

The events of his own life in 1972 resulted to a significant degree in insulating Alan from the happenings in the wider world. As the year approached its end he still had little inclination to engage in any pursuits or social activities that took him beyond the confines of his home, where he now lived alone, or his work, or in looking after his few properties. Gradually, however, it bore in on him that much of significance had been happening in Irish society, and in the world beyond, during that year. He began to notice the media's fascination with the aftermath of Vatican 2, and the stream of books that were appearing in the bookshops, with their commentaries, analysis and predictions on the subject. In simple terms it seemed that the majority of the Catholic laity, and very probably of the clerics also, looked back with great admiration and affection on Pope John XX111 for his inspiration in 'throwing the windows of the Church open'. On the other hand the conservative elements in the Roman Curia, who, in effect, governed the Church, seemed to regard John XX111 and the Vatican Council he instigated as twin disasters for Roman Catholicism. As one commentator put it, John XX111 had let the cat out of the bag, and despite the determined efforts of the dominant element within the Curia to get the cat back in again, what they didn't realize was that the cat, once having escaped, would never be quite the same cat again.

The laity was, in the main, hugely disappointed and frustrated with the pronouncements on the birth control issue, and there appeared to be significant ambivalence on the part of the clergy on the matter also. Contact with other Christian religions – previously taught to be a form of contamination, and banned under pain of mortal sin – was now being encouraged; ecumenism and reconciliation were in the air. Distain for Jews and Moslems was now to be replaced by a new recognition that they believed in the same God as Christians did, and they were to be respected with a new openness. Reading the Bible, which had long been presented as too prone to dangerous misinterpretation by the uninitiated laity, was now being encouraged enthusiastically, and Bible Study classes were proliferating. The format for the Mass had changed almost beyond recognition. From being a rather mystic presentation in a fossilized language soliloquised by a priest before a congregation on whom he turned his back, it became a community celebration spoken in the language people understood by a priest who faced them, as any respectful host would. And hell, although it hadn't gone away, seemed to have become a place that was unfashionable to draw attention to. When he thought about this, it seemed to Alan that the least ordinary Catholics might expect from those who were supposed to give them guidance was honesty. But, although Rome seemed to have decided that the preaching of hell and its horrors, which had been used by the Church to frighten generations of believers, was to be mothballed, there seemed to be something quite dishonest in ceasing to preach this doctrine without explaining why. If they were wrong, or thought that they may have been wrong in the past, why not have the decency and honesty to say so to their fellow Catholics in a straightforward way? It was as if they had decided that by not speaking about hell and damnation, as they had done with such relentless consistency previously, they could now present a more compassionate face to the world, while at the same time never admitting any change. Was it, he thought, that they couldn't, or wouldn't, bring themselves to admit that they might have been wrong? Or had they simply decided to hold on to this frightening concept and continue to dangle it over the heads of believers, like the sword of Damocles, ...just in case?

This apparent ambivalence on the part of the Church had a particular relevance for Alan because, although he had never said a word to anyone about his part in Lucy's last moments, the one person he could not hide it from was himself. It festered in his mind day and night. Interfering with human life was undoubtedly a serious business, and one that the Church certainly treated gravely. He could, he had reasoned with himself, tell it all in confession and receive absolution. The problem with that was, apart from feeling that what he had done was more an act of humane compassion than a sin, he felt he would do the same again in the same circumstances. Confession would, therefore, be a sham.

The more he analysed his emotional reactions the more convinced he became that any remorse or guilt he felt was based on fear rather than any great wrong-doing. And why, he asked himself, should he have this pervasive fear? The answer seemed almost too obvious. He feared because he had been taught to fear. He had been taught to feel guilt, and fear punishment, from his earliest days. This, he realized, had been an endemic part of the Irish culture of his youth. And all of this had been promulgated in the name of Jesus Christ and on a particular interpretation of His teachings, and had behind it not only the awesome power of the dominant Catholic Church but also of the State, which was supposed to protect and nourish the well-being of its citizens. Was it right to present such teachings as the unquestionable truth?

Was it wrong? Were they, in fact, true, or might they be false, or perhaps a mere subjective interpretation, by some ivory-towered theologians, that had taken root and spread like rampant, choking nettles, blighting the garden of intrinsic human dignity? Were the traditional Church-endorsed, fear-based teachings merely fabricated on a flimsy foundation and unprovable assumptions? Was it possible that the formidable influence of the Church had produced psychologically crippled and mentally cramped followers, incapable of independent thought, and frightened to use that most unique and precious identifier of all human beings, their intelligence, their ability to think for themselves, and not simply to hand over their minds to others?

There was, Alan realized, always the possibility that these introspective questions were merely a subconscious attempt by him to rationalize and erase the guilt that weighed on his mind relating to Lucy's death. This mood of introspection hung about him even more keenly as the Christmas period approached. Although his inclination was to insulate himself from the general air of festivity, and get through the period as quietly and unobtrusively as possible, he gave in to his Mum's persistent invitations, and spent Christmas day with his father and herself.

His Dad had retired a few months earlier and, to celebrate the event, he and his wife had gone to Rome with a group that had been organized by the parish. It had been their first time to continental Europe and they were both still excited by their experiences. His Dad talked about the amazing sights they had seen, St Peter's, the Sistine Chapel, the Trevi Fountain, the traffic and the bustle. He was greatly amused by the contrast between the attitude in Rome to the abundance of nude women on view in the paintings and sculptures throughout the Vatican, and the fact that the Archbishop of Dublin had been so horrified at seeing nude female display models in the window of a Dublin department store that he had initiated a campaign to put a stop to such shocking 'indecency'. His Mum talked about the people on the tour, and the people they had met, and seemed to recount every word that every one of them had said, and the food in the restaurants and the shops and how terribly warm it had been and the lovely clothes the Italian women wore. Alan felt a vicarious pleasure at his parents' obvious enjoyment of their adventure and their pride in their newfound status as international travellers. He hoped that they would have many more years together to enjoy lots of similar trips with such enthusiasm. Between listening to his parents' reminiscences and exchanging greetings with the other family members as they called to visit throughout the day, it was not the uncomfortable experience he had anticipated.

With the coming of the new year and the lengthening of the days Alan's spirits started to rise. Although his part in ending Lucy's life still preyed on his mind and ate into his psyche he began to feel that, if he were to have any chance of ridding himself of his continuous preoccupation with feelings of guilt and retribution he would have to take some positive and practical action. He resolved to acquaint himself with all the relevant information, theories and opinions available on the issues troubling him.

During the following months he immersed himself in scouring bookshops and libraries, secular and religious, for any available material, and read up on all he could find. The first thing that became clear to him was the enormous divergence of views, interpretations and arguments that existed in relation to the concept of the reality, or otherwise, of a place of eternal torture and punishment in the afterlife, commonly referred to as hell. Instead of the clarity and certainty he had hoped to find he discovered that the more he read, the more he had to admit to a growing sense of doubt and perplexity within himself. But, he thought, doubt - genuine doubt - must be good; it had to be the first step on the road to truth. Without examining so-called truths in an intelligent way for yourself you were little more than a robot, handing your mind over to someone else to do your thinking for you. If you did that how could you call any 'belief' truly your own?

In the course of his reading he came to the conclusion that a belief in heaven was almost always linked to a belief in hell, and didn't really relieve anxiety about death at all. The notion of heaven affected how people lived their lives, how they acted. It caused them to become constantly self-conscious, as if they were under some cosmic microscope, with every thought and action being recorded and examined and assessed. As a consequence good deeds and behaviour were not based on the altruistic love of others, but on the baser motive of selfishly helping to earn an entry ticket to heaven.

Even more disturbing was a passage he came upon in the writings of the English novelist, Samuel Richardson, commenting on the doctrine of hell

> The doctrine of endless hell has caused many to murder themselves, taking away their lives by poison, stabbing, drowning, hanging, strangling, and shooting themselves, casting themselves out of windows, and from high places, to break their necks and by other kinds of death, that they might not live to increase their sin, and increase their suffering in hell.

Richardson's editor, Thomas Whittemore, commenting on this piece, wrote

> Here we see that the same dreadful effects attended this doctrine of misery nearly 200 years ago as attend it now. It was then the cause of anxiety, despair, and suicide, as we suppose it always was before where fully believed, and as we know it has been of late years. Let posterity know, that within the last ten years, there have been a large number of suicides, which must be attributed to the doctrine

of endless torment. That doctrine makes men melancholy; it drives them to despair. Fathers and Mothers, in repeated instances have murdered their children, lest they should grow up, and commit sin, and be damned. Can a doctrine which produces such dreadful consequences be the doctrine of God?

Alan began to feel that this whole business of controlling people through the fear of being hell bound should be made a public issue, especially as it involved frightening children from the time they were very young. The problem for him was that the Church portrayed itself as the font of certainty, and had so firmly implanted the psychologically powerful notion in the minds of its followers that to question what it had to say marked you out as a very dubious type of individual.

Whether or not there was any subconscious connection between Alan's growing reluctance to accept at face value the Church's indoctrination on hellfire and damnation – which would have amounted to a sort of religious treason – and the concurrent entry in his journal, he did not know. It was dated June 1973.

> Dear Journal,
> I've been having nightmares more or less regularly since I was a boy, probably since the night I stood watching the fire that killed little Declan Millar. Not every night, or every week, or even every month. Generally they've come in clusters at particular periods. It's happening now. They seem to come marching night by night from all quarters of my subconscious. The only difference this time is that in the past I never tried to remember them, or think about them, or write them down, but now I'm trying to do just that with the current battalion. They feature frantic running quite a lot.

> Last night I was a boy of twelve again, running for my life from some unseen pursuer up a spiral stairwell in a tall, narrow, ramshackle, derelict building. The circles of steps seemed endless but I knew I must get to the top where I could see the sky. But then I ran into a room where everything was red. Red walls, red ceiling, red floor, except that most of the floorboards were missing and I could not move for fear of falling down through the gaps to the ground below. And so, breathless, and with thumping heart, rigid with fright, trapped between my faceless tormentor behind me and a suicidal chasm before me, I pounded myself awake!

Despite the guilt that nagged at his conscience and followed him about, like his shadow on a sunny day, Alan could feel an almost imperceptible brightening of his spirits as the summer progressed. The self-imposed, semi-reclusive existence he had followed since Lucy's death began to feel more like a cage than a comfort. Philip Ffrench, the person he was most inclined to socialize with, had accepted the offer of a research position with a university in Cambridge, and would be away for at least a year. He needed company, and gradually realized that what he needed most was female company..

It had been so long since he had thought of any woman, other than Lucy, in terms beyond casual friendship that the whole idea of re-entering the world of dating was peculiarly intimidating. Having dithered about for weeks weighing up the pros and cons and implications and significances that would result from or be read into asking this female acquaintance out as against that one, he decided it was more trouble than it was worth, and to forget about the whole business for the time being. It was just about then that he received a phone call from the wife of one of his work colleagues, Tom Reid, to say she was arranging a surprise 'Life

Begins at Forty' birthday party for her husband, and inviting him along. He accepted.

The party was arranged for a Saturday night and, although he had been told to come along anytime from eight o'clock he realized, when he arrived at around eight-thirty, armed with a couple of bottles of wine, that he was embarrassingly early. He was, in fact, the first on the scene, and only realized later that the current fashion seemed to be for parties never to start much before midnight. He spent the next hour making small talk with Tom's wife and drinking several glasses of wine. Happily on this occasion the guests had been instructed to be in place not later than ten o'clock as Tom, who had been entrusted to the care of a couple of his golfing pals, was due home around ten-thirty.

When Tom did arrive, he was genuinely surprised to be greeted by raucous choruses of *Happy Birthday* and *For He's a Jolly Good Fellow*. As the music and the voices grew louder, and the considerable number of glasses of wine he had consumed had their inevitable mellowing effect, Alan fell into a sort of surreal state of relaxation where he was contended to simply let life happen about him, without feeling his usual compulsion to control events. He was floating on a sort of soft cushion of happiness. Tom and his wife had introduced him to various other guests earlier in the evening and, as the night progressed, he drifted contentedly about from one little group to another, eventually finding himself enjoying the exclusive company and attention of an attractive dark-haired woman, not much younger than himself. She introduced herself as Connie, a friend of Tom's wife since their schooldays. The wine flowed and the hours drifted by. As the crowd thinned out and the mood and the music became more mellow Alan found himself, without knowing quite how it had come about, shuffling about an area that had been cleared for dancing, with Connie enfolded very comfortably in the circle of his arms. They moved quite capriciously around the floor, oblivious to tune or tempo. She clasped her hands about his neck and snuggled herself easily into his embrace. When he touched her hair she raised her face towards him, and with a spontaneity born of a mutually shared need and desire, they kissed softly and deeply.

The music, to which they had been only vaguely aware, ended and they made their way to a settee. Alan was, strangely, both tinglingly alive and profoundly lethargic. Someone handed each of them another glass of wine. As to what happened after that he would only ever have the haziest of recollections.

When he woke up from his alcohol-fuelled sleep his bedside clock showed 12.01, and brightness flooded his bedroom. Beyond the pounding in his head, he became conscious of a church bell ringing. It took him a few moments to figure out it was Sunday, and it was midday. He raised his head from the pillow and a thousand flashbulbs exploded behind his eyes. He lay down again. He was in his own bed, but had no recollection of how he got there. The party! He remembered sitting on the settee with a woman close beside him…what was her name? …Cathy?… No…, Connie? Yes, Connie. Connie, that was it. And before that they'd been kissing as they'd danced! God Almighty! I must have passed out! The panic, at not knowing what had happened between then and now, was suddenly of far greater concern to him than his throbbing head, or the nauseous feeling in his stomach. What the hell had happened? Had he…? Had they…? He opened his eyes and looked about the bedroom. He could see no evidence of anyone else apart from himself having been there. But that didn't prove anything. He tried to think back again to the previous night. He seemed to vaguely recall being in a car with other people…laughter…female laughter. Jesus! How am I going to find out what I've been doing since I sat on that settee? The blank, the lack of knowing, was unnerving.

He dragged himself from the bed and let the water from the shower pour over him for several minutes in an effort to recover physically, and to clear his head. It did little to relieve his fatigue, hangover or anxiety. He dressed painfully and made his way downstairs to the kitchen, although food was the last thing on his mind. Brunch consisted of a glass of milk and two aspirin. He went to the sitting room, switched on the T V, tuned it to a football match on very low volume, and collapsed into an armchair.

He'd been sitting there for about an hour debating with himself, drowsily and gloomily, about what he should do when he was aroused by the sound of the telephone ringing.

'Hello'. His tone indicated more of a question than a greeting.

'Hello Alan, Tom here'.

'Tom!' – was the rush of anxiety detectable in his voice? – 'How's it going?'

'I'm fine really. A bit hangover.'

'Yeah. Me too.'

'Yes, I'm not surprised. I hope it was worth it.' Tom paused briefly. 'I was just phoning to check that you got home all right?'

'Eh, well I woke up here about twelve o'clock, but to be honest I'm a bit hazy on how I got home exactly.'

'Well, you remember we got a taxi for Connie and yourself about 4 am?'

Alan stomach did a couple of somersaults.

'Eh, vaguely.'

'Well, it looks like you made it home safely.'

There was another momentary pause before Alan said tentatively,

'Eh, Tom, do you know if …mm…Connie got home okay?'

He thought he heard Tom emit a slight chuckle at the other end of the phone.

'I doubt if Connie has surfaced yet, and we haven't risked disturbing her. But I wouldn't worry too much about Connie. I think she knows how to take care of herself.'

What did that mean, thought Alan?

One thing was certain. None of what had been said did anything to soothe Alan's uneasiness.

'Okay, Tom. Thanks for the call. I'll see you tomorrow.'

The remainder of the day crawled by interspersed with waves of nagging anxieties and apprehensiveness. But there was something else he could not deny being aware of – the persistent voice in his head reminding him of how pleasurable that kiss had been. It had awakened long dormant feelings and desires.

The following day he made it his business to seek out Tom at work on the pretext of telling him what a great party it had been, but really to try to piece together the events of Saturday night with a bit more clarity. After the customary pleasantries and comments had been exchanged Tom, with a half smile, said,

'You seemed to enjoy yourself.'

'Yes. Like I said, it was a good party.'

'But you don't remember getting home?'

Alan felt it was now or never if he was to find out what he needed to know.

'To tell the truth, Tom, it's driving me mad. I remember dancing with Connie, and then sitting beside her on your settee. But that's about the last thing I remember clearly. You said on the phone yesterday that you arranged a taxi for both of us. And, to be honest, I'm afraid to imagine what might have happened after that.'

'I don't think you need worry too much,' Tom replied. 'Like I told you yesterday, Connie is not the sort to get herself into anything she didn't want to.'

This was scarcely the reassuring comment Alan was hoping to hear.

'Look Alan, in case you're worried that you got up to anything that might come back to haunt you, I can tell you my wife spoke to Connie last night and she hardly mentioned you. Connie knows how to socialize and enjoy herself. And unlike you or me, she could probably drink a distillery dry without it ever having much effect. According to herself she went directly home to her bed, and the last she saw of you was you half asleep in the taxi as it left after dropping her off at her front door.

The relief that surged through Alan almost caused him to throw his arms around Tom. In the event he simply nodded and murmured 'Thank God for that.'

It had been a novel weekend. He had made some discoveries and learned some lessons about himself. It had been an experience that had opened doors to areas of his life that had long been hidden and disregarded.

11

October 1973

After his brief encounter with Connie, and the mild reminder of the world of pleasurable sex that it had reawakened in him, Alan experienced a sort of rebirth into the world beyond work and his recent reclusive, guilt-ridden existence. Events were occurring in the wider world that had a significant relevance when it came to questioning much of what he had been taught to accept as absolutes all his life.

When in 1972, after thirty-two years as the dominant religious and political force in the country, Archbishop John Charles McQuaid's obligatory offer to resign was accepted by Rome, and he was obliged to step aside, it was accompanied by a palpable sigh of relief, and hope, by many throughout the land. This event, coupled with the filtering down of the apparently liberalizing changes advocated by Vatican Two, meant that, for Alan at least, the old rigid sureties were no longer the categorical bulwarks against alternative thinking that had previously been their unshakeable characteristic. As a Catholic, he had a very real sense of not knowing what he was supposed to believe. There seemed to be a selection of 'Catholic Churches' to choose from. Newspapers and magazines were full of articles offering a kaleidoscope of opinions, interpretations and arguments relating to the changes that were occurring in belief, attitudes and practice of 'the Faith'. Religion among Catholics was a hot topic.

All this upheaval, however, had as little effect upon Father Peter Byrne as the gentle summer breeze that occasionally ruffled his abundant silvery hair. Father Byrne was Alan's local Parish Priest. He was in his seventies and regarded with affection by everyone in the community. The fact that he preached virtually the same homily (they could hardly be called sermons) each Sunday – on love, kindness, charity, compassion – didn't seem to bother anyone. It didn't matter because the man himself was the message. He had full confidence in his able curate, Father Conor Somers, and was quite contented to leave the everyday running of the parish to him.

Father Somers was a caring, energetic man in his mid-forties, fully dedicated to the well-being of his parishioners. He had been the one who'd officiated at Lucy's funeral, and had made it his concern to keep in touch with Alan in the meantime, and offer whatever words of comfort and encouragement he could to his young widowed parishioner. Alan liked him. There was nothing pushy, intrusive or sanctimonious about him. He came across as simply being there if needed.

Alan had not had a visit from him for a few months when he called by one evening in October 1973. As usual Alan invited him in and offered him a drink and, as usual, he declined, but said he'd love a cup of tea. They got to talking about Vatican 2 and all the changes and Alan voiced the opinion that there was a lot of confusion among the laity, and a desire for leadership and clarification about what people were being asked to adapt to. The priest nodded, saying that Alan was not the first to have expressed that view. He said that various ideas were being debated within the diocese, and he had some thoughts of his own on the subject that he intended to discuss with the Parish Priest.

As he was leaving Father Somers noticed two pictures hanging in Alan's hallway.

'Are they paintings?' he asked.

'No,' said Alan with the hint of a laugh. 'I wish they were. They're only prints, but the originals are probably worth millions.'

'I've never seen anything like them,' said the priest. 'They're very unusual, disturbing even.'

'Yes, I think that's exactly what they're meant to be. They're both by Dutch painters who lived in the fifteenth and sixteenth centuries. The one on the left is the *Last Judgment* by Hieronymus Bosch. You'll notice that he depicts Hell as taking up about ten times more space than Paradise, which seems to me to be a fair reflection of the Catholic Church's traditional teaching on where most of us are likely to end up. The other one is called *Dulle Griet*, or 'Mad Meg' in English. It's by Pieter Bruegel the Elder. You'll notice that there are really two dominant features in this one. On the right there's a fiercely resolute peasant women, clad in armour and brandishing a sword, who seems to be leading an all female group of other peasant women into battle. And on the left there's the entrance to Hell, which is depicted as being horrified at the approach of the army of women. It has been interpreted in many different ways, but she seems to me to have been driven to distraction by the madness of the world she has experienced – the absence of men seems to suggest the loss of husbands and sons and fathers through the madness of the interminable religious wars of the time – and she has roused the women of her neighbourhood to take up arms themselves in a blind and furious attempt to destroy Hell itself.'

'Humm…., very interesting,' said the priest, looking a little mystified. Alan smiled at him and added,

'I like Dull Gret. She's a man after my own heart.'

Sensing that the pictures had more significance for Alan than their artistic content, Father Somers said tentatively, 'It's a subject that gives a lot of people problems. Hell, I mean.'

'I agree, me included,' Alan responded.

'Is that so? Anything in particular?'

'Well, for one thing, I could never figure out how, if heaven is supposed to be a state of perfect happiness, why Lucifer, and the angels who followed him, rebelled. Clearly, they could not have been perfectly happy. And if God created hell as a sort of prison to punish them, why does He allow them out to roam freely, and wreck havoc on humanity? It's like putting the worst criminal in charge of the prison, don't you think – not very logical?'

'All I can say, Alan,' said the priest, 'is that our idea of how God's mind works seems to be very limited. I console myself by imagining that for us to try to understand God is like a snail trying to understand human beings. I've no idea where hell is, or how the whole system operates.'

'Where it is, and all that – the logistics – doesn't bother me. It's the logic,' said Alan. 'And saying that we're too puny-minded to understand God's ways, isn't much help. He created us creatures of logic, and it must be natural for us to at least try to use that part of our intellectual make-up.'

'I don't think I can give you any great insights, Alan. I try to get on with the practical stuff – saying Mass, baptizing the newborn, hearing confessions, marrying couples, burying the dead, and trying to help people where I can. As for the rest – what the afterlife is all about – I trust in God to take care of that.'

'So you think there really is an afterlife?'

'Yes, I believe there is. But I was amused to read somewhere that Pope John XX111's last words were, 'And now to find out for certain."

'They sound like the words of an honest man,' said Alan. 'I guess mine might be, 'the next few minutes should be very interesting – or not!'

The priest laughed. 'I think,' he said, 'on that note I'll be on my way. Thanks for the tea. I'll probably see you on Sunday.'

With that they shuck hands, Alan thanked him for calling, and waved him goodbye from the hall door.

* * * * * * * * *

Father Somers comments about having some ideas regarding doing something to clarify the changes in Church thinking for the laity was not just idle talk. He genuinely felt there was a problem and wanted to do something about it. Each Monday he had lunch with the Parish Priest, over which they discussed parish affairs. At their following working lunch Father Somers took the opportunity to raise what he had in mind.

'You know, Father, all these changes that are taking place as a consequence of Vatican 2 are a bit unsettling for some parishioners. They don't really understand the whys and the wherefores. Some of them, for example, miss the old Latin Mass and can't see what was gained by doing away with it. I've been thinking to ask you if you thought it might perhaps be a good idea if we were to arrange to invite anyone who was interested to come along to a couple of evening meetings where we could discuss what's been happening, and why?'

The senior man looked slightly pained.

'You know, Conor, I'm not altogether sure I understand everything that's happening myself. Perhaps the simplest way to approach this would be to include explanations on the various issues in the sermons at the Masses on Sundays.'

Father Somers was careful not to show his amusement at this suggestion, bearing in mind the Parish Priest's less than meticulous approach to this aspect of his calling.

'I think we certainly need to do that,' he agreed, 'but I do think that a significant number of people would welcome the chance to look at what's happening in a more detailed way. I think they'd like a situation where they could discuss their concerns, and ask questions, rather than simply sit and listen, as they have to do in church.'

Again the usually serene Parish Priest looked a little uneasy.

'I can't deny that there's merit in what you're suggesting, Conor, but in my experience setting up forums, and opening up issues for debate and discussion, is a mixed blessing. Unfortunately you'll always get an element of dissent that can easily turn into acrimony. If we're going to go ahead with something of this nature, Conor, you'd have to take control of it yourself – make sure it was properly handled and supervised.'

'You think we might try it then? I'm quite prepared to take on the responsibility. I think it would do more good than harm. Yes, I'd be happy to take on the responsibility.' Father Somers repeated, anxious not to let the opportunity slip.

Father Byrne sat in thought for a few minutes.

'What I'd like you to do, Conor, is prepare an outline of items you think should be covered, and the interpretations you'd be presenting, if we did decide to go ahead on this. Would you do that for me?'

'Certainly, Father.' The curate, content with the progress he had made, went quickly on to another topic.

Three weeks later Father Somers was happy to include among the parish notices, which he and Father Byrne would read from the altar at the weekend Masses, an announcement that it had been decided, in response to requests from a number of parishioners, to arrange for a series of meetings to take place to examine and discuss the changes that were occurring in the Church in line with the recent Vatican Council. Those who were interested were invited to contact either Father Byrne or himself. The meetings, he explained, would be under his direction.

Alan had no hesitation in confirming his interest. In fact the response was such that, as Father Somers himself said at the following weekend Masses, he had 'good news and bad news'. The good news was that there had been a great response to the proposed meetings, but the bad news was that so many had submitted their names that it would be impractical to accommodate everyone straightaway. It would have to be a case of 'first come, first served', and those who could not be included in the first group would be accommodated in further sessions as soon as possible.

The first session was set to begin in mid-January 1974, and would consist of six weekly meetings limited to a total of sixteen people. Alan was among this initial group.

On the appointed night Father Somers was there at the entrance to the parish hall, ready to greet the various members of the group as they arrived, and to direct them to the meeting room where chairs had already been arranged in a circle. When Alan entered the room three women were already sitting close together. He recognized one of them, but knew her only as Joan, although he had never actually spoken to her. She was well known in the parish for the seemingly vast amount of time she spent in the church. She was in her mid-forties, but still wore her hair almost to her waist and tended to dress about twenty years younger than her age. What some people found puzzling was how she managed to spend so much time in the church, bearing in mind that she had a family of six or seven school-going children. Did 'Mr Joan', whom no one seemed to know or have ever seen – even at Sunday Mass – take care of the home? Strangely, her extraordinary partiality for the environs of the church seemed to have nothing to do with piety; she was scarcely ever seen praying or kneeling or even sitting in a pew. Although she had no official function she constantly busied herself tidying the various shrines, removing candle stubs, rearranging the books and pamphlets that were available for purchase on the bookstand at the rear of the church, and the like.

The next to arrive was a tall, thin, pleasant-looking man in his sixties, whom Alan recognized as one of the people who collected money occasionally after Sunday Mass, on behalf of the St Vincent de Paul Society. He was followed by a pale, round-faced, overweight man in his forties, who avoided the eyes of everyone as he entered the room, and who seemed to have insulated himself against the world in a heavy overcoat.

A woman of about fifty, and a man in a wheelchair, whom she was pushing, were next to arrive. She looked frail and anaemic, and bore a fixed angelic expression on her face. He was in his early twenties, and wore a black beret that was never removed. He kept his eyes downcast, and exuded the demeanour of one who was totally absorbed in other-worldly thoughts. However, he appeared anything but frail, and must have weighed three times as much as the worn woman who was pushing him about. The woman was his mother. She was well known locally for fostering the notion that her son was a living saint, whose prayers found special favour with God.

By this stage Alan was starting to develop a feeling of apprehension about the prospects for this enterprise. His anxieties were somewhat relieved by the next three people to arrive, all of whom breezed in together. There were two women and a man, all in their late twenties or early thirties. All three were the picture of vitality. They were teachers in the local schools.

A few others arrived before Father Somers came into the meeting room and started the proceedings by suggesting that it would be helpful if each one there told the group his or her Christian name. Everyone did, except the wheel-chaired man. When it came to his turn his mother, still wearing her angelic expression, speaking for both of them, said,

'Thank you, Father. This is my son John. And my own name is Maureen.'

Having fulfilled these preliminaries, Father Somers outlined his thoughts on how they might go about their reflections on the changes that were occurring in the Church. He recommended that everyone should get a copy of *The Documents of Vatican 11*, and suggested that they might pay particular attention to the sections on *Liturgy, The Church Today, Ecumenism, Laity and Education*, as these seemed to be the most relevant and of most concern.

Starting with the changes to the liturgy, Father Somers spoke about the removal of the altar rails – now viewed as a barrier between people and priest – and the fact that priests now spoke from the altar, instead of a pulpit as they used to do previously, in order to create a better sense of unity and intimacy between the clergy and the worshippers. He explained why priests saying Mass now faced their congregation instead of standing with their backs to them - 'the Mass is, after all, the sharing of a meal, a celebration, and just as one doesn't turn one's back on everyone else present when having a meal at home, or with friends, there is no good reason to do so when we gather around the altar table at Mass'.

It was when he started to speak about Latin being dropped, in favour of the local vernacular when saying Mass, that the first note of dissent was sounded. It came from the man encased in the heavy overcoat. He thought it was a 'disgrace', and truculently added that 'it was reducing the Mass to nothing more than a 'Protestant service''. Father Somers tried to calmly point out that Latin had not always been used at Mass; it had not, for example, been used among the early Christians and, as such, was not essential to the efficacy of the Mass. The insulated man was not appeased. Scowling obdurately and fixing his eyes directly on the priest, he said,

'I still think it's wrong.'

A quick gasp of apprehension escaped the lips of the wheelchair-pushing mother.

After a moment's tension and awkwardness a female voice filled the vacuum. It was one of the young women teachers, who said very pointedly,

'I think it's a great idea.'

Insulated man's mouth gaped with shock at this challenge. He looked like he had been slapped in the face. Before he could respond Father Somers took the initiative. Glancing down quickly at his watch he said,

'Ah, I see it's just 9.30. Time to finish up for tonight. Thank you all for being here. We'll meet here again at the same time next week. There's tea and biscuits outside in the hall for anyone who'd like some.'

About half of those who had been at the meeting left, including the protesting man and the mother and wheel-chaired son. Alan remained. As he turned from the table with his cup of tea in hand he found Father Somers at his elbow.

'Tricky situation there, Father,' he commented.

'Well Alan', replied the priest, 'I guess some people are bound to have strong views on these issues. It's only to be expected. Our task is to try to calm their fears, and overcome their prejudices. They've been used to things being done in certain ways all their lives, and find change very hard to understand and accept.'

With that he paused and looked about the hall.

'Would you like me to introduce you to some of your fellow 'classmates'?'

'Sure,' said Alan.

Father Somers guided Alan towards the three young teachers.

'Excuse me,' he said on joining the group of young teachers, 'could I intrude on this academic gathering for a moment to introduce you to Alan here.'

'Alan, I'd like you to meet Clare, Susan and Martin. They're all involved in teaching the Religious Education programmes in our local schools. They've kindly come along here because I asked them to give me a bit of moral support, rather than to learn anything they don't know already, I'm sure.'

The first of the three whom Alan shock hands with was Clare Murray, the young woman who had spoken up earlier. Before he released her hand he commented that he agreed with her opinion. She smiled brightly, thanked him, and made way for him to meet her colleagues.

Having finished their tea, and chatted for a few minutes, all four made their way from the hall, and parted with promises to 'See you next Wednesday'.

* * * * * * * * * *

When they reassembled on the following Wednesday evening there were a couple of dropouts, but the longhaired Joan, the St Vincent de Paul man, the mother with her wheel-chaired son, the insulated man, complete with overcoat, and the three school teachers were in attendance, along with two or three others.

The discussion, in which there was a lot more participation than there had been the previous week, centred on 'The Church Today'. All went benignly until the touch-paper subject of birth control came up. By this time the Pope had overruled the recommendation of the Commission of advisors he himself had appointed in 1964; they had advocated a liberalization of the strictures on birth-control practices for Roman Catholics, but the Pope had issued an encyclical, *Humanae Vitae*, in which he had come down uncompromisingly in favour of enforcing the Church's traditional stance.

The church-frequenting Joan was the first to venture a comment,

'I think the Church should stay out of the bedroom of married people'. This had become something of a mantra among those who did not agree with the Church's traditional position.

The St Vincent de Paul man responded heatedly, saying

'The Pope has spoken out. As good Catholics we have no right to question his directions. He speaks for Jesus Christ Himself, and we must accept obediently what he tells us to do.'

This observation was met with a snort. Alan, like everyone else in the room, looked about to see who had been provoked into this response. He was surprised to discover it was a very defiant-looking and, he thought, attractive, Clare Murray. With all eyes upon her, apparently expecting some elaboration, she hesitated for a moment before saying,

'I don't think the situation is anything like as black and white as that gentleman has suggested.'

'Yes?' It was the priest giving her the opening to continue, if she wished.

She paused for a moment, weighting up her thoughts, before deciding to avail of the spotlight she had drawn on herself.

'It seems to me,' she continued with evident conviction, 'that in the past ten years or so the Church has made pronouncements which are at variance with each other, and that have created nothing but confusion for anyone who has been following what's been going on.' She glanced about the room, apparently trying to gauge the effect of her view on the group, and then looked at Father Somers. 'If you give me a moment I'll show you what I mean.'

She bent down and extracted a book from her handbag.

'You asked us,' she said, again looking towards Father Somers, 'to get a copy of this – the Vatican 2 documents.'

She flicked through the book and, having found what she was looking for she said, 'This is what Council had to say in 1964 to parents in regard to birth control

> They will thoughtfully take into account both their own welfare and that of their children, those already born and those which may be foreseen. For this accounting they will reckon with both the material and the spiritual conditions of the times as well as their state in life. Finally they will consult the interests of the family group...

and so on. This is followed by a footnote relating to 'methods of regulating procreation', which says

> The Council states clearly that, with matters standing thus, it has no intention of proposing concrete solutions here.

It seems quite clear to me that what the Council was saying, very sensibly in my opinion, at that time was that people must take responsibility for the number of children they produce, and that the Church had no intention of telling them what they could or couldn't do to achieve this.'

'I....,' began the overcoated man, before Father Somers cut in to say,

'Sorry, Sean, could we let Clare finish her point and then we'll come to you?'

Clare was now the firm focus of attention of everyone in the room. After taking a few moments to gather her thoughts, she continued,

'The problem with all this is, as I see it, that in 1968 the Pope issued his encyclical *Humanae Vitae*, in which he overruled the recommendations of the Commission he himself had appointed, which recommended a more liberal attitude to birth-control, and basically told Catholics that the so-called rhythm system was the only morally legitimate method they could use, telling them that everything else was 'intrinsically evil'. So now we have a situation where Catholics are directed to take a responsible attitude to the number of children they can properly support, while at the same time being warned that they are doing something very evil if they use anything else besides a system which is notoriously unreliable, and which reduces something which should be a spontaneous act of warmth and affection between two people into something like an experiment in a science lab, with calculations and charts and thermometers. This, to my mind, is fuzzy and contradictory, if not quite dishonest.'

At this point she stopped short, distracted by a noise behind her. She turned to investigate along with everyone else. The frail woman had stood up and was noisily manoeuvring her son's wheelchair towards the door.

'Disgraceful! Disgraceful!' She seemed almost on the edge of tears. 'I've never heard such talk. It's not fit for decent people to listen to.'

Alan figured if she'd had a second pair of hands she'd have put them over her son's ears.

'Scandalous! I'll get John to pray for all of you', was the last that was heard or seen of her, or her putative saintly son, at the meetings.

Father Somers had stood up as she was leaving and seemed nonplussed about what he should do. But the door had already closed behind her and she was gone so quickly that he just shrugged resignedly and sat down again. It was hard to read the look he directed towards Clare – amusement? admiration? betrayal?

'We'll I guess we'd better move on to something else while we still have anyone left!' he said, trying to lighten the atmosphere.

But the insulated Sean would not let it rest. Sensing his chance to even the score for what he perceived as the young woman's impertinence in challenging his view the previous week, he announced in a truculent manner from the safety of his carapace that he was 'very much inclined to agree with that poor woman' and, looking in Clare's direction, he declared that he found it 'extraordinary that someone who is trusted with teaching the children of the parish their religious duties should hold such opinions.'

Clare did not rise to the bait.

Alan's had no difficulty analysing his own reaction to Clare's little dissertation. He was hugely impressed.

'I,' he said, 'believe Clare had a perfect right to express her opinions, as we all have. In fact,' he continued rather obliquely, 'the birth control issue is not the only area where the Church is being - to use her word – 'fuzzy'.'

When Alan did not elaborate, the priest took the initiative, and with a mixture of encouragement and trepidation in his voice, said,

'Would you care to say what in particular you have in mind, Alan?'

Alan had not anticipated being drawn into a situation like this, but rather than ducking the issue, and thus looking weak and silly he decided to carry on.

'Traditionally the Church has held its members in thrall with the threat of hell-fire and damnation. I,' he said quite emphatically, 'and I suspect the vast majority of my generation, were continuously being told that we were hell bound and were fed on a diet of what I would call 'fear and fire'. But strangely, and this is where the fuzziness comes in, if, as I've done, you check through the 793 pages of small print in this book I'm holding here, the Vatican 2 documents that we were recommended to get, you won't find the word 'hell' anywhere, and 'Satan' gets one rather vague mention. So, what are we to make of that? Has hell disappeared? Is it no longer Church teaching that hell exists? Hell, clearly, has been written out of the script, if we take these documents to reflect the Church's modern thinking. It seems reasonable to infer that this is now the case. The problem, however, is that the Church won't come out and say so. It seems that hell is not to be taught or emphasized as it used to be, but sort of kept in reserve, like a religious cattle-prod, for possible use if thought necessary at some point in the future.'

The priest looked a little embattled and crestfallen. He was about to offer some response when Alan, feeling rather sorry for him, spoke up again.

'Father, I hadn't intended getting into a debate on this issue. All I'm saying here is that people want to feel good about their Church; they like to feel that they have secure, honest leadership. When there's wooliness, or apparent contradiction, or glossing over issues, whether it's birth control, or hell, or whatever, people lose respect and start to doubt if the Church knows what it's talking about on other issues also. I didn't plan to launch us into a debate, or put anyone on the spot. It's just my point of view. The only reason it came up was because it's the same type of thing Clare was speaking about earlier.'

'That's fine, Alan,' said the priest. 'Anything you want to add, Sean?'

'No, thank you, Father.'

'Perhaps we'll come back to these issues in the future,' Said Father Somers, anxious to defuse any tension.

The remainder of the meeting passed off in a rather subdued atmosphere, and everyone seemed somewhat relieved when it was time for tea and biscuits. As Alan made his way from the meeting room he noticed Clare Murray looking in his direction. He nodded towards her, and gave her a conspiratorial thumbs-up sign. She smiled, and as if she had already made her mind up to do so, moved unhesitatingly in his direction.

'Alan, isn't it?' she checked to make sure she had remembered his name correctly.

'Yes, that's right. And you're Clare?'

'That's me,' she answered brightly through the smile that enhanced her perfectly applied lipstick and even white teeth. 'Susan and Martin and I are going for a drink. Would you like to come with us?'

After a moment's hesitation he said 'I'd love to, but I have the car with me, so I won't be drinking anything stronger than tonic.' Alan was still feeling a bit wary towards alcohol after his 'Connie' experience.

'No problem. We're driving too. We'll see you at the local in a few minutes.' With that she gave him an even broader smile than previously, and was gone.

During the hour that remained before closing time they chatted about the class, and the motley assortment of people who turned up to such events. And they exchanged the customary brief autobiographies that are part and parcel of introductory occasions. Alan told them about his work in the bank, and that he had been married, but his wife had died about a year previously. This piece of information had a momentarily sobering effect on the hitherto jovial group. Susan moved to recover the convivial mood by asking Clare to tell Alan about herself. She was, she said, a Dublin girl born and bred, from Terenure in the south city suburbs. She had been to the National University, and had qualified as a teacher.

At this Susan interjected –

'Come on, Clare. You're not telling Alan the most interesting bit. She's a bit of a celebrity, Alan. Tell him about being in the convent.'

Clare shot Susan a good-humoured 'here we go again' sort of look, and said,

'There's not really much to tell. When I left school at eighteen I thought I wanted to be a nun, and teach, so I entered the Sacred Heart Order. After six years I decided it wasn't for me, and I got out.'

Alan was fascinated.

'I'm sure there's more to your tale than you're telling us,' he commented. 'Was there anything in particular that persuaded you to leave?'

'Well, to be honest, it got to the stage where I couldn't see the point in spending my life in that cosseted, confined atmosphere. It was like living in a psychological straightjacket. And, quite frankly, I wanted sex, or, perhaps I should say, I wanted to have at least the prospect of sex at some stage in my life.'

Alan was so astonished at her frankness that he let out a short laugh. He had never heard such a forthright statement from a young woman before. He was rendered momentarily speechless. It occurred to him that she was simply being humorous, but when he looked into her eyes there was no sign of facetiousness or frippery there.

'So, here I am, twenty eight, footloose and fancy free.' She said this as if to put a full stop at the end of this particular subject.

They continued chatting until closing time, and when the call came to 'drink up folks' Alan felt a slight tinge of irritation that the evening had passed so quickly. As he drove home he felt more alive than he had been in a long time. He was already looking forward to the following Wednesday, not so much for the parish hall meeting as for the possible socializing afterwards, especially with the increasingly attractive Clare.

In the event that was the pattern that developed over the following few weeks. On the evening of the penultimate meeting Martin did not turn up and, when the time came for the, by now, customary adjournment to the bar, Susan opted out, pleading that she still had homework to correct for the following day. Alan expressed his disappointment while trying to mask the sinking feeling he was experiencing at the prospect of the evening falling flat. With more hope than expectation he asked Clare if she would care to join him for a drink anyway.

'Love to,' she replied with evident pleasure.

Their subsequent conversation that evening in the bar roamed broadly over the topical events of the day, parish politics, and what interested them in general regarding books, films, theatre and music. Again, the time flew past. When they left the bar Alan drove Clare the few hundred yards to the flat she occupied over a hairdressing salon in the local shopping area. When their eyes met as they said 'goodnight' there was one of those pregnant 'Will I?', 'Should I?', moments where instant decisions must be made between what will be considered acceptable behaviour, and what might be interpreted as downright gauche. In the event, the moment evaporated in Clare's,

'Thanks for the lift. See you next Wednesday.'

When the group assembled on the following Wednesday for the last in the series of meetings that Father Somers had arranged and hosted, the attendance was about half of what it had been originally. When Alan arrived he scanned the room; the perennially overcoated Sean, the long-haired Joan and the man from St. Vincent de Paul were earnestly in their usual places, as were two or three others. His heart sank. Not a sign of Clare or her young colleagues. Just as he thought all was lost, and Father

Somers was about to get matters under way, Clare and Martin appeared. It being the final meeting, and relatively few people being there, the event passed off uncontentiously. When it was all over, and Father Somers had commended everyone for their endurance and contributions, an air of general goodwill broke out, and even the cocooned Sean shed his customary gruff demeanour and, rather like an unctuous tortoise, wished everyone a very civil 'goodnight' from the confines of his shell.

Alan joined Clare and Martin as they made their way from the meeting room.

'Thank God that's over,' whispered Martin. 'I could use a drink.'

Alan looked at both of them, and said,

'Should we skip the tea and biscuits and head straight for the local? What do you think, Clare?'

'That's fine with me,' came the ready response.

'Sure,' said Martin.

'By the way, what happened to Susan tonight, does anyone know,' Alan queried.

Clare explained that she had called in sick that morning.

As they drank their beer and chatted Alan became increasingly preoccupied with the thought that this might be the last time he would spend time in the company of this fascinating young woman, unless he took some initiative. At closing time on previous evenings it had become the routine that Martin would drive Clare and Susan home. When Martin excused himself, to go to the men's room, Alan plucked up the courage to suggest that he could leave her home, as he had done the previous week. Her response was to look at him very directly, smile mischievously, lean towards him, and brush her finger lightly against the back of his hand, and say,

'I'd like that.'

Her tiny, exotic, unexpected gesture propelled his emotions into a whirlpool of confused sensations. He was in uncharted water and, very probably, out of his depth.

Martin, with an almost imperceptible, knowing, flicker of an eyebrow, raised no objection to the arrangement when the time arrived to leave.

As his car slowed to a halt outside Clare's apartment, and Alan was on the point of asking her if she would like them to meet for a drink the following week, it was Clare who took the initiative by inviting him in for a nightcap.

Once inside her apartment she led him into the warmth of a small, cosy sitting room, switched on some side lights, and invited him to 'make himself at home'. She excused herself saying, jokingly, that she wanted to get out of 'the school uniform' that she'd been wearing since early that morning. Alan took a seat on a plush settee, and started flicking through the pages of a copy of *Cosmopolitan* that lay on a small coffee table in front of the settee. Looking at the index he was surprised that such an overtly 'sexy' magazine had managed to breach Ireland's censorial frontiers. He noticed a feature headed *How safe is the Pill?*, and was curiously working his way through a series of multiple-choice questions under the heading *What Men Like in a Lover* when Clare reappeared. She was quite transformed. The black, long-sleeved, polo-neck jumper and fitted, cerise skirt she had been wearing had been replaced with a sleeveless, button-through, full-skirted denim dress, and her hair, which had been caught in a pony tail, was now freely falling about her shoulders. She was carrying a bottle of wine, two glasses, and an opener.

'Is this okay for you?' she asked, gesturing towards the wine, 'or would you like something else to drink. I've got...'

'Wine is fine,' he interrupted her, immediately thinking the phrase must have sounded a bit silly. She smiled, as if she had found it amusing. He noticed that she was no longer wearing lipstick. She asked if he would open the wine while she found some coasters. When she bent to, unhurriedly, place the coasters on the coffee table, he caught his first glimpse of her cleavage, and of her deep-cut lace-trimmed bra. A small, but very perceptible, dart of desire ran through him. She sat down, quite unselfconsciously, close to him on the settee while he uncorked the bottle and poured the wine. They leant towards each other to clink their glasses and, in that moment he knew that unless he risked taking the initiative, there and then, something would be lost forever. He kissed her. Her lips parted and, pressing them freely to his, invited him to continue. They broke their embrace momentarily to discard their glasses, and found each other's lips again. She pressed herself tightly to him and, wordlessly, took the hand he had placed on her waist and, with easy determination, guided it along her body until it rested, and tightened, on her breast. He clasped her thus for a few moments as if trying, through that one urgent gesture, to convey the excitement that now seemed to pervade every part of him. As she slid her hand inside his open jacket, he moved to open some buttons on her dress, until he brushed and caressed her silky cleavage with his fingertips. Responding with a small, purring sound of pleasure, she slowly let her hand drift down his body, until it found and tightened on his firm, throbbing erection.

At the same moment as his excitement surged to new heights, his hair-trigger conscience flashed its morality-questioning message across his mind. Shouldn't he back off, gather himself together, and leave? Was this not the kind of temptation – the kind of situation - he had been drilled to resist?

This incipient debate had hardly engaged his awareness before it was submerged and suppressed beneath his desire to abandon himself to the pleasure of this vital young woman, and forget the world that lay beyond that moment and that place, with all its rules and strictures. He responded eagerly to her encouragements, and gradually took the initiative as they became increasingly uninhibited in their kissing and explorations of each other's bodies. After several minutes she eased herself away, and very frankly murmured,

'Let's go to bed.'

Misinterpreting his surprise for hesitancy at the thought of her becoming pregnant, and wishing not to break the mood, she whispered,

'I'm on the pill.'

Alan, by now, was quite beyond anything he had ever previously experienced. The voice of conscience that still faintly echoed about his mind diminished to a muffled whisper, drowned out by the clamour of his senses urging him to abandon himself to the pleasure of this vivacious creature's bed and body.

She led him to her bedroom where she unhurriedly, and deftly, began to undress him, while he continued to run his hands over her hair and breasts and thighs. As he fumbled towards unbuttoning her blouse she stopped him and, quite seductively, started to remove her own clothes. It became apparent to Alan that she was a woman who favoured alluring lingerie. When he was left with only his shorts, and she with only the briefest of underwear, they stood together in a long embrace, before sliding between the sheets of her bed.

After their first impetuous climax they lay together in a state of excited sleepiness for perhaps half an hour until, once more, they started to explore each other. This second mutual giving, and receiving, of erotic pleasures was a much more leisurely experience than that which had gone before. When, at last, they drifted into sleep, it was to the sound of the distant chirping of a bird heralding the coming of a new day.

During the following day, as he tried to carry on working normally, Alan experienced, by turns, physical tiredness, the pleasurable afterglow from his exotic night with Clare and, inevitably, guilt. This guilt was like the annoying guest who spoils your enjoyment of the party by seeming to be always hovering at your elbow, no matter how you tried to avoid him. And Alan did try to avoid it, and suppress it, and ignore it as best he could. He succeeded to the extent that it did not stop him from getting together with Clare several times during the following weeks, each occasion following the pattern of that first night in Clare's apartment. He was quite spellbound and, untypically, shied away from considering the rights and wrongs of the situation. He wanted to remain enfolded in this captivating world, quite different from anything he had previously experienced.

As he sat at his desk about eleven o'clock one morning, about six weeks after their first intimacy, he received a phone call from Clare asking him to meet her that evening at a bar in the city, near his office, after he'd finished work. She would not say what it was about. He had a distinctly uneasy feeling about what to expect.

She was waiting for him when he arrived at the bar. They greeted each other, and he sensed that she seemed subdued by comparison to her usual outgoing self. When he'd ordered drinks he looked at her directly and said,

'Well, Clare, what's this about?'

She didn't beat around the bush.

'Alan, I'm sorry to have to tell you this, but we'll have to stop seeing each other,' came the reply.

The mixture of emotions he experienced in the following few seconds were many and varied – confusion, anger, disappointment, resentment….relief?

'Why, exactly?'

'Well, when I arrived at the school this morning I was summoned to the Principal's office to be told that it had been reported to them, by a parent with children in the school, that a car had been seen regularly parked overnight outside my place in recent weeks, and a man had been observed leaving in the morning – a bank manager who also lived in the area. This, it was made clear to me, if it were true, was unacceptable behaviour in my position, and unless it ceased straightaway I could not be retained as a teacher.'

She paused. He looked away from her, and vaguely registered

his own sour reflection in the mirror behind the bar. When he said nothing, she continued.

'Talk about the Ireland of the squinting windows being alive and well!'

Alan turned back to face her.

'Clare, you're a single woman. I'm widowed. We're both free adults. What the hell is going on here? Why do we have to end our relationship entirely?'

'Alan. I don't want to hurt your feelings, but I don't intend settling down anytime soon, and I am not ready to get into a long term serious relationship.'

'So, all that's happened over the last month was just a bit of recreational fun, was it?' He delivered this observation/question with a distinct edge to the anger in his voice.

'Alan, I didn't come here to fight with you, and I don't want to argue with you. I enjoyed what we did, and I think, and hope, that you did as well.'

Deep down he knew she was right. The word 'love' had never been spoken between them. He was just as complicit as she was, and it had been unfair to imply that she was the only one to have treated their affair as 'recreation'. He apologized.

They left the bar together, and went their separate ways like strangers who, coincidently, had witnessed a traffic accident, and had no expectation of ever seeing each other again.

When he got home he wished his friend Philip was around to talk to, but he was still pursuing his research in England. He went about mechanically sorting out some routine chores, and made himself some sandwiches, which he took, with a bottle of beer, to the sitting room. He selected Miles Davis vinyl recording of *Kind of Blue*, placed it on the stereo turntable, and slumped down in an armchair. The Davis' ensemble had to be one of the most soothing sounds imaginable. He could think of nothing better to calm his fractured mood on that oppressive evening.

When the music finished he switched on the television,

hoping to find something light and distracting on one of the three channels available. Before the picture appeared the sound of canned laughter, and American accents, announced another imported sit-com. He moved to the next channel, where the highlights of the day's play in a cricket match involving England were being shown, with commentary by a gentleman whose hypnosis-inducing voice and plumy English accent were on offer.

The third channel virtually exploded off the screen. It took him a few moments to realize that what he was looking at was a report on the war in Vietnam. With a voice-over by an on-the-spot Australian journalist, the horrific scene before him showed terrified people – mostly children and women, but some old men – running before huge balls of flames, amid much shrieking and screaming, the typical result, the reporter intoned, of the targeting and blanket fire-bombing of innocent civilians in a Vietnamese village. Alan shuddered at the utter depravity, the sheer evil, of what was happening. For every one who ran before the huge, engulfing tidal waves of fire, many more were roasted alive. Hell on earth.

****

The following Sunday morning Alan spotted Father Somers outside the church, after attending Mass. The priest was surrounded by parishioners, but gestured to Alan to wait a minute until he was free. They had not been in contact since the night of the last meeting on Vatican 2. Alan felt sure that the priest, through his involvement with the local schools, would be aware of the warning to Clare, and of the background and, more than likely, would have guessed that 'the bank manager' observed leaving Clare's place early in the mornings, was Alan.

'Good morning, Alan. How are you?' Father Somers' greeting was slightly guarded. 'I haven't seen you for a while.'

'Fine, Father,' Alan replied. He decided that this was not the appropriate time or place to try to determine how much the priest knew of his love affair with Clare, and quickly decided to invite him to call around to his house some evening when he was free.

'I'll come around tomorrow evening, if you'll be there,' Father Somers suggested.

'I'll make a point of it,' said Alan.

At 7.30 the following evening Alan opened his front door to the waiting curate.

'Come on in, Father.'

They made their way, as usual, to the sitting room, and Alan directed the priest to an armchair. After a few minutes of initial pleasantries and chat, which seemed slightly artificial, Alan decided to take the initiative.

'I guess you're aware of the situation between Clare Murray and myself,' he ventured.

The priest gathered his thoughts for a moment, and said,

'Well, I did hear that Clare had been spoken to about, eh, an aspect of her lifestyle outside school, that the school authorities found incompatible with her position. I surmised that the other person involved was yourself, but I wasn't absolutely sure.'

'Well, now you know it was me. And it's over. I trust Clare has made that as clear to her school principal as she did to me.' This was spoken with a slight touch of heat. He paused for a moment, before continuing in a more composed manner, ' Actually, I'm not sorry it's over. I have this weird feeling, when I think back over the past few weeks, that it's like everything that happened occurred in someone else's life.' He paused for a moment, before adding, 'It probably sounds a bit pathetic, but I feel like it wasn't 'me'. But it was me, and it was wrong, I'm sure.'

The priest shifted forward, and with a quizzical look on his face, said

'Would it help you to receive absolution?'

The question took Alan by surprise. He hated going to confession, and had been avoiding it more and more over the previous years. Still, there was something about it, a feeling of a weight being lifted from the shoulders.

'Can you just give me absolution here and now if I want it?' he asked.

'Yes. A priest can hear confession anywhere,' the priest explained encouragingly.

'But all a person's sins must be confessed for it to be a good confession, right?'

'All mortal sins, eh, all grave sins. Alan, you don't have to go into detail about you and Clare. I know all I need to know in order to give you absolution if you wish me to, and if you're sorry for your sins.'

'But there are other things, some of which I won't talk about.'

'Can you tell me what you will talk about?' prompted the priest, with evident concern.

Alan told him about drinking at his colleague's party to the point where he passed out and couldn't remember what he had being doing.

'But,' he added, 'there is something else that troubles me that I'm not prepared to get into.'

'Do you think this other matter was gravely wrong. You are only obliged to confess what is gravely wrong, and for something to be gravely wrong it must be a serious matter, and there must be full consent, and the person involved must know that they are doing serious wrong. May I ask you, was this matter serious?

'Yes, it was.'

'Did you give it your full consent?'

'I did.'

'Against which of the commandments was this offence?'

Alan considered this for a moment, while he tried to remember the sequence of the commandments he had learned in school, until he came to 'Thou shalt not kill'.

'The Fifth,'

'And do you believe that whatever you did was gravely wrong.'

Again, Alan paused to weigh up this question.

'No. In all honesty I don't believe it was.'

'In that case,' - the priest's expression brightened - 'there is no necessity to say anymore about it. Whatever it was, God now forgives you for this and for all your sins. You should focus on God's love for you, and for your penance say one rosary, the Glorious Mysteries, and ask Our Lady for her guidance and protection. If you will now say an Act of Contrition, I will give you absolution.'

While Alan stumbled through the seldom-recited, and almost forgotten, words of the prayer, Father Somers searched his pockets for a stole – a thin strip of purple silk with gold-coloured crosses embroidered at each end – which he placed around his shoulders, and proceeded to make the Sign of the Cross while saying, 'I absolve you, in the name of the Father, and of the Son, and of the Holy Spirit,....'

It was the first time Alan had heard the words of forgiveness uttered in English; they sounded, he thought, much more meaningful than the rather séance-sounding 'Ego te absolvo....' of the past.

He also felt that he had been gently, expertly, and unwittingly, navigated through a very emotionally stormy experience. His admiration for his confessor's genuine care and priestly accomplishments was greatly enhanced.

After a few moments of intense silence, which it seemed almost sacrilegious to break, Alan said,

'Thank you.'

They both relaxed visibly, and settled back into their respective armchairs. They sat in a more comfortable silence for a further few moments, as if to allow whatever tension there was in the room to evaporate.

'So, tell me, Alan,' said the priest, conversationally, 'do you see much of your family?'

'Oh yes, I see most of them fairly regularly. I usually call to my parents at least once a week, and I see my two sisters and their families – they're both married – on odd occasions throughout the year. My brother, Barry, lives in New York now. He graduated from university in – when was it – 1966 I think, the first one on either side of the family to get a degree. He's an engineer. Unfortunately he couldn't settle down here – said he needed to get better experience than he could here, so he went off to try his luck in America. He seems to be doing well. Still single. He comes home for a holiday here every couple of years.'

'Where does he live in New York?' Father Somers queried.

'Greenwich Village, Manhattan.'

'Greenwich Village, aye,' repeated the priest, as if to assure himself that he had heard correctly.

'Have you ever been out to visit him?' he asked.

'No. But I must one of these years. Have you been to the States yourself, Father?'

'I have an uncle – my father's eldest brother – living in the Bronx. I've spent a couple of holidays with him and his family over the years. He's getting on now – must be nearly eighty. He emigrated as a young man, and got into the fire service there. Married an Italian girl, but he's still dyed-in-the-wool Irish. Three sons and two daughters. One of the sons is a priest – like myself, and the other two have followed in their father's footsteps – joined the fire service.' He paused, sensing that his recitation might be becoming a boring monologue. Out of the blue he changed the course of the conversation:

'Do you not find it lonely, Alan, living in this rather big house on your own?' he asked.

Once again Alan had to take a moment to adjust his thinking.

'It's not something I've been conscious of.'

'If you don't mind me saying so,' ventured the priest, 'you seem to me the type of man who could do with company. Do you think you might find yourself a good woman and marry again.'

Alan's immediate reaction was to feel that the priest had taken too much upon himself and, had he not been convinced that the man genuinely meant well, he might have been inclined to suggest it was none of his business. In the event, having suppressed the little flair of annoyance inside him, he said, noncommittally,

'I'm not sure what I might do in the future.'

'There's an old saying, Alan – better to marry than burn.'

Again, Alan was at pains to mask his astonishment, but he decided to let the remark go without comment, and changed the subject by offering his companion a drink. For once the offer was accepted.

'That would be very nice, Alan. If you had a Hennessy that would go down very well, thank you.'

* * * * * * * *

The following day, as he drove along St Stephen's Green on his way home from work, in one of those bizarre moments that seem to dot everyone's lives, he thought he saw a familiar face among a group of three women leaving The Country Store tearooms. Was his mind playing tricks on him, prompted by the previous evening's conversation? Or was it really Heather Lattimore he had spotted?

12

November 1975

Jim Logan, Alan's father, had taken to retirement with the same easy contentment that was typical of his life in general. After their initial taste of continental travel in Rome he and Annie were now enjoying regular trips to France and Spain. In the previous few years, apart from visiting the Marian shrine at Lourdes in France, with a pilgrimage arranged by the parish, Jim had taken full advantage of the travel concessions he was entitled to as part of his job as a train driver, and Annie and himself had enjoyed several package holidays on the Spanish costas. He tended his garden, and enjoyed indulging his skills as a DIY enthusiast around the home. But it was his hobby repairing old clocks that gave him most satisfaction. He had even set up a small workshop in the garden shed to enable him to make his own individually assembled grandmother clocks. He enjoyed life at a measured, imperturbable pace.

When the phone rang on Alan's desk one Tuesday afternoon in late November 1975, and the switchboard operator announced that his father was on the line, Alan knew instinctively that something was wrong. In the twenty years he had been working he had never received a phone call from his father during office hours.

'Hello, Dad?' Alan said with some urgency.

'Hello Alan. Yes, this is Dad here. Listen, I'm sorry to ring you at...'

'That's okay, Dad. Has something happened?'

'Well, I just want to let you know that we got a phone call from New York about an hour ago, around three o'clock, to tell us Barry's in hospital. He had an accident on a motorbike this morning, and fractured his knee – multiple fractures, the man said.'

'My God! Dad. Any other injuries?'

'Cuts and bruises. Nothing else broken it seems.' He paused for a moment before continuing, 'I've had a talk with your Mum, and we've decided that I'll go over there to see him. I'm going to get in touch with Aer Lingus now to see about flights.'

Alan thought for a few moments while he took all this in.

'Tell you what, Dad, I'll come with you. I'll arrange to take a few days off. And I'll check about the flights. We'll have to get visas as well; the Yanks are fussy about letting people in. You can't expect to turn up at the airport over there and just walk through, even with your passport. I'll arrange that as well.'

'That'd be great, son. Thanks.' And then added, 'Did you know he had a motorbike?'

'No, Barry never mentioned it to me.'

'Damn things. I was always dead set against them. I asked him a million times never to get one of them. Damn dangerous things!'

Alan could not recall ever hearing such emphasis in his father's voice. 'Damn' was just about the nearest he ever came to swearing. Alan had only ever heard him use the word 'shit' once, and that was when he had hit his thumbnail with a hammer while repairing the roof of the garden shed.

'By the way, Dad, who contacted you?'

'He said his name was Bob. Shares Barry's apartment with him, he said. He gave me the name of the hospital and a phone number for them – just a second - it's the Roosevelt Hospital Centre'

Alan took a note of the phone number. He recognized the name Bob as that of the person who occasionally answered the phone when he phoned Barry.

As soon as he was off the phone Alan contacted the bank's travel agents, who were experienced at arranging short notice transatlantic travel for the bank's personnel; he explained his situation and requirements. They were back to him within an hour with everything arranged. He and his father were booked on a flight to Kennedy Airport the following morning, special visas included. Alan confirmed to the personnel department that he would be taking some of the holidays due to him, immediately, explaining that his brother had been involved in a traffic accident in New York, and had been hospitalised.

That evening Alan tried several times to contact Bob at the apartment he shared with Barry. He got no answer. He phoned the hospital and explained who he was, where he was calling from, and what he wanted to know. He was put through to Barry's ward where the female New York accent on the other end of the line confirmed, very concisely, that Mr Barry Logan had been admitted with multiple fractures to his right knee, and was scheduled for surgery the following day. Alan asked if it was possible to speak to his brother.

'That's not possible, Sir. Mr Logan is sedated right now.'

Alan made a final attempt to contact the apartment around one o'clock – 8 p.m. local New York time. He was surprised when he heard the phone being picked up promptly.

'Hello, Bob here.' The voice sounded a bit weary.

'Hello Bob. This is Alan, Barry's brother.'

'Ah, Alan. I recognize your voice. I guess you're worried about

Barry?'

'Well, yes. I want to thank you for getting in touch with my folks. I appreciate it.'

'No problem, Alan.'

'I've been on to the hospital but apart from some fairly basic information I didn't find out much about Barry's condition,' said Alan.

'There's not much to tell really,' said Bob. 'It seems that he was hit by a truck breaking the lights at an intersection, and busted his right knee pretty badly. I've been at the hospital for the past few hours, but they have him knocked out with drugs and painkillers. They have him down for surgery tomorrow morning.'

Alan explained about his father and himself flying to New York the following day. When he asked if they could use the apartment for the few days they would be in New York, it took some moments before Bob answered, hesitantly.

'Well, we've ...Well if, eh..., if you don't mind sharing a room.'

'No problem,' said Alan. 'We'll get a taxi directly to the address from the airport. We should be there around this time tomorrow – about eight o'clock your time. Will that be okay for you?'

'Yes.' Alan could not distinguish if it was weariness or reluctance he detected in the voice. Before he had time to gather his thoughts and suggest it might be more convenient if they checked into a hotel Bob added. 'See you then.' And, as an afterthought, 'have a safe trip'.

During the flight Jim Logan seemed uncharacteristically subdued. Alan tried to engage him in conversation about his various trips to Europe, but each attempt ran into a verbal cul-de-sac. After an extended period of sombre silence Jim said, quietly,

'Thank God he didn't kill himself.'

'Thank God again,' Alan responded. He sensed that his father had more to say, but was surprised by Jim's next remark.

'I suppose you know that Barry gave up practicing his religion when he was in university?'

'I knew that,' Alan replied, wondering where this was going.

'We thought at first that it was just a temporary thing – teenage independence, and all that – but he gave up going to Mass completely. His mother never stops praying that he'll come back to his religion, but he hasn't shown any signs of it even up to the last year when he came home on holidays.' Here he paused, as if waiting for Alan to comment. When he didn't, Jim continued,

'I mean, can you imagine the state his mother would be in if he'd been killed, you know, suddenly and without being reconciled to the Church.'

'Dad, if you ask me, Barry is his own man now. He's an adult – what age is he? 29? And I think he's a decent person. I think Mum and yourself should leave Barry to worry about his own salvation at this stage of all your lives.'

'I know,' Jim reluctantly conceded, 'but as a parent it doesn't matter how old your kids are, you still feel responsible, and it's always there on your mind, you know, that you didn't do enough, or do things right. Once a parent, always a parent.'

'With all due respect, Dad, that's nonsense. No one could have given better example to their children than Mum and yourself. When children grow up and become adults they have to take responsibility for themselves. In any event, Barry wasn't killed, and God knows what the future holds. Like I said before, I believe Barry is fundamentally a good person, and the main thing to worry about now is his physical health.'

'Ah,' said Jim, a bit more brightly, 'I'm sure you're right. I just hope his injuries aren't too serious.' And with that they fell into a more relaxed silence. Alan's own thoughts drifted from Barry, now lying injured in hospital, back to memories of Lucy's illness, and on to his subsequent affair with Clare Murray, which, in the inexplicable manner that characterizes the mind's grasshopper patterns of thought, triggered the image of a recent scene on Dublin's St Stephen's Green, and a face from his youth. He allowed his thoughts to settle on those bygone times as he hovered on the brink of dropping into sleep.

They cleared Kennedy Airport around 7 p.m., local time, and decided they just might get to see Barry that evening if they took a taxi directly to the hospital. When they arrived at his bedside over an hour later he was sleeping, under the influence of painkillers and sleeping pills. As they stood about Jim picked up the clipboard at the foot of Barry's bed. It gave various details, including Barry's name and age last birthday (29). The item that caused Jim to wrinkle his brow, however, was the entry beside 'Next of Kin': it read 'Bob Newton'. Alan noticed his father's puzzlement.

'Something wrong?' he asked.

Jim showed him what had caught his attention.

'I wonder why he gave that chap as his next of kin?'

'Probably, you know, for convenience. The hospital probably wanted someone local if they needed to make contact,' Alan suggested speculatively.

Jim seemed less than appeased. As he replaced the clipboard at the end of the bed Barry stirred. Alan and Jim moved up towards him, one on each side of the bed. Barry noticed Alan first.

'Alan,' Barry managed groggily.

'Hi, buddy. Look who else is here.' Alan gestured in his father's direction.

'Dad!' this came out a little more brightly. 'Bob told me earlier that you were both coming over. I didn't expect you so quickly.'

Jim put his hand on Barry's head and, bending towards him, said,

'How are you, son?'

'Well, I won't be running any marathons in the near future, I reckon.' His face clouded as he added, 'I guess you're mad at me for using a motorcycle? It wasn't really my fault, you know. A guy in a delivery truck crashed the lights and hit me as I was on my way to work yesterday.'

'Yes, Bob told us all about it on the phone. But, you know, I've said it a million times, a motorcyclist involved in an accident will always come off second best, no matter how good the driver is.' Immediately he had said this he thought it sounded a bit insensitive, and added, 'Sorry, I didn't mean ...,' he broke off in mid-sentence and, trying not to let his emotions show, said, 'Do they know how bad it is yet?'

'Not really, but they tell me I shouldn't end up with a stiff leg permanently after the surgery.'

'That good news,' Alan interjected. He sensed that Barry was struggling to stay focused. 'Maybe we should head off now and let you get back to sleep. It's getting late, and we've still got to find your apartment.'

Barry turned his head slowly on the pillow from his brother to his father, and back again. He seemed to be trying to gather his thoughts together to say something, but all that he managed to say was,

'Okay... I'll see you soon then.' After a moment he added, 'By the way, thanks for coming all the way from Ireland to see me. I really appreciate it.'

'No problem,' Alan assured him.

As they were about to leave, Jim asked,

'Do you know what time you'll be operated on tomorrow?'

'Early, they said. Around 9 o'clock.'

'We'll be in to see you tomorrow, son. I hope it goes well. You know everyone will be praying for you, especially your Mum. Goodnight now. Try to get a good night's sleep.'

'Bye Dad. Bye Alan. Thanks again.'

When they arrived at the apartment in Greenwich Village about 10 o'clock that evening, the door was opened by a slim, intense-looking, young man, of about Barry's age. His pale complexion suggested that he was not the outdoor type. He was at least six inches shorter than Barry, and his dark brown hair reached to his shoulders. Behind the wire-rimmed glasses he wore, his eyes were bright and intelligent. He was dressed in a dark blue t-shirt and jeans. He introduced himself as Bob Newton, and invited them in. Alan thought he detected a degree of apprehension in his manner, which, he figured, was understandable, considering that two people whom he had never seen before were about to share his home. Bob showed them into a compact livingroom-cum-kitchen area, and once they were seated, inquired about their trip, and about their visit to Barry. Alan thanked him again for his phone call to Ireland, and for his hospitality in accommodating them. Bob offered to rustle up something for them to eat.

'Nothing for me, Bob. I'm tired from the journey, and I'd just like to get off to bed, thanks very much' said Jim.

'Yes, I think I'll turn in too. It's actually getting on for 4 a.m. Irish time,' Alan pointed out, glancing at his watch. He asked Bob if he 'could show them to Barry's room'.

Bob led the way to what appeared to Alan to be the apartment's only other room, something which Jim did not appear to have noticed. The room was dominated by a large double bed. Alan was about to query where Bob would sleep, but immediately thought better of it. Both Alan and his father turned in quietly and without delay. Jim was asleep within minutes. Alan lay staring into space trying to piece together various things in his mind. A fractured knee was not the only issue concerning Barry that he had to think about. It would be quite a while before he eventually drifted off into a rambling, fidgety sleep.

When Alan woke, the luminous dial on the bedside clock showed 5.05 a.m. – it would have been after ten o'clock back home. His Dad was still sound asleep. After lying still for a few minutes, in the hope that he might get back to sleep for a while, he accepted that this was not going to happen, and decided to visit the bathroom. It was, he remembered from last night, located at the far side of the living area. He slid out of bed very gently, and being conscious of wishing not to waken either his father or Bob, whom he thought might be occupying the living area couch, opened the bedroom door slightly, and noiselessly. There was no sign of Bob.

About an hour later, after he had made himself a coffee and found a copy of the previous day's USA Today to read, he was startled to hear a key being inserted in the hall door. A rather tousled Bob entered, carrying a large bag of groceries. Alan's first thought was 'How did he get those at this hour of the morning.' But then he realized that this was New York, where, unlike Dublin, all-night shopping was nothing new.

After they had greeted each other rather defensively, Alan said,

'You couldn't have got much sleep, Bob?'

Bob examined Alan face for some hidden meaning.

'How do you mean?'

'Well, I assume you had to sleep on the couch here, and as you weren't here when I came out of the bedroom about an hour ago I guess you must have been up and out at some ungodly hour.'

'Actually,' Bob replied 'I didn't sleep here last night. I slept in a friend's apartment downstairs. She's got more space than we have.'

After digesting this explanation Alan said,

'Bob, I apologize for inconveniencing you like that. I didn't realize when I spoke to you on the phone that Barry didn't have his own separate room.'

'Barry and me don't need separate rooms.' There was a hint of challenge in Bob's voice.

Alan looked about the room as he took this in

'How long have you and Barry been…. together?'

'We moved in here together on April 15th 1972, almost three years ago,' Bob confirmed.

They were quiet for a few moments before Bob spoke again,

'Alan, let me ask you something. Did you not know that Barry was gay?'

'I had absolutely no idea. I don't know how the parents are

going to take it when they find out.'

At that moment the bedroom door opened and Jim appeared looking a bit bleary eyed, and the two younger men turned their heads towards him.

'You chaps are on the go early,' he observed by way of a good morning greeting.

'Morning, Dad,' Alan responded. He quickly glanced back towards Bob, and with an almost imperceptible shake of his head indicated his wish to drop what they had been talking about. Bob got the message. 'Yes,' continued Alan, 'I woke up an hour ago and couldn't get back to sleep, and Bob's been out shopping for breakfast already in the city that never sleeps.'

No one said much during breakfast. Alan was preoccupied thinking about how to handle this new revelation about Barry; should he ignore it and hope his father didn't notice, or should he try to explain the situation to him? If his father found out for himself would he be annoyed because he hadn't been told? Alan couldn't make up his mind.

Each of them went about their normal preparations for the day in a subdued, self-absorbed manner, Jim commenting every so often that he hoped Barry's operation would go well. Before he left for work, Bob gave them a spare key to the apartment, and wrote down a contact phone number for the firm on West 29th Street where he worked as an architect, in case they needed to get in touch with him for any reason. As he left he said,

'Make yourselves at home. I'll see you this evening. I hope everything goes well. Maybe you could phone me at the office after Barry's had his surgery?'

'Sure, Bob, I'll do that,' said Alan. 'See you later.'

Jim and Alan sat about until they considered it was about time to make their way to the hospital. It was around midday when they climbed into a taxi outside the apartment. They had not gone far when Jim said 'Alan', and then paused. It was his way of drawing his son's attention to the fact that he had something more than small talk to say.

'Yes, Dad.'

'That apartment seems very small for the two of them, don't you think?'

Alan began to think that his father was not as unobservant as he might have thought. It was a leading, probing question that certainly gave him the opening to tell what he had learned about Barry and Bob's relationship. But he could not bring himself to launch into the subject at that moment. All he said, quite conversationally, was,

'Yes, it does seem a bit cramped, but I suppose rents are very high in that part of the world.'

His father did not pursue the matter.

By the time they were directed to Barry's bedside, with the admonition from a nurse not to stay for more than a minute or two, the operation had been completed and he was back in his ward, very groggy, and with his right leg elevated in traction. The nurse told them that the surgery had gone well and, although it had been necessary to remove the patella, as it had been too fragmented to reconstruct, the prognosis was that Barry would eventually regain full movement in his damaged knee.

'What's the patella?' asked Jim, looking puzzled and concerned.

Both the nurse and Alan started to answer him together. Alan deferred to the nurse –

'It's the medical name for the kneecap, Sir,' she explained.

As they stood about Barry's bed, asking him how he felt, and trying to reassure him than all had gone well, Alan noticed his father again examining the notes on the clipboard that hung on the end of the bed.

At the nurse's insistence, they stayed for only a few minutes, and then left and went to look for a place to have some lunch. Jim had become uncharacteristically quiet. Despite his real concern for his younger son's physical recovery, his mind was fighting a battle within itself, between various facts that were pointing in one virtually unbelievable direction, and his unwillingness to even consider that what they pointed towards could possibly be true. He kept his speculation to himself. His only significant comment during their lunch was that he thought it would be better all round if they found an inexpensive hotel to stay in for the remainder of the few days they intended to be in New York. Alan agreed, relieved by his father's suggestion. Lunch over, they set about this task, and found a suitable place on lower Lexington Avenue. They returned to the apartment to collect their luggage. Alan left a note for Bob, from both of them, explaining what they had decided to do, and, again, thanking him for his hospitality.

It is easy to find numerous interesting things to do and sights to see in New York, but despite Alan's various suggestions his father showed virtually no interest in anything other than their visits to Barry. He had fallen into a pensive, withdrawn mood, the like of which Alan had never experienced from him before.

When they visited Barry on the evening of his surgery, Bob was already there. He had come straight from work. Alan explained about their decision to move to a hotel, and said he'd left a note back at the apartment. He apologized for their hasty departure, but Bob assured him that he completely understood. He left soon afterwards, leaving the three family members together. The visitors did not stay for long, as Barry seemed tired and in some discomfort.

They were back again during the early afternoon of the next day. Although Barry was brighter on this occasion, Jim was positively taciturn. Alan was quite sure he knew what was on his father's mind, but evaded bringing it out in the open, in the forlorn hope that he might be mistaken. Eventually, during what was their fifth visit to Barry's bedside, two days after the operation, Jim, with uncharacteristic bluntness, said,

'Barry, I notice you've put down your flatmate, Bob, as your next of kin.' It was clear from his tone that this was a question rather than a statement. Tension suddenly mounted all round.

Barry glanced at Alan, and then, as if reaching a moment of truth in his own mind, resolutely said,

'Yes, Bob and I live together.' Alan's heart skipped a beat, as he helplessly sensed that a real life drama was about to erupt before his eyes.

'I know that, but....' said the clearly perplexed father.

'Dad, we live together as a couple – I've tried to keep this from you and Mum – tried to avoid upsetting both of you and the rest of the family. But I guess it can't be avoided now. I'm sorry if this disappoints you.'

'You mean you're...' he was about to say 'queer', but stopped himself.

'Yes, Dad, I'm ho-mo-sex-ual,' Barry finished the sentence for him, with quiet, deliberate emphasis.

It was not disappointment that Jim was feeling. He was stunned and confused. There was nothing in his life to prepare him for this. The possibility of such an eventuality had simply never crossed his mind until a couple of days ago, and here it now was, unmistakably confirmed. There was silence between them for a few minutes. The father seemed to sink into a deep space within himself. His sons watched his anguished expression, one with anxiety, the other with anticipation. Jim's first words, barely audibly, as if to himself, were,

'Poor Annie.'

He gradually refocused on the reality of his surroundings. As his thoughts ran on, it seemed clear to him that whatever he said next would be important, perhaps decisive, in relation to Barry and himself.

'Barry,' he said eventually, 'this is a shock - there's no sense in not admitting that. Something like this has never crossed my mind. I don't understand how something like this happens. But I know you're my son, and this news doesn't make me feel any different towards you than I did before. I hope you understand what I'm trying to say.'

'I understand, Dad.'

At that moment the emotionally charged atmosphere was deflated by the arrival of a nurse with a dispensing trolley, followed almost immediately by Bob. Greetings were exchanged, and Alan decided to take the initiative –

'I think it's time we were on our way, Barry, and leave you and Bob to chat. I hope you have a good night's rest. You know we are due to return to Ireland tomorrow evening, but we'll be in to see you again before we leave. Okay?'

'Yes,' Jim added, 'better take your medicine.' He patted Barry on the shoulder and, turning to join Alan, said, "Night, son.' He then nodded towards Bob, and added, 'Goodnight, Bob.'

In the course of a fairly one-sided conversation on their way back to the hotel Alan said,

'Dad, you know we're due to fly home tomorrow?'

Jim nodded, quizzically, and waited for Alan to continue.

'Well, I've been thinking that I might stay on for a few days, if you don't mind flying on your own. I think I'd like to be here for Barry for a bit longer. I don't think there'd be a problem exchanging the airline ticket for a later flight. What do you feel about that?'

Jim said that was fine with him but, as for himself, he was keen to get home.

The following day, after Jim had said his farewells to Barry at the hospital, and Alan had explained that he'd be staying in New York for a while longer, Alan went with his father to Kennedy Airport. While they waited for the departure call, Jim, who had been quietly lost in thought for some time, said,

'This business with Barry and Bob….I've been thinking….I think it would be better to say nothing to your mother about it. I think she has enough to worry about at the moment. What do you say?'

'Okay, Dad, if that's what you feel is best. I'll let Barry know what you're thinking.'

Their parting at Kennedy airport was subdued. Alan suggested getting his father a book, or some magazines, to read on the plane, but Jim said he didn't need anything. Alan saw him safely to the departure gates, and waved him 'goodbye'.

He continued to visit Barry each afternoon and evening during the following days but, as Bob was virtually ever-present, the conversation tended to be light and chatty, and Alan avoided any reference to what had transpired earlier in the week regarding Barry and Bob's relationship, or Jim Logan's reaction to it.

* * * * * * * * *

New York is to jazz what Dublin is to Guinness, and Rome is to the papacy. If jazz had its roots in New Orleans, and blossomed in Chicago, it was in New York that it came into full bloom. New York became the magnet and the breeding ground for all the jazz 'greats'. Unless you made it there, you made it nowhere.

Alan realized that chance had placed him at the hub of the world of jazz, and now that he was a free agent he decided that, after the dramatic and stressful events of the previous few days, there could be no better therapy for him than to seek out what New York's jazz scene had to offer. Although the mid-seventies was a relatively lean time for the music as a popular art form, by comparison with the phenomenal success of the previous decades, Alan was gratified to discover that some of the iconic figures of the past were still about in the clubs and bars of the city. Although he was unaware of it on that Saturday night in November 1975, in years to come he would consider himself fortunate to have sought out the venue on 44th Street, and been present at one of the last performances by Miles Davis and John Coltrane, before the transcendental trumpeter would disappear from the scene for six years, to fight his own inner demons. The precise and perfect economy of each note that Davis moulded and measured from his trumpet, blended with Coltrane's mesmeric web of saxophonic improvisations, made it an unforgettable experience. There was nothing in his own life that came close to this joyous freedom of the spirit, this uninhibited inventiveness, this liberty to probe and explore, to venture and to question beyond the limits of what had gone before, which was the very essence of jazz. The music resonated against his own latent longings and frustrations.

The performance of these two jazz greats was not, however, without its unintentional humour that evening. Alan was close enough to the performance area to notice Davis's growing impatience as Coltrane's solo on *My Favourite Things* went through seemingly endless permutations and combinations of variations, extending to well over ten minutes. Eventually Coltrane returned from whatever part of the galaxy he had been visiting and, noticing Davis's exasperation, muttered,

'Sorry, Myles. I couldn't find a way out.'

'Try taking the fucking thing out of your mouth, John,' fumed Davis, none to quietly.

By the time he got to bed after this spellbinding session it was close to 4 a.m. He slept soundly until midday.

On that Sunday Alan made his usual two visits, mid-afternoon and evening, to his brother's bedside; he judged that Barry appeared to be coming to terms with the effects of his injury, and was suffering less discomfort. This apparent all round improvement in Barry's well-being, both psychological and physical, lifted Alan's spirits also. Bob, too, seemed to be encouraged by Barry's evident improvement. Alan, whose head was still full of the sound of Davis' silky notes and Coltrane's convoluted lyricism, told them where he had spent the previous evening, and of his intention to take advantage of his remaining time in New York to soak up as much of the city's jazz offerings as he could. Bob mentioned that it might be difficult to find a good jazz venue that evening, as New York tended to be fairly quiet on Sundays. Alan voiced disappointment.

'You probably won't find any of the big names playing tonight,' he explained,' but, if you're interested in a pretty good jazz session, there's a place in the Village I go to myself sometimes. They've a young saxophonist in the group who's really worth listening to.'

'I had no idea you were a jazz fan, Bob,' said Alan, obviously surprised. 'Thanks for marking my card. If you give me the name and location of the place, I'll head down there tonight.'

'Sure,' said Bob. He tore a piece from the top of a page of a magazine beside Barry's bed and wrote down the jazz bar's name and address.

As the end of visiting time approached, Alan, conscious of the fact that Bob and Barry would welcome some time together on their own, made his excuses to leave. As he departed he said,

'I'll see you tomorrow afternoon, Barry. I'm glad to see you're looking much better.' Turning to Bob, he said, 'Maybe I'll see you later at the jazz bar?'

'Maybe,' Bob responded,' but I usually try to get to bed early on Sunday nights. Work tomorrow. I hope you enjoy it.'

Alan decided to take a taxi directly to Greenwich Village and get something to eat in one of the renowned local restaurants, before finding the venue Bob had suggested.

When he entered the place the musicians were just setting up at the rear of a long narrow premises, with a counter on the right running almost its full length, and a line of tables and chairs against a wall on the left. Alan chose a bar stool close to the performance area, and ordered a beer. He liked to watch musicians as they played.

The group was made up of three middle-aged black musicians, a trumpeter, a bass player, and a drummer, and a pencil-thin, young, white saxophonist, who looked no more than twenty-five. Young as he was, it was clear from the moment they started to play that his fellow musicians regarded him 'as the main man'. His technique might not have been on a par with Coltrane's, but his ability to make the music express every feeling known to man was, Alan thought, extraordinary. Every note he shaped seemed to have a specific intent. As the night progressed, the player and his instrument seemed to merge into one fused embryo of sound and sensation. His stooped figure and hunched shoulders almost enfolded his instrument in what seemed like a lover's protective embrace. It was past midnight when, as he crept into the peripheral phrasings of *Body and Soul*, and swelled into what sounded like a bearing of the soul, and an ache for understanding, that Alan felt a profound surge of empathy with this young man about whom he knew nothing.

As the night wore on Alan got into conversation with one of the bartenders, who, it turned out, had left Dunmanway, in County Cork, for New York over thirty years earlier.

'Who's the kid on the sax?' Alan asked him.

The barman mentioned a name, and then added, 'but they call him 'Preach'.

'I guess it's short for preacher. The funny thing is, he hardly ever says a word, but they joke that every time he plays that saxophone, it's like he's preaching a sermon – you know – like he's sending a message. And he always wears black.'

'I like it.' Alan nodded. 'You know something? He preaches my kind of 'sermon''.

As he left the bar in the early hours of Monday morning, Alan felt a strange sense of liberation. Despite the raw chill of the New York November night, and the lateness of the hour, he felt like walking. He made his way towards Washington Square, and continued east. As he reached the corner of Broadway he noticed a group of three girls standing about. He figured they were in their late teens, and it crossed his mind that they didn't seem dressed for the weather. As he drew level with them, one of them left the group and approached him, saying,

'Looking for a little fun, honey?'

She took him by surprised. He'd never been propositioned like this before, and it took him a few moments to realize that the girl was selling sex. He shied away from her with a rather gruff 'No'.

As he moved on rapidly, the girl shouted after him,

'What are you, queer or somethin'?', and all three broke into a harsh cackle.

The mood of the jazz bar was broken, and Alan, suddenly felling the cold, hailed a passing taxi, and returned uptown to his hotel.

That night Alan dreamed that, as he lay on a large white sheet, four men, one at each corner, were trying to truss him up and tie him in a bundle inside the sheet, but, as one of them kept dropping his corner, they never succeeded.

* * * * * * * * *

It took him a few moments to realize that it was the sound of the telephone ringing beside his bed that had dragged him awake. As he lifted the receiver he glanced at his watch – 11.02! - hours past his usual time for getting up. An American voice said,

'Call from Ireland for you, Mr Logan.'

The next voice he heard was his father's. In the brief conversation that followed Jim said he was just calling to inquire about Barry's progress – his mother was anxious to know how things were going. Alan assured him that everything seemed to be going well, and apologized, sheepishly, for not phoning home earlier, explaining that he'd had a very late night. He was not unaware of the slight rebuke in his Dad's tone. He promised to keep them posted, and they said their goodbyes.

Before moving from where he was sitting on the side of the bed he put in a belated call to his office back in Dublin, where it was now after 4.00 p.m., firstly to check if there was anything that needed his attention and, secondly, to confirm that he would need another couple of days in New York, but expected to be back at his desk later in the week.

He stepped into the shower and, as he let its reviving water pour over him for several minutes, he thought back to the previous night. It must have been 3 a.m. before the session finished and he left the bar. Perhaps it was due to the effects of more beer than he was accustomed to, but he could not recall the name of the young saxophonist whose playing had appealed to him so much, except that he was nicknamed 'Preach'.

Refreshed, he set about getting something to eat, and buying some presents to take back with him to Ireland, before visiting Barry.

When he arrived at Barry's bedside the traction had been removed, and the patient was sitting beside his bed with a set of crutches at the ready.

'How about this?' said Alan enthusiastically.

'Hi, Alan. Yes, it's all happening today. Harness gone, and I've been told to start exercising and bending the knee. It'll be a few days before I can put any weight on the right foot, but I'll be able to hobble about on the crutches, which makes a hell of a difference, especially being able to make it to the bathroom on my own. Grab a seat. You'll have me all to yourself this afternoon. Bob won't be in until this evening. He's working.'

Alan told him how he'd gone to the jazz session in the Village that Bob had mentioned, and enjoyed the music, but Bob hadn't turned up.

'I never thought he would.' said Barry. 'He always likes to turn in early on Sundays.'

Then, looking keenly at Alan, he added, 'Speaking of Bob, did Dad say anything to you about him and me?'

'Nothing more than you heard him say yourself, except he asked me, before he got on the plane, not to say anything to Mum about it.' They were silent for a few moments before Alan said, 'Do you have a problem with that?'

'No. Like I told Dad when he was here, I tried to keep it from both of them, tried to avoid upsetting them, or anyone else in the family who might find it hard to deal with. Mind you, it was a bit like trying to balance yourself on a floating barrel in a river.'

'Tell me,' said Alan, 'did you always know you were gay?'

'Kids don't 'always' know anything, especially in the Ireland we were reared in. It only dawned on me gradually, from the time that I was in my mid-teens, that there was any real significance in the fact that girls didn't attract me in the way all my school pals seemed to be attracted by them. I knew nothing about there being such a thing as homosexuality until I was about sixteen. And even then it took me ages to realize, or accept, that it was males I was attracted to. Unless you've been in that situation I don't think anyone could realize the dilemma that causes. I was scared out of my wits that anyone would find out. I had to keep it to myself, and put on a big front for the world. And the worst part was when I gradually discovered the Church's attitude to me as a homosexual person. I felt that in their eyes I was evil just by being as I was.'

'Is that why you eventually stopped practising your religion?' asked Alan.

'I don't think it was as simple as that. When you're brought up to believe that something is absolutely right, the way we were taught that the Catholic religion was absolutely right, you sort of want it to be right. It becomes part of you, like being Irish, or being a Logan. But then, if you're like me, you discover that because of something you have no control over, the Church regards you as some sort of freak. You know what I mean. The Church tells us that we are all created by an all-powerful, all-loving, God, male and female. One or the other. Cut and dried. In other words, some of us have penises and some vaginas, and the ones with penises are only supposed to be attracted to those with vaginas, and *vice versa*. And the Church not only refuses to recognize that things don't always turn out like that, but also threatens you with hellfire and damnation if you dare to adopt a lifestyle that fulfils your emotional needs. It's like they're telling you to believe that God created your nature, but you are to blame if it isn't as they think it should be. You're told stuff like 'if you were born blind you'd have to put up with it'. Well, I have the greatest sympathy for anyone born blind but the fact is that someone in that situation does not have a choice between seeing and not seeing, whereas someone who is genuinely gay or lesbian can choose to ignore the Church's dire warnings and enter into a fulfilling relationship, and that's what makes all the difference. If you're gay the Church regards you as 'damaged' and 'fixable', a bit like one of Dad's broken clocks that can be repaired in the right hands.' Barry paused for a moment, before adding, 'You asked if being gay was the reason I stopped practising. I think it wasn't that specifically. In my case I think that when I became aware of the Church's attitude to the likes of me, it acted as a sort of catalyst to question everything else about what I'd been taught to believe.'

'I've done some questioning myself,' said Alan, 'especially about how the Church uses fear to keep us all in line, but, unlike you, I'm like the guest at the party who's not enjoying himself, but can't tear himself away.'

'Yes,' responded Barry, with some animation. 'Fear's the trigger. When I think of how the Church has frightened children with the idea of burning in flames forever, it makes my blood boil. To be honest, I think there is something criminal about it. People are hugely concerned nowadays about how children are being psychologically damaged for life after being inducted into religious cults, and subjected to systematic programming based on fear and dependency. I can't see much difference between that and what we were exposed to as children. If you feed people enough fear, they can't think straight. And fear is never far from the menu when it comes to religion, unfortunately. It's a sort of spiritual terrorism. There seems to me to be something fundamentally questionable about a theology based on the spectre of eternal damnation in fire, from which you can be delivered only if you allow your thoughts and actions to be controlled by those who preach that idea. That, it seems to me, sets up a dynamic of terror and rescue, fear followed by hope, worry relieved by reassurance and surrender, a cycle of dependency which prevents us growing up and becoming adults in our own right, because we are forever looking beyond our own conscience to someone else's moral code, which rebukes and rewards us. To my mind it's a recipe for spending your life trying to minimize fear.' This was delivered with increasing verve.

Alan had not expected such a vehement reaction from his brother. He realized that he had touched a very raw and sensitive nerve. He had never seen Barry quite so impassioned about anything before. Anxious to show his solidarity he said, pointedly, 'I can certainly relate to that.'

As if by some unspoken agreement between them there was silence for about thirty seconds, while the level of intensity of their discussion deflated. Barry was the first to speak again. In a more composed manner he said,

'Alan, I know that Mum and Dad were upset when I gave up going to Mass and confession, and all that, and they blamed it on me being badly influenced by life in the university. They were wrong. It had nothing to do with anything I was involved in at university, but I guess it suited me to let them think that way. What really happened was that I just became so demoralized by the Church's constant harping on about sin and damnation and hell, that I had to make a decision between living my life in a more or less permanent state of intolerable despair by continuing to attend church and listening to that stuff week in and week out, or by removing myself from its influence, to give myself a chance of a reasonably happy way of life. If I say I chose the latter it doesn't mean it happened all of a sudden. It's not like you 'lose your faith' all of a sudden. At least, it wasn't that way for me. For me it was more like my belief, once it had been shaken and I started to question various things, faded gradually, like when snow, that's been around for weeks, starts to melt. You can't stop snow melting. Eventually there's no snow left, and, for me, eventually the formal, organized religion I grew up with all around me wasn't there anymore. My own intelligence, my own reason, could not endorse much of what I had been taught as being 'true'. And why should it honour God to place faith above reason? Is reason no less a gift of God than faith?' He paused before adding, 'I live my life without it now'.

'A brave decision,' Alan interjected.

Barry became pensive for a moment, before responding.

'I think it was difficult rather than brave, really. It would probably have been brave in the old days when they put you on the rack for expressing such views, and kept you there until you told them what they wanted to hear, even if everyone involved knew it was a sham. For me it was a way of surviving.'

Alan was fascinated to hear these revelations from his brother. He had never before heard him express himself in such a transparent and telling manner, or expose the depth of his inner feeling. It was a side to his brother, an introspective dimension, that he never knew existed. He was learning more about him than he had learnt in the twenty-nine years he had known him. He felt an urge not to let this unique situation end. He prompted Barry with another question.

'I'm intrigued. Tell me, do you have any belief now?'

Barry was thoughtful for a few moments before responding.

'Let me put it like this, Alan. When I started to feel a sense of alienation inside me towards the formal religion I'd been brought up to believe in, I was almost too scared to even admit to myself that I had such feelings. I couldn't just walk away from everything I'd been taught. It was too important to me, too much a part of me. I realized pretty quickly that I owed it to myself to try to give what I'd been taught some serious, objective examination, rather than just ignore it and hope it would go away. I knew that wouldn't work for me. I needed to figure things out for myself. And that's what I did, or, at least, tried to do.' Barry paused.

'And?' Alan prompted him again.

'And,' said Barry, his face softening into a smile, 'right now I need to visit the bathroom.' He rose on his good leg, and reached for the crutches beside him. 'I haven't quite come to terms with these contraptions just yet,' he said, jokingly.

'Can I help?' Alan offered.

'I think I can manage, but you could walk beside me in case I need a hand.'

It took about ten minutes before they were back seated at Barry's bedside. Alan sat for a moment hoping that this interruption to their conversation would not mean the end of Barry's reflections. Again, he took the initiative.

'I hope you don't mind my persistence, but I'm intrigued by what you were saying, especially at what conclusions you came to?'

'No. That's okay,' said Barry. Again, he took a moment to gather his thoughts. 'I guess that the main thing that occurred to me was that, in the great scheme of things, the believability bar had been set too high for me to finally regard it as really credible. What I mean is, the Church teaches that God created the universe so that He could bring human beings into existence, who would have a body that would die after living for a short time on Earth, and a soul that would live forever, either in a place of indescribable joy, heaven, or unimaginable horror, hell. Essentially, the theology is, human beings are what creation is all about. But, if you imagine the whole of creation up until now as a twenty-four hour day, human beings have only been around for a second or two at most in all that time, for far less than one million of the approximately 15,000 million years the universe has been in existence. And, apparently, the chances of us, as a species, being around for any significant length of time are infinitesimal – another second or two on the cosmic clock. Well, bearing that in mind, it seems to me that it is extraordinarily arrogant of human beings to imagine or believe that they are the sole reason for creation, for the entire universe.'

Barry paused to move his injured leg to a more comfortable position..

'Then,' he continued, 'take the Earth. For ages it was believed to be the centre of the universe. But it turns out that not only is it not the centre of the universe, it is not even the centre of the solar system, and the star it spins around, the Sun, is a quite insignificant star among billions of others, with even more billions of planets spinning around them. And we are supposed to think that we are the only sentient beings in all that space, that we are the ones for which all this was brought into being. Maybe. But it does seem a bit extravagant.'

And why would an all-loving Creator decide on a scheme that included such a horrible process as death? Is it loving to subject people, every day of their lives, to the knowledge that death awaits them at any given moment, or that they may have to suffer the grief of enduring the deaths of those they love? And the concept of there being three 'persons' in God, and one of them having to come to Earth to be tortured and killed in the cruellest manner, as the only way to save human beings from hell, confuses me entirely. I can't imagine a human father, worth the name, asking that of a son, much less an all powerful, all loving God the Father, requiring such an horrific ordeal of His Son as the only way to make up to Him for the wrongs of humanity. It seems to amount to a kind of divine endorsement of torture and physical cruelty. And the same could be said about God creating and endorsing the whole concept of hell. That theology seems to me to sanction and encourage the attitude that violence and torture is acceptable in human society, to offer a great precedent to tyrants to justify their cruel behaviour – you know – an 'If God does it to punish the 'bad', why shouldn't I?' sort of argument.'

Barry paused, and looked away. Alan, who was fascinated by this insight into his brother's thoughts, made no comment, sensing that Barry had more to say. After several moments Barry turned again to look at Alan, and said,

'Having said that, it's possible that everything the Church tells us to believe may be true. But I can only say I don't know, one way or the other. I would agree that absence of evidence is not evidence of absence, but I can't see the point in saying you 'believe' in something if you don't know for sure. It's dishonest, in my view. And God, if He's about anything, should be about honesty. Gullibility is not piety. I hate the thought of living according to some false illusion - of living in a fool's paradise, or perhaps I should say a fool's hell. Is there an afterlife? Is there a heaven or a hell? I don't know. If there is, I wish God had found a clearer way to let us know. They say the three great virtues are faith, hope and charity, but faith can seem remarkably like fantasy, and hope is the gambler's best friend. It's the third one that does make sense to me, charity, love, summed up in the golden rule – treat others as you would like them to treat you.'

He became reflective again, for a few moments, before adding,

'It's a pity Jesus didn't leave His own written, clear record of what exactly He had in his mind, especially what He knew about such issues as hell and eternal damnation, if He knew about those things. It would surely have saved an awful lot of confusion and argument.'

'I never thought of that,' said Alan. 'And strange too, when you think about it.'

'How do you mean?' Barry asked.

'Well, if you accept that Jesus' mission on Earth was the most important communication between God and mankind, it seems odd that God didn't ensure that Jesus, who, according to the Gospels, was clearly able to read and write, didn't write His message down, especially when you remember that Jesus was following in a tradition that placed great value on written records, and from which Jesus often quoted, or read out passages.'

'Yes,' said Barry, ' and when you think of it, it's a tradition that was followed by His companions and contemporaries also, - Peter, Paul, Matthew, John, James, for example, and, apparently, about thirty others of His contemporaries whom the Church doesn't recognize as authentic. Why not Jesus Himself?'

'It would make you wonder,' said Alan.

'It would indeed,' said Barry, 'but, when all is said and done, the majority of people throughout the ages seem to have believed in some sort of spirit world, so I think it would be unreasonable for me to say I believe that such a world couldn't exist. I guess I get some comfort in thinking of myself as an optimistic agnostic, and I still say one prayer everyday - 'Please God, if there is a God, save my soul, if I have a soul'.

Barry's features softened again and, with a self-deprecating chuckle, he added,

'So endeth the lesson for today.'

'And very interesting it was,' said Alan. 'The thing that causes me most difficulty is the whole notion of hell. You know, on the one hand we have the central Christian message telling us to 'love your enemy', and on the other we have the notion that an all loving God condemns His enemies to roast in hell forever.'

'Yes,' said Barry, 'it seems totally contradictory. I remember reading that some scholars who've studied the gospels believe that hell is a place of destruction, of annihilation, and not of eternal torture. It all hinges on the word 'Gehenna', from which the word 'hell' comes. Gehenna was the name of a place outside Jerusalem in Christ's time, where a fire was always kept burning, and which was used as a rubbish dump for the city. So whatever was thrown in was destroyed by burning, and this was the metaphor that Christ was using.'

'It seems, if you'll pardon the pun, to be a burning issue with you,' quipped Alan.

Barry smiled, and then added in a reflective tone, 'Yes, but the pity is that there is nothing metaphorical in the Church's teaching about the burning that goes on in hell.' After a moment he added, 'Wouldn't it be ironic if God decided that those who frightened people, especially children, with visions of hell, were the ones to go there?'

Alan laughed at the notion, and said, 'Proper order in my view.'

After a moment Barry added, as if a light had been switched on in his head, 'Maybe we should start a campaign against preaching a doubtful and frightening doctrine, especially to children?'

'We could do worse,' Alan responded, infected by his brother's apparent eagerness. 'If we succeeded, that truly would be one giant leap for humanity.'

At that point a bell rang signalling the end of visiting time.

'Is it that time already?' said Alan, rhetorically. 'I'll drop in again this evening. It's great to see you on the mend.'

'Have you decided when you're returning to Ireland?' asked Barry.

'I haven't done anything about it yet. I was really waiting to see how you were progressing.'

'Well, as you can see, I'm doing fine now. I expect to be discharged within a few days.'

'Will you be able to take care of yourself?'

'I'm sure I'll be fine, especially with Bob's help.'

'Then I'd better be thinking about getting back home. I'll check out the flights this afternoon,' said Alan. The hospital bell rang again. 'I'd better be going. See you later.'

'Yes, see you later. Take care.'

'By the way, thanks for the chat. I thought it was very revealing, and interesting.'

'Me too.'

When Alan got back to his room, the first thing he did was to take a sheet of hotel notepaper and make a brief list of some of the comments Barry had made during their conversation. He folded the page in two, and left it on his bedside locker.

* * * * * * * * * *

When he visited Barry again that evening, Alan told him that he had booked a seat on the 7 p.m. flight to Ireland on the following day. As Bob was there he did not hang about for long, feeling that it was only fair to let the pair have some time by themselves.

As he left the hospital Alan felt pleased at how well Barry was recovering, and at having learned so much about his brother from their earlier conversation that he had never realized before. Feeling good, and remembering that it was his last evening in New York, he decided that he should not pass up the opportunity to immerse himself in one more of the city's jazz offerings. He bought a newspaper to see what was on offer and discovered that the inimitable and idiosyncratic Erroll Garner was performing in a club on 46th Street. He was late finding the place and it was packed when he arrived. He was lucky to get in. Garner was already at his piano, accompanied by bass and drums. As the legendary pianist fingered his way through labyrinthine introductions, oftentimes to the simples tunes, and wove perfectly intertwined progressions, Alan marvelled at the mind that could conceive such flowing and instant improvisations, and at the dexterity of the hands that could execute them with such effortless ease. Not only was this artist, who never learned to read music, technically unsurpassable, but he also possessed the rare ability to create every mood from sadness to elation with a handful of notes from the keyboard beneath his fingertips. Alan was mildly shocked to find himself entertaining the thought that the playing of this high priest of jazz had induced in him a feeling akin to the spiritual fervour he used to experience when, as a young teenager, he used to go with his mother to the Monday night Miraculous Medal devotions. The irony of two such diverse locations causing such similar feelings made him laugh quietly to himself. He glanced about to check if anyone had noticed, amused by the notion of what others around him would make of his train of thought. No one was paying any attention to him.

Again, it was well into the small hours before the session ended and he returned to his hotel.

The following morning he went through the routine of preparing to return to Ireland. In the course of packing he picked up the note he had left on his locker the previous day. He unfolded it, and paused for a moment as he ran his eye over the points he had listed -

>Frightening children – hell –burning.
>Spiritual terrorism.

A dynamic of fear and rescue.
A cycle of dependency.
A recipe for spending your life trying to minimize fear.
An optimistic agnostic.
Do something.

He checked out of the hotel shortly after midday, and went to visit the rapidly improving Barry for the last time. As if by unspoken mutual agreement the serious conversation of the previous afternoon was not referred to. They chatted about family and friends back in Ireland, and the differences between Dublin and New York. As Alan stood up to leave, Barry said,

'Before you go, Alan, I just want to say how much I appreciate Dad and you coming over, and being with me at this time. I hope you'll tell Dad that.'

'No problem, buddy. You know we're always there for you. Just try not to fall off any more motorbikes, right?'

'You can count on it.'

Barry raised himself on his one good leg, and they gave each other a bear-hug. There was a slight crack in Alan's voice as he said,

'Bye, buddy. Take care of yourself.'

It was 4 p.m. when Alan hailed a taxi outside the hospital, and headed for the busy, drab environment of Kennedy Airport.

13

November 1975

There must surely be few more soporific environments than the cabin of a plane on a long haul flight on an overcast November night. Alan had a window seat on the flight to Dublin, but there was nothing to see except the moonlight's reflections on the snowlike lining of the unrelieved cloud beneath the aircraft. He was airborne scarcely half an hour before he drifted into that condition, beyond reverie, for which there is no adequate word in the English language, when the mind severs contact with all physical surroundings, yet has not abandoned itself to sleep, and awareness still hangs by the thinnest thread to coherent thought. He gave up his vague attempts to keep his eyes open, and, aware only of the drone of the jet engines, and the beat of his heart as a sort of rhythmic opiate, followed whatever thoughts and images his unfettered mind was pleased to present to him.

Perhaps it was the scene beneath the plane that brought the winter of 1947 to his mind. He remembered Barry as a curly-haired two-year-old. He was recovering from measles, and had not been outside the house in two weeks. Alan had been left to mind him while their Mum had ventured out into the snow-covered streets on some errand. The two girls were preoccupied playing, and their Dad was at work. During the previous days Barry had been wrapped up warmly and brought to the bedroom window on a couple of occasions to experience for the first time the sight of snow. Seeing it was not enough for him; he wanted to touch it. But there was no way his Mum would allow him out of the house, even for a moment. Alan decided that, as Barry couldn't come to the snow, then the snow must come to Barry. Packing the snow hard he built a little snowman in the back garden, with pebbles for eyes, and a ball for a nose, and some buttons from his mother's sewing kit down the front, and a paper bag for a hat. And then he carried the snowman up to bedroom where Barry lay in his cot. Barry's eyes lost the dull expression they'd had for days, and lit up with excitement. He poked his chubby fingers into the snowman and sucked them to take away the cold. But snowmen don't like heat, and in no time the drips and puddles started to appear. Barry howled when Alan said he had to bring the snowman back to the garden or he would disappear altogether. The trail of evidence was all too clear when their Mum returned, and she scolded Alan. But she didn't tire of telling the story for a long time, and, it seemed to Alan, it wasn't told to make him look bad. Alan hadn't thought of that episode in years. It made him smile.

His musings drifted to the Barry he had just left behind. Barry on his crutches. Barry and Bob. Barry alone in New York with his secret. Barry and the motorbike. Would he go back to riding one again? Motorbike! Didn't I have a dream about Dad on a motorbike, even though he'd never ridden one in his life? Hated them. What was that about? Some kind of premonition? I've never had much time for all that sort of thing – premonitions, apparitions, superstitions, ghosts, miracles, astrology, fortune-telling, tarot cards. Mumbo-jumbo. None of it of any relevance in people's lives generally. If odd things happen, it's purely by chance. Mumbo-jum…his mind slipped beneath the surface of fuzzy coherence, and into the realm of dream-world images. Two figures moved against a background of white. Wearing skis. Leaning on ski poles. Barry in black, and a woman in sky-blue. Can't see her face. Barry now pointing a ski pole at the sky. He is saying something, but frustratingly, it is somewhere between inaudible and incomprehensible. The woman's face comes into view. It's Lucy. Barry shouts. Lucy falls flat on the snow and quickly sinks out of sight. And now a small child in a long, brown, fur-trimmed coat stands alone looking down into where Lucy disappeared. The dream focuses on trying to see what the child is looking at, but, despite striving and straining to get closer, the scene remains at a constant distance from the dreamer. Alan shouts out, trying to attract the child's attention…and hears a voice vaguely enter his head…

'Are you all right, Sir?'

He opened his eyes to find the bluegreen-liveried figure of a young, female flight attendant leaning towards him. 'Were you calling for attention, Sir?'

It took Alan a moment to realize what had occurred. He explained, embarrassedly, that he'd been dreaming. He was determined to stay awake for the remainder of the flight.

Gradually he pulled himself together, and regained his composure. It had been the first time he had dreamed of Lucy, and, in fact, the first time he had thought of her in weeks. And, with her memory, there resurfaced the recollection of those last few dreadful moments he had spent with her. And the old familiar feeling of guilt gripped his stomach. It was at that moment, just as he was on the point of succumbing to a bout of sullen angst, as he had always done in these circumstances in the past, that a sense of rage swept through him. His rage was swift and visceral; it ripped into what he now felt was his own weakness and dependency for allowing guilt such power over him; it flew against the misery Lucy had suffered due to her ingrained beliefs; it tore into the alienation Barry had been made to endure; it slashed and hammered against the culture of religion-based fear that reduced men and women to guilt-ridden automatons. With his rage came a feeling of power, even elation, that surprised him. He, literally, felt differently about himself, like those moments when, as a child, he had realized he could swim, or ride a bicycle unaided. He had progressed, matured. He felt as if he had made a psychological about face, as if the focus of his moral judgments had shifted its direction from being concentrated inwardly on the electric fence surrounding the forbidden territory called 'guilt', to being directed outwards towards the broad horizon of personal discretion and determination. In future he would have to have the courage to be his own arbiter, to listen to his own inner voice.

These epiphanic thoughts were interrupted by the mundane arrival of the food and drinks trolley. The ritual of dispensing the meal, clearing up, and the inevitable offering of duty free items for sale, accounted for the best part of the next hour and a half. At that point passengers settled down to pass the remaining three hours or so of the flight in their various ways, some to their books and some to their blankets, others to a glass or two of beer or something stronger, some to chat or, like Alan, to simply content themselves with their own thoughts.

As the plane droned on through the night the almost eerie quietness that permeated the cabin meant that Alan struggled to keep his eyes open. To aid his determination to stay awake, and avoid risking make a show of himself again, he kept his seat upright, and took regular sips from a beaker of water he kept on the tray he left unclipped before him. He went over the events of his New York trip, and tried especially to recall the details of all that had transpired in connection with Barry. Who'd have believed, he thought, that the brother he once knew as a curly-haired two-year-old, and as an ever-smiling, ready-to-please teenager, would have had to suffer in silence so much cultural and religious alienation, or that he'd had the depth and strength of character to confront and work out his own philosophy in relation to so many issues affecting his life. It struck Alan that his understanding and knowledge of Barry, prior to his visit to New York, was so inadequate and misguided as to be positively neglectful. He tried to imagine what it must have been like for Barry as a perplexed and anxious teenager, unable to voice his confusions to anyone. Alan could not help feeling that, had he been more observant, more caring, he, as the elder brother, should have been the one in whom Barry confided. Alan recognized this thought process as his fine-tuned sense of guilt kicking in again, and the irony was not lost on him. Anyway, he thought, this was regret rather than guilt. He refocused his mind on the conversation he'd had with Barry during the previous afternoon, recalling how his brother had explained his alienation, his fear, his demoralization, his questioning and, as a survival technique, his abandonment of formal religion, as a way of getting through this life in a tolerable manner, without worrying about whether or not he was hell bound.

He particularly recalled how incensed Barry had become when he spoke about children being subjected to doubtful and frightening doctrines about God throwing them into hellfire forever, and his remark about 'starting a campaign' against such preaching. Was that possible? Wasn't there a related precedent? Hadn't corporal punishment of children been made illegal within the Irish school system through the relentless campaign waged by Dr Cyril Daly, who had shamed the teaching profession into ceasing to beat children in school, by publicly displaying in the window of a prominent Dublin shop-front the weapons they employed, sticks and leathers of all shapes and sizes? That man never got the honour he deserved, thought Alan. A true hero. He should, at the very least, have been made a freeman of the city. But the problem with psychological abuse was that you couldn't display it graphically in a shop window for everyone to see. And there was no use appealing to the Church to stop frightening children by portraying God as an utterly tyrannical figure, Who, unlike human tyrants, did not stop at killing those He fell out with, but kept them in a sentient state forever, so that they could suffer eternally the unrelieved pain of fire. The only way the Church, or State, would take notice would be if either of them were successfully sued for causing psychological damage to particular individuals. So, thought Alan, the only hope for progress was to make it a civil issue, a mental health issue, a *rights* issue. Maybe, he mused, there might be something in the Constitution, or the United Nations Children's Charter, that would be useful. These thoughts wafted through his head as the plane flew high through the night sky. He smiled grimly to himself when it occurred to him that such notions were probably 'pie-in-the-sky'.

These preoccupying recollections were curtailed as the lights in the cabin flickered into life, and the captain announced that they were approaching Shannon Airport. Alan was aware that all transatlantic flights to Ireland had to make a mandatory stop at Shannon. What he was not prepared for, as it was his first experience of it, was the fact that all passengers, the vast majority of whom were bound for Dublin, were obliged to disembark, before resuming their journey. And so, at 6 a.m. Irish time, he, like everyone else on board, was obliged to leave the relative comfort of the plane's interior and face out into the wintry chill of a dark, cold November morning, as they made their way to the airport's bleak, cavernous holding area, where the weary, yawning, stretching travellers were supposed to be delighted to have the chance to do some duty-free shopping. Having, for the most part, sat huddled like refugees in bewildered, disconsolate little groups for an hour and a half, they were released to resume their twenty-minute flight to Dublin.

It was approaching 9 a.m. when Alan emerged into the arrivals area at Dublin airport. He was making his way towards the taxi rank, when, to his surprise, he heard his sister Terry's voice calling his name. She greeted him with a sisterly embrace and explained that she'd come to collect him, and take him to their parents' home where his Mum, Dad and Amy were waiting to hear his news about Barry. When he opened the passenger door of Terry's car a newspaper lay on the seat. As he bent to remove it she said,

'That's for you. It's a few days old, but there's an item on page five that may be of interest.'

'What about?' asked Alan.

'An old friend of yours,' was the cryptic answer.

Alan let it go. He wasn't in the mood for guessing games. All he said was,

'Thanks for picking me up. It's a nice surprise. I didn't expect anyone to be here. I'd intended to get a taxi home, get a few hours sleep, and head for the office later.'

'Well, you know Mum,' said Terry. 'She'll want to hear everything about how Barry is.'

'I'm sure I haven't anything to add to what Dad has had to say already.'

'Well, you know yourself, getting information from Dad can be like getting blood from a turnip. A man of few words at the best of times.'

As he stepped out of the car outside his parents' house he was still holding the newspaper Terry had given him. She suggested that he leave it in the car and take it with him when she dropped him to his own house later.

'If you take it into the house with you now you'll probably leave it behind you,' she commented.

Amy and his mother were already at the hall door to greet him and usher him inside. They all bundled into the kitchen, where his father was already sitting at the breakfast table. Alan and he exchanged quick nods, and a wink from his father assured him that nothing had been said about Barry being gay. Amy insisted that her mother sit at the table also, and talk to Alan, while she prepared a large Irish breakfast. As his mother sat down she nodded in the direction of her husband, and said,

'Alan, I hope you've got more to tell us than Old Chatterbox here. You'd think he was guarding state secrets for all the information we've got out of him since he came home.'

Sensing his mother's unsatisfied need for details about her far away, injured son, Alan tried over the following hour to recount everything of the smallest significance regarding Barry's accident, operation, treatment and progress. He ended by assuring her that Barry was very well and in great spirits, and was confident that he would have no long-term serious effects from his injuries.

'Oh, thank God for that. I'm relieved to hear that.' And, indeed, she did seem to be a lot less anxious than she had been when Alan first arrived.

Eventually he made his excuses to leave and, as promised, Terry drove him to his own home. It was almost midday by the time they parted company. Although he would happily have given in to his tiredness and gone to bed, he felt obliged to put in an appearance at the office before the day was out, and knowing that if he lay down then he would probably sleep for hours, he decided to take a reviving shower, put on fresh clothes, and head for work. Nothing of great urgency awaited his attention at the office, and on the stroke of five o'clock he left his desk, went home directly, and fell into bed. He slept solidly for almost twelve hours.

It was not until he got home from work the following evening that he got around to opening the post that had accumulated in his absence, and eventually to picking up the newspaper that his sister had given him. He went to page five. There, in a group photograph of six smiling people, four women and two men, he recognized Heather, whose surname was given as Pritchard. They were, the caption explained, some of the teaching staff appointed to a newly opened Community School in south Dublin. Heather was described as Vice-Principal. Alan was quite astonished, and very curious. He stared blankly at the photograph for a few minutes trying to imagine what chain of events could have given rise to this situation. Failing to arrive at any definite conclusion, he returned to scanning the rest of the news. There was nothing out of the ordinary – the seemingly endless fighting in Northern Ireland, political scandals, a murder trial, a cot death, inflation rising, an horrific car crash – except for one item that caught his eye. It was headed 'Canadian Child Sexual Abuse Scandal' and read, 'It has emerged that the Ontario Provincial Police are currently conducting an investigation into allegations of widespread child sexual abuse during the 1940's, 1950's and 1960's at two Ontario orphanages operated by separate Roman Catholic Orders.' The report went on to say that a spokesman for the police had stated that he feared that what had come to light, in their investigations to date, was probably something of an 'iceberg syndrome', indicating that they believed that only the tip of the problem had emerged so far, and that it would eventually prove to be much deeper than had been initially suspected.

Alan put the newspaper down. Inside him, a mixture of profound sadness, anger and impotence welled up. 'Was there no limit to the forms of violence that children had to endure?' Violence of the physical kind, which he himself had witnessed and been subjected to in school; violence of the emotionally and psychologically damaging kind, caused by the branding of grotesque and ghoulish images of hellfire on impressionable young minds, and the threats that went with them; and now the horror of incarcerated, defenceless, young children being sexually molested. It struck him as a sort of 'unholy trinity' of abuses – physical, psychological and sexual – all sharing the same evil nature. God help children, especially if this was what they could expect from those in society who were looked up to for moral leadership and guidance.

The thought of children and schools brought Heather back to mind. He could, he thought, phone her old home number and, if her mother was still there, ask for a contact number or address. But he dismissed this idea; he wasn't comfortable about making contact with Heather's family in this way after so many years. He thought he might phone her directly at the school the following day, just to say he had, belatedly, seen the newspaper photograph, and wanted to wish her well in her new post. He reasoned that this was a bit too overt. Finally he decided to send her a 'Congratulation' type card, care of the school, and this he did the following day, Saturday, with a short message, which read:

> Dear Heather,
>
> Congratulations, and good luck, on your new appointment. Needless to say I was surprised to see from the newspaper that you were back here in Dublin. I should say that I thought I saw you in the distance in the city a while ago, but figured that you were either visiting or that I was seeing things. I hope life is treating you well, and wish you every success in what I'm sure will be a very demanding job.
>
> Love,
> Alan.

* * * * * * * * *

If Alan had received no response to his card, that might have been the end of it, although his curiosity about how and why Heather had returned to Dublin might well have caused him to take some other initiative in order to find out. As it happened, he never had to make that decision.

On the following Wednesday at about 8 p.m., just as he was clearing up after his evening meal, his phone rang. In response to his 'Hello' a faintly familiar female voice said,

'Hello, Alan?'

'Yes, Alan here.'

'Alan, this is Heather. I hope you don't mind me phoning you like this, but I just wanted to thank you for your card and good wishes. It was very good of you'

Alan was momentarily taken aback. All he could utter initially was,

'Heather! What a surprise.' Regaining his composure, he added, 'No, I'm delighted to hear from you.'

'I thought it was better to phone and say thanks to you directly, rather than write back, or whatever.'

'I'm glad you did. How are you?'

'I'm well, thank you. But life is a bit hectic at present. You know, what with moving back to Ireland, and the new job, and getting the children settled, and a hundred and one other things that need sorting out.'

Alan felt reluctant to ask too many questions, in case it might seem like he was prying too intimately, but he did ask Heather if she had returned to Ireland permanently.

'That's my intention,' she told him.

The conversation continued briefly, and in a slightly stilted manner, but before hanging up Alan tentatively suggested that they might meet for lunch sometime.

'That would be very nice,' was Heather's encouraging response. 'Could I get back to you in a few days on that?'

'I look forward to it.'

Alan replaced the receiver with a mixture of apprehension and undeniable excitement.

True to her word, Heather phoned again one evening during the following week, and they arranged to meet for lunch the following Saturday at around one o'clock in the foyer of the Gresham Hotel, on Dublin's O'Connell Street.

Numerous times during the couple of days that intervened between Heather's phone call to him and the time they were due to meet, Alan tried to imagine how their meeting would go. What would they say to each other? Would it be all stiff and formal and tense? Would it be matter-of-fact? Had he made a mistake in suggesting it in the first place? Round and round he went on a mental treadmill.

Unlike other Saturday mornings, when he rose late and generally eased himself gently into the day, on this particular

Saturday he was wide awake from an early hour and, rather than continue fidgeting about from side to side, trying to get back to sleep, he decided to get up and get on with the day. He persuaded himself that he had a list of things he had to take care of in the city – new shirts he needed for work, Christmas cards to get and presents to look out for, and, remembering his conversation with Barry, figured he might look for copies of the Irish Constitution and the U.N. Charter. In the event he was in the city before 10 a.m., and, having quickly found the books he was looking for in Hanna's book shop, and spent a further desultory half hour browsing, he abandoned the notion of any further shopping, bought a newspaper, and by 11 a.m. had taken refuge in a coffee shop not far from the hotel where they were to meet. He 'read' his newspaper, remembering nothing. He kept considering what he would say when they met, what attitude he should portray? His mind raced along, but time seemed to be standing still. Eventually he hurried off to the hotel foyer, arriving much too early, as if being nearer to the place of rendezvous would make the time pass more quickly.

The minutes ticked past until at last the foyer clock showed one o'clock. But no sign of Heather. A dull feeling of disappointment started to take hold of him. He tried to reassure himself by recalling that punctuality had never been her strong suit. Disappointment was turning to incipient anger when suddenly, out of nowhere it seemed, she was greeting him, and all his frustrations vanished. She apologized for being late, mentioning something about children and Saturday sports. His greeting was neither familiar nor formal. As he directed her to a secluded table in the hotel's restaurant he thought she seemed quite relaxed, which made him feel more at ease.

Also, he thought she looked wonderful. It had been over twenty years since he had been this close to her and, yes, those extraordinary blue eyes were as he remembered, though a little deeper set, and perhaps a little more worldly wise. And the lovely blond hair, still striking, though now styled differently – short, instead of the flowing mane he remembered – and perhaps not quite so lustrous. Her skin still held that clear, pale, creamy quality that had so attracted him all those years ago. She was now, he thought, a beautiful woman, as opposed to the radiant teenager he had previously known, and who had disappeared so abruptly from his life so long ago. When they were seated he looked at her very directly and, almost involuntarily, said,

'You look great.'

'Thank you, Alan, but after the way I've been rushing about this morning, I'm sure I look a wreck.'

'How are you for time? Not too constrained, I hope.'

'No. I'll have to pick the children up later, but I'm free until around four.'

'Great.' This slight reference to her family prompted a host of questions in his mind. He had an almost overwhelming desire to know everything about her circumstances all at once, but restrained himself from appearing too impulsive.

He beckoned a waiter and they ordered drinks. As the waiter retreated Alan looked at her again, and asked,

'So, how many children have you? I seem to remember Philip Ffrench – you remember Philip? – telling me years ago that you had two, a boy and a girl. Is that right?'

She nodded. 'That's right. Just the two. Olive and James. Olive is fifteen now, and James is thirteen. He was named after his father.' Alan could not resist the opening,

'And your husband? A naval officer I seem to recall. How does he like it here in Dublin?'

A wry, half smile played across Heather's mouth.

'Same old Alan. You don't beat around the bush, do you?' she teased him, before adding,

'James and I split up three years ago. Basically, with his career in the Navy he was seldom home, and, after ten years of that we just grew apart. There's a pretty high casualty rate among naval marriages. Anyway, we decided to divorce. It was all very civilized. Mutual agreement, and all that.'

Alan's heart gave a little bounce at this news. Despite this he said,

'Sorry to hear that, Heather.' And immediately felt like a hypocrite.

The half smile was back on Heather's face, as if she'd sensed his less than unbiased reaction.

'Are you, Alan?'

'Well, one is always sorry to hear of relationships breaking down, especially when children are involved,' he defended himself.

The drinks arrived – gin and tonics for both of them – and the waiter presented them with menus. They raised their glasses in mutual salute and tasted their drinks. After a moment Alan said,

'How did your children react to the break-up?'

'Pretty well, I guess, all things considered. Like I said, they hadn't seen their father all that much over the years. In reality it'd been them and me for the most part, with help from nannies and child minders. But Jim – their father - was always good in terms of looking after their material welfare, and still is.'

'And how are they settling down here in Ireland?' he asked.

'Too early to say, really. Olive seems to be adjusting to the change better than James so far; she gets on very well with her granny, who spoils her shamelessly. James is missing his cricket and his football. We've only been here since June, so this is their first term at school here. They get jeered over their 'posh' English accents.'

'Did you enrol them where you're teaching?'

'No. I thought that would be a bit much for them. They're attending New Park.'

'Another community school?'

'Yes. I believe in the whole co-ed, community school approach to education. It was because of my experience in that area that they offered me the job here.'

The waiter returned to take their order, but neither of them had even glanced at the menus. Alan apologized, and asked him to give them a couple of minutes. They concentrated on the menu, and after making their selections, and placing their orders, Alan, still teeming with questions, said,

'So, how did you manage to end up teaching here? I thought the Department of Education wouldn't allow you to teach here unless you were fluent in Irish, which was the reason you went to teach in England in the first place, was it not?' This came out, unintentionally, sounding more like an accusation than a question, and Alan winced inwardly as he noticed Heather stiffen slightly. He hastened to explain,

'Sorry. There was no ulterior meaning intended there. I hope I didn't upset you.'

Heather expression softened. 'No problem, Alan. To be honest I think you have every right to be miffed over what happened at the time I went to England, but before we get into all that let me tell you how I've, as you've put it, ended up teaching here.'

She explained how she'd been teaching in a Comprehensive in Portsmouth since she'd qualified. After the divorce, three years earlier, her mother, who was living alone in the family home, but who was getting on in years, encouraged her to return to Ireland with the children, and live with her, on the basis that the family home would be signed over to her. Her two brothers, one of whom had emigrated to South Africa, where he had a very successful career as an architect, and the other, who was a lecturer in Aberdeen University, had no objections; in fact, both had given the suggestion their wholehearted support. The offer was tempting, but there was the problem of how she would find suitable work. She checked regarding the fluency in Irish regulation, and found that it still applied. But she also learned that three-month intensive courses in the language were available in Irish speaking areas. She had applied for her present job, and, on the basis of her experience in the Comprehensive system in England, and the fact that she had been teaching at A Levels standard, she had been offered the appointment subject to a proficiency test in Irish before the academic year started. She registered for a course in the Irish speaking area of Ring in County Waterford, and, along with her children, had spent the months of June, July and August there, and had reached the standard of proficiency in the language required by the Department of Education.

'And that, as you might say, is how I've ended up here,' she quipped, tongue in cheek.

Alan smiled lamely. He was pleased that she felt sufficiently at ease with him to tease him gently in this way. There was, he felt, a touch of intimacy about it that made him feel good.

Their meal arrived. After eating in silence for a few moments she said, 'You mentioned Philip Ffrench. Do you still see each other?'

'Very rarely, unfortunately. Philip was offered a very good research position in London a couple of years ago, and he's still there. We get together whenever he comes over here on a visit.'

While they ate she enquired about his parents and siblings, and he brought her up to date with the various marriages and births over the years, mentioning that it was his sister, Terry, who had drawn his attention to the picture of her that had appeared in the newspaper; and he told her about Barry's accident, and his very recent trip to New York to see him. She asked about his work, and he told her he was still with the same bank that he had left Dublin Glassware to join.

At the mention of the Lattimore's old firm a slight awkwardness developed between them. She glanced at him with some apprehension, trying to determine if, this time, there was an ulterior meaning in his comment. He realized this, but this time he did not apologize. He held her gaze and, placing his knife and fork on the table, said with quiet deliberation,

'Tell me, Heather, what happened?'

For a moment she thought of prevaricating, of pretending she didn't understand his question, but dismissed this as being childish and silly. She also put down her knife and fork, placed both elbows on the table, folded one hand into the other, and rested her chin on the arch they'd made.

'It's hard to remember exactly after twenty years.'

'That's a cop out, Heather. I have no difficulty remembering. I remember very clearly getting a letter from Southampton dismissing me from your life.'

He could see immediately that she was taken aback at his directness, and, once again, although he was tempted to say something conciliatory, he resisted. Through tight lips she said,

'You could have followed me.'

'I had the distinct impression that that would have been a complete waste of time.'

There was silence for a few moments, while the tension sat between them. She was the first to speak.

'You're probably right. You must have been very hurt if you can still be angry after twenty years.'

'I was. I think I've been angry ever since, actually.'

'All I can tell you is that my father exerted enormous pressure on me. It was made quite plain to me that if I hadn't done what he wanted, and stopped seeing you, I'd have been ostracized. Remember, I was only eighteen. I just couldn't handle it.' She stopped to take a sip of water, and then continued, 'That may sound lame now, but at the time it was hugely distressing.' After another pause, while she seemed to be visualizing the events they spoke of, she added, 'I guess I panicked. Perhaps I could have been...'

He reached across the table and took her by the arm, squeezing it gently.

'Don't say anymore, please.' He had a distinct feeling of being lighter in himself, as if by some unseen hand a heaviness he had been unconsciously carrying around had been lifted.

An emotion-filled few moments of silence settled between them. Raising her eyes to him, she said,

'I think I've been wanting to tell you that for twenty years. I hope it makes some sense. I hope you understand.'

'I do.' After pausing for a moment, he added, 'You know, come to think of it, I've also been wanting to have this conversation for a very long time.'

Any element of tension, formality or artificiality, that had existed between them evaporated. As they continued their meal they reminisced about the past. She broached the subject of his marriage, and of Lucy's death, and that of the baby, and he responded quite freely, unselfconsciously and undramatically, confining himself to the essential facts, but avoiding his role in Lucy's last moments. They talked about their plans for Christmas, now only a few weeks away.

'Have you been buying presents?' she asked, nodding towards the bag he had left on the spare chair at their table.

'No, actually. That's just some stuff I got for myself.'

'Hanna's Bookshop. Same old bookworm, then?' she said, giving him a small smile. 'Anything interesting?'

He told her what he had bought, and about his conversation with Barry that had led him to get these particular items.

'I didn't mention it earlier when we were talking about the family, but when I was visiting Barry in New York with my father we discovered that Barry is gay. We haven't told my mother, by the way. When I spoke to Barry on his own he told me that he had given up his religion. He said he couldn't deal with being reminded of the fear that had been implanted in him by the Church's teachings when he was a kid. We spoke about what a great thing it would be if the Church, or indeed Churches, could be prevented from frightening people, children especially, with dubious, unprovable notions and images of hell.'

'Wow! A weighty subject,' said Heather. 'But you were right to say 'churches'. The Catholic Church was not the only one to wallow in that type of terror tactics. My own father would have been a great follower of, you know, the Ian Paisley school of fire and brimstone.'

'Indeed?' said Alan, pointedly.

'Oh yes. A real stickler for the straight and narrow, and retribution and all that stuff.'

Alan raised his eyebrows in mock surprise, and said euphemistically, 'Not a man to be argued with, then?'

'Oh no. Not a man to be argued with,' she replied with quiet emphasis.

With that she glanced at her watch, and announced that she had to be on her way. The children would be waiting.

'Is it that late already. I can hardly believe how quickly the afternoon has slipped by,' said Alan, genuinely surprised.

As they walked from the restaurant they both said how they had enjoyed themselves. Unwilling to leave it at that, Alan asked her if she would like to do the same again sometime.

'I'd love to, Alan. Call me.'

'Great. After Christmas, perhaps?'

'I'll look forward to it.'

He arrived home in a mood of quiet elation and, feeling as if he had cause for celebration, he treated himself to a generous measure of Remy Martin, put John Coltrane's *Giant Steps* album on the turntable and, as the day faded into evening around him, fell into a pleasant reverie.

The following morning, Sunday, just as he returned home from midday Mass, the phone rang. It was Barry calling from New York, and sounding in excellent spirits, even though, for him, it was scarcely 8 a.m.

'I though this would be a good time to catch you at home,' he explained.

He was, he said, phoning to thank him again for travelling to New York to be with him in his hour of need, and to let him know that he was back walking unaided, and feeling fine. As they chatted Alan told him about Heather, and how he was hoping to see her again soon.

'Hey, that's good news,' Barry said, 'I just hope you don't end up getting hurt again.'

'Thanks for the warning! I promise to be careful. By the way, before I met Heather in the city yesterday, I got copies of the Irish constitution, and the United Nations Children's Charter. You know what I'm talking about – the conversation we had in the hospital?'

After a moment's hesitation, Barry said,

'Yes, I remember. You're taking this pretty seriously?'

'Well,' Alan explained, 'I guess I feel that frightening kids unnecessarily, and leaving them psychologically scarred for life is a serious business, and I'm curious to check if there's anything in these documents that might help to put a stop to it. That's worth doing, don't you think?'

'I do indeed,' said Barry. 'You must let me know if you discover anything worthwhile.'

When they'd finished their conversation Alan went in search of his purchases, and found them on a hall chair where he had absentmindedly dropped them the previous afternoon. He took the two items from the Hanna's bag and carried them through to the sitting room, and settled down to examine the contents. He started with the Irish Constitution. There, in the section on Social Policy, he read that

> The State shall strive to promote the welfare of the whole people by securing and protecting as effectively as it may a social order in which justice and charity shall inform all the institutions of the national life.

Strive; promote; welfare; whole people; securing; protecting; justice; charity…Fine words. Surely, he thought, under the direction of the right legal mind these words could be made to make the State responsible for protecting its citizens, especially vulnerable, impressionable children, against psychologically damaging teachings based on unprovable depictions of the horrors of hell, and if it neglected that duty it should suffer the consequences in terms of compensating those whose lives had been affected by such teachings. The issue was, it occurred to him, more one of health than of anything else, and the State should insure that there were laws in place, and enforced, to prevent gratuitous, psychological injury to its citizens, just as it had laws against physical injury. The fact that one type of injury could not be seen while the other could, did not make it any less real.

Turning his attention to the U.N. *Declaration of the Rights of the Child*, he found a few statements on the subject he was interested in

> Whereas the child, by reason of his physical and mental immaturity, needs special safeguards and care, including appropriate legal protection....
>
> Proclaims this Declaration of the Rights of the Child to the end that he may have a happy childhood....
>
> The child shall enjoy special protection, and shall be given opportunities and facilities, by law and by other means, to enable him to develop physically, mentally, morally, spiritually and socially in a healthy and normal manner and in conditions of freedom and dignity....
>
> The child shall be protected against all forms of neglect, cruelty and exploitation.

Again, thought Alan, surely any lawyer worth his or her salt could demonstrate that indoctrinating young minds with horrific images of possibly being thrown into fire forever when they died, was a clear breach of the rights of children as set out in this

Charter? He marked the relevant passages. He'd photocopy them in the office and send them to Barry.

* * * * * * * * * *

Although Alan was kept busy at work during the following days with various items that needed his attention after his trip to New York, he found himself regularly preoccupied, either thinking about Heather or with the question of how to go about finding out if it were possible to do something effective about the issues he had discussed with Barry. After mulling this over for about a week, he decided to seek the advice of Peter Baxter, a solicitor whom he had known for many years. Peter was a partner in the firm of Wilson, Lawford and Good, that acted for the bank. Alan had first got to know him during his days in the bank's Audit Department, specifically regarding matters of fraud that were discovered occasionally. Later, on the few occasions when Alan bought property, it was Peter who handled the conveyancing. The two men got on well together, and Alan had a high regard for Peter's ability.

'Good morning, Alan. Bought another house, have you?' Peter's first words, when he took Alan's call, were typical of his breezy manner.

'Good morning, Peter. No, actually. But I'm not phoning on bank business either. I wonder if you might be free sometime during the next few days? There's something I'd like to get your opinion on.'

'Sounds intriguing?'

'Well, it's just something I'd like to talk to you about privately, rather than on the phone.'

'I know I'm in court in Cork tomorrow. The case could take a couple of days. Just let me check the diary for today.'

Before Alan could respond, he was gone from the other end of the line. When he returned he explained that he'd be tied up until around 5.30.

'I'd be happy to see you then, if that suit's you?'

'That would suit me perfectly, if you're sure you don't mind being delayed?'

'No problem. I'll see you then.'

The offices were closed when Alan arrived, but Peter was waiting in the foyer to open the door. Peter was of medium height, pencil-thin, wiry and dapper. He always looked liked he had just stepped out of a draper's window, Alan thought. They had not seen each other since Lucy's funeral, and as they went up in the lift to Peter's room, he asked Alan how he was coping. Alan, avoiding detail, assured him he was doing fine.

When they reached his room, Peter indicated that they'd sit at the small conference table that stood to one side of the office.

'I appreciate you seeing me like this, Peter. The matter I'd like to ask you about is not urgent. It won't take long.'

'I'm in no hurry, Alan. Take as long as you like.'

Alan explained what was on his mind, while Peter listened attentively. He then handed Peter an envelope with photocopies of the relevant extracts from the Irish Constitution and the U.N. Children's Charter, and said that, specifically, he would like an opinion on whether or not they could be used to bring about the change he had in mind, and if so, how to go about achieving that.

'I'll just take a look at these,' said Peter.

He read through the photocopies and, placing them on the table before him, said,

'You've given this some serious thought, haven't you?'

'Well, I believe it's a serious matter. It's about time human beings got past inflicting gratuitous, and pointless, anguish on each other, and if we're not yet civilized enough to stop doing that voluntarily, then I think it's reasonable to investigate if there might be some other way, or ways, to make those who promote this kind of abuse accountable for their actions.'

After a moment's quite consideration, Peter bent over the table and started to fold up the papers Alan had brought to him. As he did so he said,

'I'll tell you what I'd like to do, Alan. I'd like you to leave this with me for a few days – let me think about it, and speak to one or two of my colleagues here in the firm. You know I'll be away tomorrow, possibly the following day also. Perhaps if I were to get back to you after the weekend – how does that sound?'

'Sounds fine, Peter. I didn't expect any instant answers.'

Their business finished for now, Peter accompanied Alan to the lift. As they descended Alan became conscious of being flushed with a sense of excitement at having, at last, done something positive about this issue. They shook hands at the front door, and Alan stepped out into the chilly December evening. An Angelus bell in the vicinity announced that it was six o'clock.

* * * * * * * * *

Although he felt quite confident that Peter would do as he had said, Alan was surprised when two weeks passed without any contact. It was now mid-December, and Christmas was rapidly approaching. On the third Friday after their meeting, just as he was preparing to leave the office for the weekend, his phone rang. The switchboard operator told him there was a Mr Peter Baxter on the line.

'Peter, good to hear from you.'

'My apologies, Alan, for taking so long in getting back to you. I can only offer the excuse that I've been extremely busy, but I have not been idle on your behalf.'

'I'm delighted to hear that.'

'I wonder if 11 o'clock on Monday would suit you to drop in here?'

'That'd be fine, Peter. I'll see you then.'

'Good. We'll have a look at the pros and cons then. See you Monday morning.'

* * * * * * * * *

An eight-foot high Christmas tree, discreetly decorated, in the foyer of Wilson, Lawford and Good, was the only visible evidence of the festive season to be seen when Alan arrived at their offices for his appointment on Monday morning. He introduced himself to the receptionist. He was expected, she said. He told her he knew his way to Mr Baxter's office.

When he arrived there, Peter had been joined by another man, Cyril Aylward, whom he introduced as his colleague. Cyril was a large, treble-chinned, rotund man, with black hair, parted to the side, and a small moustache. Looking at him beside the lean, dapper Peter, Alan could not help thinking – 'Laurel and Hardy'. He managed not to show his amusement. They sat at the conference table, and Peter explained that Cyril was more *au fait* with the law in the particular area of interest to Alan.

'I must say,' said Cyril, 'I find your query fascinating, but I'm not sure if I can give you much in the way of encouraging news.'

Sensing the deflating effect his remark seemed to have on Alan, he continued,

'However, there are angles that may be worth exploring. Perhaps we could talk about the United Nations first?'

'Yes, by all means,' Alan encouraged him.

'As I see it, there are two issues to examine in considering whether or not the U.N. could be useful in protecting people, especially children, from the harmful effects of frightening theology. The first is in relation to its own *Declaration of the Rights of the Child*, or, indeed, any other article of its various charters. Could anything in these documents be judged, legally, to provide the protection we are talking about? That's a question that would have to be decided upon before a court of law. Unfortunately, the U.N., as an entity, is not answerable to any court, and therefore there is no mechanism for following that course. We must bear in mind that the U.N. is an association of nations – the ultimate 'country club' if you will.' He chuckled, and wobbled slightly, at his small joke. 'This, in effect, means that if any member nation, Ireland for example, desired that the U.N. should spell out more explicitly this type of protection, it would, through its U.N.

representative, be required to go through the proper procedures - propose a motion, get the necessary backing *et cetera*. So, in our case, our first port of call would be the Department of Foreign Affairs here in Ireland. Quite frankly, in my view, the chances of the Irish government taking any initiative, which might put it on a collision course with Roman Catholic theology, is extremely unlikely. The Department, on behalf of the Government, would, if they were to give it any consideration at all, regard it, I believe, as stirring up a hornets' nest with the religious powers-that-be, from which they have nothing to gain in the present religious climate in Ireland.' He paused to consult some notes that lay on the table in front of him, before continuing.

'Is there,' he asked, rhetorically, 'any possibility of some other nation taking up the proposal – the U.S.A. for example? Equally unlikely, I believe, bearing in mind that the politicians would consider themselves quite mad to even think about taking on Bible-belt U.S.A. And, more than likely, the same rationale would apply to the other Christian member states. And the issue would be of little or no interest to non-Christian member nations, I'm fairly sure.'

At that moment he broke off, as tea arrived. When they were on their own again, he continued,

'In any event, even if the present regulations were regarded as strong enough to provide a basis for action, or if they were strengthened by the addition of a more explicit article, the procedure would be for one member state to propose censuring another. If that were carried, all that would happen is that some form of sanctions would be imposed on the offender, which, more than likely, would never be implemented. The fact is – the U.N. is ninety-nine per cent aspiration, and one per cent implementation.' He paused before adding,

'All in all, I'm afraid the U.N. doesn't seem to be of much use to us.'

'Which leaves us with the Irish Constitution,' said Alan

'Indeed, the Irish Constitution,' said the corpulent solicitor, happy to agree. 'And here we may be on slightly more fertile ground, but, I fear 'slightly' is the operative word. The first question we have to consider is if the wording of the Constitution is strong enough for a plaintiff to succeed in an action for damages against the State, on the basis of the State's failure to protect him or her against the alleged harm done by permitting religious institutions to teach hellfire and eternal damnation? To find out the answer it would be necessary for an individual to take an action against the State. Apart from being very expensive – the case would probably run for several days in the High Court and even one day there would cost about two years salary for the average man - it would, I believe, be extremely difficult to prove psychological damage which could be specifically related to such teachings.' He paused to drink his tea.

'And there's no other way?' Alan asked, disappointedly.

'Well,' said Cyril, flopping back on his chair, 'one could consider lobbying the government, to introduce specific legislation. The chances of that having any success in present-day Ireland would be about as good as the proverbial snowball's chance in hell, if you'll pardon the quip.' Again he chuckled and wobbled, as he glanced about seeking acknowledgement of his little witticism. 'I have no doubt that the vast majority of politicians, and political parties, in this country, would regard getting into a theological row with the Catholic hierarchy as political suicide. They will do nothing voluntarily. No. The only way to make either the State or the religious institutions pay attention is if they can be persuaded that by doing nothing it is likely to cost them money, or votes. If they see a bottomless pit, in terms of compensation for psychological damage, opening up under their feet, they'll react pretty quickly, more than likely. But, I fear, the time is not ripe for that. Not yet, anyway. But political, and religious, climates change. History has taught us that. Who knows what opportunities a change of mood in the country, at some time in the future, might bring with it?'

'Yes,' said Alan, after a moment's consideration, 'but sometimes we need to give the future a helping hand.' After a few moments' consideration, he added purposefully, 'From what you've been saying it seems that the best option is to bring an action against the State?'

'Yes,' the portly Cyril replied, somewhat surprised at the evident earnestness in Alan's tone. 'But I would emphasise again that if the plaintiff – you in this instance – were to lose such a case, you could very likely be held responsible for both your own costs and those of the State, which could amount to a very significant figure.'

Alan lowered his head and seemed to fix his gaze on a point in the middle of the table. After a few moments Peter broke the silence.

'Perhaps you'd like to think about what Cyril has told us for a while, Alan, and come back to us when you've considered the pros and cons?'

'No,' said Alan, almost inaudibly.

'No?' queried Peter, looking puzzled. 'You mean you've made your mind up not to pursue the issue?'

'No,' said Alan again, more determinedly. 'I mean I don't need a while to think about it. I'd like you to go ahead. I imagine we'll need a sympathetic barrister, and an expert in child psychology or child psychiatry. You could start the ball rolling in that direction now, if you would. I believe this needs to be done. If I lose, I lose. I'm fortunate to have property I can sell to cover the costs. It's worth the risk. Too much harm has been – is being – done through this type of abuse to let it go on any longer unchallenged.'

Both solicitors' eyebrows had shot up perceptibly during this little speech.

Peter looked from Alan to Cyril, and back to Alan, and said,

'Fine, Alan. I suggest that Cyril write to you confirming what he has outlined here, and you could then confirm your instructions to him to proceed. Are we agreed?'

'Certainly,' said Cyril. 'I'll get working on it.'

'Agreed,' said Alan.

'Good, that appears to be it for now,' said Peter, 'unless you have any more words of wisdom, Cyril?'

'No, that's about it, I think,' said the Hardy look-a-like, taking this as his cue to leave.

As he rose from his chair, the other two stood up also and, shaking his soft, plump hand, Alan thanked him for his explanations and advice.

As he accompanied Alan to the front door Peter expressed his admiration for Alan's courage. They wished each other 'Happy Christmas', and, with that, Alan was on his way.

Outside it had become unusually dull and warm for the time of year. A long peel of thunder rumbled in the distance, and seconds later sheet lightening flashed across the sky. Alan quickened his pace, hoping to make it back to his office before the inevitable cloudburst.

14

December 1975

In the weeks following their lunch together Heather was never far from Alan's thoughts. He realized that his attraction for her was as strong as it had ever been. He felt drawn to her like no other woman he'd known. But there were so many questions and complications. Did he really want to get involved again in a serious relationship? Life was quiet and uncomplicated right now. Did he want to risk changing that? She was a divorcee now. She had teenage children. She was probably still married according to the Catholic Church, and the State in Ireland. And then there was, of course, the question – would she be interested in anything other than friendship? The more he considered it the more he realized that two very distinct thought processes were vying for his endorsement; one had to do with all the prosaic practicalities and strictures of life; the other came down to one very simple fact – the attraction of one person for another. No matter what else she was – married, divorced, a parent of teenage children – Heather was Heather, a woman to whom he was attracted, and with whom he wished to be. It did not take long before he knew he would have to follow where that reality beckoned. He knew he would have to find out if she felt the same way. Otherwise he would spend the rest of his life haunted by the gnawing regret of never knowing.

As it turned out Alan did not wait until after Christmas to contact Heather again. At around 4 p.m. on Christmas Eve, just as the street lights had been switched on, he pulled his car up outside the Lattimore residence and, armed with a greeting card, a bunch of flowers and a box of chocolates, walked to the hall door and rang the bell. The girl who opened the door caused Alan to do a double take; she was a virtual clone of the teenage Heather he remembered.

'Yes?' She looked at him as if she suspected he was trying to sell something.

'Oh, you must be Olive,' he said.

The girl's face softened, but remained quizzical.

'My name is Alan. I'm a friend of your Mum's. I've brought these for her. Is she in?

Without answering, the girl half turned and called back through the hallway,

'Mum, there's someone here to see you.'

Heather emerged from the rear of the house, wiping her hands on a towel.

'Alan! What a surprise! Come in please.'

'Hello Heather. Really, I'm just dropping by to give you these, and to wish you a 'Happy Christmas'. I'm on what I call 'the grand tour' – I try to visit as many relations and friends as I can each Christmas Eve. I'm sure it's a very inconvenient time to be calling.'

'No, no. Not at all. Please come on in. Look at these!' she enthused, as she took the flowers and chocolates he held out to her. 'What a surprise! They're lovely. By the way, this is my daughter, Olive.'

'I gathered that. She is the image of you at her age. I'm very pleased to meet you, Olive,' he said as he extended his hand in greeting. A slightly bemused Olive shook his hand, said 'Hello', and retreated out of sight.

All this was happening as Heather simultaneously ushered him into a large, comfortable, antique bedecked sitting room, and directed him to a plush armchair.

'Please take a seat, and I'll be back in a moment.'

A few minutes later she returned, without her apron and the towel she'd been using, and with her hair fixed to her satisfaction. She was carrying a bottle of sherry and two glasses.

'You have time for a drink?'

'Well, I honestly didn't intend to interrupt your afternoon, and I am driving.'

'You're not interrupting anything. And it's lovely to see you. Just a little glass to celebrate?' This was said as she raised the sherry bottle in his direction.

They sipped, and chatted, for about twenty minutes, during which she enquired about his family, and especially about Barry. Alan told her about the phone call he'd got from Barry.

'He told me he was on the mend – back walking unaided, and feeling fine.'

'That's great news,' said Heather.

'Speaking of Barry,' said Alan, 'you remember I told you in the Gresham why he'd given up his religion, and about what I'd bought in Hanna's before we met for lunch that day?'

She nodded, not knowing where this was leading.

'Well,' Alan explained, 'to cut a long story short, after reading through the U.N. Children's Charter, and the Irish Constitution, I decided to take some legal advice, to check out if there might be any way to bring pressure to bear on the State, or the religious institutions, to make them responsible for the psychological damage being caused to people, especially children, through filling their heads with all that awful stuff about hell.'

'And did you have any success?' she asked.

'Well, in a nutshell, I've just instructed a firm of solicitors to start proceedings.'

Suddenly feeling a bit sententious, he added, with a wry grin, 'Not a very festive subject?'

She smiled too, but the tone in her voice was serious when she said, 'Well, I think it's a very worthy issue to take up.'

'Thank you,' said Alan, feeling pleased by her endorsement.

'You must let me know how you get on.'

With that she picked up the bottle of sherry, and indicated that they might have another drink. He suggested that it might be wiser to have coffee instead. She agreed, and went to prepare it.

When she returned she was accompanied by a tall, slim boy, whom she introduced as her son, James. He, like his sister, seemed slightly bemused, but went through the formalities politely.

'James, like you, is an avid reader. Aren't you James?'

James gave her a sort of 'let me out of here' look, but said nothing. Heather gave an awkward laugh and, turning her head towards Alan, said,

'He's probably anxious to return to his latest adventure story.' James was happy to take this as his cue to leave his mother and her friend alone. At that moment a key could be heard in the front door, and a female voice called out, 'I'm home'.

'That will be my mother back from her last minute Christmas shopping,' said Heather as she went to the hallway to meet her.

'Come and see who's here, Mum.'

A rather flustered lady of about seventy appeared in the sitting room, followed by Heather. She studied Alan inquiringly, but clearly without recognition.

'Don't you remember Alan, Mum?'

'Alan?'

Alan extended his hand in greeting.

'How are you Mrs Lattimore. I'm Alan Logan. You may remember I was at some parties here in your home many years ago with my friend Philip Ffrench, before Heather went to England?'

'Oh, yes. I remember you now. You worked for my late husband.' She looked rather quizzically from Alan to Heather.

'That's right, Mrs Lattimore. All of twenty years ago.'

After some polite small talk Heather's mother excused herself, and, plainly puzzled by Alan's visit to her daughter, left them together.

When they were alone again, Alan decided to take the plunge and ask her if she would have dinner with him some evening.

'I'd love to,' was her bright response.

They arranged for him to collect her the following Friday, as they both had family gatherings to attend during the intervening Christmas period.

And so, at 7.30 on that Friday evening, when she answered his ring at her door, Heather and Alan started their first date in over twenty years. They drove in his freshly washed and vacuumed car to one of Dublin's most prestigious canal-side restaurants, where Alan had booked a table. The meal was wonderful, and the conversation easy and interesting, and, when their waiter enquired if they would like to select a complimentary liqueur, they were surprised to see that it was already past midnight. Reluctant to break the mood of intimacy that had developed between them, they lingered over their drinks for a further hour before making their way, from the cocooned cosiness of the restaurant, to Alan's car.

When they reached her home he walked her to her front door. She found her key and, as she turned to thank him for a lovely evening, he bent and kissed her cheek. She tucked her head into his shoulder, and then, with quiet deliberation, raised her lips to meet his. They held their kiss just long enough to intimate that it might be opening a door into their future. And with that she was through her hall door and gone. When he reached his car he glanced back at the house; the hall lights were already switched off. He was alone in the crisp clear January air. But the bright brilliant stars above him never seemed so near.

It was mid-February before he got a letter from Cyril Aylward to say that he had been assigned to the case. A sympathetic barrister who specialized in constitutional law had been engaged, and was studying the brief. He would be in touch with Alan as soon as he knew the outcome.

During the weeks before Cyril Aylward's letter arrived Alan and Heather had started to see each other regularly. Each Friday evening after their week's work Alan would call to collect her from home and they'd set off to spent the evening sharing a meal, and perhaps to enjoy a concert, or a film, or a play together. What Alan enjoyed most was simply being in Heather's company, and felt happy in the knowledge that she seemed to enjoy his also. He felt enriched by the time they spent together. Occasionally, as he took his morning shower, he would smile at the realization that he had, unconsciously, been humming or whistling some old jazz tune, something he could not recall doing in years. There was, he thought, a sort of joyous background music pervading his life, since he had started to see her again. As if it was as natural as flowers appearing in the spring, the phone calls and the meetings became more and more frequent. But - and there was a but - beneath the surface of his comfortable feelings of well-being, there lurked some issues that niggled and nudged away at the back of his mind, issues that his fine-tuned Catholic conscience would have to face eventually. But for now they were rather vague and unfocused, and, like Scarlet O'Hara, he put off worrying about them 'until tomorrow'. For now life had taken on a sparkle, an interest, an excitement that he wanted to prolong, and luxuriate in, just as it was. It was a state of being, a wholeness of spirit, that he did not want to risk upsetting, or disturbing, by thinking about the wider implications of their relationship. Heather was back in his life, and he knew that he had not felt this good since the time he had first known her.

Usually his ring at Heather's front door was answered by Olive, who seemed to have made this her own special job. Her girlish, welcoming,

'Hi Alan. Come in. I'll tell Mum you're here,' always made him feel good.

James was seldom to be seen on these occasions, but a couple of times, just as Alan was closing the hall door behind him on his way in, he noticed the tall figure of Olive's younger brother leaving the sitting room, and scampering up the stairs.

After one such occurrence, as they were driving away from the house, Alan said,

'How are the kids taking to us seeing each other?' As he glanced momentarily in Heather's direction, he saw a slight look of concern cross her face.

'Oh, Olive thinks you're great. And she loves the idea of a bit of romance in her mother's life!'

'And James?'

'James, I'm afraid, is a different story. He hasn't said anything directly, but it's obvious he's not happy about it.'

'Not happy?'

'Well, kind of sullen. Seems to shun my company at the moment, and doesn't talk to me as much as he used to do. It's a bit upsetting, really.'

This news did not come as much of a surprise to Alan. But he did feel a sense of disappointment, and of concern for Heather.

They were quiet for a few moments, before Alan said,

'How about your Mum?'

'Oh, she seems to be taking it in her stride, thank goodness. You mightn't think so to look at her, but she's pretty broad-minded for her generation really.'

Alan laughed, and hearing him, Heather laughed too. To himself he thought, 'two out of three. Could be worse.' They remained quite for a while before Alan said,

'Maybe we should think about trying to do something together with the children – you know, the four of us.'

'Yes,' said Heather, as if weighing up the suggestion. 'James will be fourteen in a couple of weeks – March 22nd – it's a Saturday

– maybe we could arrange something around that?'

'Sounds like a good idea,' Alan agreed.

During the following week Alan noticed an article in *The Irish Times*, encouraging people to visit a Spanish naval ship that was due to pay a courtesy visit to Dublin on the weekend of James's birthday. He phoned Heather and asked her if she thought the children, James in particular, might be interested? They could visit the ship, and then go for a meal in the Bianconi Grill in Dawson Street – nice food, nice atmosphere, not too intimidating for kids. They could invite Heather's Mum to join them for the little celebration in the Bianconi? Heather thought it sounded like a possibility. She'd talk to the kids and see what their reaction was.

In the event James responded to the suggestion with a grudging 'Okay.' Olive and Mrs Lattimore were both pleased with the idea.

As usual, when Alan rang the bell on the Lattimore hall door around 11 o'clock on the morning of James's birthday, it was Olive who opened the door, and once again he was struck by her remarkable resemblance to the Heather he had first met. Even her open, pleasant manner and the bright intelligence reflected in her eyes, were, he thought, extraordinarily reminiscent of the teenage Heather he had known.

Everyone was ready and waiting to leave. Alan wished James a 'Happy Birthday', and handed him a present. The boy looked at the parcel, said 'Thanks', and then put it on the hall table.

'James, aren't you going to open it?' said Heather, trying to keep the irritation out of her tone.

'Oh! Okay.' He unwrapped Alan's gift. It was a set of *Biggles* books by Captain W. E. Johns. He put them back on the table, and stared at them awkwardly.

'I hope you like *Biggles*,' Alan said, pretending to ignore the uncomfortable situation.

'I do. Thanks.' Three syllables, but it was the longest string of words he had ever directed towards Alan.

As they made their way from the house, Mrs Lattimore appeared from the direction of the kitchen to say she'd meet them for lunch around two o'clock in the Bianconi Grill. And with that they left to make their way, in a rather edgy atmosphere, towards the Dublin docks, and the Spanish naval ship.

They spent about an hour touring the ship, during which James was usually about ten paces ahead of the rest of them. He seemed genuinely interested in the workings of the vessel, and, although Alan was also curious, he found it difficult to concentrate because of the boy's aloofness. Heather and Olive did their best to appear impressed with what was, for them, a less than enthralling experience.

When, as they reached the bottom of the gangway, Alan asked James if he'd enjoyed looking around the ship, he was rewarded with another monosyllabic reply. At least it was a 'Yes'; be thankful for small mercies, he thought to himself.

They drove in relative silence towards the city centre, and parked the car. As they walked to the restaurant they passed Elvery's sports shop, which prompted Alan to ask,

'Do you like sport, James?'

'Yes. I used to play cricket and football for my school in Portsmouth.'

Encouraged by the impressive length of this statement, Alan pressed on –

'Which is your favourite?'

'Cricket.' Once again James had moved far enough ahead of the group to make it virtually impossible to continue the 'conversation'.

When they reached the restaurant, on the dot of two o'clock, Heather's Mum was already waiting for them. She immediately sensed that all was not well, and avoided the obvious enquiries about how the morning's trip had gone. Although the place was bustling, they had to wait only a few minutes before being directed to a table. James sat looking about him, appearing to be fiercely interested in everything else in the place except what was happening at their table. Heather was about to loose her patience when Alan caught her eye and, with a slight shake of his head, indicated to her to hold her fire. Speaking to the side of James's head he said,

'Would you like to join a cricket club, James?'

With a distinctly disdainful look, James retorted,

'They don't play cricket in Ireland.' The implied 'you stupid person' was obvious.

At this, his grandmother who, as a rule, made a point of leaving it to Heather to deal with the children's behaviour, said, quite sharply,

'James, you're being very rude!'

The shock of his grandmother's rebuke seemed to startle the fourteen year old.

'Sorry,' he said sheepishly.

'It's Alan you should say you're sorry too,' said the grandmother, firmly.

James looked at Alan directly for the first time that day.

'Oh, I'm sure he didn't mean to be rude,' said Alan. 'Actually, James, there are quite a few cricket clubs around Dublin. In fact, a very good friend of mine, Philip, played for the Pembroke club for years. He's probably still a member, although he's been in London for the past few years. The thing is, I've met some of the people there, through Philip, and, if you like I could make enquiries about getting you in?'

James looked nonplussed. To break the silence, Heather said, 'Well, James?'

'That'd be great,' he managed, and when his mother continued to glare at him, he looked at Alan again, and said,

'Eh, thanks.'

From that point on, the atmosphere became a little easier. Later, however, when Heather and Alan were at last on their own, she summed up the day by saying,

'My God, that was uphill.'

'Yes,' Alan agreed, 'but I think it was worth it. I'll follow-up on the cricket idea. At the very least, if we can get him into Pembroke he mightn't feel quite so alienated.'

'I'm sure you're right. I just feel that his attitude today may have more to do with his reaction to you than to do with missing cricket.'

One week later James joined Pembroke. Alan had taken him down to the club on that Saturday morning, introduced him to the officials, some of whom he remembered vaguely. The man in charge of the 'under sixteens' took James under his wing, and gave him all the details about practice times, and showed him around the premises. As he drove him home, Alan talked about how he enjoyed watching cricket, or listening to it on the radio, how he was fascinated by the game's emphasis on numbers, - ten wickets per innings, six balls per over, how the runs clicked up – and its innumerable strategies, field placings, types of bowling, the effect the weather conditions, or the type of pitch, had on the game. As they parted, James said he'd cycle down to the ground the following Tuesday after school, for practice.

'Do you know how to get there?'

'I'll cycle over there tomorrow to make sure I'll know the way.' Was that a hint of excitement in the lad's voice? Things, Alan thought, are looking up.

Two weeks later, at about 10.30 on a Sunday morning, the phone rang in Alan's house. When he answered it, he was astonished to recognise James's voice, sounding quite animated.

'Hi, James.'

'Hi, Alan,' ('Alan!' - that's a first, he thought to himself) 'I'm just ringing to tell you I got picked for the under sixteen team yesterday.

'That's great, James. How did it go?'

'We won! I scored nineteen. But they let me bowl, and I got three wickets in my first over!'

'Hey, that's terrific. Thanks for letting me know.'
''Bye, Alan. Mum's here.'
'Morning, Alan.'
'Morning, darling. How about that? I'm not sure if I'm still dreaming. I'll bet you put him up to making that call?'
'No. Amazingly, you're wrong. It was his own idea. I get the impression that he's now something of a minor celebrity at the club, and he feels he has you to thank.'
'God be praised!' he said, with exaggerated animation. 'Champagne tonight, right?'
'You're on!'

* * * * * * * * * *

As the weeks passed Alan and Heather were spending more and more time together, perhaps driving out beyond the city's suburbs and strolling in the foothills of Dublin's Three Rock Mountains, as they used to do when they first met, or walking Dun Laoghaire's east pier, before settling down to a drink in a quiet corner of the Marine Bar. These evenings would invariably end in Heather's sitting room, and, although the children had usually gone to bed by then, and Heather's mother would, with unfussy old-world consideration, leave them to each other's company, inevitably they were quite constrained in showing their feelings for each other. They enjoyed the physical pleasure of their closeness as they held each other in intimate embrace; their kisses became at once less urgent and more passionate and deep; their touching and gentle stroking filled them with a warmth that pulsed through their veins like tropical heat. But there the intimacies ended.

They had been following this pattern for about three months when, one Friday evening, as Alan was parking the car outside Heather's home after being to the cinema, Heather said,

'I have a question for you which has been bothering me.'

Alan felt his heart sink.

'Tell me,' he said, fearing the worst, but anxious to know the problem.

'Well, I've been wondering why you've never invited me to your home?'

It was something that had gone through his mind many times already, but each time he argued with himself that his desire for her was too strong to be resisted in that situation, and he did not want it to happen like that; if they were ever to make love he wanted it to be an act of true significance, of commitment, not a mere sensual encounter. Or so he had told himself. But beyond this there was another reason.

He stared into the distance for a few moments, and then turned to face her directly.

'Believe me, Heather, it's not that I didn't want to. It's something I've been debating with myself, but I've kept putting off in case you might think the wrong thing.' He hesitated for a moment. 'What I want you to know is that I love you very much. I don't think I could bear to be without you again, and I simply did not want to risk doing anything that might put pressure on you, or be misinterpreted by you. It is so important to me that you think well of me. I guess it's just me being cautious – trying to make sure I get my timing right...'

As he felt her move towards him he spoke again.

'But there is something I must confess to you.'

She drew back slowly, and looking at him with uneasy and confused curiosity, simply said, 'Yes?'

In the next few minutes he told her about the last stages of Lucy's life, and his part in ending it. Finally he said,

'The fact is, I 'pulled the plug' on Lucy's life. I've never told anyone else about that before tonight. But I feel I must tell you now, otherwise I'll feel like I'm hiding something from you which you have a right to know about if we are to have a true and happy relationship in the future.'

Heather had listened patiently, and without interruption, and now, with a catch in her voice, and with an expression of compassion in her tear-moistened eyes, she said,

'Alan, how awful for you. I think what you did was heroic and humane. And I want you to know that there is no one in the world I think better of than you. There's nowhere else I want to be but with you. I love you too, very much.'

He put his arm around her and drew her close, and as they held each other tight, he whispered,

'I cannot express what a relief it is to me to hear you say that.'

She drew away from him, and smiled.

'Now do I get an invitation to your place?'

'With pleasure.'

'How about tomorrow night then? I'll make dinner. You get the wine, I'll get the food!'

'Wonderful.' They both laughed out loud as they exited the car.

When he arrived home that night he was on something of a high. The fact that he had unburdened himself of the decision he had taken in Lucy's last moments, and Heather's sympathetic reaction, left him feeling like he was no longer carrying a dead weight. As he sat contemplating the evening's events, he remembered the journal he had taken to writing during the very stressful period after Lucy's death. He went in search of it, and eventually found it in a banker's box in the bottom of the wardrobe in his bedroom. Flicking through it, the first thing he noticed was that the last entry had been made over two years previously. He sat on the bed and started to read the entries. It didn't take more than a few minutes, and when he'd finished he decided that the best thing to do was to get rid of it. The contents could be of no benefit to anyone who might discover them later. And he no longer had any need of them. There and then he tore the pages into tiny fragments and dropped them into the pedal-bin in his bathroom.

The next evening, Saturday, as he watched Heather make herself at home in his kitchen, and expertly prepare dinner, he felt that everything that was best about the world had come his way.

'Can you manage a glass of sherry between all that activity?' he asked jokingly.

'Most certainly!' she responded with mock emphasis.

He poured the sherry, and handed her a glass. He raised his glass towards her, and said,

'Thank you for being here.'

As they clinked glasses she said, 'I wouldn't want to be anywhere else. And now, you had better go and sit down well away from me, or goodness knows how this meal will turn out!'

For the next couple of hours they relaxed into the enjoyment of the food and the wine and, most of all, the unique pleasure of each other's exclusive company. They had finished one bottle of wine and were half way through a second when they decided to take what remained of it, and their glasses, with them as they made their way to the comfort of the sitting room couch. She snuggled close to him as they finished the wine in a silence of contentment that no words could have surpassed. Free of the glasses, she rested her cheek on his shoulder and, taking his hand, pressed it to her breast, and said, 'Kiss me.' He kissed her many times, and as they kissed his hand moved from her breast, through the curve of her waist, and down along her thigh, and up again, slowly and tantalizingly, until it again cupped her breast. At that moment she raised her head from his shoulder and, looking unwaveringly into his eyes, she, with quite sudden determination, undid the buttons of her blouse and, slipping her hand inside her flimsy bra, freed her breast from its lacy restraint. Her eyes, wide and full with unmistakable intent, revealed more than a host of impassioned words. This, he knew, was her clear challenge to him. This was a life defining moment. Refuse this offer, this token of her very soul, and the promise of what could be theirs was surely lost beyond recall. His response was devoid of deliberation, beyond even the most fleeting conscious consideration. His fingers barely brushed the warm silky valley of her cleavage, and delicately caressed the excited, and deliciously exciting, erect nipple that had become the very essence of her desire, the physical presentation of her inner self, her heart, her will, her mind, all that was her at the deepest level of her existence. And there and then, unstoppable as a torrent cascading down a waterfall, in a wonderfully spontaneous choreography, they unhooked, unbuttoned, unbuckled, unzipped, untied their way to exquisite unison.

During those long insubstantial moments after culmination they clung together in drowsy contentment. Eventually the mundane realities of life, like tiny waves sneaking their way on to a beach, started to insinuate themselves into their reluctant consciousness. It was very late, but, unwelcome as the thought of facing out into the night might be, Heather was expected home. Alan insisted on her taking a taxi, as it wouldn't be safe for either of them to drive because of the amount of alcohol they'd had earlier.

When she'd gone the house seemed unnaturally quiet. Disinclined to go to bed he returned to the sitting room, took Kenny Davern's *Soprano Summit in Concert* from its sleeve and placed it on the turntable. He donned a pair of earphones, pressed the start button, stretched out on the settee, and sank into a mellow reflection of the previous few hours. Two hours later, the sound of a passing siren – police car? ambulance? fire-engine?, he couldn't tell - roused him from a curious dream: he had stepped into a lift, but instead of a floor he found himself on a narrow, descending stairway which, within a few steps gave way to what looked like a playground slide that, in turn, quickly disappeared into a dark void; stricken with uncertainty, he turned hastily to see if he was in time to exit the lift before the doors closed on him. It was at that moment, as he emerged from that sifting period experienced between sleep and wakefulness, half shadowy, half real, when images overlap each other as the mind swims towards equilibrium, that he became conscious of the siren.

* * * * * * * * *

They were never quite sure afterwards how the subject came up – it seemed to have presented itself spontaneously – but within days of that first evening at Alan's they had decided that they must be together, although as regards marriage, and the practicalities of living arrangements, they had no clear idea. When Heather asked him if he would have a guilty conscience if they could not have a Church wedding he said,

'I hope God has bigger things on His mind.' Heather was not entirely convinced.

When Heather got home at around 11.30 on the evening they had come to this decision, before going to her own room, she put her ear to her mother's bedroom door. Mrs Lattimore enjoyed watching old films, last thing at night, on the small black and white television she'd had installed in her room. Heather could just about hear the low-volume television voices. She knocked gently on the door, in case her mother had fallen asleep while still watching the programme, as she sometimes did.

'Yes,' came the mildly surprised sound of her mother's voice. Heather opened the door slightly, and said,

'Just checking if you're awake, Mum. May I come in?'

'Yes, of course, dear.'

Heather slipped into the bedroom, and sat on the edge of her mother's bed.

'I've something to tell you, Mum.'

Her mother gestured towards the T.V.

'Turn it down, please, dear.'

Heather went to the television and turned down the volume, and sat down beside her mother again, and took hold of her hand.

'The thing is, Mum, Alan and I are considering getting married. We know there are a lot of things to be sorted out, but that's what we've decided we want to do.'

'I'm not at all surprised, dear. In fact, I've been half expecting something like this. You do seem to be suited to each other.'

'You're not upset, then?'

'No, dear, of course not.'

Despite these reassuring comments, Heather knew there was

one issue that would be bothering her mother, and decided now was as good a time as any to bring it up.

'Mum,' she began, 'I know that when I came back from England it was on the understanding that the children and me would live here with you. I just want to assure you that, no matter how we figure things out, we'll continue to do that.'

'Thank you, my dear. I'm so glad to hear that.' She gave her daughter's hand a little squeeze. After a moment she said,

'Actually, I've been anticipating this for a while, and if I may make a suggestion…?'

'Go ahead, Mum.' Heather was inwardly amused at her mother's perceptiveness.

'Well, I'd be quite happy to have Alan move in here with us – it would cause the least disruption to everyone – provided that…,' and here she hesitated.

'Yes, Mum, provided that what?' Heather encouraged her.

'Well, what I would like is my own self-contained space. I've been thinking about it, and there's plenty of space at the side of the house for a granny flat.'

'That sound like a great idea, Mum,' said Heather, feeling relieved and pleased by her Mum's reaction.

She couldn't wait to tell Alan about her conversation and, late though it was, she telephoned him right away. When he answered the phone with a puzzled 'Hello', she said,

'Hi, darling. It's me. I hope I didn't wake you up.'

'No, love. Is something wrong?'

'No, no. Not at all.'

She went on to tell him about her conversation with her mother, and of the granny flat suggestion she'd made. Alan agreed that it sounded like an excellent arrangement.'

'I could even keep this place. I'd have no difficulty renting it out.'

They agreed, there and then, to start putting plans in motion straightaway.

Before saying 'goodnight', Alan asked her about letting the children know what they planned to do?

'I'll talk to them tomorrow evening when I get home from work. I've asked Mum not to say anything until I get a chance to talk to them myself.'

* * * * * * * * * *

The marriage issue was resolved when they learned that, because Heather's first marriage had been in a Registry Office, and not in a church, the Church, despite its professed emphasis on the importance of the family unit, had no difficulty in solemnizing a marriage between a Catholic and a divorced mother of two children, who's father was still alive, provided she had not been married previously in church.

At midday on the last Saturday in June 1976, the wedding took place. It was a small affair, officiated at by Father Conor Somers and, on behalf of Heather and her family, the Reverend Gerry Grimes of the Church of Ireland. Mrs Lattimore was there, never having been in a Catholic church before, together with Heather's children. Olive was the picture of excitement, and even James seemed to be enjoying the occasion. Alan's parents, along with his sisters and their families were also there, and Barry had made the trip from New York, but, much to his father's relief, without Bob. Apart from Philip Ffrench, who acted as best man, there were less than half a dozen other close friends. The entire church ceremony took scarcely twenty minutes.

After the reception, which was held in a private function room in Dublin's Royal Hibernian Hotel, Philip drove the new bride and groom to Dublin Airport, from where they flew to Barcelona, where they spent their first night as husband and wife, in an old-world shore-side hotel. For their honeymoon they had decided on the novelty of a Mediterranean cruise as neither of them had been on that type of holiday previously. They joined the gleaming, white liner, *Valhalla*, the following afternoon and set sail within a couple of hours.

During the following days, although trips ashore were available at the various ports of call along the French Riviera and the Italian coast, they were content to remain on board and enjoy the magnificent panoramic views of the blue waters of the Mediterranean and the sheer pleasure of each other's company. They made love many times.

Each morning Alan awoke with a feeling of immense well-being. The woman he loved, and who made him feel whole, and wanted, and approved of, and loved without reservation, lay contentedly beside him.

They left the ship for the first time at Naples and strolled about its ancient streets and drank coffee at a small café in the shade of the Duomo. They ambled to an elevated spot where they could admire a view of the world-renowned bay. As they stood there an elderly Neapolitan appeared beside them and, spreading his arms as if to embrace the scene before them, said, 'Is very nice-eh, yes?'

Heather's eyes sparkled with mischief as she smiled at him and said, 'Yes, is very nice-eh.'

Later that evening, midway during a leisurely dinner, Heather leaned across the table towards Alan and, lifting her glass of wine, smiled and said,

'This will be my last alcohol for some time.'

Alan's puzzlement quickly turned to realisation.

'You're sure?'

'Oh yes. Quite sure'

'How long?'

'I haven't had a period since March.'

Surprise, apprehension, but most of all, pure joy, all coursed through him.

'Darling, this is wonderful. How do you feel about it?' he asked.

'Happy. Very happy.'

The apprehension that had flickered through his mind was at the memory of baby Christine. But looking at Heather now he had the strongest feeling that this time everything would be perfect. He bent towards her and, taking her hands in his, said,

'Me too.'

It had been a full and exciting day, and they retired to bed early. Aided by the almost imperceptible motion of the ship Heather was soon asleep. As he lay listening to her gentle breathing Alan thought of the new life that had been conceived between them. A new life. And what sort of life would this new life have? What influences would shape it? The same as had influenced his? Not entirely, he vowed quietly to himself, if he could help it. And now he stood at the foot of a rugged mountain with a blond haired toddler by his side. He looked up towards the cloud-covered summit and hoisting the boy on to his shoulders set off along the steep mountain track. They had gone some distance and Alan's pace was slowing from the effort when the boy said,

'Where are we going, Daddy?'

'I have to find something.'

'What something, Daddy?'

'I'm not sure. Something for you, I think.'

The going was getting tougher, but Alan knew he must press on. He had no choice. On and on upwards along the track he toiled until a voice called him from his sleep.

'Are you all right, Alan?' asked Heather anxiously. 'You seemed to be breathing very heavily.'

'Yes dear. I was having a dream. Sorry to wake you. Go on back to sleep.'

He lay quietly for a while until she had fallen asleep again, and then slipped silently out of bed. He found his bathrobe with the aid of the dim moonlight that infiltrated the room, draped it over his shoulders, and stepped through the sliding doors that led to the cabin's small balcony. And there, as the liner scissored its way southward along the Italian coast, he saw in the distance Stromboli's infernal volcanic display. The fiery scene seemed like an apocalyptic vision. Although the night was warm Alan shuddered as he gazed at the black shadowy mass with the glowing tip. Turning his back on Stromboli's smouldering inferno he stepped back into the cabin, slid the doors closed, shook the robe from his shoulders, and crept back into bed.

'Are you sure you're all right, darling?' Heather asked as she snuggled her back into him.

'Yes, dear. Never better,' he answered with a tone of resolution.

And, as *Valhalla* entered the Straits of Messina, Stromboli fumed, and faded, into the distance.

ISBN 1425111475